'What a debut - and what a rich, beautifully written, gothic treat.'

Derren Brown

'I was instantly drawn into the mystery and swept along by the shocking twists and turns. A beautifully written novel.'

Jodie Whittaker, actor

'A.J. West has history at his fingertips and writes brilliantly - so clever it makes your head spin!'

Jeremy Vine, journalist

'Dark, powerful and twisting - *The Spirit Engineer* will leave you wondering what is real and what is illusion.'

W. C. Ryan, author of *A House of Ghosts*

'An atmospheric and entirely gripping chiller that calls to mind the best of M.R. James and E.F. Benson, without in any way paling in comparison... A fantastic read, and perfect company as the evenings start to close in.'

**Billy O'Callaghan,
bestselling author of *Life Sentences***

'A marvellous and menacing gothic chiller, filled with secrets and soaked in atmosphere, in which the ghouls and fiends are not of the other world, but this one...'

**Neil Blackmore,
author of *The Intoxicating Mr Lavelle***

'With a skilful misdirection that any Edwardian spirit medium would be proud to demonstrate, A.J. West turns the screw in this fascinating novel.'

Essie Fox, author of *The Somnambulist*

'Gripping from the outset – A.J West immerses readers in the spiritualism of 1914 Belfast with great skill. A wonderful debut.'

Sam Hurcom, author of *Letters from the Dead*

THE SPIRIT ENGINEER

A. J. WEST

DUCKWORTH

To William, Kathleen and Elizabeth. I'll forever be haunted by your story

This edition first published in the United Kingdom
by Duckworth in 2021
Duckworth, an imprint of Duckworth Books Ltd
1 Golden Court, Richmond, TW9 1EU, United Kingdom
www.duckworthbooks.co.uk

For bulk and special sales please contact
info@duckworthbooks.com

A catalogue record for this book is available from the British Library.

Printed and bound in Great Britain by Clays.

9780715654330

PART ONE

THE END

CHAPTER ONE

Bangor, Northern Ireland, 30th July, 1920

A wave crashes onto the rocks. I scrabble backwards, shoes scraping over wet stone.

Take it, William. Drink it quickly.

I pinch a paper envelope from my pocket, tap the potassium cyanide crystals into a bottle of scotch, rolling the mixture until the poison drowns and vanishes.

A spirit to create a spirit.

I whimper, burying my face between my knees. I am afraid, yes. Afraid of death after so many years communing with the dead. The water whispers from rockpools, slaps between legs of sharp stone. I listen for voices, but there is only the sea. How wretched, to study the afterlife for so many years, only to end here, gripped by a realisation more terrible than anything beyond the grave.

I am a failure, a fraud. I have travelled so far to arrive nowhere; to become nothing.

So, let it be.

I squint towards the horizon, grimace at the sea where the slate waves whelm and roll and remember those promising words: *death is a beginning.*

Out there, at the far reaches of the world, I can imagine nothing at all.

I sniff the scotch. Almonds. Shivering, I place my spectacles beside my jacket. My throat tightens. I catch sight of my pipe. Spring to my feet. Fling the blasted thing to oblivion. Lost forever. Not so lost as I. A seagull stands in the shingle, wings open, head cocked. It yawns, regarding me with a yellow eye.

'Is it time?' I ask the creature, disgusted by the sound of my own treacherous voice. 'Is the final experiment about to begin?'

I grip the glass. Chill breeze on my neck. *Must I do this horrible thing?* To the crash of wind and water, beside the creeping tide, I rub my thumb over the mouth of the bottle, rap it three times.

Knock. Knock. Knock.

So, I am done. There is no escape now. In a moment, I shall listen helplessly to my own voice, crying out in agony. How appropriate.

CHAPTER TWO

Belfast, 1914

An almighty racket came from the upstairs of our little home. I sighed, searching for my damned pipe. An argument had been going on; something to do with the destruction of my daughter's painted eggs. Until recently, the housemaid Hazel would have calmed the children's squabbles, yet confound the woman she had left us without any notice. I ran my finger over the mantelpiece, tutting at the grey-blue fluff collected around my fingernail and sighed. 'Damned inconsiderate,' I muttered to myself, before scanning the floor. My pipe had most certainly been in my jacket pocket; I had picked it up in my study. It was in the peculiar character of the Crawford family for inanimate objects to go wandering about only to show up in the strangest of places.

'Father?' called Elizabeth from the landing. 'Will you come upstairs, right away?'

Her tone was strained and impatient, scratching on my already sensitive nerves. *Right away, indeed?* She had been in a sharp mood since a cold and lumpy breakfast, which I ought not to have mentioned, yet I was so deathly tired myself, the pressures of the day having met me like a doomish friend in the grim hours of a drizzly, unpromising dawn. I took a long breath and considered my wife's own predicament: three children to raise, a house to keep, food to cook, and a disappointment for a husband. She had grown brittle since Hazel's departure, dark cushions gathering beneath her eyes. I crouched down, searching under the armchair, blindly running my fingers over the carpet. She was supposed to be preparing for our guest, sweeping, dusting, tidying, yet between the children and her efforts with the sandwiches she had completely lost control of the time. I closed my eyes, then headed for the stairs, willing myself to keep my temper. 'Coming, my love.'

Standing at the nursery door, I surveyed the evidence, pulling at my moustache. 'Well then, what's the matter, Elizabeth? I'm very busy.'

'Oh, William, there you are,' she said. 'Look at what he's done, honestly.'

I searched for the boy amidst the rubble of abandoned toys and gave my best impression of a concerned father. 'Has he turned transparent as well as obstinate?'

'Oh, do be quiet, William,' said Elizabeth, rubbing her hands together in a fit. 'I haven't done a thing to prepare; not a thing and where have you been?'

I bounced on my heels, staying my tongue. Where had I *been?* In my study, that's where, working on my textbook and troubling over bills, not to mention wiping dust from the parlour mantelpiece. Margaret, my eldest, was in the corner with her hands on her hips, concerned and practical. She was very much like her father, sharing my dark curls and clever eyes, while young Helen, at seven, could not have been more like her mother: slight, fanciful and cursed with an incorrigible weakness for the dramatic. She watched me, half-hidden behind Elizabeth's skirts. My wife scratched at her wrists.

'William, please take a stronger hand with Robert, he's such a wilful thing, you're too soft with him.'

I chewed my cheek, looking around the room, mint green, covered in childish paintings with building bricks, miniature cooking implements, tin motorcars and horses strewn about the unswept floor. The decapitated body of a doll lay beside the fireplace, her skirt rucked above the waist. I wrinkled my nose.

'Elizabeth,' I said. 'I realise the household is missing a maid, but these toys won't tidy themselves.' She gave me a look, which I chose to ignore; turning to Margaret as I rifled through my pockets, yearning for tobacco. 'Child, have you seen your father's pipe?'

'No, Father,' she said, tapping the headless doll with her toe.

I nodded. 'And I suppose this is Robert's victim, is it?'

'Oh no, Father, the dolly lost her head last week.'

I glanced at Elizabeth. 'She's not the only one.'

'William, I am doing my best,' Elizabeth replied, turning on me with the unmistakable expression of someone about to succumb to their feelings. 'But little Robert has managed to outdo himself this time, and I specifically asked you to watch him for me.'

'I was watching him from the study, dearest.'

'You were doing no such thing, you were scribbling away in your book.'

I chewed at my tongue, searching the nursery, looking for clues yet found no evidence of disorder until Margaret stood aside to reveal an act of vandalism, four putrid eggs smeared in a zigzag pattern across the wall. I scratched my nose. 'Has Jack the Ripper been making an omelette?'

'Oh, don't be funny, please,' chided Elizabeth, wrenching at her sleeves.

'No, Father, it isn't a laughing matter at all,' agreed Margaret. 'Helen spent hours painting those eggs and they were very splendid, weren't they, Helen?'

Helen made to answer, but threw herself against Elizabeth's skirts with a wail; the opportunity for melodrama all too tempting.

'Oh shush,' I said rubbing my temples. 'The chickens haven't stopped laying, have they? You can paint new ones. Now tell me, where is the little crook?'

Margaret pointed to the door, from where there came a snivelling, muttering sound, followed by the scuffling of a tiny shoe.

'Dear, oh dear,' I said to Margaret with a wink. 'Where is Robert? Has he gone to the races?'

Margaret grinned. 'No, Father.'

'Has he gone to the Houses of Parliament, perhaps?'

She shook her head.

'Damned pity,' I said. 'He should get on well there.'

Helen wiped her nose, her eyes pink, and I recalled the day of her birth, my darling Elizabeth's eyes streaming with relief when the noisy ordeal was over. Baby Helen was such a poorly little thing then, while Elizabeth had suffered some sort of woman's injury which had remained a mystery to me ever since, such was the chilly torpidity of our marital relations.

Elizabeth went to the window. 'He's behind the door,' she said. 'Honestly, I am at my wit's end. Aunt Adelia will be here in an hour, or have you forgotten?'

I raised an eyebrow. 'If only.'

She turned to me, glaring. 'You will be polite,' she said. 'Don't forget who pays for the coal.'

'I believe I pay for the coal.'

'Yes, William, when there aren't pipes to fix or roof tiles falling on our heads or money to be spent on tobacco.'

'Speaking of which, have you seen my pipe?' The house creaked and we all looked up, waiting for the ceiling to come in. I smiled. 'Darling, I shall make the sandwiches for you.'

'You will do no such thing.'

I gave a long sigh, resigned to her irrational mood, and pulled away the nursery door to see my darling son, only five years old and small even for that. His face was buried between his knees, his strawberry comfort blanket covering his head in a cowl.

'Robert,' I said sternly. 'What about these eggs then, eh?'

'I din't do nuffun,' he sniffed.

Helen stepped in, arms crossed, feet stomping the floor. 'Yes you did, Robert, you naughty little thing. You must have, or who else was it?'

Robert lifted his head from his blanket, squealing, 'I didn't touch your bloody eggs!' He leapt up, scraping his feet over the floorboards, before circling the nursery in an imaginary motorcar, making loud raspberry noises.

'Robert, your language!' exclaimed Elizabeth turning after him like a ringmaster. 'Were you not listening to the minister this morning? Let your speech always be gracious, seasoned with salt. Who taught you that word?'

'Farfur says it,' said Robert, parping on an invisible horn, bashing into the egg-daubed walls.

I inspected my fingernails. 'The boy's throat is an open grave,' I said. 'He uses his tongue to deceive.'

'I din't do nuffin to them stinky old eggs!' Robert bellowed, parking up beside the dollhouse, his blanket wrapped around his face. I could feel a headache coming on. Helen began wailing again and I could almost have lost my temper.

'Enough,' I said, clapping my hands. 'Robert, my boy, apologise to your mother for smashing Helen's silly eggs.'

'I told you, I din't do it,' protested the lad. 'Honest, Farfur, I din't.'

I rubbed my nose, smiling in spite of myself. 'Then damn it, who did?'

'I don't know, Farfur,' he said. 'They was smashed in the night-time, I heard them. Bang, bang, bang!'

I scratched my chin, studying the ceiling as a tapping sound started up, like gravel on boards. 'There are some funny noises in the house of late,' I said. 'Bats in the loft, I expect.'

With that, Robert set to flapping about his sisters, nibbling at their arms, Helen screeching, Margaret aloof and observant like a tennis umpire. Elizabeth covered her ears. 'Enough of all this, please,' she said. 'I am going to the kitchen with the girls, you can give your son a smack.'

'A smack, Elizabeth?'

'Yes, William, a smack.' She looked at Robert. 'Perhaps a sharp tap on the bottom, at least. You can use one of your precious books.'

Helen sniffed. 'Aunt Adelia says you deserve a smack on the bottom too, Father, for not looking after us better.'

I made to protest, only to see Elizabeth covering a smile. 'Oh don't look so grumpy,' she said. 'You're as bad as Robert. Aunt Adelia means you no harm.' She led the girls past me to the hallway, brushing my hand. 'You must bite your tongue when she arrives.'

I watched them go, before turning to my son, who was backing into the corner of the nursery, his hands on his backside, that silly comfort blanket under his feet. I crouched in front of the scoundrel, a sharp pain throbbing in my head. I had longed for a peaceful family life in our new home at 1 Park Avenue, yet the increase in space had served only to amplify the noise. Our previous home had been beset by sticking doors and strange noises but, thank goodness, my pay rise at the Institute had allowed us to move up a rung, albeit a rotten, dilapidated rung, and I had the ticklish excitement of any man poised, after years of hard toil, on the verge of success. Soon my textbook would be published and we would no longer require Aunt Adelia's benefaction.

'Now,' I said, lifting Robert's chin. 'Who smashed Helen's eggs, eh? The pixies in the garden?'

His eyes fixed on a spot beyond my shoulder, his finger outstretched. 'It was the lady in the white dress.'

I scoffed, looking to the hallway, expecting to see my wife standing there, but it was empty. 'You mean your mother smashed the eggs?'

The boy squinted at me, nibbling his blanket. 'Silly old Farfur.'

I studied him for a second, wondering what he was thinking, the funny little animal, then shook my head. 'It would be an awful lot easier to tell the truth,' I said. 'Why tease your poor mother?' I straightened up, my knees clicking, and walked to the nursery window, peering down at the road.

'What messes we men make,' I said, tutting to myself at the grim prospect of a wasted afternoon. Robert toddled to my side as below, a woman in a huge plumed hat came marching towards the house. I clipped the lad's ear, then ruffled his hair. 'There, you have had your punishment; alas, mine is about to ring the doorbell.'

CHAPTER THREE

I drummed the arms of my chair, the interminable minutes passing at such a sluggish pace, the revelation might have arrived before the sandwiches. All my mind was tobacco and smoke. The mantle had been dusted at last, though Helen had made a rather sloppy job of it, fluff clinging to Elizabeth's sparse collection of figurines.

'Thank you for your visit,' I said, smiling as best I could.

Lady Adelia Carter nodded. 'The pleasure is mine.' I saw her grimace and shift uncomfortably in her chair. 'Is this furniture of yours second-hand?'

'Certainly not. Is your hat?'

She scowled, rocking uncomfortably like a chicken on eggs, then thrust her hand between the arm of the chair and her skirts, before tugging out my pipe.

'Aha!' I cried, leaping to snatch it from her fingers. 'I am much obliged.'

Instantly, I was packing the dear thing with tobacco with trembling fingers, catching Lady Adelia Carter's beady eye. I took a deep, crackling puff, engulfing her in a thick cloud of blue smoke.

'Such a lovely house,' she said, coughing and rearranging her ample skirts. 'The late Lord Carter smoked a pipe.'

'Is that so?' I said. 'He sounds like a discerning fellow, Aunt Adelia.' I tasted her name on my tongue like bitter ashes. She was no true aunt of ours; more a meddlesome old crow who also happened, by grievous circumstance, to be our family's benefactress.

She raised her head in thought, wrinkling her nose. 'I did not approve of his smoking on account of the smell and the dust.' She glanced at the figurines on the mantel. 'I believe it killed him.'

But for the ticking of the clock, the room fell silent. I longed for Elizabeth to return. Where were those blasted sandwiches? Where was the damned tea? Adelia coughed again, preening herself. 'Your housemaid has deserted you, I hear.'

'She left us last week.' I nodded. 'She gave us no notice, but the women of the house are coping admirably.'

A muffled cry came from the kitchen, followed by the clatter of porcelain. Adelia smoothed the feathers in her hat. 'I am so pleased to hear it. Tell me, how does my dear Albie do at the Institute?'

Young Albert Blithe had joined us late in the previous term, having graduated from St Andrews with dubious honours. Still, what qualifies a man better for a career in advanced mathematics than well-connected relatives?

I sniffed, picking at my knee. 'He does well enough, by all accounts. Though the students have little respect for him.'

'He is a childish boy, persisting with his ridiculous jokes. Then again, show me a man who *isn't* childish. I believe Lord Carter was the very last of the adult men.'

I looked at her wedding band, trying to imagine the brain-boggled individual who had been fool enough to place it on the old buzzard's bony finger. Outside, a fine drizzle was beginning to fall, the rumbling sky promising a storm. 'It is horrid weather for June,' I said.

Adelia chuckled. 'This is Belfast not Dunedin, William. I expect your upbringing in the colonies has lumbered you with a foreigner's perspective when it comes to our weather.'

'I left New Zealand more than a decade ago and the weather is not dissimilar.'

Adelia made the indulgent expression of a governess asked to believe in pixies, yet her riposte was lost to providence for just then, Elizabeth arrived, carrying a large pot of tea, followed by my daughters presenting plates of meagre sandwiches like pages at a pauper's wedding. They placed the sad assortment onto the occasional table, my heart breaking as my poor wife took her seat with a strained smile. She fussed over the plates apologising, the sore skin of her wrists showing.

I caught Adelia glaring at them, then flicking her eyes at me in the throes of some preposterous allegation. I was about to take her on, when a shot sounded from a distant street, the lot of us leaping from our chairs in surprise before freezing, listening for some cry or boom. Such bursts of violence were becoming more frequent with every passing day, Belfast growing menacing as though, in hiding its own madness, the city might scream at any moment. The Ulster Volunteer Force was armed now, of course. Rumour had it they had procured some 25,000 rifles and at least three million rounds of ammunition from the Germans.

I drew a healthy puff on my pipe to calm my nerves then stood at the window, looking out across the black cranes and skeletal ships, tracing the distant hills looming dark beyond the violent far reaches of the city. I had a premonition that Ulster would soon be manufacturing ghosts as fast as rivets. How insignificant the loss of the doomed Titanic would seem then. I was about to say as much when a second gunshot cracked over the rooftops and, at that very moment, the swollen clouds burst as though the very heavens were punctured.

'These gunshots,' said Adelia, shaking her head. 'I do hope the prime minister ignores them. If London insist on us being Irish again, I shall be moving to America.' She took a deep breath, studying Elizabeth. 'I have friends there who say it is the only place for money these days; though you will understand better than anyone, Elizabeth, I do worry about the ships.'

Elizabeth closed her eyes, stroking Helen's hair, as Adelia looked on in conspicuous sympathy, dabbing a dry eye with a laced handkerchief. 'I still think of those poor people bobbing about like corks in the Atlantic. Two years it's been, and I simply cannot bring myself to forget it.'

Elizabeth watched the rain, her eyes welling up as she fiddled with her sleeves. None of us in the Crawford household was yet comfortable speaking the liner's name aloud. The city's stately leviathan had turned out to be a terribly poor swimmer. Such shame we felt; such embarrassment. Lost work, lost pride and, in Elizabeth's case, a drowned brother. She, one of so many living with the spectre of a deceased relative; no body to bury, no peace. Arthur had been trapped in the lower decks of the liner, or so a cursory letter from the White Star Line had informed us a few weeks after the tragedy. Trapped or imprisoned, I wondered privately, for I had secretly alerted the ship to his various misdemeanours by telegram when they had departed Queenstown. He was a rogue so I carried no guilt and, in her innocence, Elizabeth seemed content to imagine the boy sacrificing his own life for the safety of the women and children. Such is the comforting mythology of the deceased. I touched Elizabeth's shoulder and she looked up, eyes sparkling, the sunlight tracing the line of her cheek. What was she doing with such a plain, forgetful man as I?

'Precious in the sight of the Lord is the death of his saints,' she said, kissing my fingers.

'Death is not an end, Lillie,' said Adelia with a meaningful look. She touched Elizabeth's knee. 'Remember what we have been told at our church meetings, child. Death… is a *beginning*.'

I huffed on my spectacles, blowing dust from the lenses. What rot were they being fed at these Presbyterian church meetings now? Adelia eyed me dangerously as though reading my mind, then sniffed. 'How those poor souls crammed themselves into the lifeboats, all classes mixed together, I shall never know. I experienced something similar in the opera house last Tuesday evening, though at least we were dry. Poor Mr Ismay; I hear he weeps at the mere sight of an ice cube.'

'The man is a coward,' I growled, standing beside the long curtain separating the dining room, its pattern of faded peonies and ferns suffused with the collected memory of so many candles, dinners and dust. I willed the blasted woman to leave us alone before Elizabeth fell into another of her nervous moods.

Adelia gave me a thin smile. 'Only poor men are brave, William; rich men have no need to be. Ah! What charming tableware.' She leaned towards the sandwiches as though they were scorpions, cooing. 'Tell me, are they bone china?'

'Oh,' said Elizabeth, returning to the room with a blink. 'No, Aunt Adelia, they are porcelain. We bought the set for the new house when we visited Bangor last Christmas. We thought it was from China but we were wrong, weren't we, William? It was made in Plymouth.'

'Plymouth!' said Adelia. 'I have never been to Plymouth. Are they very like the Chinese on the South Coast?' She took a triangular sandwich, nibbling at its corner, then placed it ceremoniously back on the plate. 'Now, tell me, dear Lillie, are we attending our evening meeting this week? I do think it wise, given your state.'

'Oh yes,' replied my wife, looking up at me hopefully from her chair. 'I would very much like to. That is... William, will you manage, alone with the children, do you think?'

I gave her a wink. 'I should hope so, my dove. I am a teacher after all.'

Elizabeth had been attending her church meetings with increasing regularity of late, though I worried they were serving to amplify her disquiet, rather than quell it. 'Aunt Adelia, where are these church meetings held, might I ask? Perhaps I might join you both one evening?'

Suddenly, there came a loud thump from somewhere high in the house, followed by a mournful wail. I dashed to the hallway, the girls close behind; but before I could investigate any further, Elizabeth was scuttling up the stairs, calling up, 'Robert, Robert, whatever is the matter, are you hurt?'

Exasperated, I returned to the parlour, hands clasped behind my back, our guest observing me with a suspicious eye. Presently, she stood from her chair, patting down her skirts, her bent body weighed down by so many preposterous folds of material. She spoke to me in a low tone, stepping close enough to smell the soapy perfume of her wrinkled skin.

'William, I do hope you understand...' She paused, her eyes searching mine. 'I mean to say, it is kind of you to allow Elizabeth the privacy of her church meetings, especially taking into account my generosity. After all, if you are able to neglect your writing to join us at our church meetings, perhaps the Crawfords no longer require my financial assistance...'

'Indeed no, Aunt Adelia, that is not the case. Your support is most welcome.'

'Aha,' she said, tapping my cheek with a gloved hand. 'All is well then. You ought to know, women need *space* to grieve, William, not husbands. Please ask Elizabeth to wait for my word.'

And with that, she ruffled away, singing to the girls, 'Now then, young ladies, will you give your Aunt Adelia a kiss? I believe it is time for me to go.'

I raised an eyebrow, searching my pockets for my pipe. 'What a pity.'

CHAPTER FOUR

Dusk came quickly that evening, weighed down by a heavy curtain of rain which swept in from the hills, smacking against the roof like a shower of lead weights. The window in my study shook, and when I held my palm to it, I could feel a coolness passing through the glass.

I pushed my spectacles to my brow and looked gloomily at the manuscript for my new book, *Calculations on the Entropy-Temperature Chart*. It was almost complete yet, for the life of me, I could not write the introduction. I rubbed my eyes, too tired to make another attempt. It was almost the end of term, though I was surely more exhausted than my students.

I scratched a few rudimentary sketches onto a page then stood to try on my top hat, fetching my cane from the wardrobe. I inspected the brooding reflection in the window, posing to the side, lifting my chin, turning slowly to face my mirrored self as though greeting an old friend at the club. Bidding the imaginary fellow adieu, I straddled my cane like an East London rogue, baring my teeth. There in the black glass, stood the world-renowned Professor William Jackson Crawford, legendary scientist and engineer. Such sophisticated eyes, such a sharp brow. There, the gracile cheekbones, the neat jawline, the urbane demeanour. I unbuttoned my jacket. Other men my age seemed to be bloating out like pickled eggs, while I was growing lean and lithe. Why, I could feel my muscles flexing and twitching under the loose waist of my trousers. We were all growing spry in the Crawford Household, even Robert was fast losing his puppy fat to ribs.

Just then, an image flashed into my mind: Elizabeth lying in a summer field, her hair loose, laughing, inviting me to lay with her, skirts lifted. I followed her petticoat between her legs then looked up to find my wife's face replaced by Adelia's smile: 'William, women need *space* to grieve, not husbands.'

Disgusted, I threw away my hat and drew the curtains, dumping myself into my chair. Damn the woman and her influence over my Elizabeth. Oh, but really what did an old dowager matter anyway? Let them have their church meetings. There was I, a young, successful man with nothing ahead but prosperity. Yes, prosperity. I leaned back, and lit my pipe, my heart soothed by the thought. Perhaps one day, Principal Forth would invite me to the top table at the annual gala. A delightful tableau came to mind: I standing before a hall filled with admiring peers as they cheered, their glasses raised in admiration of my latest feat of engineering. A dirigible perhaps, with a hotel attached to its belly plated in steel.

The Institute's 1914 gala was to take place the following week and I had made a mental note to make a few casual observations to Principal Forth. He had been impressed the previous month by my somewhat lonely but exculpated position on rubber washers for the belt-driven water pumps. Yes, I would look the man directly in the eye and tell him about dirigibles. If only he didn't speak to me as though I were a gun dog in training. It quite undermined my confidence.

I lit my pipe, thinking of my children resting their little heads on their pillows as Elizabeth played some faltering hymnal on the piano downstairs. The pipes rattled against the walls outside and a creaking came from above as a gust of wind blew through the glass into my face. Another promotion at the Institute would help the Crawfords to live a more comfortable life, not to mention a more independent one. I gritted my teeth at the thought of the woman. *Aunt* Adelia, the poison in my wife's ear.

A new housemaid would do nicely for a start. It was four days since Hazel had disappeared. Why had she left in such a rush? She had always been a most reliable housemaid and had never been careful about voicing her demands for new cleaning utensils or household wares. Why, only the previous month, she had complained of a twisted hip caused by a broken spring in her mattress and what had I done but ordered a replacement straight away.

I scratched my head. Why should anybody demand a new mattress, at no little cost to a stretched household, when they had already made up their mind to leave? I found the whole thing utterly bizarre. Had Robert bitten her again? Elizabeth had claimed absolute ignorance but then, on considering the possibility of such an attack, she had suddenly decided it was a very likely explanation after all. I searched for my spectacles, yanking drawers then slamming them again, tutting, twisting about and under the desk to look into the darkness for a shimmer of a lens. Blast it. I shook the ache from my head, focused my eyes as hard as I could against the blur, and flashed my pen.

Wanted
In a professional gentleman's family, a short distance from the centre of Belfast in a smart area, a good Protestant MAID-OF-ALL-WORK. She must be accustomed with the care of plate, glass, waiting at table, the care and instruction of three young children and the cooking and laundering of clothes and all linen. There are seven rooms to keep warm with stoves or fires. A thoroughly respectable and DEPENDABLE young woman desired, preferably of Presbyterian character. Uniform not supplied. Apply for name and address at the office of this paper.

I read it back a couple of times, mumbling the words as I often do, then placed it in a drawer for the morning. The dull ache of a tiresome day drew down my shins to my feet as I made my way to the landing, looking up at the maid's room, blurred as though underwater, at the top of the bare attic stairs. Is that what Arthur had seen as the ship had plummeted to the ocean floor? It occurred to me I had not inspected the room following Hazel's departure.

Desperately weary, I climbed one gloomy step after another, the rain still drumming angrily above my head. I whistled to myself as I turned the handle, yet to my surprise it was stuck. I tried again with a push from my shoulder, but the door simply would not budge. I heard some movement and looked down to see Elizabeth's hazy silhouette at the foot of the stairs, her face in shadow, lit by the lamp at her back. 'The damn door is stuck,' I said, offering it another hefty budge with my hip.

Her voice was almost lost in the noise of the rain. 'Not stuck, William. It is locked.'

I felt for my spectacles, fingers pressed deep into my trouser pockets, admiring the soft glow of her hair, her body revealed within her high-collared blouse.

'Locked?' I said. 'Nonsense, how is it locked?'

'Oh honestly, there has been a lock on the door for months; as you would know if you'd ever checked on the roof as I asked.'

I could hardly believe it. 'You mean our housemaid locked her own sleeping quarters without telling us?'

'No, of course not. I called a man in when Hazel requested it.'

'A man?' I turned about, thrashing my fists in my infernal jacket. 'Is there no man in this house? It should not have been done...'

'It had to be done.'

I stared, incredulous, at my wife. 'I am an engineer, Elizabeth. Am I not capable of fitting a damned lock without the expense of a locksmith?' She said nothing, turning her hands about her wrists. 'Then where is the key?' I demanded.

'I do not know,' she said. 'It went missing when Hazel left.'

'Oh, how careless of you.'

'Your spectacles are on your head, William.'

'I know!'

I took a deep breath, rubbing the bridge of my nose, so awfully tired. She came into focus, her eyes darkened by circles. I smiled. 'My love,' I said, descending the stairs. 'Worry not. We shall find the key and open the door soon enough.' I kissed her head.

'Thank you,' she said, stifling a yawn, pulling her warm body away. 'I am so very tired and I must pray before bed.' She slipped from my arms to her own room, turning back at the door. 'Goodnight, dear father.'

I smiled. 'Goodnight, precious wife. Sweet dreams.'

She closed her door. There was I, alone in my socks on the landing. I considered knocking gently at her room, asking whether she was cold and in need of company... no, it would cause her alarm or, worse still, amusement. Besides, she had already begun her prayers...

'Be pleased to keep me so chaste and unpolluted, not less in mind than in body, and safe from all dangers...' Her voice was insistent. Any foreigner would have assumed she was begging for her life. '...by the darkness of the night, so let everything that is sinful in me lie buried in thy mercy.'

Not a woman alive felt so deeply for the good of her family, I mused. No woman in Belfast was so vigilant and so handsome. It was a quality to admire, particularly amidst such grief for Arthur, not that the reckless boy deserved it. Her pure spirit was a quality to be protected by her husband. I made my way to my room, changed into my nightclothes and climbed into bed, goaded by a sinful, nagging ache. Next door, beyond the thin walls and moaning pipes, her prayer finished with one final, supplicant entreaty. I mimed to it in the moonlight, arms pinned to my sides, resolved to a solitary, sinless sleep.

'Hear me, O God,' came her voice. 'Father and Preserver, through Jesus Christ thy Son. Amen.'

CHAPTER FIVE

A week passed, and then another, the issue of the lock relegated by corroded gas pipes and leaking window frames. So it was, burdened by a mass of unfinished tasks, that I woke on an inconspicuous Monday in an agitated mood, greeted by a headache, anxious before my eyes were open, as though my ankles were gripped by some half-forgotten dream. There was a voice, was there not? And the familiar faces of strangers. There was something approaching; something unwelcome.

I scratched the razor across my neck, the dull blade nicking my skin, then splashed my face with cold water. Straightening up, I caught my eyes staring back from the cracked mirror above the sink, sunken and bloodshot. *I had the expression of a man in great pain,* I thought, as little spots of blood blossomed around my Adam's apple. Pressing my fingers into my cheekbones, I gurned and mugged away the chains of the nightmare, dressed and made my way downstairs, inspecting the troops as I took my seat at the breakfast table.

'Good morning, all.'

'Good morning, Father.'

There were knots in the girls' hair and where there were no knots, there were tangles. How crumpled their clothes were. I was about to pass comment when I caught sight of Elizabeth at the end of the table, her chapped fingers bothering her cuffs. She looked even more wretched than I, her own hair loose, lips dry, skin and eyes flecked with broken veins. *We should sleep better*, I thought, *if we shared a marital bed.* Yet too much time had passed between us, our estrangement stiffened and calcified since Robert's arrival, and she had grown alien to my touch. I had forgotten how she smelled, lost the brush of her skin. She was growing plain, I noticed, troubled with so many chores. A new housemaid could not come soon enough, though no applications had been made following my newspaper advertisement.

Elizabeth entreated us to recite a desultory prayer before we began picking our way through dollops of grey porridge. Margaret listened attentively as I offered a few updates on the Institute, while Helen slopped a cold drip of porridge into her bowl. Robert sucked his blanket, covering it in milky slime. I reached over and pulled it away from his mouth.

'Robert, you really are too old for that silly blanket. You're not a baby anymore; you are a Crawford man.'

'Oh, Father,' said Elizabeth, covering her mouth to yawn. 'Please do not excite the child, he is tired.' She set down her spoon, blinking. 'We are all tired.'

Helen spoke into her lap. 'The lady was crying on the stairs again, Mother. I heard her. She sounds very sorry.'

I gave my wife a testing eye. 'You must stop reading them such silly bedtime stories. All those impatient rabbits and madcap fairies, it only encourages them. Honestly, Helen, whatever possesses you to turn creaking pipes into white ladies?'

'I have heard her,' said Margaret, folding her arms. 'You must have heard her too?'

I thumped the table. 'Oh, for goodness' sakes, not you as well? Mother, will you kindly have a word with our children, this really is too much.'

Elizabeth yawned. 'They've been scaring themselves with ghost stories.'

'Mother, we haven't!' protested Margaret, Helen and Robert, jumping from their seats in unison.

I turned to Robert, his little hands still gripping his blanket in a tug of war. 'I tell you to cease that shouting and grizzling or I shall give you something to grizzle about.' The boy bit his thumbs. 'Better,' I said. 'I ought to take the blasted rag to the garden and burn it right away.'

I snatched it from him, rocketing a slop-filled spoon onto Elizabeth's blouse with a wet smack. She looked at the mess slipping down her chest, then wiped it away with her fingers, flicking it into her bowl, before walking silently to the kitchen, her mouth set hard. Robert looked at the blanket in my hand in a state of horror then flew into hysterics, screaming until I was forced to hand the damned thing back to him, porridge slime smeared over my jacket sleeves. Hang it all.

Duly, I finished my breakfast in three gulping spoonfuls before dashing upstairs to carry out a secret task while the rest were distracted with the clearing up. In ten minutes, I was back down the stairs for my coat, hat and umbrella, and out through the door with a meaningful slam, leaving the cries of Bedlam behind.

Patting myself down on the doorstep, I enjoyed a deep breath making my short way to the tram stop just in time for the six fifty-three via City Hall. It arrived in the dawn sunshine, gleaming and empty. I gave the conductor his penny-ha'penny fare and no sooner had I crossed my legs than the wheels of the tram were rumbling down the hill to the river. As we neared the Lagan, the electric lights buzzed, an uneasy tension rising in my stomach. My conscience perhaps... or congealed porridge. Perhaps I had been a little harsh after a late, somewhat disturbed night, pestered by my own desires and troubled by my dreams. I knew the cause of my rotten mood. What sort of man did Elizabeth think I was, unable to fit a blasted lock? I sighed, shaking my head. It mattered not, we would have the door open at last and she would remember my talent for invention and more besides.

The tram passed over cobbled streets, flanked on both sides by identical terraced houses, so close by I could almost have tapped on the windows. Gangs of labourers trudged towards the shipyards, cloth-capped and greasy-haired, cigarettes twitching as they conspired. It was a troubling thing, so many of them en masse. Pack-horse royalists hell-bent on committing treason.

A great beast of a young man caught me spying him, his sleeves rolled high, a blurred mermaid tattoo on his forearm. He studied me directly with gimlet eyes, fists in his pockets.

How small I felt then. If only a man's physical size were matched by the measure of his intellect; then William Jackson Crawford would be a giant! I saw myself straddling the river like Colossus, picking up a half-clad hull from the shipyard, crushing the men beneath it like ants beneath a shoe. As things were, any one of them – even the boys – could have reduced me to tears with a single thump. I knew it. They knew it. Such is the currency of manhood.

A morning shower of rain began to fall, and I pretended to study the houses on the near side of the carriage as the crowd thinned, the tram carrying me away. We clattered over the Lagan, the shipyard retreating into the thickening downpour, ribs of half-built boats cowering beneath monstrous baskets of iron.

What a glad sight, as we rolled down Chichester street and Donegall Square with the Robinson & Cleaver department store to our right. Pretty girls in smart housemaids' uniforms ran laughing through the rain for refuge beneath awnings, unfurled by beanpole shop boys. To our left, the dome of City Hall swung into view, men greeting one another, newspapers over their heads. A delivery boy waved as we passed by, almost clattering into a barrel-laden cart, headed no doubt for the drinking houses of the Ormeau Road. On we sailed to the Scottish Provident Building before hoving-to beside The Municipal Technical Institute.

I disembarked, thanking the conductor, and looked up at the grand building rising into the rain, smart as any London address with its imposing stone walls, soaring windows and copper cupolas. Immediately, I was across the pavement, head bowed, slapping up the steps into the entrance hall. I closed my eyes, breathing in the familiar scent of plaster, oil and varnish. My polished shoes sang like nails on glass. The Institute lay silent beyond the unending columns. A warren of bright corridors stacked in cavernous floor after cavernous floor, every inch crammed with state-of-the-art machinery. I took it all in as though it were my first visit. Within that marble cathedral hung the very beating heart of British invention. One day, I hoped, I would be its grandest patron.

'Professor Crawford!' called a voice from above. I searched hopelessly for somewhere to hide, but I had been spotted. 'Romeo, Romeo where for art thou, Romeo? Ho-ho!' I looked up to see Seamus Stoupe, the photography lecturer, leaning over the little stone balcony waving a peacock-blue handkerchief. 'Wait there, William, I shall come to you.' He scampered away to the stairs.

Damn it, there was no escape, and no creature on earth moves so quickly as an irritating man. He danced over the tiles towards me, grinning, all arms and sweat, dressed preposterously in a baggy velvet suit, pursing his lips like a kissing pig. He gave a courtly bow before standing far too near, smelling of lavender, whisky and damp, short tufts of blond hair sticking up from his round, pink head.

'Oh, Professor, how lovely to see you. My aren't you wet?' He patted his pudgy little fists over my waistcoat as I stood back, knocking him away.

'Let me go, Stoupe,' I barked. 'I have work to do.' I made to leave but he grabbed my hand, spinning me back like a Spanish dancer.

'What table are you on for the gala, Professor Crawford? You must tell me.'

'Thirty-two.'

'Thirty-two! What a relief, so am I.' He tickled me on the ribs. 'We shall make all sorts of mischief back there, eh, Prof? Hidden away from the top table.'

I frowned. Why *were* the Crawfords placed so low?

Just then the entrance doors swung open, hitting their frames, the principal appearing in a triumph of galoshes, flashing rainwater from a rubber hat. A young man followed close on his heels, sweeping his blond hair back with one hand, patting his fine suit down with the other. He was tall, lithe, with green eyes and a broad smile – every bit the Adelphi hero. Albert Blithe, our preposterously young mathematics teacher, barely twenty-five years old and some form of relation to the principal, though quite how they were connected was a mystery. He belonged to that peculiar cohort of young men who invariably turn out to be the sons, cousins, brothers, husbands and nephews of every prestigious person in the country. I pushed Stoupe away, arranging my tie.

'Aha! Good morning, gentlemen,' said the principal with a jolly smile. 'We are returned from some fishing on the Quiggery, what?' He looked me up and down. 'Are you a man for trout, Crawford?'

'Trout, Master?'

'Yes boy, trout. Trout!'

'Yes, Master, as a boy in Dunedin...'

Young Blithe cut in with an infantile cockney accent, waving his hat about like one of those awful stage performers in London. 'Here, I took my stepmuvva freshwater fishin' once, me ol' mucka,' he declared, beaming from ear to ear. 'She wouldn't eat the catch though. Oh, no. Said it needed a good wash!'

For some reason, the principal roared with laughter. 'A good wash? Oh, that is good, Albie! Wherever do you pick them up?' he bellowed, holding his stomach, Stoupe tittering like a sycophant.

I frowned, turning between them. 'Why ever would a freshwater fish need a wash?' I said. 'Was the water polluted?'

The principal slapped me on the back. 'Ha ha! That is what I like about you, Crawford. Always thinking, ever serious. Crikey! Look at your coat, all wet, lad.' He ruffled my hair. 'You shall have to dry off before class, there's a good boy.'

'Yes, Master.'

Stoupe wiggled his fingers. 'I was just asking Professor Crawford about the gala, gentlemen.'

The principal turned to me. 'I hope to see you there, Professor?'

He hoped? Was it such an uncertain thing? 'Yes, Master, of course.'

'Good-oh,' he said with a wink. 'Now I think of it, Crawford, I have a very important job for you, what? Come a little early if you can.'

Blithe raised an eyebrow. 'Important job, Frances?' he said. 'I could come early if...'

'No, no. This one's a job for Crawford, no doubt about it.'

My chest swelled. Oh, glorious providence. 'Yes, leave it to me, Master,' I said, smiling at Blithe. 'I shall arrive early as you wish.'

'Excellent, Professor, excellent,' he said, leaning back on his heels to take me in. 'You shall do well here, Crawford. Keep that mind of yours sharp.' He pulled a boiled sweet from his pocket and popped it into my unsuspecting mouth, patting me on the head. 'Good boy.'

I watched him stride away to his office, followed by Blithe, before spitting the sweet into my hand. Stoupe winked at me, lips pouting. 'Teacher's pet, my dear. Never fear, you are a favourite.'

I rolled my eyes, making my excuses, then climbed the central staircase to the fourth floor, revived by the pleasant tap, tap, tap of my shoes on the terrazzo. The engineering lab' and lecture rooms were at the far end of the corridor and I was upon the department in brisk fashion. Before turning the handle, I made a private wish that my colleague Professor Fforde was at home, sick after a damp weekend. I was to be disappointed.

'That blasted ballerina Stoupe catch you?' he growled from behind the great wheel of a steam pump. He leaned heavily on his walking stick, looking at me through wires and belts, heavy lips hanging low, hammocked between silver-whiskered jowls. Would he ever retire? For someone so unwell, he seemed preposterously healthy. 'This place is a damned mess of idiots.'

'And a very good morning to you, Professor Fforde,' I replied curtly, hanging my umbrella above the door. 'Forgive my tardiness, I was just discussing important matters with the principal. He has some vital work for me and requests I arrive early at the gala.'

'Is that so, Professor?' he said, raising his bushy eyebrows. 'Important donkey work, more like.'

I popped my coat on the stand. The laboratory was just as I had left it the previous Friday afternoon; pumps and engines polished, belts greased, the legions of bottled chemicals, wires and tools arranged in perfect order around the high shelves circling the panelled walls. I took a fresh piece of chalk from the box on my desk as Fforde hobbled away to his rooms. I sighed, relieved to abandon my petty troubles and focus on something light.

I snapped the chalk, merrily swooping across the board: *The tensile strength of steel (yield, ultimate, breaking) and the relative elongation of inferior materials at break*. It was to be another invigorating lesson. Now then, where was my pipe? I knew instantly; it was sitting on my desk in the study at home, just where I had left it.

CHAPTER SIX

I talked through heat radiation in under three hours, making satisfactory time to nose into convection before the day's end. There was a little trouble from an irksome boy, Samuel-something-or-other, who spent much of the day larking about, distracting his peers with paper cannonballs and a strange muttering sound, which caused great amusement behind my back. I ordered him to be quiet on three occasions, my every nerve tightening around the absence of tobacco.

Eventually, as the last hour of the day drew in, I sensed that my students' appetite for fluids and gases was waning, so I decided to loosen our figurative belts with a practical experiment. I clapped my hands. 'Who would like to give one of the new machines a run?' I said, to a gasp of collective delight.

We collected around a gleaming steam pump, as one of the sensible boys filled the water tank, checking the pipes were clean. With a bubble and push, the machine was thumping away quite happily. 'See how the rod glides?' I said, enjoying the slip of polished metal into the hungry mouth of the greased cylinder. 'Every angle, every seal, every point of friction must be engineered to within a fly's whisker if we are to create maximum energy.'

'Sir?' said the irksome boy, pushing to the front. 'What would happen then, if thon bit wasn't greased right, so?'

I looked to where he was pointing. How filthy his skin was; his nails and hair so caked in soot. I thought he must be a chimneysweep when he was not disrupting my lessons.

'This piston rod here?' I asked.

'Ay, sir.'

'Well, young...?'

'Goligher, sir,' he said in a husky little voice, staring at me with black eyes, his fists deep in his pockets.

'Ah yes, quite so. Master Goligher, that is a fine question,' I said. 'If the piston rod lacked grease, then of course it would rub.'

'Is that right, sir?' he interrupted. 'And what if thon rod was too thick, like?'

There were more stifled chuckles at my back as the wheel span faster.

'Well, Goligher, if the rod were too thick then it would split the valve.'

The boy cried out, clutching between his legs. 'Oh, sir, nai, I'll bet that's what happened to my sister last night!'

I frowned as the boys turned their backs, their shoulders shaking while the more serious students tutted and shook their heads. I tugged at my moustache, quite befuddled. 'I don't understand, Goligher, does your sister have a pump in her bedroom?'

'Ack, sir, yes. Most nights!'

And with that the entire classroom fell about laughing, slapping him on the shoulder, hanging from one another, cradling their bellies. I stood up, exasperated, ready to give the little toad the back of my hand for such vulgarity, but, before I could reach him, the bell called them away and in a minute flat they were gone, chanting and calling to one another, voices echoing down the corridor. I shook my head, smiling as I ran a dirty rag over the greased piston. Sexual congress is a fine source of amusement to a blushing boy until he realises how shamefully ill-equipped he is for the job. Split valves, indeed.

I twizzled my moustache, standing back as the machine let the last wisps of steam escape, then locked the laboratory door, skipping back to my desk in an excited little dance. Looking through my drawers, scolding myself for not ordering things better, I found what I was after: a short brass rod with a blank paddle at the end. I lit my magnifying lamp, reaching into my pocket to pull out a piece of card cut into the crude shape of a key. The end was covered in a coating of dark blue ink, impressed with a geometric pattern. I held it up to the blank with a satisfied smile, the brass winking at me in the light. 'Right then,' I said, one eye closed. 'Let us see.'

That very morning, while the family were clearing the breakfast plates downstairs, I had taken a knife from the desk in my study and cut a piece of card to the exact shape I needed, then painted it with my own concoction of Prussian ink and grease. Then, I had crept up to the maid's locked door before slowly, ever-so-gently, placing it into the keyhole, careful to avoid contact with the brass escutcheon. An inch or so inside, I had felt the makeshift blank pressing against the hidden plate. My breath held, my eyes closed, I had proceeded to turn it further, pressing the card firmly against the sensitive mechanism within. After a short while, I withdrew from the lock, padding softly back to my study where, behold! It had worked! For there, upon the flat edge of the card was the unmistakable imprint of the pins, like castle crenulations, revealing the shape of the concealed mechanism of the lock.

I worked at the lathe, humming to myself, vents whispering from the Institute walls as I cut into the metal. The engineering lab' seemed such an eerie place with the lights turned out, the machines casting unnatural shadows on the walls, the overwhelming sense that the room was nothing but a small pocket of air in one vast cavern of brick and marble. Thankfully, the job did not take long for soon enough I held between my thumb and forefinger a perfectly polished key.

Merry as an apprentice, I popped it into my pocket and stepped into the deserted corridor humming a timid hymn to myself for company, then paused... had I heard something? Away to the far end of the corridor perhaps... or closer maybe, beside the tall windows? It was a clicking sound, like the hard boots of a small child walking slowly towards me. A queer chill passed over my bones as I listened. There! I strained my eyes in the dark, for I felt sure of three things all at once: that nobody was there; that somebody had most certainly *been* there moments ago, and that they were watching me now.

'Hello?' I called, my voice echoing against the high ceiling. 'Hello?' I crept along the corridor, and there it was again. I froze. The eyes play such devilish tricks at low light, yet whether it was the fall of a shadow from the far window or some other troubling of the light, there was surely the indistinguishable form of a stranger at the far end of the corridor.

'Hello?' I called again, reasoning against my quickening heart that they might be a student. 'Are the doors still open?' Yet there came no answer, and I felt another chill pass over my back as I neared the stranger. 'Turn around, whoever you are,' I said. Yet the closer I drew, the less their outline seemed to impress itself against the wall, and, by the time I edged within ten feet of them, there was nothing there but plain white plaster. I smoothed my hair with shaking hands, turning the corner to the grand staircase. 'Bloody fools,' I muttered to myself, comforted by the sound of my voice. 'Silly children.'

I stepped from the corridor, humming for reassurance, then walked towards the stairs, doing my best to control my rising disquiet – yet, all of a sudden, another shiver coursed through me for I was absolutely certain that someone, some cold *thing* was following at my back. I did not turn, but sprinted full pelt down the stairs, clattering, barely holding on to the bannister as the shadow of another person ran after me, barely an arm's length behind my back. I sensed their fingers on my shoulder as I reached the lower staircase, felt them tugging at my jacket and I squealed, tumbling through the entrance doors to the street where I hunched over, hands gripping my still-quivering knees, the spookiness of the great empty building washed away by the ordinariness of an evening's drizzle. Looking up, I panted, laughing at myself in my foolishness, wiping sweat and raindrops from my damned traitorous eyes. Get a hold of yourself, man, you are no better than the children.

CHAPTER SEVEN

I was through the front door of our home in twenty minutes, calling over my shoulder, 'Hello all, Father is home.'

'Hello, Father.'

I nearly jumped out of my shoes, for Elizabeth and the children were standing directly behind me at the parlour door.

'Goodness me, Crawfords!' I said, shaking my coat. 'What is all this then?'

'Did you have a lovely day, Father?' asked Margaret.

'Yes... thank you, I did as a matter of fact.' What the blazes were they doing, standing there like the Coldstream guards? I reached for the parlour door only for Elizabeth to jump in front of me, crying out in a state of glee that dinner was on the table. I looked her over, removing my hat. 'Good God, Elizabeth,' I said with a nervous laugh. 'Why such excitement? Is it lamb?'

'No, Father,' she said, wringing her hands with a peculiar smile. 'You are late again, are you feeling well?'

'Well, my love? I should say so.'

'Oh good. Come to the dining room straight away and you shall see.'

'I must fetch my pipe first, I...'

'No, no! I have it for you.' She thrust it into my hands, then tugged at my arm as I followed on, the children under my feet.

'You remind me, we must find ourselves a new housemaid and cook. A young girl perhaps, smart and practical.'

Robert snorted as he dashed past me, earning himself a sharp, whispered rebuke from his sister. I tutted at them as we arrived at the dinner table. 'What a silly mood you are all in this evening.'

Elizabeth disappeared to the kitchen, returning with a platter which she placed at the centre of the table, standing back, beaming. Margaret removed the lid from a pot, while Helen placed a jug at my side. I was taken aback, for laid before me was a glorious assortment of roasted potatoes, buttered green vegetables and strips of flaky white fish, pale flesh shining happily in the candlelight, all of it cooked and presented to perfection.

'My goodness!' I exclaimed. 'What's all this?'

'Dinner, Father,' said Helen. 'Isn't it wonderful?'

'It is. My, my, haven't you been working hard?'

Elizabeth took her seat, beckoning the children to follow and oh, what a cosy little family we were settling into the sound of the crackling fire in the parlour. I sniffed our steaming supper, rubbing my hands together, only to find my fellow Crawfords staring at me with fixed smiles, as still as dolls. Even Robert was without a wriggle, hands pinched beneath his bottom, blanket tucked to one side. So, my harsh words at the start of the day had achieved their desired effect? Father knows best.

'Prayers, Elizabeth?' I said. 'Christ must be thankful for what we are about to receive.'

'Yes, Father, of course. Come, children, let us pray.'

She chanted her invocation with great enthusiasm, the corner of her mouth twitching, fingernails scratching nervously at the sore skin on her wrists. 'Gracious God, we have sinned against Thee, and are unworthy of Thy mercy...' The children followed along, I miming as much as I could manage, inspecting them from beneath a suspicious brow. '...help us to eat and drink to Thy glory, for Christ's sake. Amen.'

'For Christ's sake indeed,' I said, taking up my fork. 'Elizabeth, you have done yourself proud. How lucky we are, children, to have such a clever mother. Come along then, let us eat.' We tucked in hungrily, any pleasantries lost to our enjoyment of the feast.

'Yummy,' said Margaret in an uncommonly loud voice. 'It is delicious, thank you. We are not difficult to cook for at all and truly very polite and grateful.'

'Indeed we are...' I said with a raised eyebrow. 'There is no need to shout, though. What say you, Robert? Have you paid your compliments to the cook?'

'She's ugly,' he said, laughing to reveal a tongue caked in white slime.

I slammed down my knife. 'How dare you, Robert. Apologise to your mother at once. Your mother is easily the most beautiful lady in Belfast.' I gave her a wink.

Robert bounced in his chair, waving his fork over his head, only to have Margaret's hand clapped over his mouth. 'Be quiet,' she snapped. 'Don't be rude.'

Elizabeth coughed, picking at her peas, her eyes darting from the table to the parlour curtain and back, delivering slivers of potato to a watery smile. I jabbed my fork at her. 'The family bond is the greatest ingredient in any home-cooked meal, I say. That is the key.'

The key indeed. Just then I remembered my plan and sniffed casually, feeling the brass rod in my pocket. 'Tell me, dear, will you be going to a church meeting this evening?'

'Yes,' said Elizabeth brightening up, only to sink again. 'Though now... perhaps not.'

I was pleased to have her home for the evening. She could witness her husband using his marvellous key to open the locked door; all against anybody's expectations. On we ate in a queer sort of mood, the silence only interrupted by the sound of knives sliding over plates. Elizabeth finished her dinner first, resting her cutlery neatly beside a delicate arrangement of fish bones. She sat with her hands fidgeting beneath the table, watching me as I mopped up my potato.

'Was work very interesting today?' asked Margaret.

'It was, it was.'

I was just lifting a potato to my mouth when there came a dull thump from the parlour. I stopped to listen, frustrated by the chatter around the table which seemed to grow in volume precisely as I strained my ears. 'Hush,' I said. 'What was that sound?'

'The pipes, I expect,' said Elizabeth. 'Come, Father, finish your dinner.'

I did so, chewing a lump of fish, wondering whether the entire house would need replumbing, when I heard another thump from the parlour, this time followed by a stifled yelp and a sort of sniffling. I threw down my cutlery. 'What was that?' I demanded, standing from my chair. Margaret froze, eyes wide, Helen whispering to her mother. I placed my napkin on the table and went to the curtain, yet before I could pull it back, Elizabeth sprang forwards.

'No, don't!' she said, knocking a glass of water across the tablecloth. 'Finish your dinner first, please.'

'First?' I said, aghast. 'First? What is *after,* pray tell? Is there some murderous pudding lurking behind here?' I tutted at her. 'Come now, Elizabeth, what is going on, you've been as guilty as priests from the moment I arrived home.' I parted the curtain, poking my head through to the lightless room.

Only the low flame of the fire could be seen, its amber glow barely reaching the tassels of the Persian rug, nothing illuminated but a few sparks floating over the grate. As I parted the curtain further, some dim yellow light crept over Elizabeth's phantom figurines, giving the room the personality of some late-discovered crypt. 'Now then,' I said in a low voice. 'What do we have in here? If it is another stray cat, Helen, she shall have to go.'

'William, come back in here, please,' said Elizabeth.

I ignored her, catching sight of something shifting in the armchair beside the window and I jumped backwards, overcome by an involuntary shiver, knocking one of the ornaments to the floor with a smash. 'Hello?' I whispered, stepping gingerly towards the chair, my arm shielding my face. 'Hello, who is there?' The thing, whatever it was, shifted once more as I edged towards it. My eyes grew keen against the shadows, for I could see what appeared to be two thick legs sticking down from the chair to the carpet. I turned on the lamp, the pungent hiss of coal gas mixing with my own agitated breath, the crackle of the fire, the thump of my heart.

'Darling Elizabeth,' I called back through the curtain, 'Darling, there is someone in here, is there? Who is it, please?'

I had a sudden memory of her late brother, Arthur, playing a similar trick, hiding in the parlour of our old home as a surprise guest. A familiar chill struck me as I imagined him in the chair, face swollen, lips and fingernails blue, bright-red hair floating in slow-dancing fronds over a barnacled, eyeless skull. Oh my poor shaking heart, for I felt lost in the silent house, not a light penetrating the room, not even a glimmer beneath the door to the hallway. Trembling, I searched my trouser pocket for my matches. 'Arthur?' I whispered, my voice high. 'Is that you, Arthur?'

There was no answer; only a terrible gargling sound like the last dribble from a draining sink. I gulped, ready to escape, for who could say what I was about to discover? Forcing myself to be brave, I struck a match, spying in the flash two huge eyes glaring at me from the chair.

'My Lord!' I exclaimed as the curtain swished open behind me, filling the room with light. The thing gave a strangled cry as it recoiled, covering itself with a muscly arm beneath a pile of bags. I gripped my heart, near dead from surprise, for it was not a *thing* at all, no spectral visitation from a buried wreck. Rather it was, at least from what I could make out between handles, straps and corners... a *woman*.

I stumbled backwards into the curtain, catching my heel on the swinging material and with the sound of an almighty *rip*, crashed to the floor. There I lay groaning, spectacles askew, my pipe balanced over my ear, the children staring down at me.

'Silly old Farfur,' said Robert.

CHAPTER EIGHT

'Her name is Rose,' said Helen. 'Might we keep her?'

'Rose?' I said, lifting myself from the pile of dusty curtains on the floor. I rubbed my aching backside, catching sight of my reflection in the mirror, one length of heavy material draped over my shoulder like a Roman senator. I threw it off. 'Where is your mother?' She was standing in the doorway. 'Who is this?' I demanded. 'Tell me at once.'

'Do you not know, Father?' said Margaret in a business-like tone, already rescuing the girl from the rubble of luggage on her lap.

'Do I not know? What on earth is that supposed to mean, child?'

The naked gaslight danced on the wall, three fingers guttering and springing. What an unfortunate air of evil it gave to the young woman's profile, for her visage was strangely twisted, larger on the left side than the right as though two faces, malformed in their own individuality, were squashed into one. She regarded me fearfully as I stepped closer, shrinking away with the same awful gargling noise. I snorted, for the ghoulish sound in the dark was nothing less than a sniffle in the light. Helen stood beside me.

'She is such a sorry thing, Father, don't you think? Please be kind to her.'

'Who on earth is she?' I asked.

Elizabeth crossed the room, took me by the hand, peered intensely into my eyes. 'Give thanks to the Lord, for he is good,' she said. 'Rose has come to join our family in answer to our prayers. You will be kind to her. We all will. You advertised for a new housemaid and here she is, a blessing we can afford.'

'We are... blessed by this... by this...?' I was quite lost for words, mesmerised, for my beloved wife had never held my eyes with such purpose, not even on our wedding day. The great miserable goat on the chair was crying silently now, tears rolling down her cheeks.

I clicked my fingers at her impatiently. 'Housemaid indeed. Do you have a letter of application? Hand it over, let me read it.'

'I don't believe she can write,' said Elizabeth.

'Whyever not? Is she foreign?'

'I don't think so.'

I nodded. 'Catholic, no doubt. It is a peculiarity of theirs you know, to be persistently threatening and habitually terrified. Do you come with any experience?' I lit my pipe, turning to Elizabeth. 'Why won't she speak?'

'I believe... I believe she is a mute.'

I laughed, only to see the expression on the girl's face. 'She is a mute?' I said, looking between the children. Margaret nodded and I knew it to be true. 'We have engaged a mute, illiterate maid with no references? Good Lord, the Crawfords have outdone themselves this time.'

'Oh, William, shame on you,' said Elizabeth. 'You wouldn't wish her harm.'

'Yes, Father,' said Helen. 'We like Rose, don't we, Margaret?'

'Oh yes, certainly,' said Margaret, lifting an assortment of boxes to the stairs. 'I suppose we must.'

I massaged my poor, throbbing temples, facing the queer visitor, hands on my hips. 'Well then, let us see you.'

She rubbed one heavy boot over the other, then stood up smoothing her skirt. What an impression she made. Two powerful, bowed legs, wrapped in thick woollen stockings; her dress, a crumpled, grey thing, stretched tightly around a dome-like stomach with breasts like sacks of sand slung across a mule. Why, she must have been six feet tall. I looked up at her, clearing my throat. 'My goodness,' I said, tutting to myself, thinking of the pretty things I had seen outside the department store that very morning. 'Rose, is it?' I shook my head, standing back, for I had never encountered a woman less like a flower in all my life.

Elizabeth squeezed my arm. 'How good and pleasant it is, when God's people live together in unity.'

'I think she is beautiful,' said Helen, trimming Rose with ribbons plucked from her dress while Robert tried to climb her, his blanket aloft like a flag. All the while the visitor looked at me, oblivious to anything but my own deliberation. I raised an eyebrow. 'A week's trial,' I said.

'Oh, thank you, Father!' cried Helen, dancing in circles, while Margaret lifted one of the larger bags to the hallway with a long-suffering sigh. 'Wherever do we bed her down, Mother? Shall I carry her bags to the nursery?'

'Yes,' said Elizabeth. 'Rose, you shall sleep in the nursery tonight with Robert; we shall organise your room first thing tomorrow. Quick, children, take her things upstairs, then it is time for bed.'

I allowed them to chatter, enjoying a wry smile at their expense. What a propitious moment for our new housemaid to have joined the Crawford household. Here she was, barely an hour under our roof and already a demonstration of my ingenuity.

'Why should she sleep in the nursery?' I asked, nonchalantly picking at a loose thread on the back of the armchair. 'After all, we have the maid's room, do we not? Where better for a housemaid to sleep?'

Elizabeth rubbed at her brow. 'Oh, for goodness' sake, William, your memory. Hazel's room is locked.'

'Ah yes, so it is,' I said, nodding before spinning about flourishing the key from my pocket with a triumphant aha!

'What is that?' asked Elizabeth, eyeing the thing nervously, her face ghostly pale.

I laughed, turning about the room in amazement. 'If you cannot recognise a simple key, it is little wonder you lost the original.'

'It won't work.'

'Oh pish, have some faith in your husband. Come on all of you, let us find out...'

'No, please,' said Elizabeth, blocking my way. 'Do not open that door, I beg you.'

I can swear now, this was my very first comprehension of my wife as a villain. Until that point, from the moment we had met, I had no reason to doubt her motives, her behaviour, her honour. Yet there, in that queer, flickering moment, watched by the children and our strange new housemaid, I beheld for the first time the possibility of a second woman in my wife; neither a better one nor anything like the woman I had loved, and whether it was the heat of my fingers combined with the fire or something more unnatural I cannot say, yet the key in my fingertips grew scalding hot and it was all I could do not to drop it. I pushed my way past her, leaping up the staircase, tripping on the runner as I rounded to the attic room stairs, Elizabeth close at my heels calling all the while, beseeching me to wait. No, I would not, for I realised that if I reached the room second, I would never know the truth. I took the bare staircase two steps at a time to the maid's room, jabbing the key into the lock. At first it stuck, damn it, Elizabeth panting behind me.

'You see,' she said, tugging at my sleeve. 'It cannot open, please come away.'

Yet with a deliberate wiggle and a sharp turn, I felt the key bite, the door shuddering with a hollow, satisfying *click*. I turned the handle, Elizabeth crying for me to give in.

'Forgive me, Lord,' she said. 'Forgive me.'

CHAPTER NINE

The attic room was lit by the open window, the drapes pulled out by a breeze. I stepped inside, searching for some lurking intruder, some scandal. The lamp shone, revealing nothing more than an undressed wire-framed bed, a bare floor, an empty wardrobe and a writing desk beneath a white sheet. I turned to my wife, who was looking into the room with haunted eyes.

'William,' she said. 'It is my shame. Oh, Christ, forgive me for my sins, I repent.'

I frowned, searching the room. 'Is it... the desk?' I said, and she nodded. I stepped over to it, pulling the sheet away. There was a candle, almost burnt to the quick, cold wax frozen over a cracked saucer. Beside it, a bald carnation in a porcelain vase, petals scattered around a folded letter with a heading stamped across its top: *WHITE STAR LINE.* Propped against the back of the desk, a photograph of a young man staring out, the formality of the picture doing little to hide his low character. I picked up the photograph. His name was written beneath it, in Elizabeth's hand.

ARTHUR JOLLY

Hello, Arthur, I thought. *Strange to think of you, far beneath the sea.*

A tear rolled down Elizabeth's cheek.

'My darling,' I whispered. 'What is all this?'

'It is Arthur, of course.' She stepped closer to me, looking at the photograph. 'Don't mock me. I should like to hear him again, that's all. I worry for him. I should like to know whether he's safe.'

I rolled my eyes, tutting. 'He is not safe, he is drowned.'

Elizabeth pressed past me, fetching the portrait, clutching it to her chest. 'Stop it, don't say that, please.'

I took her in my arms, but she pushed away. 'Don't touch me, William. I didn't want you to see it. I needed to be close to him, that's all. He died alone in the dark, with the sea all around him. It was so cold.'

'It might not have been so dark.'

'There were no stars, he told me.'

'It was a clear night, filled with stars. I read it in the newspapers.'

Elizabeth squealed with frustration. 'Oh, spare me your wisdom! Will you quarrel with him even when he's dead? Don't do this to me tonight, I couldn't stand it. Is it any wonder I locked the room? If you care for me at all, care for anybody but yourself, you will leave him be. I know what you thought of him; why could you not be his friend? He looked up to you.'

'When he wasn't looking up skirts, perhaps,' I laughed. 'He was a waster.'

I regretted the words as soon as they left my mouth and went to hold her, only to have my hand slapped away.

'He was a boy. He was my brother. If it hadn't been for your constant lecturing I might have seen him before he left.' She kissed the photograph and I felt a jealous temper rise.

'He did not run from me, Elizabeth. He ran from the law.'

She looked up, bitter loathing written in every line of her face. 'My mother begged me to care for him,' she hissed. 'And she begged me not to marry you. I should have listened. Did you know, he called for me as the ship sank? For the children too. But he called for you last, William Jackson Crawford. You had better hope he stays in the sea.'

I stood frozen, my body tingling with rage. 'Enough,' I said, my voice high. The light outside guttered, our new housemaid blocking the doorway, her silhouette filling the frame. 'That is quite enough. I shall be in my study.'

***

The following morning, I rose, hands and feet aching, bones brittle with cold. My head was terribly sore. When I looked in the mirror over the sink, I felt sure my own skull was no less split than the glass. I looked down at my bed in disarray, trying to remember my dreams. I could recall a moment, buried deep in the early hours of the morning, when I had sat up, my heart pounding, to see a pale figure slipping through the bedroom door. I pressed my fingers into my eyes, a sick feeling in my stomach. What on earth did I have to feel guilty for? I slapped my face, taking up my razor, irritated by the sight of my sheets in the mirror. Every night, I would slip into bed like a penny in an envelope, only to wake up tangled in bedclothes.

I thought of the previous evening's revelations with the new housemaid and Arthur's shrine, wondering at the absurdity of it all. Me, creeping into the parlour in the dark, that gargantuan girl hiding beneath her luggage. If only *that* had been a dream. I groaned, scratching my whiskered face. My eyes were bloodshot, my skin dry. I heard Elizabeth on the landing, speaking to the housemaid in a clipped voice. She had some errands to run with the children; Robert needed medicine for a tummy complaint. A few minutes later, they were all thumping and squealing from the house, Robert stamping his feet down the stairs. What time was it? Nine o'clock, and still I was undressed.

I washed myself with a cold flannel, mumbling about women and their tantrums, as my mind wandered to the annual gala. It was almost upon us and what a couple we would make. We would have to put on a show of unity, there was nothing else to be done. Elizabeth would look back one day, aghast at her reckless behaviour. I imagined a future where I, a celebrated professor dripping with accolades, would sweep my eyes across a room filled with humble admirers. Principal Crawford, the respected – nay *renowned* – leading light in engineering: inventor of an unimaginably luxurious airship. I imagined a letter from the king above my desk thanking me for my services to the Empire. *Sir William Jackson Crawford.*

I pulled my underwear up, before lathering my face and scraping my whiskers away with the dullest razor in Ireland. How profitable life promised to be; and then she would be sorry for speaking to her husband so. I smarted, catching my cheek with the blade. The only thing required of me was to follow my own sedulous ingenuity with good faith and hard work, whilst younger men clapped my back applauding my inexorable rise to fame and fortune. I nicked my cheek and tutted. What exactly had I expected to find behind that door anyhow? A daemon? A murderer? A lover? All the while, nothing but a ridiculous shrine to her mongrel of a brother. Why, Elizabeth's behaviour would have made even the most sceptical detective search for a pile of bodies. I cut myself beneath my earlobe, growling with frustration, swishing the blade in cold, pink water. I mean, to keep the room locked, to order me not to look inside. To *order* me! Scandalous behaviour; if only I had a friend to complain to about it. I cut my lip, blood trickling to my chin. Had she not said something strange when her shrine was uncovered? Well, she had been in such a hysterical temper, I had barely listened. Something about Arthur... something that didn't add up. I tugged a wayward hair from my moustache, cutting my neck before throwing the damned useless blade into the sink with a plop. A knock came at the door.

'Go away, God damn you!' I shouted, but she appeared all the same, her hair tied into a cap designed for a smaller skull.

'Oh, it's you, Rose. Didn't you hear me? I said go away, or are you deaf as well as dumb?'

She hovered, looking at her feet, before edging into the room. I was about to splash my shaving water on her like a stray cat when I noticed she was holding out a soft towel, a new razor laid upon it. Our eyes met and she looked away, scuffing the floor with her shoe.

'For me?' I said, and she nodded, still staring at the floor. 'Well, I suppose it must be for me; Robert is a few years from shaving.'

I reached out for the razor, and she backed away. 'Come now, Rose. I'm not such an ogre. My wife tests me, but she is a good woman.'

She moved to the door, tall as any docker at the yard, the feminine frills of her apron a mockery of her shoulders.

'Do you have the measure of things?' I asked kindly and, to my relief, she nodded. 'Good, good. If there is anything I can show you at all, I'd be perfectly willing. I am a respected engineer and a *professor*, don't you know.' She looked down at the ash pan, still unable to meet my eye. I smiled. 'I expect you're not very used to men. I was taught to "keep home" by my late mother.' She flushed, flicking her eyes to the skirting board. 'Mother needed the help, you see. I had to wash the beds...' I thought of pink water being squeezed from grey linen. 'Do you have a mother, Rose? What was her name?' She stood still, ignoring me as a puff of ash fell to the rug from her pan. Immediately, we both bent down to fetch it up, bumping our heads. She gave a startled grunt then disappeared from the room, as I dropped my shaving brush and followed her out. 'Agnes,' I called.

She turned to face me and I leaned against the wall. 'That was my mother's name. Agnes.' She nodded, wringing the towel in her hands. 'Thank you for the razor, Rose. I think I would have cut my throat if you hadn't come.' She raised her eyes to me at last, and we stared at one another to the sound of the parlour clock, horses clopping beyond the front door. To my delight, she smiled. It was like a great tree coming to leaf, not a graceful thing, nor gentle, more sturdy, like the ruddy health of freshly carved meat. 'Listen, Rose,' I said. 'Forgive me if I startled you last night. I admit I was rather manic when I discovered you there. After all, what sensible man enjoys surprises?' I pointed my new razor at her with a wink. 'I say behind every war, baby and aneurysm there is a surprise.' She looked at me with a queer expression, eyes fixed, as though every word I uttered was her first hearing of the gospel. I wondered what brutish behaviour she had suffered in her childhood. Awful boys, no doubt, abusing her. 'Work downstairs for the time being please. I require absolute silence in my study.'

She left to empty the pan, the kitchen soon clanking to the sound of scrubbed plates. Once fully washed and dressed, hair tamed, I stood on the landing, wrestling with myself, looking up to the attic. It called to me, the housemaid's door. How different the flight of stairs seemed in the daylight. How innocent, open, ordinary. Just a set of narrow stairs to a sparse bedroom. Was

Elizabeth's shrine still there? Surely she had cleared it all away by now, ashamed of her childish performance. I pursed my lips. I simply had to prove the room's innocence to myself before I could let it be. One look, one *quick,* unobtrusive glance would not hurt a soul.

I padded up the stairs as quietly as my socks would allow and peered inside. The curtains were open; Rose had made her bed with particular care, the corners of her sheets folded back over a smoothed eiderdown; the thin, flowery pillows squared at the corners, neatly piled, the bedspread placed deliberately over the foot with all the care of a Japanese paper-folder.

I stepped across the room to the escritoire, pleased to see the shrine gone. Foolish Elizabeth, tormented by the thought of her beloved brother sinking with that ship into the icy darkness. He didn't deserve a moment's thought; not after all he'd done. The newspapers at the time of the sinking had told of countless mottled bodies being tugged with sodden ropes from the water. Not Arthur's, mind you. His corpse remained submerged, picked to the bone no doubt by the fish. I had a vision of him down there; one ankle tied to the murky seabed by a chain, fingers forever reaching up from the darkness. How the city had mourned, streets filled with weeping mothers and even weeping men. Belfast had turned a deeper shade of grey that day, and it was yet to cast off its weeds, hanging on to grim storms year on year.

I sniffed. What had Elizabeth said about Arthur's shrine? Had she not mentioned something about calling my name? I had been distracted. I peered into the escritoire, opening the central compartment. The space inside was bare, save for a sheet of blue lining paper, dotted with faded yellow daisies. I went to close the drawer then stopped, catching sight of a sheaf of writing paper, hidden at the very back. It was creased, covered in a dense scribble of smudged blue handwriting. I pulled it out, held it up to the light, reading something that troubled me for... damn it, footsteps were approaching from below. Quickly, I shut the drawer, then tiptoed down to my study, just as Rose passed by.

Panting, I moved to my bureau, fetched out my reading spectacles, flattening the letter on the desk. The author had been in a terrible rush, that much I could see; the words were backed into one another, crammed impatiently into the edges of the page yet, in spite of the frantic hand, I recognised it instantly. The author was none other than Hazel our former housemaid, and her words were damning:

Forgive me, Mrs Crawford... but I can lie no more.

CHAPTER TEN

I tried my darndest to decode the rest of the maid's handwriting, reading it fully three times, nose right up to the paper. I screwed the thing into a ball with a growl, stopping myself just in time from tossing it onto the fire. I retched over the wastepaper basket before slumping at my desk once more, steadying myself as the room spun.

At last, I wiped my brow, returning to the letter, my eyes now grown accustomed to certain characters. Some of the words were impossibly blurred, like old Delftware porcelain. I removed my spectacles with a groan. *Hazel, confound you,* I thought. *What are you trying to tell me?* I squeezed my eyes shut, shook my head, then, at last, some of the words began to lift from the scrawl.

Dear Mrs Crawford,
I am sory to have to give you my notis. I hav give much thort to my disishun. My sisters have a plays for me so I will stay ther. Plese, dont think badley of me Mrs C, and it is for you to say what you lyk to Mr C.

Iv left sum cold meets for the childrin and all the washerin has bin done and the hose is cleen so don say it waznet. I am sorry to leeve you in a fix.

49

I cant sense what I saw last nite and what I hav herd and it is not riet for a God-fearsum women such as myself to be part of it.

I mak no jujmet, that is not my plays, you now me and I hav lived a lyfe and I now yore intenshins are not evil but ther can com no god of theese secrits.

I now you have bin unhapy Mrs C but I cannt help but pity pore Mr C for not nowing about Angels.

Do not play games with love, Mrs C I saw you meetin that man. You are a marreyed women and Mr C will discuvver what he has bin doin with you sooner or layter and then what will you do?

Think of the childrin. You told me when I saw evrythin that you love him and nede him but is that enuff to rooin what you hav with yur husbind?

I cant pritend no longer. Yesterday, you ask me to kip another secrit and I will not. If you love Mr C, you must tell him the trooth about Angels. Say goodbie to Margritt, Helin and poor litle Rob for me. Tell them not to be afrayd of the voyses at leest?

Plees do not to contact me. You can do wot you think about a new made. Be carefull, Mrs C

Hazel Conneely

I tapped my pipe before folding the letter into the desk drawer. What on earth did it all mean? Hazel pitied me. She *pitied* me? I pitied myself. Elizabeth's actions were not right for the family, so Hazel had written. Elizabeth had been unhappy. Well, that was hardly a revelation. What *had* Hazel seen exactly? What had she heard? And *Angels*, for crying out loud. What on earth was I to make of *Angels*? I put my head in my hands, tugged at my hair, whimpering like a sorry schoolboy. My spectacles pressed hard into the bridge of my nose, pushing them deeper still, finding some purpose in the pain. The words, they were already stained on my very heart, quite impossible to forget. *I cant sense what I saw last nite and what I hav herd and it is not riet for a God-fearsum women such as myself to be part of it.*

I was about to retch some more when the front door opened, filling the house with shouting. I dragged myself from my desk to the landing, stretching the anguish from my face, determined not to let on. 'What ho, returning adventurers,' I said, descending the stairs, gripping the bannister to keep my balance. Robert came bounding past me in blind tears holding his tummy, followed by Rose. The girls were singing, Helen boasting about a new dress while Margaret instructed Elizabeth on her unsatisfactory mothering skills. I found them in the parlour, stepping inside, swinging my arms.

'A successful trip, my dear?' I asked, casually.

Think of the childrin. You told me when I saw evrythin that you love him and nede him but is that enuff to rooin what you hav with yur husbind?

'Oh, William, there you are,' said Elizabeth, removing her hat, throwing it to the armchair. 'I suppose you could say that, though Robert *will* keep running away. Rose shall have to come with me next time. It's good to have some help with the children at last. Have you been kind to her? I wouldn't want you scaring her away.'

'I have been a master, if that is what you mean.'

Elizabeth raised her eyebrows, taking a bottle from a paper bag, setting it on the table. 'Thank goodness we managed to get Robert's medicine before his accident,' she said, grimacing as a howl rang out from the nursery followed by a great splash of water from the bathtub. 'The poor thing had an embarrassment.'

'We visited Fusco's for ice cream,' said Helen, all too eager to tell the story. 'Robert had far too much butterscotch whip, and I did warn him, Father. Then we visited Robinson & Cleaver's and he ran straight in front of a motorcar and almost got squashed. He was crying like a baby when I told him off and if he hadn't been naughty enough, he made a mess in his shorts which was bright green and everyone was looking at us and the nice man with the tape measure around his neck had to take us to the back of the shop to fetch tissues and towels because it was going all down his legs and then we had to come straight home on the tram with Robert crying all the way wrapped in a much bigger boy's shorts from their lost items box which was strange really because what sort of boy loses his shorts?' She pinched her nose, her voice like a muffled cornet. 'There was the most awful stink, Father, and the tram was terribly busy and...'

'That's enough, Helen, please,' said Elizabeth, rubbing her wrists. She turned to me, flushed to her chin. 'William, it was such an awful mess. He has his poorly tummy again and it seems worse than ever.'

I heard my son bellowing upstairs. 'Rose is on the case, by the sounds of it,' I said. 'Come, such things happen, darling, it isn't your fault.'

'I know it isn't my fault.'

'Are you still using boric in his milk?'

'Of course I am,' said Elizabeth. 'I have been using more than usual, but he only gets worse.' I looked at her, quite disorientated. How could she be capable of the shameful visions conjured up by Hazel's letter? Was there something more than grief for her brother and women's troubles keeping her from me?

'Girls,' I said. 'Take your new things upstairs and give your mother and I a moment.'

Margaret shrugged, taking Helen upstairs. I waited for their footsteps to recede before closing the door. 'Elizabeth,' I said, standing at her back as she fussed with a hairpin.

'What is it? More of your wisdom to share? I half expected Rose to be gone when we got back. It's a wonder Aunt Adelia puts up with us, you're so horrible to her.'

'Why must we call her *Aunt Adelia*, anyway?'

She paused. 'I swear, I shall stick this pin in your eye.'

I sighed. 'My love, I merely want to ask you, after last night, is everything as it ought to be?'

She frowned, busying herself with a ribbon. 'As it ought to be? What a funny question.'

I shifted my feet. 'I mean, as it ought to be between a husband and wife.'

'What is this?' She turned to me, her face strained.

'I mean to say, happy as a family,' I said, fumbling over my words.

'Well, I must admit I wasn't too happy when Robert had his accident.' She raised her eyebrows, turning back to the mirror with a pin in her teeth. 'I couldn't bear to see him looking so sad.'

'I just wonder...' I stopped as she pressed the pin into her hair, the cuff of her sleeve pulling back. We both saw it, the dark-pink finger mark on her skin. She lowered her arm, pulling her sleeve down, the pin dropping onto the mantelpiece.

'Those children,' she whispered with a dry laugh.

I narrowed my eyes, watching her face as I quoted the letter. 'I make no judgement,' I said. 'That is not my place.'

Elizabeth pursed her lips. 'What was that?'

'Think of the children,' I said.

She looked at me, perplexed. 'Think of them? All I ever do is think of the children. They are my reward from God, so says the minister, though what we did to deserve Robert I shall never know. Adelia says three children are far too many for a middle-class family and we ought to have had Robert first, skipped over Margaret and stopped at Helen.'

I paced to the window, staring at the distant shipyard. 'Angels,' I said.

Elizabeth smiled. 'Hardly, William. Angels do not go to the toilet in the umbrella department of a department store. Have you been drinking?'

I gritted my teeth. 'I need you to tell me this instant if there is anything I ought to *know*, Elizabeth.'

She regarded me in the mirror, her lips parted, then shook her head. 'No, dear, of course not.'

'I...' I strode to the fireplace and touched her elbow. She gave me a queer look as Rose appeared from the hallway, her hand gripping Robert's wrist to stop him from running away, the boy sucking on the corner of his blanket. His hair was still damp from the bath, his face pale.

Elizabeth brushed past me. 'Robert, do you feel better, my darling? Your father has been so worried about you. How is your tummy?'

'It hurts really much,' he sniffled, looking furtively at me, straightening his back. 'But I will be a big boy now.'

I folded my arms. 'Quite right, young man,' I said, bouncing on my heels. 'Crawford men do not behave like farm animals in public.' I gave Rose a stern eye. 'I think it is time we took that blanket away from the boy.'

Robert squealed, clutching the rag to his face. I took out my pipe. 'It will be gone by bedtime, Robert, then it will go into the fire. You can say your goodbyes this afternoon.'

I regretted my decision as soon as I'd spoken, not least for the fresh chill which passed behind my wife's eyes. Woeful shrieks filled the house, Robert's despair echoing down the stairs as he was dragged, kicking and screaming to the nursery. I climbed after him, closing myself into the study without a word, before leaning against the door. I must not allow myself to show my feelings. I must not comfort the boy, just as there was nobody who could comfort me. *Elizabeth, what are you hiding from me?* I dried my eyes, swallowing deep breaths. Be strong, Robert, we must all experience such pain in childhood, for without it who could survive the torture to come?

The afternoon passed in uncomfortable silence. Trapped by my own indecision, my guilt, my raging imagination, I refused to allow myself another look at the letter, focusing instead on writing my children's textbook, ready to send to the publishers. That, at least, was within my control. At last, as the evening drew in, we came together for dinner in an unbearably tense mood. I could not meet Robert's eye as he glared at me, gripping his blanket so tightly his little knuckles were white. I did not care, for all I wanted was to reach out to Elizabeth and beg her for an explanation. What *had* she told Hazel for so many years that she could not tell me? I chewed my potato, studying her, yet I could read nothing in her face.

After dinner I stepped into the back garden for some air, drawing long puffs on my pipe as I looked at the moon, contemplating my troubles and thinking of a woman, long dead to me, but still my only true friend. I looked back towards the house, making sure I was alone, then spoke to her, voice low beneath the breeze. Such things I did when I was at my worst. How the pain of her death clung to me still after so many years.

'Mother, I do not know what to do. I believe I have lost Elizabeth. She is lying to me.' I sniffed, scuffing my toe into the damp grass. 'I have been very foolish and not much of a husband. I do try, Mother. I try my best but I cannot seem to get anything right. I will do better. I shall make you proud.'

I could still see her face, looking up at me in the candlelight, the tendons in her neck pressing like razors through her skin, the sheets crimson. There was something not right about the baby, the bundle being rushed away, likely to choke. Mother had sung a lullaby to me as she had left us, her damp fingers brushing my cheek, her eyes flickering until her last breath departed to a faint tune. I had forgotten the melody. I had forgotten the words. I had forgotten her face. Oh, my poor mother, whose very last wish, was for her son to look after his sisters. I told her I would. A boy making a man's promise. Who knows what happened to those children after I left New Zealand? I had written to them as a young student in Glasgow, but never received a reply. In the end, as my own family had grown, I had stopped writing to them altogether. They were strangers to me, our only connection a father who cared little, and a dead mother. I sucked on my pipe, the bowl empty and sour.

Just then, something caught my eye from the study window. There was something there, buried in the black glass, hovering over the desk. I looked up, trying to see better, but the window reflected the sky, masking the room beyond. The letter! Elizabeth was attempting to steal my evidence of her wrongdoings. I tore across the garden into the house, mounting the stairs and bursting into the study, only to find it empty. I dashed to the bureau, wrenching open the drawer, certain to find the letter stolen, yet there it was, exactly as I had left it. I collapsed into my chair, pressing my knuckles into my temples. 'Good god, Mother, I am going mad,' I said. 'What on earth can I do?'

'Farfur?' I turned to see Robert standing at the door, his little face frowning. 'What was you doing, Farfur? Was you crying?'

'Certainly not,' I snapped. 'Crawford men do not cry; your father has a headache, that is all.' I gave him a stern eye. 'How long have you been standing there?'

He shrugged, biting his lip, then with terrible effort, offered me his blanket. 'Here, Farfur. Mother says I must.' I looked at the little fellow, half-illuminated by the window, eyes brimming.

'Come, come,' I shushed. 'All is well, don't cry. Here.' I took the blanket, scooping him to my knee. 'This is for your own good. We mustn't cling to comforts but grow up strong.'

He yawned, nestling into my chest.

'My precious mouse, it has been a long day for us all. Shall we get you to bed?'

He nodded, looking up through his curls.

'The lady in the white dress came again last night,' he said.

I chuckled, stroking his fringe. 'That was Rose. Remember she is living with us now?'

'Silly Farfur.' He yawned. 'The lady wasn't Rose, she was talking.'

'Talking?'

'Mhmmm,' said Robert, in his dreamy little voice, breathing softly. 'Talking, talking, talking, Farfur. Talking on the stairs. I will be a big boy now.'

I thought of the figure I had seen from the garden, moving about in the study. Was Elizabeth stalking the house at night? Or was it one of the girls? Someone else, perhaps? The maddening thoughts of a man so deadly tired. I cradled Robert to the nursery, laying him gently in his bed, before tucking him into his blankets. 'Goodnight, Robert,' I said. 'Dear boy, be brave.'

Quietly, I tiptoed to the fireplace, rubbing my thumb on the comfort blanket, steeling myself to do what must be done. I looked back to Robert's face on his pillow, half-lit by moonlight. His little paw reached out, fingers searching. He grunted, caught in an unhappy doze, then rested his cheek into the pillow and fell into a deep slumber. I crouched down, my poor knees cracking, then pressed the blanket onto the coals. The material was stubborn at first, refusing to burn, yet finally with some blowing and poking, the thing slumped and glowed orange, the material at last giving in to the heat. I looked back to see Robert's face caught in the emotion of some private adventure, then kissed him goodnight and took myself to bed, weeping into my pillow as my own troubled dreams drew closer.

CHAPTER ELEVEN

It was the night of the gala. I arrived early at the Institute just as the principal had requested, excited to see what task he had in store. Perhaps he required me to cast my expert eye over the plans for the extension? Or, with tensions growing in Europe, he might be interested in dirigibles. I would give him my mind on anything he asked, desperate for something to occupy it.

After much deliberation, I had resolved not to speak of the letter to Elizabeth. Is it cowardly to hide from the truth or better to live alongside it; to be haunted by it for the rest of one's life, without pursuing it or tempting it into the light? To simply accept it and move on? Better, I thought, to be the timid man who hangs back at camp rather than the bold explorer venturing into the jungle only to be eaten by cannibals. There could be no profit in pursuing the letter. No hope for glory. And what was 'glory' anyhow? When it comes to a marriage, which statues immortalise men for being good husbands? Not enough of them, I reasoned.

I placed the previous evening's paper on the staffroom coffee table, then left the common room to find the men's lavatories, which were empty, thank goodness. Rose had pressed my evening suit and shirt, my white collar starched and ironed into a sharp blade. I checked my teeth and nostrils in the mirror, pinching the corners of my moustache. Normally, I would have used the cubicle to avoid embarrassment but the Institute was empty so I moved to the urinals, desperate for relief. 'Dirigibles, Master,' I murmured to myself, practising for our confidential tête-à-tête. 'Dirigibles are the new weapon in modern warfare, though they suffer a few weaknesses, namely the envelopes the Italians currently use are...'

The door opened and young Blithe strode in, instantly freezing my bladder. 'Hooha! You're early, Prof.'

'You will remember the principal has a special task for me,' I replied curtly, covering my shyness with my hand, staring directly at the tiles.

'Oh yes,' he said, knocking me with his elbow as he unbuttoned his trousers. 'Yes, I remember now. Well, you are the best man for the job, I suppose.'

'I suppose I am.'

He shuddered as a great gush of piss burst forth with all the punch of a fire hose. I looked down at myself, groaning inwardly at my shy bladder, unable to go. Had he noticed? Did he think I was there simply to expose myself to the tiles? He looked around the bathroom, almost straying from the pan. 'Here, Prof, want to hear a joke?'

'Not particularly, no.'

'Very well, as you please.' He cleared his throat. 'Oh, by the way, did you hear about the girl in Women's Work who swallowed a pin?'

'Swallowed a what?' I said. 'Is the principal aware? She ought to be taken to hospital.'

'Her father won't hear of it.'

'Whyever not? The girl will be injured...'

'He says she's not allowed to feel a prick till she's married.'

I huffed, bouncing on my heels. 'Oh really. For goodness' sake, Blithe.'

'Here, Prof,' he said, nudging me, 'talking of girls, I thought you'd snuck one of them in when I heard you chatting to yourself just now. What on earth were you whispering about?'

I sighed. 'Dirigibles, if you must know.'

'Oh...' He nodded sagely, waggling his member. 'Yes, dirigibles indeed, hmmm. Wonderful things. Will your handsome wife be joining us this evening?'

'Indeed she will.'

'And what table are the Crawfords at this year?'

'I believe... I don't recall,' I coughed, leaning in as though enjoying my own relief, whistling to mask the absent splash in the plughole. *Why would he not leave?*

'No matter,' he said. 'The top table really is a terrible bore. You'll join me at the summit in a few years, then we shall have a jolly old time together, eh? Everyone here is so pasty and old.' At last he buttoned up, stepping to the sinks to wash his hands, before returning to clap me on the back. 'I find it helps to think of a waterfall,' he said, before marching from the lavatories chuckling to himself.

Naturally, the moment he left, my bladder relaxed, emptying itself in a splash which sprayed my cuffs and trousers. Running late, I washed my hands, drying myself with a pile of paper towels, before skipping across the corridor to the principal's office where, no sooner had my knuckles rapped on the door, I was bade to enter. 'Come, boy.' Inside, I was directed to a chair from behind a huge oak desk. 'Sit,' he said and I did as I was told. I looked at the framed certificates covering the walls. There was a decanter on the desk and two glasses. I smiled.

'Master, may I express my humble...'

He waved my words away like so many flies. 'Hush, boy. I have a very important mission and you, Crawford, are the only soldier for the job. I needed someone of the necessary rank, you see?' I smiled, counting his medals and trophies in a glass cabinet. 'We shall have some very important guests this evening at the top table. I need you to help me impress them.'

I looked away bashfully. 'Principal, anything I can do to help. Are they men of Science or Engineering? Perhaps I can clarify some of their questions around airships...'

'Airships, Crawford?' he frowned. 'Airships? No, no, enough of that floating nonsense, leave it to the birds I say. It isn't for a teacher to tell the Government how to win wars, Crawford. No, these men are the very paragons of Belfast business and culture.'

'I see.'

He lowered his voice. 'We must make the right impression on them. These people think we're a bunch of nuts and I need them to understand this is a factory of the arts as well as of industry. Only...' He looked around the study as if checking for spies. 'It is rather delicate work.'

I leaned in. 'Is it?'

'Yes, it is, very fragile indeed. I might have asked Mr Stoupe to do it, but I don't think he's strong enough to carry the weight, if you know what I mean. Same goes for old Fforde.'

I took out my pipe. 'Not Blithe?' I asked nonchalantly, crossing my legs.

'I believe you are better placed, Professor,' he said with a wink.

I nodded, our shared judgement of the man unspoken. 'I understand completely.'

'Good, good, wonderful, tip top,' said the principal, suddenly jumping up from his desk. 'No time to lose then,' he said and I looked around to see him standing beside the open door. 'You will find them at the back of the building by the boiler shed. I had them moved from the old School of Art on North Street this morning.'

I frowned. 'Them?'

'Yes, boy, yes, have you not been listening? There are six statues that need shifting to Antiques, on the third floor. As I say, very delicate, very weighty, very fragile. I need them in place before the gala begins so young Master Blithe and I can give our important guests a tour.'

'You want me to move some statues?' I said, looking at the bottle of port and empty glasses. 'That's the important role you have for me?'

'Yes, yes, yes,' he said impatiently, flicking his hand along the corridor as if throwing an invisible ball. 'Quick now, fetch!'

I stepped into the corridor only to see Blithe waiting outside, arms folded, leaning against the wall. 'Hallo, Prof.'

'Blithe.'

The principal ushered him inside, closing the door behind them to the sound of instant laughter and chinking glasses. I stood alone for a while, unsure what to do with myself. I had half a mind to go home, but then I remembered how uncomfortable it was at Park Avenue with the strange maid, Robert's weeping for his burnt blanket and Elizabeth, who had fallen into a tight mood. Besides, she would be arriving at the Institute soon, to enter the gala on her husband's arm. In the end, I realised there was nothing I could do but get along with it and so, presently, I reached the very back of the building, where the corridors were gloomy and forgotten, no grand windows, no fresh paint, the walls thrumming to the sound of the boilers. For all the world, I might have been standing in the engine room of a great liner. Well, if a blade of ice had sliced through the wall at that very moment, sinking the building beneath the frozen Atlantic, I should not have been sorry. Poor, hopeless Sir William Jackson Fool.

I stuck my hands on my hips, inspecting the cargo. There were not six statues at all, only one; a pomegranate-breasted woman with a double-chin in *contraposto* pose. Muttering to myself, I manhandled her onto a trolley, rolling her along the corridor. As I passed the principal's office, I could hear a low, serious conversation.

I rolled the woman into the cramped lift, caring little for her fingers and elbows, before riding up through the building, her leg cocked against my groin, her nipples protruding uncomfortably at my cheek. The lift shuddered, doors opening to quite the most unexpected sight. There was a naked boy by the opposite wall being held around his slim waist by a crooked man. I had heard of such things going on in private schools, but nothing of that kind at the Institute. We didn't even have a rugby team. As my eyes adjusted, I realised it was Professor Fforde with another statue, wings in his hair, a severed head held out like a lantern.

'Perseus, this one,' Fforde said, resting his elbow on the statue's shoulder, his arthritic knuckles gripping the ball of his cane.

'Is that so?' I muttered, impatiently pulling the woman from the lift.

He cleared his throat. 'The principal told me about his job for you. Thought you might need a hand.'

I rolled my eyes. 'You can leave it to me, Professor. The principal has asked me to get this done for him before his important guests arrive.'

Fforde snorted, raising a bushy eyebrow. 'Couldn't get a janitor to do the job rather than a professor? Sure, he thinks we're nothing but lackeys.'

'He needed someone of the necessary rank.'

He stopped himself, pursing his wet lips. 'I see. Ack, come here.' He stepped over, freeing a stuck wheel with a yank on the woman's knee. 'So, where are we taking them?'

'The antiques room down there.' I pointed to the end of the long corridor. Together, we rolled our statues over the terrazzo, trolley wheels squeaking. We were about a third of the way along when Fforde spoke, his breath short. 'Dirigibles,' he said.

'I'm sorry?'

'You were discussing dirigibles in the men's room with Blithe. I heard you as I passed with one of the wee statues.'

'Not so much *discussing*,' I said.

Fforde gave a dry laugh. 'The boy wouldn't know a Zeppelin if it flew up his arse.'

We passed the tall windows halfway along the corridor. Far below us, over the courtyard, guests were waiting inside the anteroom to the Central Hall, checking their reflections in the dark glass, quite unaware they were being watched. I saw Elizabeth, smiling as she corrected her hair. Adelia appeared, taking her forearm, whispering something highly confidential behind a gloved hand. Instantly, Elizabeth's smile disappeared, her body stiffened, clutching the woman's fingers, shaking her head, caught in the throes of some passionate entreaty. Was it the letter? *Do not play games with love, Mrs C. I saw you meetin that man. You are a marreyed women and Mr C will discuvver what he has bin doin with you sooner or layter and then what will you do?*

Who was this 'he'?

'Come, Fforde, let us get on,' I said, turning back to the statues, yet Fforde did not budge.

'Zeppelins, nai, that's what the Germans call them, not dirigibles.'

'What's that?'

'Great big leviathans hidden in the clouds, bristling with guns and bombs in their bellies like fish roe.' He shook his white head. 'The stuff of nightmares, Professor. Bad enough, death being thrown at you from the ground, I should know, but imagine shells thundering straight down at you from the skies.' He slapped his statue's buttock. 'Not even the gods dreamed up a diabolical thing like that. There is nothing in

Heaven and Earth so evil as mankind.' He sniffed. 'Man*kind*. There's a joke.'

Far below us, across the courtyard, Principal Forth and Blithe appeared behind Adelia, greeting guests. I stood beside Fforde, watching Elizabeth dab at her eyes, before making her way into the hall. The old man spoke in a low voice. 'The deaths powerful men dream up for other men,' he said, his breathing shallow.

'You have seen them?' I said. 'These Zeppelins?'

'Read about them,' he replied. 'The Italians have used 'em for bombing raids, but the Hun are building monstrous things the size of ocean liners, they say. Ack, and with today's news...'

I frowned. 'Today's news, what's that?'

'Have ye not seen the evening papers, nai?' he said, lifting his eyes to the sky. 'Oh well, best not to I suppose. The Arch eejit of Austria's got hisself shot in Sarajevo. The wife's dead too, so I hear. How old are ye, Professor Crawford?'

'Thirty-four.'

He nodded. 'Thirty-four, that ought to see ye right. And yer wee boy?'

'Five and a half,' I said.

'God help us if that in't young enough to save his bones. Ack, ye should both be fine. No parent should lose a child.'

Indeed, I had made my own calculations as the years had passed since boyhood, understanding the grim expectations of my sex. It was equally a relief and a surprise to have found myself spared by the giant tread of fate's jackboot as it had marched towering above me, the monstrous, insensible colossus, leaving those born in my inglorious decade cowering in its path, relieved though somewhat ashamed on a bubble of untrammelled dirt. While all around us men slightly older, and mere months younger, were squashed face first, bones snapped, into the puddled trenches of its staggering tracks. Then, what an extraordinary gift from God, to see little Robert and those of his age spared too, supposing this war ended quickly and the next came late enough.

I waited for Fforde to continue, for I felt he intended to do so. Together, we watched as a squat woman appeared, dressed in black weeds, her head bowed to the floor. For all the world she might have been the late queen. 'Terrible thing, losing a son,' Fforde whispered to himself. 'Ruins a mother.'

He sniffed, then straightened up, dusting his trousers and smacked his stick resolutely on the floor. 'Mrs Fforde needs her husband,' he said, nodding. 'You do the rest, Professor, then get yerself to yer good woman, she will be pining for ye no doubt.'

Away he went, clacking to the end of the corridor, leaving me alone but for the statues. I took their hands, admiring the marble woman's curves, jealous of the boy's physique. We travelled a little further, the wheels squeaking over the floor past a second set of tall windows. A solitary bird jumped from the roof, circled the tiled walls then swooped into the leaves of a cloistered tree on the opposite wall. Above the canopy, I could see to the opposite side of the courtyard where the east corridor was unlit. I moved away, afraid of what might be there, laughing at my own superstition. A scientific man spooked by shadows! Yet just as I neared the end of the corridor, I heard footsteps close by.

'Hello?' I called. 'Fforde, is that you? Stoupe? Blithe? Master?'

I turned back to the statues, my heartbeat quickening, sensing an approaching terror I had suffered before. The stone woman looked back at me with a faint smile, only... were her eyes somehow changed? And the boy; his lips were parted when before, were they not closed? The head, held aloft in his hand, blinked. There came another patter of steps at my back, closer this time. 'Who goes there?' I called, spinning around, my voice echoing down the passageway. How cold it was all of a sudden, air pressing from the windows as though the panes of glass were gone. I gulped, forcing myself to be calm, shaking the visions away. Breathe, William. You are tired and under stress.

I rolled the statues further, humming a prayer, then froze, looking through one of the windows and how I wish I had not looked, for there now stood the unmistakable silhouette of a person, staring out from the empty east corridor at the opposite side of the courtyard. Empty I say, for their presence did little to occupy the space in which they appeared; yet still, horror in my turning belly, whoever they were... they were most certainly looking at me. Slowly, I raised my hand to them and nodded, whispering 'who are you?' then watched, mesmerised as they reached out their own hand and pointed at me, a strange, plaintive cry drifting across the abandoned courtyard. I knew their voice, though could not think who it was, and Heaven save me, for that is when I realised something was shifting in the corner of my eye.

I turned, shaking in every bone of my body, to see the female statue rotating slowly on her trolley wheels, her marble eyes meeting mine. The boy too was rolling towards me, the wheels at his sandals squeaking as he came, his mouth grinning, eyes stretched wide. I backed away. 'No, no,' I whispered. 'Get back.' The statues faced me, their expression something ghoulish, the woman's carved eyes two balls of white fury. I felt for the wall, tripping, turning to run. 'No, no, get away!' I cried over my shoulder. I looked back across the courtyard but the strange figure was gone.

Unable to hold my wits any longer, I let out a high-pitched cry, running down the corridor as fast as my slapping feet could carry me, tearing down two flights of stairs before skidding to a halt at the little balcony. There, I leaned out, panting, gasping for air, waiting for a cold marble hand to place its fingers on my shoulder...

'But soft, what light through yonder window breaks?'

I looked down to the Entrance Hall, where Stoupe was leaning against one of the pillars, peering up at me with a coy smile, holding his hanky aloft, his face half-illuminated by the lights. 'It is the east, and Professor Crawford is the sun. Arise, fair sun, and kill the envious moon, who is already sick and pale with grief that thou, William dear friend, art far more fair than she.'

I turned, damp at my collar, to the top of the deserted stairs. My poor, exhausted mind. There was nothing there.

'Will you deliver me to the hall, Professor?' Stoupe called, lifting his arm with a curtsey.

'Yes,' I replied, brushing down my shirt, never so grateful to be in another man's company.

CHAPTER TWELVE

We stepped into the Central Hall, our breath caught by the wonder of the great room, dressed in its finery for the annual gala. It ranged about us like a lantern, the stained-glass windows glowing in myriad shapes of emerald, amber and scarlet and where the glass was clear, the starlight mixed with plumes of cigarette smoke in pink and orange clouds. The electric chandeliers were hung with frosted snowdrops while the atmosphere was heavy with the perfume of beef and tobacco. Tables were arranged in long banks, covered in white tablecloths, each set for dinner with crystal glasses and napkins folded in clean white crowns. All was perfect symmetry while, already, the hall was filled with men in their black and white dress suits, women milling about in twinkling dinner gowns. At the far end I could see palm trees lining the stage; behind them, an unseen musician playing a piano sonata.

The warmth of the room eased my anxiety, and I was about to make some jolly remark to Stoupe when I caught sight of Elizabeth amidst the crowd. She was glaring at me, Adelia at her shoulder staring in my direction, her expression a grisaille of reproach and self-satisfaction. I made my way to them, offering a courtly bow and a happy smile.

'Good evening, ladies,' I said, holding out my hand. 'Will you do me the honour?'

Elizabeth sniffed and turned away. What had gotten into her? Still in a temper with me, no doubt. I looked about for some water. My heart was unsettled, fearful of another hallucination. Might pixies dance across the ceiling in nutshell hats? Would pink elephants swim about the walls, chased by dancing pastries? I took a reassuring puff on my pipe. *Relax, William, for goodness' sake.* 'You look very lovely tonight,' I whispered to Elizabeth, for she certainly did, yet she shrugged my hand from her shoulder.

Adelia huffed. 'Which table are you sitting at this evening, Lillie?' she asked, pushing between us.

'I don't know,' said Elizabeth, searching the room. 'William has the invitation.'

Adelia glowered at me. 'Table number, William?'

'Thirty-two,' I said, reaching out once again to take Elizabeth's hand, only to be tapped away.

'Are there so many tables?' Adelia replied. 'Lillie, I shall be joining my nephew and the lord mayor. They attended Harrow with the late Lord Carter.' She slanted an eye in my direction. 'Do not fear, I shall be watching *him* like a hawk.'

Up at the top table, young Blithe was already making himself at home with a glass of champagne and a fat cigar, joined by two gentlemen I thought I recognised from the newspapers.

I managed to find Elizabeth's wrist, only to be met by a suspicious eye. Outraged, I stood back. 'Why are you being so cold, Elizabeth?'

She faced me, brimming with tears. 'Why are *you*?' she said. 'Let us not walk in sexual immorality and sensuality, William Jackson Crawford.'

'Let us not indeed,' I bit back. 'Nor in quarrelling and jealousy. Or have you forgotten your duty as my wife?'

'Sometimes I wish I were still a Bullock,' she hissed.

'Well then, be a blasted Bullock for all I care.'

I looked about, nodding politely as two of my fellow lecturers passed by. So, there it was, the truth of the letter. Elizabeth had as good as confessed to her adultery as easily as spilled milk.

Elizabeth's eyes hardened and she walked away, pressing through the crowd.

'William,' squawked Adelia. 'You must explain your shameless behaviour at once.'

'Shameless behaviour?' I spat, struggling to control myself as a pack of nail-biting weasels from the plumbing department smirked at me from a neighbouring huddle. 'What are you talking about?'

Stoupe stepped up. 'I am sure William has done nothing wrong, Lady Carter.'

'Mr Stoupe,' said Adelia. 'I am afraid he was *seen* this evening. Caught red-handed, in fact. I always suspected you were up to something, William. I knew it the moment I met you. *There is a rogue,* I thought. And his trousers are too long.' She glared at me triumphantly.

'Seen?' I said. 'Whatever are you talking about, red-handed?'

'What did you see, Lady Carter?' asked Stoupe, rather too excitedly.

Before she could answer, Professor Fforde appeared with his wife at his side. 'Fancy do,' he said, only for his smile to fizzle away under Adelia's caustic glare.

'I can hardly say what I saw,' she began, only to be cut off by Elizabeth, who returned to the group with her shawl.

'William, I want to go home.'

'Whyever should we go home, dearest? What is all this?'

Adelia looked at Stoupe and Fforde, her gloved hand to her chest. 'I am sorry you have to hear this, gentlemen, but your esteemed Professor Crawford has been having an affair.'

I could have fallen on the floor. Fforde's wife shook her head, while Stoupe gasped, his handkerchief flying in the air.

'Please, William, can we go?' said Elizabeth, unable to meet my eye.

'Not until he confesses,' said Adelia. 'I shouldn't think it safe to spend another moment with him alone. William, I saw you, barely half an hour ago with a naked woman. Right in front of the windows, touching her all over.'

Mrs Fforde choked.

'Good Lord,' said Stoupe. 'Why, Professor, I didn't think you had it in you.'

'Strange,' said Fforde, his bushy eyebrows low. 'I think you have it wrong.'

'Not at all,' interjected Adelia in an unnecessarily loud voice. 'He was touching the poor thing all over with those dirty little rodent hands of his. Elizabeth, you and the children shall have to live with me.'

Elizabeth groaned. 'Thank you, Aunt Adelia, but I am quite safe. Now please, William, let us go.'

I gawped at Adelia, lost for words. I, dallying with naked women? What utter nonsense was this? Her words bore no greater relation to reality than the creeping statues. 'My darling Elizabeth,' I said. 'Where is all this coming from?'

Adelia offered a pitiful smile to Mrs Fforde, who clutched a miniature Bible on a chain about her neck. 'The late Lord Carter was a faithful husband, Mrs Fforde. There was certainly no dallying with other women in his case. Indeed, there was very little dallying at all. Company was our chief distraction; company and the enrichment of the mind. He pleasured me nightly with his thesaurus.'

Professor Fforde stepped in, resting his cane in the crook of his arm, taking Elizabeth's hand. 'Mrs Crawford, calm yerself. Yer man has done you no wrong, not unless a husband can commit adultery with a lump of stone.'

'Stone?' said Elizabeth with a sniff.

'What is that supposed to mean, Mr Fforde?' snapped Adelia.

'A statue,' he said. 'Yer husband was manoeuvring a busty statue about, that's all. I was with him.'

Stoupe chuckled, positively brimming with scandal. 'Less an *affaire de coeur*, rather an *affaire de pierre*! I once enjoyed one of those in Montmartre.'

'Yes,' I growled, staring pointedly at Adelia. 'I was moving a statue for the principal though, Christ the dignity it has cost me, I ought to have stayed at home.' I turned to Elizabeth, emotion rattling in my chest, twisting my voice high. 'There you are then. You will be accusing me of having an affair with the Elgin Marbles next.'

Adelia, ever quick to shift attention to her next victim, waved above our heads. 'Oh look, there's Mrs Weebly, I must say hello to her. I shall introduce you later, Elizabeth; she is ever so dull, it's fascinating.'

And away she bustled, leaving us to suffer the most intolerable embarrassment. I caught young Blithe looking over at us with a half-smile, doubtless having seen the whole thing.

Fforde cleared his throat. 'Well. Shall we sit?'

My temper bubbled as we found our table at the very rear of the hall right beside the exit doors, the Gala already ruined with shock and crying injustice. I sat with my head down, struggling to control myself and was about to leave in a fit of pique when Elizabeth squeezed my hand beneath the table.

'Dear husband,' she said. 'Can you forgive your wife? She has forgiven you.'

I bit my lip, looking up to see her eyes filled with contrition. I shrugged. She took my hand more tightly. 'Things have been so difficult lately, what with Robert's poorly tummy and the house, I think I would have believed anything Adelia told me. The children are such hard work, even with Rose's help. How silly of me, I am ashamed of myself. Isn't it funny, how the mind plays tricks?'

I toyed with my napkin ring, trying to hold a steady voice. 'Perhaps...' I looked her in the eye. 'Perhaps I am a very inadequate sort of husband.'

'No,' said Elizabeth. 'You are a fine husband.'

The murmur of polite conversation hummed around us, our friends having moved discreetly to the end of the table. I held her hand, only to see a flash behind my eyes of blue handwriting on crinkled paper.

Do not play games with love, Mrs C. I saw you meetin' that man.

The words burnt my tongue, desperate to be spoken. Why, oh why must I torture myself further on such an important night? Did I not have enough to worry about? After all, as Elizabeth said, if the evening had taught me one thing, it was to beware my own traitorous imagination. If my addled mind could conjure up living statues, then why not misconstrue the meaning of an innocent letter? I screwed up my eyes, kissed my wife's cheek, awakening my instincts, and for the first time in months, she blushed.

'You look very beautiful this evening,' I said. She was wearing a loose cream evening gown spotted with yellow flowers; an inheritance from a larger friend. Still, she was undoubtedly the prettiest woman in the hall, her copper hair set in gentle waves, framing her intelligent eyes, their purple rings artfully hidden beneath a touch of makeup. She smelled of jasmine.

'And you look rather dashing,' she said, squeezing my knee, sending a tingle up my leg. She pulled a curl of hair from my forehead and placed it behind my ear as the musicians picked up a waltz. I had the sudden urge to dance with her, remembering our romantic evenings, long before the children were born, before Belfast, before we lost ourselves.

Seeing we were friends again, Stoupe leaned in. 'Are the love birds cooing? Honestly, if I don't eat soon I shall collapse onto the floor. Vegetable soup first, apparently, but that won't fill the hole, eh, Professor? Might as well pour a cup of tea into the Albert Hall.'

'People do not live by bread alone,' said Mrs Fforde, fiddling with her tiny Bible, her chins squeezed in an effort to read the pages.

Elizabeth nodded, completing the recitation from heart. '...but by every word that comes from the mouth of God.'

'If the word of God comes with potatoes, I shall gladly eat it,' said Stoupe. 'Though I wager beef will go better with the wine.'

Luckily for Stoupe, the food arrived quickly, Fforde making conversation about new belts for the machines, I answering him as best I could, hardly taking notice while Mrs Fforde and my wife carried on a polite conversation about their church meetings. I could think of nothing but returning home to bed; though to which bed was a tantalising question.

'Mrs Crawford,' I heard Mrs Fforde say. 'Have you been unwell?'

I strained my neck to peep at the top table. The principal was engaged in an intense conversation with the smart gentlemen at his side, Adelia butting between them. Young Blithe was somewhat adrift at the far end, desperately leaning in to be heard by his superiors. He rather reminded me of Bartholomew at the Last Supper; a thought which gave me cause to laugh, sharing my witty observation with Stoupe who pinched my arm, calling me 'perfectly wicked'.

'Unwell?' I heard Elizabeth say. 'No, thank you, Mrs Fforde, I have been very well.'

Just then, Principal Forth said something to the men which caused them both to crane their necks to the ceiling. Whatever he'd said, it seemed to have caused some discomfort to one of his guests, because he excused himself from the table mopping his eyes, leaving his dinner behind. I tried to catch some word or clue from his fellow diners, yet Mrs Fforde was still prattling away in my ear.

'We have missed you at our church meetings these last few weeks, that is all,' Mrs Fforde was saying. 'We thought perhaps you were too weak to attend.'

'No, Mrs Fforde,' I heard Elizabeth reply. 'Tell me, did you ever identify the shrub in your front garden?'

I felt a nudge beneath the table. It was Stoupe, catching my eye. He gave a furtive nod to a glass beside my left hand, which was filled with a small measure of red wine. I took a deep breath, winked at him and enjoyed a sip. Gradually, the hall became warm and smoky, the sharp edges of the evening drifting from my mind. I watched as the well-to-do man returned to the high table as a quartet played a chatty little sonata. Mr Robinson, that's who he was. Mr Robinson of Robinson & Cleaver, Belfast's premier department store.

'I didn't take you for a singer, Professor,' Stoupe chuckled, pouring a little more wine into my glass. I realised I was humming along to the music.

'I sang countertenor in the choir as a child,' I said. 'My mother enjoyed listening to me, but I haven't sung in years.'

Stoupe tutted. 'That really is too tragic, we must clean out your pipes and get you going again.'

And so the evening passed, filled with merry chatter, some collegiate discussion between myself and Fforde about the mechanisation of the agricultural economy and Stoupe regaling us with tales from his travels to Florence as a young artist. 'I should like to paint your portrait, William, you have such fine lines. I'd paint Fforde too, but I'm not sure I have the strength for his nose.'

'Are you not married, Mr Stoupe?' asked Mrs Fforde. 'You must miss the care of a good woman?'

'A good woman? Heavens, no,' he replied. 'I prefer the bad ones. No, no, I make do with my male companions.' He winked at me, filling my glass. 'A wife, indeed. You might as well ask me to marry a macaroon.'

After dessert, Elizabeth became very sleepy, asking whether we might take our leave, so we made our apologies, escaping the stifling clatter for the cool air of the entrance hall where we collected our things. I lifted Elizabeth's coat, squeezing her shoulders.

'I am very sorry for what I said about Arthur last night,' I told her. 'I believe a man must be held accountable for his actions, but I am sorry he is gone. Truly I am.'

She raised her eyes to the little balcony, searching the high ceiling. 'Well... perhaps he isn't gone.'

The door swung open from the hall and out stepped Mr Robinson, wiping his brow. We nodded to each other politely, only for his face to light up.

'Professor Crawford?'

'Yes.'

'Aha! Professor Crawford and his darling wife, how wonderful to make your acquaintance. I have just been talking about you, young man.'

Elizabeth squeezed my hand. 'Is that so?' I asked.

'Yes, indeed. Principal Forth was telling me about his dirigibles. Apparently, he's been lecturing you about their use in war, no?'

'Oh... yes indeed he has.'

Mr Robinson leaned in with a wink. 'Come now, Crawford, we both know that isn't true. Forth's a good man, but I can tell a public school cheat when I see one. I wager you're the real mastermind here.'

'I wouldn't say that exactly, I...'

'I should like to know more about these airships. Forth says airborne warfare is the next frontier, and I'm minded to agree. What a pity you're not on the high table with us, would you like to join?'

I turned to Elizabeth, who was stifling a yawn. 'Forgive me, Mr Robinson, but we must get be getting along.'

'Quite right, old man, quite right. Another time perhaps.'

'Another time.'

We didn't have to wait long for the tram, which rocked like a cradle as we rolled past the outline of the City Hall then over the broad black river, the shipyard lamps reflecting in the water. Elizabeth dozed happily on my shoulder, a pair of older women cooing over us as though we were a pair of kittens in a box. At last, we reached our stop at the top of the hill, climbing from the tram to meander together the short way to our door. Elizabeth could hardly walk, leaning her weary head on my shoulder.

'I do care for you, Elizabeth Jackson Crawford,' I said. 'Ever so much.'

She kissed my shoulder, clinging to me. 'I know you do.'

We stopped beside the garden wall. 'Elizabeth?' I said, playing with her hand.

'Yes, dearest?'

'I would never hurt you.'

Her eyes flickered. 'I know that.'

'And you. Would you hurt me?'

Before she could answer, the door opened, Rose standing in the hallway. She ushered us inside, taking our coats before guiding us to the parlour where she served up cups of hot milk and biscuits. Elizabeth took a sip. 'Are these bone china?' she asked in a perfect impression of Adelia.

I chuckled. 'Are they very like the Chinese on the South Coast?'

We laughed, snuggling together, sharing old secrets, then at last climbed the stairs to bed, checking on the sleeping children before parting on the landing with a kiss.

'William?' said Elizabeth.

'Yes, dear?'

She smiled, her eyelashes low and together, we crept into her room, stripping away our clothes in the flicker of the lamp. I took her in with shaking fingers, moving onto her, bed springs creaking, her face growing distant. So beautiful a creature, her hair splayed over the pillows, her eyes closed. I believe she found her pleasure before I completed and she fell asleep, her face to the wall, praying under her breath.

I lay awake as she slept in my arms, thinking back over the evening. How strange the encounter with the statues had been. Suddenly it did not matter, for I had taken my wife back and somehow the world felt as though it had been fixed like one of my machines, the cogs turning gently, efficiently as they were designed. Such warm contentment filled my heart, I began to fall asleep, admiring my good fortune to have taken ownership of such a gentle wife. Had she not been as patient as a saint with the pious Mrs Fforde at the gala? I yawned and turned over, yet something niggled at me just as my eyelids closed. A thought struggling for attention. What had Mrs Fforde said to Elizabeth at the table?

'We have missed you at our church meetings these last few weeks...'

I frowned. She had *missed* Elizabeth at the meetings? How could that be? Elizabeth had been to a dozen church meetings in a month. Or so she claimed.

Troubled, I crept from Elizabeth's bed to my own room, where the sheets were cold. Another happy night stolen away by the lurking spectre of some hidden truth. I took to sleep, drowning once more in paper and blue ink.

I now yore intenshins are not evil but ther can com no god of theese secrits.

CHAPTER THIRTEEN

The next evening, I troubled my memory, fishing out a melody from my dream, peeping at Elizabeth over my newspaper. An unsettled sleep had given in to another difficult day for the Crawfords, my wife rising late with pains, the children prattling on, making a game of their ghosts.

'The white lady!' they shouted, chasing each other screaming until Robert vomited across the stairs. I would have given anything for Elizabeth to stay at home so we could share another contented evening, but it was not to be.

'I must go to my church meeting,' she announced when dinner was done, rushing to the hallway before reappearing in her coat and hat and dashing from the house. As soon as the door was closed, I sprang from the table myself, throwing on my hat and coat, explaining breathlessly to Rose that I had an errand to run; she would have to put the children to bed. She said nothing of course, nodding her head in mute understanding, while the children begged me to stay.

'Please, Farfur,' said Robert, twisting his shirt, looking rather incomplete without his blanket. Helen nodded, grabbing Margaret's hand. 'Yes, Father, please stay. We don't like it here alone.'

I knelt down and pecked them each on the cheek, hugging them close. 'Be brave, my children, I shan't be long.'

I looked at their faces and could almost have cried with them, yet suspicion tugged at my arm so fiercely I was drawn away. Searching my pockets, I turned to see Rose, holding my pipe with a pouch of tobacco. 'Thank you, Rose. Splendid work. Remember to give Robert his boric.' I stepped from the front door, catching sight of Elizabeth as she disappeared around the corner at the far end of the Avenue. I followed her in the dusk, skipping between steps, pulling my hat low. 'Go to the church, my love,' I whispered. 'Go to the *church*.' Yet she checked her purse, turning in the opposite direction towards the Newtownards Road. A grease-stained boy at the gates of the old Kane scrapyard watched her pass, smirking at me as I followed on, my back scraping over the bricks. She rushed through a maze of terraced houses before crossing Conn's Water, where she stopped. I dipped into an alleyway before skulking to the main road, then skidded to a halt beside a cart. On Elizabeth walked, with the certainty of someone who had followed the same route a hundred times. She crossed the Albert Bridge, then turned up the Ormeau Road.

Men were beginning to congregate around the public houses as Elizabeth walked on, the shipyards and factories not long closed. A tram passed by, ringing its bell and causing me to jump back into a puddle of horse piss. 'Drat,' I said, as Elizabeth drew away. I followed a skeletal donkey pulling a cart that wheezed and clopped over the cobbles as Elizabeth walked past a gaggle of boys carrying scraps of wood fashioned to look like rifles.

Elizabeth, I said to myself. *Where are you going?*

It dawned on me then, the true danger of where I was. Those soggy-bricked terraces were riven with sectarian fighting, street against street. The gun shots we had been hearing from the safety of Park Avenue had rung out from this ramshackle maze of terraced homes. A gang of children watched me pass, bare feet ankle-deep in a grimy ditch that had been cut into a side road. One of them, a girl no older than two or three, gave a gap-toothed grin then toddled to a woman standing in a passageway, holding her swollen belly, a babe in each arm. She looked at me suspiciously, then pulled her shawl over her face, stepping back into the shadows.

A voice called from across the street. 'Here, you, peeler.' It was a man of around forty, an iron pole swinging by his leg. 'You don't belong here, right?' He stepped into the road, just as two constables from the Royal Irish Constabulary appeared around the corner.

I bowed to them, walking back onto the main road, aware I had lost track of Elizabeth. I straightened my clothes, skittering up the low hill until, thank goodness, I caught sight of her, standing in front of a hardware shop with a tall young man, sleeves rolled up, a tattoo of a mermaid on his arm. His shirt was open, revealing leather-brown skin furred in thick black hair, his barrel chest yoked by broad, muscular shoulders. He stood before a heap of rusted scrap. The man laughed, guiding Elizabeth inside, his hand splayed across her back. I dashed to the opposite side of the road unseen, cowering behind a wall of stacked barrels.

Morrison's Quality Hardwares read the sign above the doorway, filthy beneath a ripped awning. The frontage was strewn with lengths of rusting pipe and broken engine parts. The building was three stories high with a steep roof, a cracked chimney pot smoking away at the gable end. The lamps were out, the windows black. I strained my eyes, trying to see some movement within, but everything was still. My wife must have passed into the living quarters at the back of the building. So, this was where she had been sneaking to? An old shop on a miserable street for fun with a fancy man from the yards. I felt nauseous. Was I so unsatisfying? Was last night all for show?

In disgust, I moved away, just as a light appeared in the roof. I had not noticed the small attic window. It flickered, then grew, casting a streak of Turkish red over the broken tiles. I could just make out the shadows moving inside. It was impossible to see who they were or even how many people were in the room, yet I could judge there were more than two. I ought to have marched over the road, rapping on the door, *beating* it open, dragging my wretched wife home to her children. I laughed bitterly. If I so much as tried to overcome the larger man, I would end up pressed into the kerbside like putty, nose split, trousers soiled. The alternative was to stand there, the dutiful husband, waiting for my wife to finish her whoring. A decent man must be stoic.

O Lord, to know that one is not allowed to be afraid; it is the most frightening thing of all.

I watched the window as the figure of the man passed before the red light. Was Elizabeth safe in there? Had she thought of him the night before? The light dimmed. I looked at my shoes with a sniff. It was beginning to rain, my clothes growing heavy on my back. I turned home, drowning in miserable thought yet, just as I did so, the strangest thing happened. I looked up at the attic window to see something behind the glass. I stared at it, blinking through the rain. It was a girl in the window, staring directly at me. She had a pale, almond-shaped face with dark hair and wire-rimmed spectacles. Her dress must have been as dark as the light behind her, for her head appeared to float. As I watched, the sound of the rain faded away while the cartwheels passed by, muffled as though submerged in water. The light at the girl's back grew darker still. She touched the glass with the tips of her fingers, opened her mouth once, twice, then a third time, turning at last into the room with a lingering glance. She was singing, I realised, for I could hear a congregation of voices, rising together in melody.

Transfixed, I waited for her to return, wondering if Elizabeth was with her. Was this a church meeting after all? I considered crossing the road to take a closer inspection of the shop, but the large man appeared at the attic window, looking down into the road. I ducked behind the barrels then peered back, hoping to see the girl again, only to realise a curtain had been drawn. I suppose I stood there for another hour as the night came in, sharp and wet. I sneezed, grousing at my damp feet.

Suddenly there came a great clatter from the downstairs of the shop, the lights came back on. There was an elderly woman grabbing at the counters, shrieking as she ran; whirling, bent-backed, towards the door. She almost fell, sending a box flying from a shelf as she tottered, crying out, a terrified expression on her ashen face. She stumbled towards the doorway, clutching her shawl, pulling at her grey hair, clasping her heart, panting, shrieking in prayer. The young man appeared behind her, his eyes cold. The crazed woman wrenched the shop door open, pulled her shawl about her head, scrambling into the dark, then disappeared into an alleyway with a final, distant shriek.

The man stood in the street, drizzle landing about him in sparks, watching her with an amused sneer. There was some movement from the back of the shop, a congregation of people making their way onto the street. A queer church indeed. Elizabeth appeared, looking pensive, holding herself back until a woman guided her, rubbing her arm as she wept. The girl was nowhere to be seen. I realised there was hardly a minute to lose if I was to get home before my wife, so I wrenched myself away, running low behind a slow horse before jumping onto the back of a passing tram. Inside, I nodded politely to my fellow passengers, who slid up the benches tutting at my sodden coat and the puddles which followed my shoes. I took my seat puffing on damp tobacco, inhaling hungrily to calm my troubled heart. I sneezed, my head throbbing as I thought of Elizabeth in that horrid place. Not only Elizabeth, mind you. I closed my eyes to bring her back. The girl. At the window. Staring down at me with a strange smile. Yes, the girl. With the almond face and the spectacles... had she seen me?

CHAPTER FOURTEEN

When I woke the following morning, I might have been a living corpse. My bedsheets were twisted around my legs, soaked with sweat, my neck locked fast against the pillow as I garbled in and out of consciousness, singing every thought in my clotted head. When I cried out for help, my voice was strangled with fever, glands like croquet balls beneath my jaw. Damn those plague-riddled streets.

In such a state I barely existed, imprisoned by my own body, in my bed, in my room, in the house... a viral nesting doll, cavities filled with sticky sweat and aggressive germs. A poorly man nursed alone by a mute maid, for I had chosen to separate myself from my family, particularly from poor Robert, who was equally ill with his stomach. *Let Elizabeth care for them all without me*, I thought, *if she could bear to stay away from her secret rendezvous.*

Hour after hour the maid and I stared silently at the corners of the room as the daylight moved interminably about the walls. The ache left my bones after a few days, the headaches softening and departing quickly after; yet I could sense contagion loitering at the door, threatening my fragile humours and I was sure my condition was far more serious than my symptoms implied.

Thus, I ignored the doctor's entreaties, taking the decision to practise further solicitous distancing from the family, nursing myself with a selection of newspapers and fascinating books. Oh, Christ, for an active man to be encased in his own quarters for any length of time is a wretched punishment indeed. Rose proved a diligent nurse nonetheless, fluffing my pillows, refreshing my pipe and bathing me daily with a sponge dipped in hot water. She even shaved me, her powerful hands slipping the razor about my neck and cheeks with all the confidence of a Turkish barber.

On the eighth day I was able to harness my soldierly spirit and install a makeshift writing desk across my bed, busying myself with diagrams, finding pleasure in the truth of each sketch, wolfing down macaroons dipped in steaming cups of malted milk. How productive I was, away from the Institute and my poor abandoned colleagues. Were they managing without me? I wondered many things, the inactivity of my body lending unhealthy energy to my imagination. What of the children's white lady talking on the stairs? Was my wife unfaithful to me, or was she a convert to some pagan religion? What had Hazel seen? What did Rose really think of us all, behind that silent, gurning jaw and why did she look at me so strangely? *There are great mysteries in this world of ours, but a mystery is only a fact in disguise. One day there will be no mysteries, only truth.* This I noted down, late in the evening, before fortifying myself with a very dark sherry.

On the ninth day of my laying-in, the doctor came to see me, talking some nonsense about my being on the mend, no matter my fainting and shivering. When he was gone I had to post Rose at the door while Elizabeth pleaded from the hallway for me to come out.

'William,' she called. 'I'm coming in. I've never seen Robert so ill. You have to get out of bed. The doctor says Robert is young and strong and he seems to be getting better, but he has been calling for you day and night. He misses his father so terribly, as do we all.'

So desperate was she to show me her impression of a concerned wife and mother, she took to bashing the door and I was forced to stand, losing my place in my books, reprimanding them for wishing a sickly man to endanger their own feeble lives with his deadly disease. No, it was out of the question. I would sacrifice my own pleasure to serve their best interests by remaining a little longer in bed, not least to recoup some energy lost by their interruption. 'I am dangerously poorly,' I shouted, climbing back beneath my blankets. 'My whole body is riddled with phlegm.' Besides, I could have added, who was to blame for my wretched state after all? Force a husband to stand in the pouring rain, ankle-deep in piss, you shall soon find him ill. There was nothing for me to feel guilty about, Robert was obviously on the mend; his crying had ceased. No, I told her, if she persisted with her rapping I would throw Rose out of the window and she would be a convict's wife. It seemed to do the trick, Elizabeth calling an end to her nagging, though Rose managed to imbue herself with a silence more profound than before.

On the tenth day, I received a most kind letter from the principal, reassuring me that I was not expected at the Institute. The world would wait for me, so he said. I placed his letter beside the marmalade and biscuits, picking my way through the *Daily Telegraph*, puffing on my pipe for medicinal effect. It was reassuring not to see any alarming headlines about the great European disagreement on the front pages. I read with interest an opportunity to buy shares in J M shock absorbers, then skimmed over the latest on the money markets. Seemingly they were suffering declines after Austria–Hungary's declaration of war on Serbia, but nothing too concerning. I thoroughly enjoyed chortling over a glorious WAR MAP of the various squabbling nations, admiring nonetheless the considerable engineering feat of building serviceable railway lines over the Carpathian mountains. I demanded a pack of the children's coloured chalks, colouring in the map with key geographical features for Rose's entertainment. Kutnow's Powder Eradicates Constipation declared the next page. I wondered if Mr Kutnow had a powder for the opposite effect that might help poor Robert. I turned the paper over, reading a very interesting update on divorce law reform. A bill had been proposed putting men and women on an equal footing in cases of adultery. The issue was apparently *a bitter grievance* for women who, I supposed, felt injured by the undervaluing of their own sexual infidelities.

'Rose,' I said, tucking the paper between my hot water bottle and slippers. 'Is a man's infidelity equal to a woman's, would you say?' She stared at the pile of darned socks scattered across her Olympian knees. 'I mean to say, if a husband has an affair would you *really* think it as shameful as his wife doing the same thing? It says here that to put men and women on an equal footing in such terms would lead to disastrous consequences. I quite agree.'

She said nothing. How small she made her chair appear. I folded my arms, sinking deep into my pillows. If Elizabeth was pursuing that young brute, it would do my reputation far greater harm than if I had been visiting prostitutes like her beloved brother. The very thought sent me frigid. I resolved to rest another few days. She would be glad of it, no doubt. I lifted my knees, snatching the newspaper back with a sniff, searching for something to calm my tempers. Sir Edward Carson, the great Unionist leader, was to be awarded the freedom of Belfast, much to the disturbance of the nationalists. Meanwhile, in Dublin, a rather feeble-sounding 'mob' had been shot by riflemen of the King's Own Scottish Borderers.

'Strange,' I said to Rose, holding up the article for her to read. 'These men were shot from behind; is it common for mobs in Dublin to attack backwards?' Rose stared at her sewing, harder still. 'Never fear,' I said, imagining a pendant of St Mary hanging against her breast. 'There is no sectarianism within the Crawford household. Union, Home rule or Rome rule, I could care less. In Dunedin we were all Presbyterians you know, so families were free to hate each other as they chose.' I laughed myself into a burst of hacking coughs, a gobbet of phlegm hanging like an emerald earring from the lampshade until Rose bore it away with a handkerchief.

Two more days of lying-in gave the dreadful *Telegraph* report: *The fairer prospects of yesterday have suffered a fatal eclipse to-day,* began the somewhat alarmist article. It continued: *The first dreadful fact is that war has begun – it has been formally declared by Austria–Hungary.*

I smiled at Rose. 'We shall soon be at war, do you think?' I imagined the whole of Europe as some diabolical clockwork machine. Never was there such a doomed contraption as Europe. Here a piston rod punching a bent chamber; there a cog grinding against a smaller cog, all sorts of pulleys twisting and rubbing against one another with this treaty and that rattling loyalty, forcing the lot to overheat until it erupted in one inevitable, almighty explosion.

Shouts came through the wall; it was the children's room, Margaret and Helen crying, Elizabeth banging preposterously at my door before bursting in, begging me to help her care for the children or at least relieve Rose of some of her nursing duties. Outraged, I threw myself against the mattress prostrate in my sickbed, pimple-skinned and croaking like a dying goose, hardly able to defend myself until she ceased her raving to mop my poor head. 'William, will you ever be better do you think? I see your cheeks have colour, are you certain you're ill?'

'My cheeks?' I said, eyes struggling to focus on the ceiling. 'My cheeks! I am pleased my cheeks are well, Elizabeth. I fear my lungs however, are giving out.' She looked me over then dropped my head to the pillow like a brick before heading back to the nursery.

I drew deep beneath the sheets that night, thinking of the girl at the window. Elizabeth's peculiar meeting with the man. A fitful dream rose to my mind: the shop lit by a burning yellow wind, the rooms glowing from the inside, strewn with a slow tornado of copy after copy of Hazel's letter. At some late hour, I awoke to hear Elizabeth singing Robert's favourite lullaby, Helen and Margaret singing too until the room swam. Again, I fell asleep, deep in fever.

On the thirteenth day, I woke with a start to the sound of screaming. I managed to prop myself against an arrangement of pillows, covering my ears, wondering where Rose had gotten to with my eggs and bacon. She was normally very prompt. I called for her, banging my heel on the floor, but she did not come. 'Rose,' I shouted. 'Rose, where is my breakfast?'

Still there was screaming and crying outside, so I shifted my aching legs from the bed and hobbled to the door. Outside, there was pandemonium, the girls holding each other in floods of tears, Rose standing beside the closed nursery door, face drawn, hair loose. I stepped onto the landing.

'What is all this racket? What is going on? Girls, stop all this crying.'

The nursery door opened and the doctor stepped out, dabbing his brow with a handkerchief, shirt sleeves rolled to the elbow. 'Mr Crawford, I came as quickly as I could.'

'Well you needn't have bothered,' I said. 'I have recovered.'

He gave me a sorry look. 'I am pleased to hear it. Robert, however, took a turn for the worse in the night.'

'He is still sick?' I asked.

The girls stopped crying, Margaret ushering her sisters into their room. I smiled, waiting for the doctor to continue.

'I am terribly sorry, Mr Crawford. Robert is dying.'

How quiet it was all of a sudden; only the sound of birds from the garden; the distant thrum of a motorcar engine. I looked at him in disbelief. The air turned grey. 'Dying?' I said.

'He is very weak. I felt sure he'd make it through with prayer, but there is little hope now.' He removed his spectacles. 'Your son has been very unwell. It was quite right to keep you away in case your fever made his condition worse.'

I stepped forward, the walls tilting. 'I must see my son,' I said. 'He needs his father, he must be afraid.' I lurched towards the nursery, held by the doctor who stepped with me, gripping my elbow. Rose stood away from the door, her head bowed. Inside, I saw the floor covered in stained towels, strewn with bowls and pans filled with water. The window was shut and the heat from the fire made the putrid air unbearable. Elizabeth was stretched over the bed, whispering gently to the boy who was buried deep in the sheets.

'Let thy mighty hand and outstretched arm, O Lord, be still our defence; thy mercy and loving-kindness in Jesus Christ, thy dear Son, our salvation.'

She looked up. 'William, our little Robert.'

Though I could hardly bear it, I forced myself to look at him, choking at the sight, an inhuman sound drawn from my throat like wet thread. How does it feel, to see a dying child? One does not feel at all for there is nothing in the mind to make sense of it. Nothing but one's own death. For a moment, I fancied there had been some mistake, for the collection of bones lying in the sheets hardly resembled my son at all. Hollow, purple eyes, sunken cheekbones, lips curled in. I knelt beside him, kissed his damp skin, took his tiny hand in mine, prised open his cold fingers. I looked at my wife. 'I did not realise. I did not know. You did not tell me...'

'I tried, but you wouldn't come out. He has been asking for you.'

I turned back to my son, holding his skeleton through the sheets, pulling the cover to his lips for comfort.

'Robert,' I whispered. 'Robert, your father is here. Take this, it is your blanket, look.'

His pale eyes opened, a bubble at his lips. His voice was tiny, his once-dimpled cheeks transparent to his teeth. I brushed his hair, kissing his forehead.

'Robert, take your blanket, look. I did not burn it after all. You see?'

His eyes slid down and smiled.

'Silly Farfur,' he said.

And then, he was gone.

CHAPTER FIFTEEN

Elizabeth stopped as she neared the hardware shop; fidgeting with her black gloves and hat in the reflection of a neighbouring window before clasping her hands in prayer. She looked up to the sky, then back along the road. I shrank into the shadow of a doorway, thankful for my unkempt clothes, my bushy hair covering my eyes.

Robert was barely a fortnight dead. The house was a morgue, the body of the child still haunting the nursery, his death alive in the girls' eyes, the rooms a measure too quiet, the table, a chair too empty, and, all the while, my wife took herself away to that tawdry place day after day. Thank goodness for the boy's penny policy, for we had lost the hot water the night we lost our son, and only the insurance would cover the cost of his burial in the end. It had caused such a quarrel, but I had stood my ground, refusing to have my boy entombed for ever in yet another debt to Adelia. I would take her money for a water tank, but not my child's grave. I had been sure the last few days were a dream, a nightmare, waking every morning like Scrooge, expecting a new chance to leap out of bed and find Robert dashing about the house in his imaginary motorcar. Yet no, it was all too real and there was I, cowering behind the barrels, their damp bellies against my hollow bones.

Elizabeth walked straight to the shop door. No sooner had she entered than an old woman guided her by the hand to the dim recesses of the building. I straightened up, striding over the road, almost stumbling into the side of a passing tram, not thinking what I was doing. It was as though my feet had a life of their own as I marched inside, straight into the path of the young man.

'Here nai, watch it!' he said.

He must have been over six feet tall and every bit as broad as a shire horse. At close quarters, I realised the red-haired mermaid on his arm was bare breasted, which scandalised my addled brain into a fit of stammering chirrups and sniffs, wiggling my moustache, searching for my pipe. I stopped, closed my eyes to quell a wave of nausea, stood back, then spoke in an unexpected falsetto.

'Sir,' I said, swallowing deeper. 'Sir, I am here to collect my wife.'

'Is that right nai?' he laughed, chewing a match. 'Did ye place an order?'

'I... of course I didn't; I did no such thing. You have my wife back there.'

'Yer wee wife is it, nai?' He turned his back to me, scratching his chin. 'Yer in the wrong place, wee feller. None of those in stock. Only screws and pipes, the like.'

I pushed my spectacles up and turned back to the door, whining. 'You have my wife; I saw her enter not a minute ago. Where is she, where are you hiding her? I am not looking for trouble...'

He leaned in, a glint in his eye. 'Shame, we have enough of that.' He raised his eyebrows, gestured about the disarray of torn boxes, overflowing shelves, peeling walls, grease-slathered floor and cigarette-stained ceiling. 'No wives though.'

Before he could stop me, I dashed behind one of the tables towards the back of the shop, legs shaking.

'Here what's this, ye crazy wee bastard?' he growled.

Though I was half his size, I had the measure of him quickly enough for even in my feeble health, I was far too nimble to be caught by such a lumbering buffalo. I was able to sweep a pile of hammer handles under his feet, sending him crashing to his back.

I took my moment to scurry into the back quarters of the shop where I found a young woman with bony shoulders, working at an ancient ship's stove, her back turned. The kitchen resembled a makeshift galley, bent water pipes leading across the ceiling, bandaged in places with tar and linen, a deep metal sink the size of a bath filled with pots, plates and strips of cloth. Wet clothes hung from poles against the dripping walls, the table at the centre of the kitchen strewn with cheap lace. Quickly, I disappeared through a tattered curtain unseen, mounting a narrow staircase which led up a passageway to a windowless landing. I could hear the man's voice below, arguing with the woman as I rushed to a second staircase, even narrower than the first, that wound up to the next floor. There were faint voices somewhere above my head as I crept along a tight hallway, the walls leaning drunkenly towards one another, wallpaper spotted with black mould. The floor sprang under my weight, tipping precariously to one side as I steadied myself. At the end I opened a cock-eyed doorway – the letter 'S' carved clumsily into the bare wood – and peered inside. It was a sorrowful, uncarpeted room, bare of anything but a boy's clothes strewn over the boards beside a bricked-up fireplace, a ladder leaning against a curtain pole.

I spun about as someone thudded up the stairs behind me. I might simply have waited for my punishment, were it not for a voice coming from above my head. A woman's voice, repeating the same phrase...

'Robert, are you there, Robert? Come to us...'

I noticed a crooked door on the landing, half as wide as the rest, squashed into the very corner of the wall, part-hidden by a black curtain which revealed a set of tiny stairs climbing a steep, twisted passageway, which was so narrow I had to ascend sideways, pulling myself up with my hands against cold brick. At the top was a small door. Gently, I pressed it open, my heart drumming in my ears. How fearfully dark it was inside, a red lantern projecting shadows against the far wall.

'Robert, are you there, Robert? Come to us...'

In the haze of the peculiar light I recognised Elizabeth, sitting at a small table, holding the hands of an elderly woman, their faces burning amber.

The stair squeaked beneath my shoe, and the old woman's head snapped up, eyes white. Her voice crackled, words stretched so thin she might have been singing.

'We have a visitor, Katie.'

I stared across the room as a shape emerged from the darkness. A figure, its head covered by a long, black shroud. Slowly, a set of pale fingers appeared from beneath the table, pulling away the material to reveal a crown of dark hair, parted at the scalp as if scratched into the air with chalk. It was the girl from the window. Her eyes sparkled in the flicker of the lamp, hands rested on the arms of her chair. She cocked her head with a curious smile.

'Hello, Professor,' she said. 'You have come at last; we have been waiting for you.'

PART TWO
EMANATION

CHAPTER SIXTEEN

I sat on an unsteady chair, taking in the room and its strange inhabitants. So, this was the answer to Elizabeth's mysterious church meetings? I could have laughed. My once-pious wife, she of constant morals and incessant incantations, was not unfaithful to me, but to God himself, dabbling in the occult, calling out to the dead no doubt with ringing bells and floating trumpets. Suddenly, Arthur's shrine took on an altogether more sinister meaning. I straightened my jacket, smoothing my moustache. 'Elizabeth, for shame.'

I took in the room as best I could. The attic window was blotted out by a blackout curtain giving the sensation that, even though it cannot have been much later than half past four in the afternoon, it might have been the witching hour. The room was of no particular character, but for the dim outline of a fireplace on the opposite wall. The bare floor was around two-thirds the building's width, ample for a party of four, though the space was claustrophobic beneath the low, gabled ceiling. The lamp beside the table was a rudimentary thing, made from an old biscuit tin, glazed on three sides with panels of ruby glass, and lit by the constant glow of a bat's-wing gas-burner. There was, I noticed with an inward smile, no direct illumination on the girl medium. Each of us was sitting on a standard kitchen chair, while the table at the centre of the circle was, to my engineer's eye, a simple thing of low-grade, unvarnished wood, approximately two feet in height. The girl lifted her veil from her lap, draping it over her head.

'Come,' she said, as the ruby lamp turned low. 'Our friends are growing impatient.'

She took my left hand, my right gripped by the old woman's bony claws. Elizabeth stared at the table, swallowing her tears, not meeting my eye.

'Elizabeth, we should leave at once.'

'No, William,' she said. 'I want to speak to Robert. He must be terribly afraid, don't you think?'

'He is in Heaven.'

'Ack, you can't be so sure a' that,' said the old woman.

'I believe I can. If anyone is in Hell, it's me.'

'Hush, Mr Crawford,' said the young medium in a soft voice. 'Can't you hear your wife weeping? We will find your son. In fact I believe... yes... he is in the room with us now. I sense him, over there beside the door. Do you feel him too?'

I jumped up in disgust, sending my chair clattering. 'We are going, Elizabeth,' I shouted. 'This is madness, how dare you?'

'Sit down,' barked the man who was standing sentry at the door.

'I will not!' I said, wrestling my hands free from the circle. 'You cannot order me about, I am a Professor of Engineering, not some weak-minded fool. Elizabeth, my poor darling, I understand everything now, but we know precisely where Robert is. He is in the grave.'

'No,' came the girl's voice from beneath the shroud. 'He is here. Come to us, Robert, do not be shy. Please, Professor, listen for him and he will speak to you. Death is a beginning, not an end. You will see.' She moved her veiled head in circles, her voice deep. I looked on, unwilling to sit, unable to leave.

'Robert,' said the girl, staring fixedly towards the door. 'I know, poor child... I know... we see you... you have begun a new journey. Dare you remove your fingers from your eyes? There is no need to be afraid. There now, that's better. You are afraid but you are not alone... you must move towards the light... do you see a light, Robert?' Her cloaked head turned towards me. 'What are you saying, Robert? Is it... feather?'

I looked around the room, huffing at the silliness of it all, wondering if the man at the door would let me leave, and was about to instruct him to stand aside when there came a voice from the darkness. A voice I knew.

Farfur...

I lost all strength in my trembling legs, righting the chair and sinking down slowly as though shot through the heart. No sooner had I fallen, than my hands were gripped once more by my fellow sitters.

Farfur...

The voice was soft, buried somewhere beyond the walls. There came a distant banging noise. The girl shook her head. 'No... poor Robert, do not be angry with us. Who are you searching for?'

'Elizabeth,' I muttered fearfully, my wretched voice shaking. 'We must leave, this minute, I beg of you. What have you done?'

But Elizabeth did not reply, her hands holding onto the circle in the red light. Somewhere above the table, a bell rang, followed by further rapping sounds from various parts of the room. The girl spoke, her voice lower still.

'Stay, Professor. Robert is here. He is asking for you.'

There was a dull sound, low beside the door, like something soft, rubbing on wood.

Farfur...

'Stop that!' I bellowed. 'Who is doing that? Stop that this instant!'

'Quiet!' said the medium, removing her shroud, eyes closed. Slowly, she rose from her chair, tapping old Mrs Goligher's hand as she searched the lightless room. 'Did you hear the voice, Mammy, was it the little boy? Where did it come from?'

The old woman glanced nervously around the room, before settling her pale eyes on me. 'I'll say somewhere close,' she croaked. 'It's him, sure.'

I gave a wild, incredulous laugh. 'Here? My son! What would he be doing in your blasted attic?'

The medium took her seat and leaned towards me, her face looming through the murky air, searching my eyes.

'Professor,' she said. 'Tell me truthfully, did you hear the voice?'

'Of course I heard it,' I scoffed. 'Who was it?'

There came a scratching beside the fireplace, like a mouse in straw. The girl turned away, her face in shadow.

Farfur, where are you?

I slammed the table. 'Stop that at once. Who is it? Elizabeth, was that you?' It could not possibly have been, for my wife was breathless from weeping, quite unable to speak. The girl had a faint smile on her face. She narrowed her eyes. 'Professor, are you here to make fools of us?'

'I am here to confront my wife. Whomever it is, pretending to be my son, I ask them to stop at once and set my good wife free. What will it cost? I shall pay.'

The girl raised her eyebrows, shrugging at her mother who squeezed Elizabeth's hand, coddling and whispering to her. 'Poor Mrs Crawford, you said he would come. Will we carry on or no?'

'Yes,' said Elizabeth. 'Yes, do carry on, please. Ignore my husband. Dearest Robert, you are here. I knew you would be. Are you hungry? Are you safe?'

Noooooooo...

The medium cleared her throat, pulling the shroud over her face once more. 'The spirits search for unfinished business, Professor. Your boy must have left something behind. He is so frightened. What did he leave?'

'Robert,' said Elizabeth, staring at the empty space beside the door, smiling through her tears. 'He is there, I believe it. Robert? Will you find your Uncle Arthur? He will take care of you.'

I snorted. *Uncle Arthur, that drunken yob?* The room rattled as a tram passed along the street below.

'Darker,' said the girl, as her mother turned the lamp down, the shadows pressing in until only the tabletop was visible. 'I sense Robert is in some danger, there are many spirits here today, though one is cold and cruel.' She shivered. 'He is very angry.'

'Cruel?' said Elizabeth. 'Robert, you must go to Arthur. Quickly, my darling!'

'Yes, Robert,' said the medium. 'I sense you are unsafe, something is approaching. Be quick!'

I tutted. I should have preferred an affair. Sighing, I prepared to stand when, suddenly, a powerful jolt coursed around the circle, wrenching my arms, followed by a flurry of hard raps bouncing from every wall. I saw the old woman's eyes staring white in the darkness. Elizabeth cried out as the banging gave way to a scraping noise beside the fireplace. A loud boom rang out behind my head, footsteps clattering across the roof, the table tilting into the air before tipping violently to one side as though thrown by some hostile force. Startled, I sprang back in my chair, twisting to see who was there, pulling my hands from the circle, swinging them in blind, empty space as the medium cried out, 'Professor, look out!'

Beneath my chair, something grabbed my ankle as I fell to the floor. 'Get off me!' I cried. 'Let go!' The table, or something like the table, hit my shoulder, swinging above my head, bashing my ear with a swiping leg. I rolled backwards, covering my face with my arms. 'Do not hurt me, please!' I squealed. 'Keep away...'

Silly old Farfur...

I strained my eyes, a thousand shadows dancing across the ceiling, the memory of the statues looming towards me, stone eyes and stone mouths set in furious energy, their hands stretching towards my throat.

Please help me, Farfur, who is that man? He is coming to get me.

I felt the wall at my back, flailing blindly to keep the demons away when, suddenly, the room was flooded with daylight.

Panting, I looked through my arms to see the bony woman from the kitchen standing at the window, one hand clasping the curtain, the young man beside her, his eyes wide. Elizabeth was half-sitting on her chair, gazing about the room, awestruck. The old woman, rigid as stone, knuckles blanched at the edges of her seat, stared blindly around the room, her face a perfect mask of terror. The medium was quite still, her heavy, scuffed boots planted on the floor and her long, delicate fingers relaxed over the arms of her chair. Her head was bowed to her lap yet, as I crawled from between the table legs, she raised her chin beneath her veil, took a long, deep breath and sighed.

Elizabeth was wringing her hands, nodding. 'Yes, Robert, we heard you. Oh my poor boy, you're afraid, I knew it. We shall find you. Yes, we shall help.'

I jumped up before anyone could stop me, leaping towards the medium, and snatched the hood away from the girl's head.

I cannot say what I expected to see beneath the material. A triumphant gypsy, perhaps, with a sly, squinting eye. Yet there was nothing in the chair but a bewildered, exhausted-looking girl.

CHAPTER SEVENTEEN

'Bullshit.'

Professor Fforde lowered his newspaper, his long, wrinkled face glowering at me through the smoky light of the men's common room. I had been telling him about the séance. What had I expected him to say? After all, it is one thing to find oneself caught up in the queer atmosphere of a ramshackle attic with a family of common, occultist shirt-cutters, quite another to share my experience with the learned men of the Institute. As I recounted the bumps, the raps, the red lamplight and the extraordinary change in the girl, the whole thing seemed perfectly absurd.

Absurd, and yet... I remembered the girl's limp body after the shroud had been pulled away. The smoothness of her wet skin. The vacant look in her limpid, petrified eyes. The fine lines, the sweeping curves, filled with mystery. The poise. She was quite apart from her frowsy coven. No woman of such a tender age, even if she had grown up in the circus, could possibly have affected such a convincing approximation of horror. And Robert. His voice had seemed so present, so real; as though he was speaking to me from behind a curtain. Alive.

Of course, the details of the sitting were ordinary in their own right: a tilted table, bangs all about the room, floating objects. I had read about such poppycock in the newspapers. And yet, the sum was so much greater than the parts, for the séance had made its impression, not so much on my senses, but on the very imagination of my soul. How could she have lifted the table so violently? She simply could not. The man, Noah, was strong enough of course, yet he was stationed beside the door. Meanwhile, the elderly woman lacked the necessary strength to perform such acrobatics, of that I was sure. Someone else then. The man's wife perhaps? I had seen her downstairs at the sink. Thin but lithe. Even so, I would have sensed her in the room. Besides, to create so many effects at once, she would have needed eight arms or at the very least, some system of pulleys and magnets and all this stagecraft, simply to fool a man and his wife, who paid not a penny for their seats?

'Perhaps,' I said to Fforde, returning to the common room. 'Perhaps, if you had been there...'

'That is the point, Crawford,' he snapped. 'I would not have been there, would I? You are nothing but a madman to have gone in the first place, and one of a growing number.'

He jabbed the newspaper on his lap, disturbing the brittle atmosphere in the common room. It was a somewhat jumpy day, Britain having mobilised to join the war. Fforde threw his newspaper to the floor. 'I have heard them in my class today boasting about joining up to fight the Krauts and now here's you with your bumps and levitating tables. Have you all taken leave of your senses? Half of our young men throwing themselves into Hell, the other half trying to speak to them when they get there.'

He puffed on his pipe, stopping the stem at his large, wet lips just long enough to mutter, 'Idiots.'

'Well now, hang on a second,' I said. 'I am not suggesting that there was anything of the paranormal about it. Quite the opposite, in fact. It was clearly all a performance of some kind of...' I laughed, fiddling with my pipe. 'Well, I cannot say.'

Fforde humphed, shaking his head.

'Oh now, Fforde, don't be so dismissive of the lad,' said Stoupe, turning to me excitedly. 'How I wish I had been there with you, my adventurous friend! I've been invited to these sorts of things in the past, but I'm far too nervous to go. Imagine all those lost souls trapped beyond the veil, watching us as we go about our lives. I think I should like to die a grizzly, unavenged death in a hotel room, wouldn't you? Imagine the scandalous things one would see, floating above the bedrooms.'

Fforde tutted loudly, hunkering ever deeper into his chair. Stoupe chuckled at him, wagging his finger. 'There are many mysteries still to be explained, old man. Besides, there isn't enough magic in the world as I see it. All these arguments between kings and kaisers would be gone in a wisp if we just listened to the wisdom of our dead. Your sort like everything to be as mechanical as your pumps and thingamajigs, but give no credit *at all* to the unknown. There are more things in this world than we could ever understand; such wonders!'

'Such bloody wonders,' barked Fforde. 'Such as?'

Stoupe prodded a fresh gobbet of sponge into his mouth, flitting his eyes about the room, searching for inspiration. I willed him to say something profound; something that would appeal to that nagging, vaporous question at the back of my mind: could it be possible? Was Robert in trouble? I had failed him at the end; was I failing him in death?

'How about butterflies?' said Stoupe.

'Butterflies, ha!' said Fforde, his face disappearing into his collar like a contemptuous tortoise. 'If it could be demonstrated that any complex organ existed, which could not possibly have been formed by numerous, successive, slight modifications, the theory would absolutely break down. Mr Darwin's words, not mine.'

'Oh, Darwin, Darwin, Darwin,' said Stoupe. 'The very enemy of magic himself. Very well then, perhaps not butterflies but even Mr Darwin would struggle to explain where we go when we die. He might be up there now, in fact, sitting on a woolly mammoth and thinking himself a perfect clown.'

Fforde grabbed his cane, muttering at us both. I offered him some assistance, only to be growled at. 'Enough of this nonsense,' Fforde said. 'You are a fool to let your wife go anywhere near those charlatans. You're an even greater fool to talk about it here. You meddle with dark magic tricks if you want to, but it's no place for science and no place for a reputable man.' His face shook as he spoke, his voice hard. 'Our boys are dead, Crawford. They are not coming back.' He looked around the common room, a group of apprentices poring over an advertisement to join the ranks. 'Nor will any of them by this time next year, mark my words. You can take it from me. Death is death.'

I stood up, shaking. 'Perhaps you are wrong, Fforde,' I stammered. 'Perhaps death is a beginning.'

'The beginning of madness!' the old man cried, banging his stick to the floor. 'Mark my words, if you truly love that boy, you will leave him buried in the ground where he belongs and be thankful you know where he is.' He hobbled to the door before turning back. 'Forgive me, Professor Crawford,' he whispered. 'But you are too late.'

The door closed behind him, the sound of his stick receding down the corridor. I watched him go, thinking of my own words. *Death is a beginning.* Had I meant it? I could not be sure, though I had said it with all the certainty of a priest. I looked around the staffroom at the faces of my colleagues, who were speaking to one another behind their newspapers. Stoupe offered me a handkerchief, pouting.

'No need to look so glum, Professor. Whether little Robert was at the séance or not, he will be up there now, ever so proud of his father.'

Just then the door swung open, banging against the wall. It was young Blithe in an army uniform, breeches flapping triumphantly. 'Ha ha, gentlemen, great news!' he cried, waving his cap above his head. 'I have been called up to fight for King George! Will you join me?'

The apprentices jumped up, applauding, cheering him with cries of 'Hurrah!' and 'Hooray for young Blithe!' and 'Take that, Fritz!'

As Stoupe applauded, I crept quietly to the door, only to be caught leaving by the hero of the hour. 'Here, Crawford, won't you join me?' Blithe called over. 'I would be a proud officer to have a man like you in my platoon.'

'Me?' I said.

'Ha!' cried one of the men from carpentry. 'Crawford? Ye'd be better throwin' dandelions at the Hun!'

Blithe laughed. 'Dandelions, really? No, come on, Crawford, why not show Jerry what we've got, eh? I'd say you're just about tall enough.'

'I'm sorry,' I said. 'I cannot I... I am very sorry.'

'Coward!' called one of the men as the door closed behind me, Blithe calling to the crowd: 'Would you like to hear a joke about Fritz?'

I stood in a daze. I had always slept poorly, suffering my usual headaches, yet the last week had proved nothing short of torture, the world somehow spinning against my feet. I would wake, every morning for no longer than a second, carefree as a child, only to be gripped by fear and sadness dragging me back to the same, repetitive thoughts, the long wait for the next fitful sleep.

I wandered to the end of the corridor, nodding to students as they walked by, feeling the tears build then ebb only to return again in a wave until I realised there was nothing I could do but run to the gentlemen's lavatories. Locking myself into a cubicle, my hands shook as the unbearable grief threw itself from me like vomit. Wretched tears, wretched weakness, wretched sobbing. I looked at my blurred shoes, whispering to my boy.

'I love you still, Robert. I miss you, I do. I am so very sorry for abandoning you. I hope you are not alone. Perhaps Arthur will find you, or even she might... Were you afraid when you died?'

A door opened.

'Hello? Professor Crawford? Are you in here?'

It was Stoupe. I lifted my feet, holding my breath, gulping until he left. I crept out of the stall, splashing cold water on my face in front of the mirror, massaging my cheekbones, pulling the skin around my eyes. When I looked up, I was struck by the sight of myself. It was as though the face staring back belonged to another man entirely, his skull wrapped in sallow, crinkled flesh. His cheeks were sunken, his skin flaking. A single white hair coiled from his fringe, two sharp lines running from the corners of his eyes. I should never have recognised myself, were it not for the fact that my own lips moved as I whispered in a high, brittle voice: 'Robert.'

CHAPTER EIGHTEEN

Stoupe burst back into the photography lab' on tiptoes, carrying a mahogany camera on a tripod. 'Oh no, Stoupe,' I said. 'I couldn't possibly have my portrait taken, I'm exhausted.'

'I've been wondering where you were, Professor,' he said, setting the tripod on the floor, humming to himself as he adjusted the legs. 'Grief does funny things to a man, you know. I have an uncle who lost his cat last Christmas and all he does is meow.'

He disappeared under a black cloth attached to the back of the camera, his head moving under the material like a levitating ball.

'Now listen, you shall call me Seamus from now on, not Stoupe.' He reappeared, leaning clownishly on the tripod. I laughed in spite of myself, lighting my pipe as he nipped into the darkroom, calling excitedly. 'Honestly, Stoupe is such an ugly-sounding name, don't you think?'

He returned holding a short wooden pole with a brass bracket fixed to the top. 'My flash powder lamp,' he explained. 'I charged it with magnesium this morning, so we shan't be long.' He inspected me with a serious eye. 'You know, I once met a very sour-faced chap with no teeth called Christopher

Lemon. How I laughed, but look at me now. A bent old fatty called *Stoupe*.'

I laughed, pushing my spectacles up my nose. 'You certainly are fat, Stoupe.'

He frowned, fingers frozen on the camera lens. 'I am cursed with bad looks, it is true,' he said. 'Not that you believe in curses, of course.' He winked at me mischievously, dashing to a tall cabinet. 'Unless you've come round to the possibility of the paranormal?'

'Certainly not.' I laughed, watching him rifling through a box. It felt good to shake off the grimness of my thoughts. He may have been older than myself and quite a funny old stick, yet still, I felt an unexpected kindness towards the man after so many days rattling about my study.

'Aha!' said Stoupe, fixing me with a beady eye. 'Almost there.'

I sat back as he danced behind me, lowering a wooden pole towards my head.

'It is a posing stand,' said Stoupe, holding the back of my neck. 'You mustn't worry.' He pushed the contraption until its arms pressed lightly behind my ears. 'It is merely there to prevent your head from moving. Not always necessary, but for you... well, you are a rather animate fellow.'

He snatched my pipe from my hand, tutting, and I took a long breath, blinking my sleepless eyes. We had emptied the nursery of Robert's things on Sunday, attending church in the morning whereupon the minister had held my hands, pleading with me not to blame myself. I had resolved to follow his advice, channelling my grief into anger towards the family of swindlers on the Ormeau Road. People like that deserved to be flung in jail. They may not have channelled my son in their paltry little attic, but they had most certainly hypnotised my wife. I could barely get a word from her.

Stoupe clapped his hands, ducking beneath the camera hood once more, lifting the flash powder above his head. I yawned, straightening my back, feeling a tingling sensation beside my ear. It felt almost as if someone was touching their mouth to my neck. I turned to look, only for Stoupe to shout out, 'Stay still, William, please! Just as you are. Hold there.'

The room flashed with a shimmer of green stars and I screwed up my eyes, head swimming, as Stoupe appeared in front of me like blots of ink in milk. I rubbed my neck, laughing. 'What a strange sensation,' I said. 'Did you pass behind me? I could have sworn there was someone there.'

'Pass behind you? No, no,' he said. 'Just you, Professor Crawford. Now, I must develop the image in my dark room, it may take a few days, but I'll show you as soon as I can.' He added with an impish smile, 'You look very dapper. I am certain it will cheer you up no end.'

I straightened my jacket, bidding him adieu, then made my way outside. It was a warm, clear evening, and I decided to wander home rather than take the tram. My head felt tight and packed with chalk dust and I fancied some time to think. An hour or so later, I reached the end of our street, gazing down at the shipyard where mighty brown hulls sat like slugs beneath the cranes. Just then, a low thud rolled up the hill. I wondered whether it was the crash of a steel plate or a makeshift bomb from the houses across the water. Perhaps the shop was lying in a heap of rubble, the family twisted amongst a pile of shattered bricks, a chimney pot on the young man's head.

I smiled, kicking a stone along the path into a tuft of long grass. On reaching our door, I stopped. The walk had been so lovely, I hadn't given a moment's thought to my troubles. I simply had to put my foot down. Those crooks could swindle any innocent, broken-hearted family they liked for all I cared, but not the Crawfords. Yes, I was pleased that Elizabeth was faithful to me after all, but she had still lied, concealing her intentions from her husband and that was a form of infidelity in its own right, was it not?

I looked up at the nursery window to see my daughters watching me, Rose standing behind them. I waved as a cool breeze passed over my neck, disturbing the leaves of a neighbouring tree. I remembered the voice calling from the attic room, the lights low, the white eyes in shock, the loud bangs, the ringing bells. The girl beneath the shroud.

Farfur.

The family must be exposed, I thought. And exposed they would be, or Robert would never find peace in his grave.

CHAPTER NINETEEN

I had not told Elizabeth of my plan, for I knew if I did, she would set herself against it. As we entered the shop, the brawny man, Noah, greeted me coolly.

'Mr Crawford, nai,' he said, squaring his shoulders. 'Wot about ye?'

I offered my hand. '*Professor* Crawford, please.'

'Ay, Professor Crawford it is. And I'm Noah Morrison, leader of the Goligher Circle. You met my wife.'

The bony woman was standing beside the counter, her pinched face inspecting me with button eyes. I removed my hat, wishing her a good evening.

'Yer late,' she said. 'Back for yer dead boy, so y'are?'

The shop was every bit as chaotic as before, the stench of damp wood, plaster dust and tobacco filling the air. There were fresh curls of razor-sharp metal strewn about the floor while lengths of wire, chain and string tumbled from an assortment of boxes.

I gave Noah a friendly smile. 'I work with metals myself, you know. At the Municipal Technical Institute.'

He turned to Elizabeth. 'Here, Mrs Crawford, how are ye?'

My wife smiled, her neck blushing.

'Mrs Crawford is doing perfectly well,' I said. 'Our prayers have given us some peace.'

'Ay,' came a croaking voice. 'But what peace has the boy?' The old woman with the clouded eyes was standing in the corner of the shop beside a tower of pots. Her clothes were so tattered, they were quite perfectly camouflaged amidst the clutter. 'Didn't expect yous back, so we didn't,' she said fearfully, licking her long, yellow teeth. 'Ack still, the lost child will be grateful, nai. That's if he's escaped the demon that's after 'im.'

A soft, sweet voice came from the back of the shop. 'Good afternoon, Mrs Crawford. Good afternoon, Professor.'

The medium, Kathleen, was standing at the bottom of the stairs wearing a white blouse, hair tied high. She pushed her spectacles up her nose with a long finger, nodding to me with a smile. 'Welcome back, Professor. Someone special is waiting for you.'

'Robert,' whispered Elizabeth, rubbing my hand. 'Robert, he needs to tell us he is safe; he must have found Arthur.'

'Nonsense,' I scoffed under my breath. 'You mustn't hope for such things.'

'Oh, go home, please,' said Elizabeth, pulling away. 'You didn't have to come.'

'Ah, but I did,' I said, levelling my eyes at the wretched cast.

'I don't trust the wee man, so I don't,' said the old woman. 'What's his face tell ye, Kat? I say he can't join the circle, there isn't room.'

The girl shook her head, assessing me. 'We have nothing to fear from the professor, Mammy. Come, let us begin.' She gestured for us to follow, disappearing through the tattered curtain.

I followed Kathleen up the damp stairs, covering my nose with my sleeve against the fetid air. Just as we turned onto the second staircase, a small boy clattered past, delivering a sharp elbow to my ribs as he shoved through, calling back in a familiar voice: 'Hallo, Professor, ye big ballacks!'

It was none other than Samuel Goligher, the filthy boy from my class. I could not believe my eyes. So, the perverted ferret was one of them, was he? Instantly, any shred of remorse for the family's fast-approaching shame was gone in a flash. Let them boil in their own stew.

The young medium moved quickly, disappearing ahead of us as we rose through the house, reaching the tight stairwell to the attic. I hit the walls with my fists as we ascended the stairs, kicking the door when we reached the top.

'What are you doing?' hissed Elizabeth.

'Hush, my dear, never mind.'

Satisfied, I stepped into the attic, where the medium waited in the daylit room, already seated in her sturdy chair arranging her long skirt over her boots in front of the black curtain. Beside her sat none other than Adelia.

'William,' she said, barely concealing a look of triumph. 'I thought you were a sceptic.'

'Oh, well of course you're here.'

'Take care, William. One could easily mistake your excitement for hostility.'

'Not at all. I came here expecting delusion and delusion I have found.'

The woman bristled, nostrils flaring. 'Lillie,' she said. 'I should hate to find myself unable to pay for your children's new shoes.'

Elizabeth clenched my hand. 'Do be quiet, William,' she said. 'Robert will hear you.'

I bit my tongue and looked away, concealing my rising temper, for my plan required a cool head.

'There, William.' Adelia smiled. 'We are good friends, after all. What on earth was all that knocking just now? Oh, no matter, no matter take a seat, everyone, I haven't long, the draper is coming at four.'

The medium spoke up. 'Lady Carter, as you well know, this circle is managed by Noah Morrison, not you, and blessed by the spirits. I have asked you before to stay silent.'

I could almost have kissed the girl and laughed in spite of myself. Why, with the air of a strict nanny, she had scolded Adelia and the woman had taken it! She gestured to me. 'Professor, you will find a better connection there. Hands on the table please, where we can see them.'

Elizabeth was duly asked to sit to the girl's left while old Mrs Goligher was guided to the chair beside a visibly wounded Adelia. Noah stood in the doorway as before, his wife taking the seat to my right. The window was covered by the blackout curtain, the only light coming from the powerful glow of the ruby lamp at the side of the room.

My heart thumping, I prepared to end their charade.

'Welcome, everyone,' said Kathleen, her voice slipping down her throat like an oyster. 'Welcome, spirits. Stand, please, to call forth our friends.'

Six chairs scraped over the boards as we raised to our feet, holding hands in the red light.

'He is here,' said the girl. 'Close your eyes, quickly, let us sing.'

We duly raised our voices as one, filling the tight space with a hearty rendition of 'Glory, Glory, Glory', the very rafters of the roof elevated by our song. The spirits, I speculated, must have enjoyed my harmonies, for I found myself the most qualified vocalist of the group. On the second chorus, I took a peep, catching sight of the girl who was watching me with a curious expression. She pursed her lips with a playful, disapproving glance, before singing on with a knowing smile.

I took the opportunity to inspect the room a second time. I had already checked the door on the way in. It was made of solid wood with a brass handle, the frame sturdy. The passageway was built of solid brick, no cavities as far as I could tell from my thumping. Inside, the fireplace on the far wall was empty with a vase of dead flowers on the mantel, cobwebs covering the surround, encrusted with plaster dust. There was a gas pipe running in clumsy fashion from the lamp to the wall where it disappeared behind the long curtain, that fell from the low end of the gable ceiling to the floor at the girl's back. The walls themselves were of no particular note, covered in curled wallpaper, seemingly damp. I looked up to the ceiling, tracing over the plasterwork in the hope of finding some small holes or hooks from which objects might dangle. Dark though it was, I could see none.

I blinked as the hymn ended, pretending my eyes had been closed. Presently, we were instructed to return to our seats, Noah turning the lamp low before processing back to the door, folding his arms like an executioner at the block.

He will beat me to a pulp, I thought. *Have courage, William, for yours will be the greater blow.*

I felt the grip on my hands tighten. The medium rolled her head, removed her spectacles, pulled the shroud over her face, then spoke in a clear, confident voice. 'Good evening, friends, are you there?'

The circle jolted.

CHAPTER TWENTY

Elizabeth gave a startled yelp as a trio of sharp raps sounded from the back of the room. As before, I could feel no movement beneath the table. I looked over my shoulder at Noah, my hands held fast by the circle. I could barely make him out.

The girl spoke. 'Friends, will you acknowledge Mammy?'

Silence.

'The Lady Carter joins us too. We are honoured by her company.'

Adelia called out, 'George, are you there?'

'Patience, Lady Carter,' said the medium firmly. 'Lord Carter will find us, if he is looking for you.'

I watched the girl's faint silhouette across the table, wondering what she was up to in the dark. I would know soon enough. I had hidden a box of matches in my jacket pocket. Just at the right moment, I would strike one of them, catching her in a damning flash. The thought of her exposed sent a dangerous thrill through my body. I would have to be quick of course, for my fingers were gripped tightly in the circle, yet I was certain the opportunity would arise, if I could only hold my nerve and stay alert. There was something about the room, something about the hushed nature, the stillness, which managed to drug the senses, inflaming them to a point of almost unbearable sensitivity.

'And Elizabeth,' said the girl, her voice lower still. 'Poor Elizabeth is searching for her brother, who was drowned at sea. Also her wee boy, Robert, who died not two weeks ago.'

I imagined Elizabeth in the dark, looking about the room and mouthing silent words of prayer. Finally, there came a faint scrape from the far wall. I heard Elizabeth whimper. The medium made a high singing sound as her black form shifted before the curtain.

'Come now, guides,' she sang, her tongue slipping between her words. 'Will you help Mrs Crawford tonight?'

There were three clear knocks and I smiled. *Keep us on the hook*, I thought, nodding to myself. I could hear Elizabeth whispering. 'Lord, when I am afraid, I put my trust in you. Please. Oh, please. Arthur, where is dear Robert?'

It was almost too much to bear. I prepared myself, for I knew I would have to expose them soon. Alas, nothing came, no further raps, no scrapes. Why was the medium not answering my wife? *Give the woman some comfort*, I thought, *so that I might disabuse her*. Still the silence drew on, Elizabeth becoming ever more upset. *Make a sound, God damn you. Whoever you are; whichever one of you it is, make a sound, if you have any humanity at all.* Nothing still; only a distant cheer from the street below. A rumbling motorcar passed by. My arms tensed. Who was it then, torturing my wife? Who was sitting in that blackness, sniggering at us as the empty silence drew on? I thought of them in turn. The girl, the mother, the sister, the brother-in-law, even Aunt Adelia. It might be every single one of them. They would be unmasked soon enough. I would have them flung in jail the moment one of them conjured up a trick. It was a game of patience for, if I struck too soon, the humiliation would be mine. My wife spoke in a pathetic whisper.

'Please. My poor Robert, I beg you, tell us you're safe?'

I pulled my hands away, tired of the game. 'Oh, to hell with the lot of you,' I said. 'Oh, great and powerful ghosts! If you are real, then speak now. Is little Robert in the bloody room or not?'

No sooner had I spoken than a thunder of explosive raps stampeded above our heads filling the blackness as the table rose up from the floor, hovering beneath our hands, tipping violently from one corner to the other. Suddenly, with huge force, my chair was dragged backwards, crashing into Noah who yelped in pain.

'Here, Christ, what's that?' cried the old woman.

There was another great crack above our heads and before I could reach my matches, my chair shot forward, tipping me onto the table as it levitated sideways like a wild horse, throwing me to the floor. I toppled downwards, hitting my jaw on my knee as a bony limb collided with my cheekbone. I managed to scrabble the box of matches from my pocket, scattering them over the floor as a thud of footsteps passed around the walls.

Farfur!

I found the matches, striking them frantically as an army of unseen feet thundered across the floorboards.

Farfur, help me!

At last one of them struck, illuminating the medium's face. Her shroud was pulled away, frightened eyes gazing at me, hair loose over her white blouse. The match burnt my fingertips, fizzling out as I spun about, blindly searching for my spectacles.

Someone is coming, Farfur, help me! I don't like him. I won't go. I won't go!

Raging, I leapt to my feet, crashing the table to the wall. I struck another match, only for it to be blown out a moment later, but, in the brief flash, I caught an impression of bodies moving across my vision, startled faces, the table floating upside down. Beside the fireplace... a tall figure... or perhaps it was my imagination... but no, it could not have been, for I felt certain the man standing before the fireplace, staring directly at me, was...

'Quiet!' someone hissed. 'Listen.'

I heard it then, the faint sound of a woman singing, not in the attic, but somewhere far off, beyond the walls. The voice tinkled merrily for a few seconds, then stopped.

'Another spirit!' said Adelia.

The girl spoke up. 'Child, where are you? Who is coming for you?'

I can see him. He is coming for me. I won't go, Farfur. He is a bad man.

'Where, Robert?' Elizabeth called out. 'William, ask him where he is going. Ask him if he's safe.'

'Where are you going, Robert?' I cried, unable to control myself.

The table slammed to the floor. No sound but heavy breathing.

'Is it finished?'

It was a fearful, shaking voice and I realised, to my surprise, that it belonged to the young medium. Her composure was gone, replaced by the timid whispering of a frightened child. I held my breath, straining to catch something in the darkness. The singing perhaps, or Robert's crying. Please not the man at the fireplace. Yet all was strangely still.

'Find the lamp,' said Noah, but, before he could move, the attic was split by an invisible force which struck at me from every unseen wall as though we had been dropped into a tank of broiling, electrified water. The amend to phenomenon could not be seen, nor heard, nor touched, yet nothing was more real to me. I threw my hands to my ears, crashing to the floor, for the sensation was so fierce, so enormous, I could not think or breathe. And then, in a moment, it was gone, replaced by the breeze of some distant fields.

A woman's voice.

I recognised it, from many years past.

She was singing a plaintive melody, her voice threading through the unseen attic, curling about our heads in smoke.

The Elfin knight stands on yon hill,
Blow, blow, blow winds, blow
Blowing his horn, so loud until.
The wind has blawin his blanket away

'No,' I whispered. 'No it isn't possible.'

CHAPTER
TWENTY ONE

Noah turned the ruby lamp as high as it could go. The room flickered into view: chairs, people, hats, hair in complete disarray, as though the attic roof had been torn away by a whirlwind. I looked at the faces of my companions, gripping my shirt to my heart, gasping for air. They were, all of them, staring fearfully at me. Had they heard it too? Felt the electricity?

'Who was that?' I demanded, scrabbling to my feet. 'Enough of this now, who was it?'

Elizabeth shook her head, petrified. Adelia looked away, her expression something between fear and curiosity. The young medium's chair was empty. I found her standing beside the fireplace, gripping the wall, shaking.

'You?' I demanded. 'Admit it, now. The game is over.'

'No, Professor,' she said. 'You should not have lit the matches.'

'Wrong,' I said. 'I ought to have lit a thousand matches!'

'Oh, William,' said Elizabeth. 'What were you thinking?'

Old Mrs Goligher stepped into the lamplight, her hands feeling for me. I had never seen such a perfect picture of madness.

'The spirit cried yer name, Professor,' she said. 'You heard the words yerself.'

'Oh, I heard the words, alright!' I snarled, dodging her claws. 'I am asking who *spoke* them.'

'Robert spoke them,' said Elizabeth. 'Didn't you hear his voice?'

I threw the box of matches down in frustration. Noah righted an upturned chair, hunched forwards in it, staring at the floor. I was surprised, for his hands were trembling. Elizabeth whispered in prayer, oblivious to her humiliation. 'Robert, Robert, Robert. Our Father who art in Heaven, hallowed be thy name...' She looked at the matchbox beside my shoes, lifting her red eyes to mine, shaking her head. 'You must have frightened him away.'

Disgusted, I marched across the room, tearing open the door. The passageway was empty, the floor below deserted. Slamming the door shut, I marched to the window, ripping the curtain back, half-expecting to stare into the face of some floating apparition. Outside, the stars shone like pins above the tenement houses. Below, the cobbles were flooded with pools of fresh rainwater. I thought again of the woman's song. I had not heard it since childhood.

Could it be? Was it not the very last song *she* had sung to me, just before she had died? If so, then someone in the attic had chanced upon something exquisitely private, for I had shared nothing about her with my wife nor any living soul. I turned around.

'Frauds,' I barked through gritted teeth. 'Nothing but frauds, the lot of you.'

'Well!' said Adelia. 'How rude.'

'I'll give you rude,' I said, walking around the table, snatching up my bent spectacles, keeping a safe distance from Noah who was rising to his feet. 'Yes,' I said, wagging my finger at him. 'I do not need matches to see a bunch of treacherous imposters. Mr Morrison, I saw you skulking by the fireplace. What? Did you think I would take you for a spirit? Where have you hidden your wig? Police! Police!'

I stepped over to the window, attempting to throw up the sash, only to find it painted shut. 'Damn it, police!' I thumped on the glass, before snatching at Elizabeth's hand.

'Come, Elizabeth,' I said. 'Come at once.'

'Let go, William. Stop this. You frightened him away. He called for our help.'

'Who, Elizabeth? Who called for help? That was not Robert... that was... that was...'

'Who was it?'

The medium had her hand to her throat, her shroud piled around her feet.

I laughed. 'You!' I snarled. 'It was you, girl.' I pulled Elizabeth up by her arm as she tried to wriggle away. Let my fingers make marks on her wrists for once, instead of the spirits. 'Come, my darling, enough of these petty thieves. Let us leave them to their costumes and silly voices.'

Noah slammed his foot into the floor. 'Out,' he growled.

'Much obliged,' I said with a bow, yet he shook his head. 'Not you, Professor. Kat, Rebecca, Mammy, Mrs Crawford, Lady Carter. Leave me alone with him, all of you.'

Elizabeth shook me off as I backed into the wall. 'Darling, please. You cannot leave me alone with him.'

She looked back, already being pulled down the stairs by the old woman.

Noah curled his lip at Adelia. 'I'm sorry, Lady C, this'll be yer last sittin'. You an' Mrs C.'

'Come now, Mr Morrison, what have I done?' said Adelia, fishing in her tasselled purse. 'I'm sure we can come to some arrangement.'

Noah snorted. 'Get out.'

Adelia glared at me. 'Another fine success for the professor, then. I wonder, is there anything you cannot ruin? We shall have to lock you away at this rate, lest you inflict yourself on another unsuspecting achievement.' She touched Noah's shoulder with a gloved hand. 'Mrs Crawford and the children require William to work. Do not make her a widow.' She looked at me as I searched for escape. 'Goodnight, William, and good luck.'

I kicked the fireplace in frustration as Noah shut the door.

'Ye can stop that fer a start, ye blasted fool!' he snapped.

I inched along the wall as he approached me, cracking his knuckles. In a moment of sheer panic, I thought I might have to jump through the window. I laughed, my voice hollow.

'You are all charlatans,' I said, fumbling my pipe to the floor. 'Kill me if you wish, you belong in prison. One thing is for sure, that harpy will never get a penny from me.' He stepped towards the upturned table, righted it with one hand, his eyes hard.

'Say that again, nai,' he snarled.

'You are frauds,' I said. 'The rapping noises; they are nothing but heels on the floorboards or a stick against a wall.'

He took a long, slow breath, cracking his neck.

I continued, 'Do you seriously expect me, a Professor of Engineering, to believe a table is floating through the air? Well, I don't.' I cackled at him. 'Tell me, who was it singing?'

He narrowed his eyes. 'Who was it? Are ye askin' me that?'

'Yes, and who was speaking for my son? Come on now, answer me, man. I demand you tell me.'

He closed his eyes, rubbing at his whiskered jaw. I pressed back into the fireplace. 'You are cruel, taking advantage of a grieving mother.'

'Ack, cruel, am I?' He smiled. 'Hard words from a man who let his wee un shite hisself to death while ye were drinkin' sherry and readin' feckin' newspapers.'

'I... I...'

His nose was almost touching mine as I fished desperately in my pockets, eyes closed. 'Here, is this enough?' I said, holding out a shilling, trying to find his hand. I opened one eye to see a pair of black eyes, large as plates. I felt my veins fill with a crazed panic, my arms and legs shaking all the way down to my shoes.

'No,' I begged. 'Do not hurt me, please.'

'Noah, stop.'

We both turned. The girl, Kathleen, was standing at the attic doorway, slender arms folded. The man lowered his fist with a snort.

'The professor wants to pay us a shilling, Kat,' he said, spitting on the floor by my shoes. Only then did I realise hot urine was running down my leg. Noah snarled. 'Ye won't be commin' back here again, right?'

'I won't.'

'I will drown ye if ye do.'

'You'll drown me, yes, I believe it.'

He leaned in, hands either side of my head. 'Get out, nai, before I change me mind.'

I slid down the wall, cold trousers clinging to my legs, then scuttled to the passageway past the girl. I half-fell down the stairs, shoes slipping, bashing my knee, then tumbled onto the landing. There came the clatter of small boots, the boy Samuel pointing at my groin, cackling in his gritty voice.

'Here, Professor Crawford, yev only pissed in yer trousers, so ye have ye big ballacks! Wait till the lads hear this, nai!'

I pressed past him in a daze, running down the last flight of stairs and out through the shop into the road where the cold air nipped at my prickling legs. There was nobody waiting for me; Elizabeth was gone. I stumbled a little down the road, before stopping to look back at the attic window. The panes of glass were barely held by the rotting frame in the middle of the bowed roof. It was empty, the black curtain drawn. Above the tiles, silver clouds dropped spots of rain into the smoking chimney. I went to find my pipe for some solace, realising it was on the floor in the attic, swimming in a puddle of my own piss.

CHAPTER
TWENTY TWO

Elizabeth did not speak to me for three weeks following my ill-fated intervention; not until I abandoned any last vestige of dignity and begged for her forgiveness. At last, she thawed, if only to make our home more bearable for the children. She would be my wife, she said, only if I would accept that the séances were real and promise to make amends with the Golighers. I acquiesced, knowing I could do no such thing. How had I come to such a state? I was a man of science, an educated, middle-class professional, renowned at the Institute for his exactitude, his intellect, his calm nature. Naturally, the girls could sense our disquiet, playing up with ever more elaborate stories of the so-called white lady and her night-time visitations. Such fancies are so often a child's way of handling grief. If ghosts are real, death is not. 'Father, is Robert in Heaven?' Helen had asked me one afternoon, as she cradled a painted egg in her lap. 'I think I was cruel to him.'

'Cruel, Helen? When were you ever cruel to anybody?' I said, and she had looked up at me, eyes brimming with tears, sniffing her wet nose. 'It wasn't Robert who smashed those eggs on the wall,' she said. 'I made it up.'

'Well that was very naughty of you,' I said, glancing at the nursery door, imagining his little toes sticking out. 'You ought not to blame others for your own misdeeds.'

'Oh I didn't smash them either, it was—' and at that, I had left her to it. Meanwhile, Rose had grown a habit of staring at me for long periods, appearing unexpectedly in the corners of rooms or at the top of the stairs, often with items I'd lost, though I would have preferred them to stay that way, rather than spend another moment in her unsettling company.

Naturally, I had returned to Hazel's letter. Her words were fairly seared into my memory, its revelations more present than they had ever been...

I cant sense what I saw last nite and what I hav herd and it is not riet for a God-fearsum women such as myself to be part of it... I mak no jujmet, that is not my plays... I now yore intenshins are not evil but ther can com no god of theese secrits... I now you have bin unhapy Mrs C but I cannt help but pity pore Mr C for not nowing about Angels... Do not play games with love, Mrs C. I saw you meetin that man. You are a marreyed women and Mr C will discuvver what he has bin doin with you sooner or layter and then what will you do?

I had studied the letter again and again, obsessing over it as though every reading offered fresh meaning.

I sighed, looking around the common room. The Institute seemed so quiet. A good number of the younger men had been recruited into the linen factories to work on the machinery, while a hundred or so of the boys had joined the Army, some of them far too young. It didn't take many to leave a noticeable gap, but they would be back soon. I pushed my spectacles up my nose, folded my newspaper, and set off in search of Stoupe, finding him in the photography lab', arranging some tropical plants in front of a painted jungle scene.

'Ah, William!' he said brightly. 'Welcome to the Amazon.'

'Hello, Seamus,' I said, inspecting a clothes line of recently developed photographs. 'I was wondering whether you'd developed my portrait yet? I plan to give it to Elizabeth as a keepsake.'

'A keepsake? Are you going somewhere? Oh please, don't go to the war, Professor, I should die here, if you leave me on my own.'

'No, no, not that.'

'Ah, thank goodness; you really don't have the legs for marching. Alas, I've had no time at all, with the boys requesting photographs for their sweethearts and mothers, poor darlings. I've been asked to take a portrait this afternoon in fact, though the sitter is neither mother nor sweetheart.' He shook his head, laughing at some private joke.

'Did I tell you?' I said, nonchalantly. 'I returned to that family of supposed spiritualists on the Ormeau Road.'

'No?' he said, lips pursed.

'Yes, yes. Fakes, the lot of them, just as I thought. Nothing but a bunch of amateur beggars. The usual nonsense, really. Unconvincing illusions, floating tables, disembodied voices, ringing bells, that sort of rubbish. Raps and the like.'

'Nothing to trouble a scientific mind such as yours,' said Stoupe, buried in a plant.

'Certainly not. Laughable really. I told them as much. Put the fear of God into them, actually.'

'Is that so? How frightening you can be. You shan't be going back there then?'

'Oh no. Nor will Elizabeth. I have forbidden it.'

'The master has spoken.'

'Yes. Only...'

Stoupe turned around, eyebrows raised. 'Only?'

I coughed. 'Well, I must concede, there was this moment... it was the queerest thing. Such silliness, but I *had* to tell you about it. Honestly, it is rather funny, really.'

I told him about the séance. He hung on every word as I relayed the voices, raps and footsteps, and, as I spoke, I found myself laughing, embellishing the story to make it even more ridiculous until I reached the point at which my own words failed me.

'And then what happened?' he asked in wonder, nodding me on.

'Well...' I stumbled. 'Well I suppose everything grew quiet, really until...'

'Yes?' His eyes grew thirsty.

'Until somebody began singing.'

He clapped his hands to his face. 'Singing? Was it a message from the other side, do you think?'

'That was undoubtedly the intended effect, but of course it was someone in the room. They were lucky too because they chose a song which, by sheer chance, has some sort of, I don't know, meaning to me.'

Stoupe stepped closer. 'What did they sing?'

I was about to tell him when the door banged open. 'Blow, blow, blow winds blow!'

Adelia, strode into the studio in a vast canary hat, shedding yellow feathers. 'Good afternoon gentlemen. William, how fortifying to see you in one piece. Such a sweet song, I cannot seem to forget it.'

I chewed at my tongue. 'Aunt Adelia.' I nodded curtly. 'I must go.'

'No, no!' said Stoupe. 'Lady Carter, were you there at the séance, too? William was just telling me all about it. You must tell me what happened, both of you!'

Adelia fixed me with a vespine smile, seating herself on the posing chair. 'Go on, William. Tell Stoupe exactly what happened; tell him everything. I shall make sure you don't miss a detail.'

'Very well then,' I said, gritting my teeth. 'You were taken in by a gang of cheats, then threw a grieving, impressionable woman to a pack of wolves. It was a reckless act, Adelia. You ought to be ashamed of yourself.'

Adelia took a deep breath, before fixing me with a contemptuous glare. 'A reckless act? I should be ashamed? I believe in Heaven, William. I do, and I will not apologise for it. There is too much in people for them to end so suddenly. I believe beauty outlives the body. I believe your poor wife, like too many women, hungers for the love stolen from her by the grave and by her marriage. I should say that *you* are in need of love yourself, perhaps more so than any of us, though you would far rather uncover mean explanations than accept beauty.' She laughed. 'You're nothing but another arrogant man, telling the world what is right and what is wrong, what is true, what is shame. Creating problem after problem, then busying yourselves with solutions. Lord Carter is bumbling about in the afterlife somewhere no doubt, too lost to find his widow, precisely because of young men like you. Oh, yes! The clever doctors had clever designs, ingenious plans. Do not worry, Lady Carter, we shall fix your frail husband with drills, chemicals, scalpels. Science, William. Medical science took him from me, when love and prayer would have kept him at my side for another year at least. So please, do not cast your scorn at me, you cowardly trouser wetter.' She jabbed a painted talon to her chest. 'I have been to more than twenty séances. More than twenty! I have not heard a single word from my George. But you are visited by not one but two of your loved ones and thumb your nose at the blessing.' She covered her face with her shawl before looking back at me. Her eyes were wet, face determined. 'Who was she? The woman, singing?'

'Someone from my past,' I said. 'Someone very dear to me. I suppose that's the intended impression, at least.'

'She has returned to you, then. The medium was right. She predicted it all.'

'My goodness,' whispered Stoupe.

'She needs William's help, that is what the medium says. I've been back, though it cost me dearly after your nasty little trick.'

'Help?' I said. 'You cannot believe that. Help for what?'

'To save Robert, of course. Little wonder his soul is trapped in Limbo; Elizabeth told me you didn't guide him to the glory of our Lord God. He was a sinner. He vandalised everything he touched, just like his father.'

Stoupe lifted his hand, a band of sunlight artfully contrived across his face. 'He is trapped,' he said. 'Trapped between this world and the next.'

I scratched my head. 'Damn it, Stoupe, you cannot honestly think that.'

'I do think it, Professor. We believe in life after death, do we not? We believe in angels? It isn't so ridiculous...'

It *was* ridiculous. Of course it was. Yet still I wanted to believe that Robert's voice was real. That *she* had indeed sung her song.

'The girl claims you are special,' said Adelia. 'I was there last night and the spirits were silent. We sang for over an hour and they did not come. They have abandoned the poor family ever since your stunt. She says they will only speak to you. Desperate thing; her sister and that giant of a man are treating her very roughly for it.'

I checked my pocket watch. I was late for my next class. 'I must go,' I said.

Adelia reached out to me. 'She sends you this,' she said, placing a piece of paper in my palm. 'She begs you to go to her.'

CHAPTER
TWENTY THREE

I entered the lecture room without my usual greeting, scrubbing the previous lesson's notes from the board, muttering to myself all the while as the class looked on in silence. I fetched a fresh piece of chalk. *Mensuration: circumference of a circle, areas of a triangle, rectangle, parallelogram, circle...*

'Last week,' I said, my back to the class lest they catch sight of my mood. 'We calculated the area of a regular solid. How then might we calculate the area of an *irregular* figure without a planimeter?' I held my hand up, waiting for someone to call out the answer. I took a deep breath and straightened my mouth, turning to see Samuel Goligher smirking at me from the back row, whispering. I resolved to ignore him. 'Come now, answer me. What if a circle is flawed?' I demanded, impatiently, dotting the board with the chalk. There was some commotion. I waited for silence. 'Take out some squared paper, be quick about it; we are well behind.'

I leaned my forehead on the blackboard, the cool surface comforting my aching head. Some muttering started up. I turned in a fury to see the same filthy little woodlouse deep in conversation with his neighbours, his hand covering his mouth. His hair was sooty, his skin grey, eyelashes of black grime trapped beneath his fingernails. 'Goligher,' I barked. 'You will be quiet and pay attention, damn you.'

He sneered at me, leaning over to his classmate in the row below. 'Here, Noel, gimme yer paper, so.'

'Where is *your* paper?' I demanded. 'I suppose you lost it along with your soap?'

I turned back to the board, trying hopelessly to calm myself, drawing a large circle. 'Who will tell me what shape this is? Come on.'

'A circle, Professor,' said one of the boys, nervously.

'It may well be a bloody circle to a mere surgeon or a measly chemist,' I snapped. 'However, to a modern engineer with an eye on the *truth*, it is not a circle, is it?' The boy looked at me, then to his classmates, stammering. I removed my spectacles, rubbing my nose. 'Forgive me, gentlemen,' I said. 'Let us begin again. This appears to be a circle to the trusting eye, indeed, yet in fact it cannot be. Think about what is hidden from view. A clock face may appear circular to the layperson's eye. Yet, in fact, if you were to inspect such things under a microscope, one would understand quite rapidly that they are slightly *asymmetrical*, filled with tiny imperfections. If an engineer cannot know for certain the precise nature of the elements with which he is working, then he risks his two mortal enemies: assumption and inaccuracy. And the inaccurate engineer is deadly not only to himself, but to all those who trust in him. So, we must find a way of calculating the area of an imperfect shape. Therefore, we can learn to use...' I underlined 'Simpson's rule'.

William.

I spun around. 'Who dares call me by my Christian name?' I demanded. The boys stared at me with apparent bemusement. I raised my eyebrows, returning to the board, coughing on chalk dust.

'So,' I said, attempting to regain my thoughts. 'If we have an integral rule to an equivalent area and, of course, the trapezoidal rule, which we looked at yesterday, is different from Simpson's rule, then...'

William.

'If we have an integral rule to an equivalent area...'

William.

I turned to the class, launching the chalk over the boys' heads, cracking it against the far wall. 'Enough, Goligher!' I bellowed. 'You will stop disrupting my lesson or I shall report you to the principal, do you hear me?'

Goligher lifted his grimy head from the desk. 'Me, sir? I ent said nottin.' His eyes slipped to my groin. 'Yer wet you are, Professor Crawford.'

The boys around him snorted.

'Stop it,' I said. 'Stop laughing.'

I faced the board. 'Where was I? Remembering that the trapezoidal rule is not the same as Simpson's rule...'

Farfur, who is he?

I punched the board, jolting the boys in their seats as they leaned away from me, marching myself up to where Master Goligher was sitting. I grabbed him by the collar, dragging him stumbling down the shallow steps to the front of the class before flinging him hard into the wall.

'Professor Crawford?'

I turned to see Fforde standing at the lecture room door.

'Yes, Professor Fforde?' I panted. 'Can I help you?'

He looked at the boy. 'I heard... a commotion.'

'As did I. This boy has been disrupting my class with voices.' Samuel Goligher made to speak but I clicked my fingers, grabbing his wrist as he struggled and twisted.

'Professor Crawford, man. Have a care,' said Fforde, taking my arm. 'He's only a wee'un.'

'The boy is a pervert, a liar and a bad influence on my class,' I said, defiantly. 'Thank you for your concern.'

I nodded curtly, before throwing the boy outside and slamming the door on them both, clapping dust from my hands and returning to my lectern, determined to finish the lesson. I looked up at my class, straightening my jacket. 'Well now, there is no need to look so terrified. Let that be a lesson to you all. Professor Crawford is no fool. Not to be toyed with. Not to be mocked.'

I retrieved a piece of chalk from beneath my shoe, straightening up to realise that the boys were staring at the blackboard, mouths hanging open. One of the boys slowly lifted his hand and I turned to follow his outstretched finger.

Three words were written there in a sweep of chalk dust, as though blown onto wet glue:

WILLIAM
MOTHER
ROBERT

'Out!' I shouted. 'Get out, get out, get out all of you! Enough! Get out.'

The boys leaped from their seats, climbing over one another, looking back with fearful eyes. Once they were gone, I locked the door before sitting at one of the long desks at the back of the room, staring at the strange words.

Would the Golighers ever cease torturing me? What unknown curse had I earned for seeking the truth? It was clear, they were determined to discredit me before I could discredit them. It was then that I remembered the note from the girl. I reached to my pocket, missing my best pipe, and pulled it out.

I will be waiting in the Botanic Gardens at six. Please meet with me, we must talk alone.

CHAPTER
TWENTY FOUR

I jumped from the Stranmillis tram, striding through the iron gates into the Botanic Gardens as the light turned low. The trees rustled in a growing wind as drops of rain pattered over beds of faded marigolds. Turning along a winding path, the curved dome of the Palm House rose up ahead, steel basketwork gleaming white in the dusk.

I pulled out my pocket watch, tutting. The dilapidated glasshouse would close in half an hour; likely she was not there and the whole thing would turn out to be another waste of my time. Mind you, what if she *were* there, waiting alone... for me? A strange meeting indeed. There was only one way to be sure.

The heavy glass door closed behind me with a sucking noise, my skin prickling in a curtain of tropical air. 'Come along then, girl, where are you?' I said to myself, my spectacles steaming over. I paced around the beds, shoes brushing past ferns, clanking over steaming grills. I craned my neck to the crystal roof as a panorama of impossibly tall palms ranged above my head, their ungainly fans reaching far into the sweltering air. 'Ms Goligher?' I said, swatting at a leaf the size of an umbrella. 'I received your note.'

It occurred to me, my clothes already damp with steam and trepidation, that Noah might have tricked me with Adelia's connivance. Perhaps this was an ambush, lest I reveal the true nature of the séances. I looked over my shoulder, my back tingling. 'Ms Goligher? Are you here?'

There was a rustling as I moved deeper into the building, tracing past parrot-coloured blooms. I stepped around a cactus the size of a foot stool and there she was, in a plain grey dress, waiting for me. The lenses of her round spectacles were no less occluded than her mother's eyes.

'Ms Goligher?'

'Professor Crawford, you came? There isn't long.' Her hair was knitted into curls by the humidity, its dark gloss tangled like sheep's wool on barbed wire. She ran her hand across her brow, droplets of water slipping along the edge of her hand to her sleeve. 'I am glad Lady Carter gave you my note.'

'That woman would do anything, if she thought it might cause me stress.'

'Do I?'

'Do you what?'

'Cause you stress, Professor?'

'More than you could ever know, child.'

'Then I'm sorry. How is Mrs Crawford? I hope you haven't fallen out.'

'That is none of your business,' I snapped. 'Mrs Crawford and I are very happy; more so than ever.'

'She is a good wife.'

I huffed. 'You must stop pretending to be a spiritual medium, Ms Goligher. That is all I have come here to say. It is immoral. For my part, I must apologise. I made a fool of myself with my matches... and my accident, of course. I was not myself.'

She stroked a pane of glass with her finger. 'Noah is a monster. He controls people, hurts them.' She looked up, holding her hand out. 'Professor, I do not pretend to be a spiritual medium. At least, I don't think so.'

'What is that supposed to mean?'

She removed her glasses, caught by some private grief. 'You heard the voices. Where did they came from?'

'I have told you. You are making the voices beneath that hood of yours. It could hardly be more obvious. Next you will be playing trombone under there, expecting us to believe in phantom marching bands.'

She examined me closely, eyes searching. 'Perhaps... perhaps I ought to hold a circle without my shroud... would it be safe? I cannot tell.'

I laughed. 'Ho-ho, yes. And get your sister or some other hack to do it for you. I am a charitable man, but you cannot expect me to believe in your...' I waved my arm about '...amateur theatrics.'

'My spirit guides were the first voices I ever heard, Professor. They have been my closest friends at the darkest of times.' She fiddled with the cuffs of her blouse. 'Only...'

'Only what?'

'Only like you, I had begun to doubt whether any of it was true. Do you know, my older sister Rebecca was a medium before me? So was Mammy once, but she lost her second sight and now she's losing her first as well. I began to wonder whether I was hearing spirits at all. Perhaps my family were playing tricks on everybody. Maybe I was mad.'

'You admit it then. All of it is make-believe? There are no spirit voices.'

'That's not what I'm saying, Professor.'

I removed my hat in frustration, my hair springing up. She giggled. 'Your hair tangles like mine.'

'It does.' I stepped closer, shoes ringing, sweat bubbling across my shoulders.

'She always told me you would be handsome, Professor.'

'I, handsome? Who told you?'

'You know who, if you'll only allow yourself to admit it. She's been speaking to me for many years.'

I searched the girl's face. 'Stop. It.'

She looked down, embarrassed. 'I'm sorry. Sure, I am. I'm only telling the truth.'

'It's impossible, child.'

A dragonfly landed on her shoulder, cobalt blue with yellow stripes. 'I was seventeen yesterday,' she said. 'Hold out your hand, Professor. Gently now.' The insect fluttered between us, before landing on the tip of my finger. 'I'm a good age, so Noah says. I know what that means.' She stroked her finger over the insect's back, its body rolling up at her touch. 'Look.

Is he not the most impossible thing you have ever seen? But he's real.'

'Why did you ask me here, Ms Goligher?' I said, flicking the insect into the air. 'You have admitted the sittings are false. How did you guess my mother's song? I have never shared it with anybody.'

'Listen,' she said, eyes darting. 'They'll be searching for me already. I told you, I'd grown suspicious of my powers. Then, when I saw you that night in the rain watching us from across the street behind those barrels, I knew it was you.'

'Elizabeth told you precisely who I was.'

'She told me she had a husband, yes; that he was a kind but troubled man. That is all I knew. But when I saw you that night, I realised I'd seen you a thousand times before. You were *hers* and now, at last, I could bring her to you.'

I turned away. 'I believe the voices are a performance on your part, Ms Goligher. I am sorry. I have come here to ask you never to speak to my wife again. I believe she may be mad with grief.'

The girl placed her hand on mine. 'You are right to be doubtful, Professor,' she whispered. 'That is why I asked you here. What if everything is a lie as you say? What if I am mad? I am not here to convince you of my powers. I am here to beg you to convince *me*. I do not know what I am.'

There came a call from beyond the vines. 'Anyone still here? Closing time.'

'Yes,' I called back. 'We shall be leaving shortly.'

'Very good, sir, take your time.'

The door closed and she laughed. 'Are you concerned about being seen with me, Professor? Elizabeth would be happy to see you here, I am sure. Lady Carter too. She was in a horrible temper last night, desperate to hear from her husband. She doesn't understand. All her money means nothing to the departed. They would scream till the gravestones shattered for a penniless widow before making a sound for a king. Isn't that strange?' She looked up. 'If my voices are false, Professor, if the circles were a trick played on me until my body could be sold for profit, would the spirits not perform best for those offering the highest fee?'

I could smell her damp skin in the air, the faint scent of almonds. She was dewy, her frantic hair dusted with sparkling droplets. She shifted, blushing. 'I feel as though the spirits are trapped inside my body, Professor, waiting for you to cut them free. That is why you were sent to me. To prove me a liar or discover the truth once and for all.' She nodded, turning to play with the finger of a palm leaf. 'It is your destiny.'

'You have read too many fairy tales, child.'

She snapped the leaf away, folding it with her long fingers like a spider on a fly. 'Stop calling me that, Professor, I am not a child. You must listen to me. Noah says he won't allow you to investigate me, but there is another way. Lady Carter has an evening planned with some rich gentlemen. She refuses to invite you, but I will insist. I will be there alone.'

'Your mother will be with you, surely?'

'No, she won't.'

'Your sister then? Noah at least?'

'Lady Carter was very clear about it. None of them would be welcome in great houses.' She sniffed. 'If she could have my spirits without me being there, she would. It's lucky my guides taught me to speak better, and how to behave like a lady.'

'Whoever taught you, they did a worse job with young Samuel.'

'The boy means you no harm.'

'He means me all the harm in his malicious little head. Tell him to stop playing the fool in my classes. He has been mocking me with voices, you know.'

'I will, if you come to Lismarra House. Allow yourself to believe, Professor, then all will be true. If the spirits are silent, then I will run away somewhere. There's a girls' home in Bangor by the sea; I always thought I would escape there if anything bad happened to me. If not there then... well, I am a blouse-cutter. A young woman. I have enough to sell.' She touched my chest, her eyes slipping inside my jacket, eyes imploring. I pushed her away.

'I told you, I want nothing to do with your séances,' I said. 'They've done enough damage to my family already.'

Kathleen stood away, tracing her finger sulkily over a pane of steamed glass. 'It is too late. She has found you with her song. She will not let you go now. I believe she is searching for Robert. He is alone and frightened and calling for his father.' She looked up at the crystal dome above our heads, the evening turned indigo, rain drumming on the glass. Together, we stared towards the sky in silence until, with a sigh, she spoke, her voice solemn and soft. 'There is an ocean of souls coming, Professor, can you feel them? So many dead. More of them every day. Listen to your lost ones, before their voices are drowned in the flood.'

She lifted her spectacles, the lenses dripping with condensation, then stepped past me. 'Lismarra House,' she said. 'Our host is Mr Robinson of the department store. Friday, at eight o'clock. Please be there.'

I watched her slip through the wet leaves, moaning to myself. I had come to that place searching for a confession, an apology, a promise to stay away. Somehow I had accepted an invitation to another damned séance. I carried my exhausted, sweating bones to the exit, nodding at the caretaker, who smirked before jangling his keys.

'Night, sir.'

Outside, the peaceful light moved low, solemn and soft. I wandered through the park, kicking fallen leaves. Would I go? I reached for my pipe, forgetting it was lost, then touched something in my jacket pocket. I pulled out my hand and laughed to see the very thing, along with a box of matches and a pouch of tobacco tied together with a band of cheap lace. Clever girl. Clever *woman*.

So, a dinner party with Mr Robinson of the famous department store. He was already an acquaintance, after all. Of course I would go.

CHAPTER
TWENTY FIVE

The shops were horribly busy, people pushing by on the street as we made our way, Rose and the girls following behind us laden with bags and boxes. I strode as quickly as I could, Elizabeth skipping to keep pace.

'But what is all this for?' she said. 'We haven't the money.'

'I've told you, it's a surprise. And have some faith in your husband for once, my textbook is published next month.'

'I hope it sells.'

'Of course it will sell; the publisher is very confident. Now then, you have your coat and shoes, what else do women wear?'

'A frilly dress, Father,' said Helen, dancing along like a ballerina.

'I suppose I could wear the one I wore for the gala,' said Elizabeth.

'That mangy old pair of curtains? No, no, I want you looking your very best. Come.'

We stepped through the doors of the Robinson & Cleaver department store, the doorman tipping his hat as we made our way to the central atrium, peering up at the vaulted ceiling. I turned about to get my bearings. There were polished glass cabinets packed with everything from gloves and ties to bracelets and bows, walnut counters running in every direction between marble columns, each with an attendant waiting to serve us.

I clicked my fingers at Rose as she collided blindly into a portly man carrying a standard lamp. 'Do look where you're going,' I said. 'Honestly, I've never seen someone create so much fuss carrying a few boxes.'

I marched away to the stairs, pulling Elizabeth and the children with me. A matronly assistant was busying herself with a box of silk flowers. 'I need a dress,' I said looking over her shoulder.

'For your wife, sir?' she replied.

'It isn't for me, is it? Come, come, dresses where are they?'

'The first floor, sir, allow me to help you.'

'Fine,' I said, snatching a pale-blue rose from a countertop. 'And we'll have this too.'

Helen ran up the white marble staircase before us, Margaret trying her best to play chaperone, as Elizabeth scolded me for being brusque. I tutted as the woman climbed to the first floor, noticing an empty plinth with two abandoned circles where the busts of Kaiser Wilhelm II and his wife had once stood.

'You've removed your most illustrious customers, I see?'

'Oh yes, they went last week after the kaiser's nose was chipped off. The empress will be missing her favourite Ulster marmalade.'

'Messrs Robinson and Cleaver must be smarting.'

'Patriotism before profit, that's what they say.'

'Fine, gentleman,' I said, stopping myself from bragging that we would soon be dining with her employer. I wanted it to be a double surprise for Elizabeth: dinner with distinguished new friends and a reunion with Ms Goligher to boot! Just the thing to set us back on track.

We found our way to the Women's Evening Wear Department, and I left Elizabeth with the assistant, taking Rose in search of Men's Formal Wear. How I loathed shopping for suits, all that standing about and fussing over buttons and collars. We passed a counter arranged with an assortment of brightly coloured umbrellas, a man about my age deciding between racing green and a particularly garish yellow. He had his son with him, a boy in shorts and a blazer, his teddy bear cuddled under his arm.

A vision of Robert came to mind, standing beside the counter, strawberry blanket in his hand, excrement running down his legs. I blinked and picked up my pace.

The menswear department was a peaceful affair, carpeted in swirls of burgundy, high shelves packed with the latest trend in 'ready-to-wear' shirts for the professional man. I nodded my approval, catching sight of myself in a long mirror, my trousers rumpled over my shoes.

'Do you think my trousers are too long, Rose?' I asked.

She looked at me, uncertain, placing the hat box and bags on the floor, then smiled, pointing at a mannequin dressed in a splendid tuxedo and satin-striped trousers.

'Midnight blue? I should look a perfect fool in that,' I said, fingering the finely tailored cuffs. 'I look a fool in anything I wear.'

She shook her head, frowning, then pointed to another mannequin wearing a fine shirt with a wingtip collar. Well, it *was* a special occasion. I allowed myself to be measured up by a pimpled boy, though I refused to have his tape measure anywhere near my inside leg. When all was ordered, I marched back to find the women, harrying Rose to get a move on with our ever-growing mountain of packages.

I found them huddled around a mirror, Helen and Margaret smiling as the woman busied herself with pins.

'Isn't she pretty, Father?' said Helen.

Elizabeth turned and shrugged, letting her arms drop to her sides. The dress spilled from her shoulders in leaves of white lace, cascading from a cameo brooch, furls of delicate blue silk setting off her pale skin and copper hair.

'My darling,' I said. 'You have never looked more beautiful. Why, you shall make me the envy of every man at the party.'

'Party?' she said. 'Is that what all this is for? I daren't ask what it costs?'

'Oh now,' said the assistant from the floor. 'What does it matter when your husband has such a look in his eye?'

'His eyes don't pay the bills.'

I grinned, taking her hand. 'My sweet wife, relax. We've endured so much lately. Besides, if I don't buy you this dress, you'll never forgive me come Friday.' Rose held up the blue silk flower, which I placed behind Elizabeth's ear. 'You look fine indeed, and we shall match. I have ordered a tuxedo and trousers in midnight blue.'

Elizabeth's eyes grew wide. 'Will you heat the house with midnight-blue trousers, William? Or pay for the gas? Or buy us food? The girls need new shoes and Aunt Adelia hasn't said a word this month about money.'

'I've told you. The book will sell, have faith.'

'I have faith, you know that. Faith is not what I need. I need a sensible husband. Oh, don't look at me like that, I can't bear it. I know your book will be wonderful, but all this?' She turned in a circle, admiring herself in the mirror. 'And what party are we going to? I hardly need to dress up for Mr and Mrs Fforde.'

'The Ffordes! Heavens, they won't be there.'

'Well then, tell me where we're going or I shall go straight home.'

'Very well then, if you must spoil the surprise. We are invited to dinner with Mr Robinson and his prestigious guests.'

The woman got to her feet. 'Not Mr Robinson of the department store, sir?'

'The very same.'

Elizabeth clapped her face. 'My goodness, whatever for?'

'Dinner, I expect. Is that not implied?'

'But why?'

'Darling, I must say your low opinion of the Crawfords is bordering on offensive.' I turned to the woman as she returned with a pair of embroidered silver gloves. 'Tell my wife. Most women would be thrilled to go to such a party, wouldn't you say?'

'I should say so, sir; there isn't a lord or lady he doesn't count as a personal friend. Here, let me fetch you some jewellery, I have a perfect pair of pearl earrings...'

'No, no, no,' I said. 'We're not the Rockefellers, Elizabeth has her mother's jewellery.'

'I do,' said Elizabeth. 'My goodness, Mr Robinson. He must have taken to you that night at the gala. He'll want to know more about your balloons.'

'Dirigibles, Elizabeth. I expect so.'

'The gloves, too?' asked the woman, her pencil eager at her book.

I laughed. 'Yes, yes, the gloves too.'

Together, we headed to the counter as a silver-haired man in a waistcoat and half-moon spectacles totted up our purchases.

'Elizabeth,' I said. 'Take the girls to look at the dolls, will you?'

'Dolls?' asked Margaret. 'What do I want with dolls?'

I crouched down, rubbing my chin thoughtfully. 'Dolls for Helen, then. Books and the like for Margaret.'

Away they went, skipping and cooing with excitement. I watched them go, filled with the drunken joy of a man unused to pleasure, then returned to the counter.

'Here you are, sir, will you be paying now or shall we send a credit note?'

I looked at the piece of paper beneath his thumb and almost fell over the balcony. 'Is that... I believe you have made a mistake.'

'Really, sir? No, no, it's quite right. Is there a problem?'

I looked at Rose, who was staring at the note with a face like a Japanese samurai mask. I gulped. 'I... goodness me, that's quite a bit more than I'd expected.'

'I see,' said the man, giving the assistant a knowing look. 'Ms Morris, would you kindly place these items back where they came from?'

She looked at me, then at Rose. 'Are you sure you can't afford it, sir? Your wife will be ever so disappointed, don't you think? You both seemed so happy, it was a joy to see such love between a young couple.'

I looked along the row of cabinets to see Elizabeth holding the girls' hands, pointing at a crowd of dolls in frilly dresses. Our eyes met and she smiled, her cheeks flushing. Something touched my arm and I looked to see it was Rose's hand. She was nodding, parting her hands like a butterfly, miming a word.

'Boot?' I said, frowning. 'Book? Ah, yes, my book! I am to be a published author next month, you know.'

The man raised his eyebrows, impressed. 'Congratulations, sir.'

'Thank you. Yes, now I think of it, I shall take credit. Crawford is the name. Number 1, Park Avenue.'

CHAPTER
TWENTY SIX

Friday came soon enough and I whooped like an excited boy as we raced over the bridge in a taxicab, air billowing through the open sides of the canopy. Lismarra House was some way outside the city, so I had indulged in a little luxury. I was impressed by the machine, a Unic imported from France. The engine chugged up a low hill as we whistled past the Harbour Commissioner's Office.

'Do you think I will fit in with the other women this evening?' asked Elizabeth. 'Aunt Adelia says Mr Robinson from the department store has the smartest friends in Belfast.'

'And now, so do we!'

The taxicab careered past an exhausted horse pulling a cart piled high with broken chairs. I smiled at the thought of the Goligher family huddled in their damp hovel above the shop while we drifted towards our high-society dinner. The girl clearly thought she had me wrapped around her little finger at the Palm House. All that nonsense about voices and my mother. Well, if she wanted proof that her séances were bunkum, then so be it; I would give her such proof.

Elizabeth squeezed my hand, curling into my shoulder as the engine rattled, a fresh gust of wind billowing into the cab. A few miles along the Shore Road, the car took a sharp turn onto a long driveway lined with cedars, a fine panorama opening out to sea. Lismarra House must have been one of the grandest mansions in Ireland, rising in one square block of shining sandstone above a broad, manicured lawn.

I paid our fare, adding a generous tip for the driver if he would return for us at ten o'clock. As the motorcar left, honking its horn, we climbed the broad steps to the polished doors, rubbing one another's arm for reassurance. Before we had even pulled the bell chain, a portly butler opened the door in long tails, hair shining in a centre parting.

'Good evening?' he said in a thick, Continental accent. 'Can I help you?'

Elizabeth shifted behind me nervously, wrapping her shawl around her shoulders.

'Why, yes,' I said.

His waspish eyes landed on my hair, then crawled down to my overcoat. I ought to have spent more at the department store. He sniffed. 'Might I ask for monsieur's invitation?'

I looked at Elizabeth, panic rising in my throat. We had no invitation. The entire evening was planned on trust. On the word of... oh good God, was this entire thing some sort of revenge, designed by Adelia and the girl?

'I... we have no invitation...'

Instantly, the door began to close.

'Oh no,' whispered Elizabeth.

Just then, a man's voice came from behind the butler's back. 'Parra, who are you keeping at my door?'

The butler stood away, revealing a man with a kindly face. I recognised him instantly from the gala.

'Mr Robinson, sir. Professor William Jackson Crawford of the Belfast Municipal Technical Institute. This is my wife, Elizabeth, she is wearing one of your dresses.'

The butler began closing the door again, only to be stopped by Mr Robinson, his face lighting up. 'Aha! Professor Crawford! Well now, you must forgive me. Parra, invite our esteemed guests in at once.'

Presently, the butler stepped back, inviting us inside. Our hats and coats were taken as we turned together, cooing at the electric chandelier and gilt mirrors, a record player on an ebony table surrounded by fragrant lilies. 'Fascinating,' I said.

'What, that thing?' said Mr Robinson, clipping a cigar into a silver tray. 'We sell phonographs in the shop; would you like one?' Before I could take a closer look, he clapped me on the back, leading us towards the sound of polite chatter and clinking glasses. I caught sight of my hair, jumping to see how large it had grown in the wind. Frantically, I tried patting it down, nodding to our fellow guests.

'I shall leave you to mingle,' said Mr Robinson. 'Parra, where are the drinks?'

'William,' whispered Elizabeth. 'What should I talk about? The women look so proper.'

'Well, what do *proper* women usually talk about at parties?'

'Their husbands, I think.'

'Perfect, then talk about that.'

I accepted a glass of champagne as we approached a mother and daughter with matching teeth, standing awkwardly beside a table of hors d'oeuvres.

'Good evening,' said Elizabeth, fiddling with her dress. 'Are you here for the dinner party?'

The woman exchanged a queer glance with her daughter. 'Yes, of course,' she said. 'Aren't you?'

'Yes.'

'Lovely.'

'We came here in a motorcar.'

'Oh.'

I took in the surroundings, humming to myself, sipping at my champagne. A gilt chandelier at the centre of the room hung low above intricate plaster cornices, the walls patterned with green leaves. I thought of the Palm House, wondering whether the medium had arrived yet.

A group of well-to-do gentlemen were standing in a circle beside the fireplace, talking in low voices with concentrated eyebrows. I was about to drum up the courage to approach them when Adelia entered in a bustling dress of emerald silk, her neck and décolletage hung with swags of Victorian jewellery. Evidently bored by her company, she moved on to a group of women in long, shimmering gowns, holding court with them before spying us across the room with a great cry of delight.

'Elizabeth, you have come!' she said, her eyes darting over our clothes as she approached. 'How fine you are in your dress,

Lillie. Of the hundreds of women wearing it, you must be one of the prettiest. And William,' she turned to me, teeth bared. I felt like an apple about to be bitten, but she seemed to stop herself, settling into a sing-song voice I found even more unsettling than her usual bark. 'You are here too.'

The older of the two women with the teeth gave a little curtsy. 'Good evening, Lady Carter.'

Adelia affected a smile. 'Mrs Weebly, how lovely to see you. And your beautiful daughter too; I do hope you are well after your loss?'

Content to leave Elizabeth, I took myself to the edge of the room, keen to inspect the phonograph, yet Mr Robinson spotted me and called over. 'Professor, do not stand alone. Come here, old chap. Gentlemen, make room for Professor Crawford, please. What's the use of such a large house if we're all huddled together like penguins?'

A second man reached out, gripping my shoulder as he sucked on a cigar. 'A pleasure to meet you, Professor Crawford,' he said. 'Cleaver's the name.'

I shook his hand, accepting a second glass of champagne from the butler. 'I am honoured to meet the famous Robinson and Cleaver,' I said. 'In fact, I must thank you for dressing my wife.'

Cleaver guffawed. 'Well as long as we didn't *undress* her.'

Robinson wagged his finger at his associate, turning to me with an earnest eye. 'Professor, I have been hoping to cross your path ever since the gala. What can you tell us about this book of yours?'

I took another gulp of champagne to steady my nerves. Already, I could feel my blood beginning to fizz. 'It is a simple book really, though not so simple perhaps for the average mind; that is to say not the *average* mind but the untrained mind, if you know what I mean? Never mind, what am I trying to say? It details, to use layman's terms, the various tabular calculations, formulas and such that any engineer must learn if he is to... well...'

I stopped. While my tongue had skittered on its wayward course, one of the men at the far side of the room had approached our circle. It was Principal Forth! Before I could stop myself, I was speaking again, plucking the monocle from the eye of a young man at my side, before holding it aloft. 'For instance, what would you call this?' I asked, turning to the rest of the men.

'My bally monocle, that's what it is,' exclaimed the young man. 'Here, can he be trusted? What is he, some sort of parlour magician?'

Principal Forth took a sip of his whisky, watching me closely.

'I am asking about its *shape*,' I said. 'Not its purpose.'

The young man sniggered. 'It's a circle, of course.' He turned to the other men. 'Are we to name farmyard animals next?'

I smiled patiently. 'I'm afraid it is not, in fact, a circle.'

The men muttered to one another, leaning in to inspect the glass ring between my fingers.

'At least, it is not a *perfect* circle, that's what I mean. With the precise magnification offered by the very latest microscopes – which, needless to say, can be found at Principal Forth's Municipal Technical Institute – you would discover that this apparently smooth, clean disc is no less riven with fractures than Donegal Bay.'

The young man snatched the monocle back, inspecting it closely before poking it into his pocket with a flounce. 'Fractures,' he said. 'What rot.'

'Not at all,' said Principal Forth. 'Professor Crawford is one of the finest minds at the Institute. Something of a rising star.'

I smiled, filled with the most glorious pride. 'Thank you, Principal Forth,' I said with a bow. 'Though I ought to point out that a star cannot rise. It is, of course, another illusion borne of the limitations of the human mind.' I lifted my arm towards the glittering chandelier, spilling a little drink on my sleeve. 'We perceive the firmament moving across the sky when in fact it is we who are rising, turning and falling, viewing from the axis of our own perspective.' I offered a little belch to my fist. 'Thank goodness, the practical, dispassionate application of scientific inquiry is telling us more than ever before about the world and the heavens around us.'

A small, jug-shaped man in a minister's collar spoke up. 'Be careful, lest your science offend the word of the Lord our God.'

I smiled. 'Minister, we engineers must obey mightier Gods than yours.'

'Ho-ho,' said Mr Cleaver, winking to his business partner who was listening intently.

'My gods,' I pronounced, jotting in the air. 'Precision. Perseverance. Pragmatism.' I took another gulp of champagne. 'My nemeses? Inexactitude. Inexperience. And...' I poked the young man on the breast pocket where he kept his monocle. 'Ignorance. Just as we witnessed with that evidently all-toosinkable ship, inaccuracy can only ever beget catastrophe for those who harbour it.'

A gentleman standing beside Principal Forth, who had been nodding along quite appreciatively until my last words, turned puce. I must have sensed danger, but still on I sailed.

'Wars,' I declared. 'Are lost by politicians and army generals, yet they are won by engineers. That is why the teaching of our young minds should form the very foundation of our war effort. A nation's greatness depends on the education of its people.' I hiccoughed, realising I had won the attention of the room. The butler was watching me from the hallway, directing a meaningful look at Mr Robinson, while Elizabeth stood beside Adelia, imploring me with her eyes to shut up. 'I mean to say,' I added. 'If we cannot sail past a few icebergs then what possible hope do we have against dreadnoughts?'

I laughed, though nobody joined in. In the cavernous silence, I smiled at Principal Forth who was glaring at me, astounded. Mr Cleaver pointed at the beetroot-coloured man. 'Here, Lord Pirrie,' he said with an impish look. 'Did you hear that?'

My veins froze. Baron Pirrie? The former Lord Mayor of Belfast, Pro-Chancellor of Queen's University and Chairman of Harland and Wolff shipbuilders, the very architects of the *Titanic*. I thought I might be sick.

'Do forgive me,' I spluttered, stepping towards him, champagne spilling.

Mr Cleaver guffawed. 'Pirrie, you old sea dog, you ought to draft Professor Crawford here to design your ships.'

Adelia had the malevolent look of a crone at a public hanging. Time itself stopped. Oh Christ, what had I done? People murmured to one another, turning their backs and then, as though the words had come to me from another mind altogether, I began to speak again, quite beyond my own control...

'My mother used to say that I would be a great inventor one day... silly really, but that is what mothers do, is it not? Believe in their sons? She couldn't see that my designs were flawed... I remember her face... I remember her voice... how proud she was when I offered her one of my new contraptions. She would pretend to make use of them, though they only ever made her chores harder. In truth, though I never speak about her, I have spent my life living up to my mother's expectations, haven't you? We men are all the same, surely? If we can accept our mistakes and work hard to approach even the feet of our mothers' expectations, then even when a glorious ship confounds its own brilliant designers... even if the world falls apart, the Empire shall never sink.'

My heart was drumming. I closed my eyes and remembered her last breath.

The Elfin knight stands on yon hill...

Where was the medium, was she here? Why had I followed her to yet another indignity? *Help me, Mother*, I thought, my eyes closed.

Clap.

I opened my eyes.

Clap.

Mr Cleaver was beaming at me.

Clap.

He was applauding, nodding his wonderful, bald head in approval.

'Hear, hear,' he cheered. 'What a magnificent man you are, Professor Crawford. My goodness, Forth, you canny old dog, you must be proud of this one?'

'Yes, well put!' said Mr Robinson, joining his associate in clapping his hands, encouraging the whole room to applaud me, before raising his glass.

'A toast to the Empire!' he cried. 'And to our mothers!'

Everyone cheered; the women congratulating Elizabeth on her fine husband, pulling her away from Adelia and the Weebleys to join them in conversation. I snatched another glass of champagne from a passing tray, trembling with the sheer energy of the room's delight. Mr Cleaver slapped my back. 'Forth is very lucky to have you, Professor Crawford. Here, Lady Carter, why has he never been invited to one of your tiresome evenings before?'

Adelia swished over, placing a bejewelled hand on my sleeve. 'Mr Crawford is a treasured friend of mine; I have been sponsoring his little family ever since I met his gentle wife at my church meetings, adopting them as my dear pets. Professor Crawford always brings a certain *je ne sais quoi* to any event he attends. It is quite thrilling; one never knows what will happen next.'

The dinner bell rang, the butler calling us through to the dining room, Elizabeth finding my arm as we passed through. 'Never do that to me again,' she whispered in my ear. I looked at her, concerned, only to see that she was smiling. 'I'm so proud of you tonight, my clever husband.'

We gasped when we saw the table, set with gilded crockery, crystal glasses, folded napkins on a crisp white tablecloth, embroidered with foxes chasing hares beneath silver dishes. The candles wore little shades matching the apricot petals arranged in a bridge over a pond of green bay leaves. I ate hungrily, hardly able to bear the tiny morsels, yet still, the food was rich and varied, matched with fine sherry, white Burgundy and two champagnes beside a selection of light meat dishes. We tucked into great platters of lamb and poultry before finally embarking on balls of delicious iced cream and port. My lips prickled as Elizabeth and I answered excited questions from our new friends. The conversation swung around the happy table so quickly it was hard to keep up, serious one moment, uproarious the next. I spoke earnestly about dirigibles and flight, new mathematics, steam power, diesel engines, electric motors, magnets, lightbulbs, phosphorescent clocks. I believe even Baron Pirrie had warmed to me by the time the cheese plates were cleared, Principal Forth coming under great pressure from Mr Robinson to admit me to the high table at the next gala.

'Oh, he will be promoted,' he said. 'We are training the boy up well. Still a few tricks to learn though, eh, Crawford?'

'Yes, Master Forth.'

'Major Forth now, boy,' said Mr Cleaver. 'Here, Forth, surely young Crawford is prime officer material? You run Irish recruitment, after all. Or is he too short to fire a gun?'

The principal laughed. 'No, no we need men like the professor at the Institute. As he said, wars are won by engineers. I told him so myself, did I not, Crawford?'

'I... yes, Master.'

Just then, Adelia chimed on her glass. 'Dear guests, forgive me for interrupting your *fascinating* conversation. How you men like to talk.' She flicked an accusing glance in my direction. 'I hope you enjoyed the meal; congratulations, Mr Robinson.'

'Ah, no, Lady Carter,' said Mr Robinson. 'It is to your credit alone. I could never have organised such a splendid feast. Alas, my dear departed wife, Caroline, would have been proud to have prepared such a meal.' He looked away from the table, lost in grief.

Adelia replied that she was – her voice catching, lip wobbling in a poor approximation of authentic grief – bereaved of her own husband, while Mr Cleaver – exchanging a sympathetic look with more than one of the men around the table – spoke about no fewer than three children lost to his family in the past five years. It transpired that, between us, we had lost some thirteen family members to various illnesses and accidents over the previous year, a quite sobering number. Mrs Weebly revealed that her daughter had been a twin until the previous March. Elizabeth spoke at length for the first time about Robert before mentioning Arthur, causing one of the maids to leave in tears, she having lost her husband to the very same tragedy, Baron Pirrie excusing himself at this point, bidding us a good night.

Mr Robinson dabbed his eye with the corner of a napkin. 'I take great comfort knowing that my dear Caroline is in Heaven looking down on her sorrowful family. I should dearly like to speak with her again.'

Adelia gave him a charged look. 'Perhaps you shall.'

'Oh no, Lady Carter,' said Mr Cleaver. 'Please, not your spiritualism again. It cannot be wise to meddle in such things. Surely we can join the dead when we get the chop ourselves.'

'Very wise, Mr Cleaver,' I said. 'My dear wife was momentarily hoodwinked into believing in Adelia's ghost whisperers and I had the misfortune of meeting them myself. I can report with absolute confidence that they are frauds.'

I felt Elizabeth shift at my side. Adelia smiled. 'I am sure the professor is right. Perhaps, then, it is time for our little curiosity?' She rose from her chair, beckoning for us to follow.

'What is happening?' asked Elizabeth as we climbed the sweeping staircase to a set of French doors on the landing.

'I am by your side, my darling,' I said. 'There is no need to fret.'

At the top of the stairs, we filed into a large, panelled room with mullion windows looking out to sea. The space was cast in a red glow from a familiar ruby lantern. I eased past my fellow diners to see Kathleen Goligher, her shroud over her shoulders, grey eyes flitting between us with a look of benign curiosity. Her voice was soft yet insistent, people duly hushing as she spoke.

'Ladies and gentlemen,' she said, resting her eyes on me. 'Come, be quiet, take a seat. My friends are waiting.'

CHAPTER
TWENTY SEVEN

The table jerked, but no sooner had it moved than it sat dead again, refusing to respond. Already some of our party had given up while the vicar and the principal had immediately headed downstairs, expressing their disdain. I would have followed them, were it not for my peculiar meeting with Kathleen at the Palm House. The proceedings were, of course, tiresomely familiar. I waited, silently, for each of the supposed phenomena with a grim, impatient smirk, my head swimming with drink.

'Friends,' said Kathleen beneath her shroud. 'Where are you tonight?'

I was about to suggest a theory when the table pressed upwards, rotating clockwise beneath our fingertips. The younger Ms Weebly gave a whimper, her mother similarly impressed. I watched the medium suspiciously, noting her ability to perform her trick without a flicker of movement in her upper body. Eyeing the circle, I fancied I could get away with a basic investigation to satisfy my curiosity, removing my hand from the circle.

'Hands on the table, or the connection to the spirit world is broken,' came the young medium's voice. I gave a relaxed yawn, sitting back in my chair. Presently the table jumped higher by about a foot, tipping to one side as though carried by a pair of invisible, clumsy porters. The Weebly girl squealed, my neighbours tightening their grip on my hands. With feigned innocence, I raised my right foot from the floor, poking into the unseen space with the toe of my shoe. Evidently, I brushed Mrs Weebly's shin, for she yelped, her fingers trembling. I moved my toe across, touching what I supposed to be Mr Cleaver who spluttered, only for Kathleen to speak.

'Calm, everyone, please. My guides are timid tonight. They may not be used to disturbances in this house. I sense it has been many years since they walked as flesh. Some are as ancient as the rocks beneath our feet.'

I snorted.

'Mother,' whimpered the Weebly girl. 'I'm afraid.'

I straightened my leg, pressing my foot towards Kathleen, waiting to feel the soft meat of her thigh. My shoe must have been halfway beneath the table, yet nothing was there. Deeper I probed, sliding down in my seat until my toe must have been barely an inch from Kathleen's midriff. Just as I was wondering how on earth she was managing such a trick, I realised with a jolt that she was staring at me through the dark, her eyes sparkling, shroud pulled back.

'Professor,' she whispered. 'What are you doing?'

'Exactly as you asked,' I hissed under my breath. 'Exposing the truth.'

Just then, there came a tinkling sound from somewhere beyond the room, Mr Robinson jumping forwards. 'My God, will you look at that!' he said as a little brass bell travelled across the ceiling above our heads, the table still rocking between us in the air. The bell tinkled merrily as it moved before melting back into the curtain. A line of wire, I thought, like a fishing rod. So, Kathleen was not alone after all. Hardly surprising; we had not witnessed her arrival at Lismarra House. Doubtless that French butler had accepted a bribe to keep his nose out. A chill came over me, imagining who was skulking behind the curtain, barely three feet from my shoulder. Was Noah lurking back there? Or her sister Rebecca, perhaps? I studied the drapes as best I could, though the light was too low to discern any presence within the folds. Duly, the table floated back to the floor.

Mr Cleaver chuckled. 'Well, well. How extraordinary. I cannot think how it was done.'

Adelia cut in. 'No mortal can understand the ways of the spirit world.'

'Hush,' said Kathleen. 'Spirit friends, do not be alarmed.' Her voice became croaky, her breath shallow. 'You are doubted by some tonight. Are you still there?'

A trio of low thuds echoed from somewhere above our heads. So, someone was posted upstairs.

'What does that mean?' whispered Mr Cleaver.

'Three bumps are "yes", one is "no",' said Mr Robinson, nodding sagely.

'Tell me, spirit, are you frightened?' asked Kathleen. Three sharp taps could be heard from the windows, though they appeared empty but for the broad black sea. 'Shall we leave you in peace?' We all jumped in unison as a single hard knock slammed into the table. 'Will you speak to us?'

Kathleen shrank into her chair, rolling her head towards her lap as a scraping noise grew from a corner of the room.

'Will you look at that?' whispered Mr Cleaver. On straining my eyes, I saw a grandfather clock in the far corner of the room, just visible in the gloom. The scraping became a faint squeaking.

'Good gracious,' whispered Mr Robinson as a shape emerged from the chest of the clock, a panelled door swinging out, hinges squeaking.

'It is a child,' said Adelia. 'Lillie, could it be?'

Kathleen shifted, a low moan growing beneath her hood, her long fingers rigid on the arms of her chair.

'Robert?' said Elizabeth. 'Is that you?'

Such is the nature of charged imaginations in the dark, that certain shapes can gather in the mind as truthfully as if they were shifting in reality. For how many times has an intruder turned out to be nothing more than a coat on a hook or a branch at the window? Thus, I could not be certain whether the silhouette of the small boy standing beside the clock was real or merely some invention of my champagne-soaked brain. And then, it spoke. Timid... drifting through the lightless air as thin as cotton...

He is coming. Who is the man, Farfur? I am frightened.

'Who is it, child?' asked Kathleen, her voice buried beneath her hood.

The man with the hanging bones, Farfur. He is closer now.

'Where is he?' asked Kathleen.

He is watching me, through the window.

Elizabeth whimpered, the Weebly women cried out, yet nothing could be seen at any of the windows, but for tendrils of ivy tapping against the glass in the wind.

'There is nobody there,' said Mr Cleaver.

The outline of the child stepped back towards the clock, faint moonlight picking out the curls on his crown. The voice was a bare whisper, hardly audible above the sound of our breathing.

He is inside the room now. Where are his bones? Please, Farfur...

Mr Robinson sat up. 'Here, what is that awful odour?'

'It smells like rotten fish,' said Adelia. 'Oh, how horrid.'

Indeed, it was awful; an almost unbearable stench of rotten fish and seaweed filled the room, crusting the briny air. There came an ominous thud beside one of the windows at the far corner of the room, followed by a scuffing sound like a long coat rubbing along the wall in shifting, lumbering steps. It moved towards us, closer and closer until—

'Mother,' Ms Weebly spoke, her voice shivering. 'Mother, there is someone behind me.'

Three dull thumps appeared against the skirting board at her chair.

'Mother, I can feel him.' She sat straight as a pin, her teeth chattering. 'Mother, it... it is touching my neck.'

I peered at the terrified girl through the darkness, trying to see if someone was there. Mr Cleaver shrugged. 'There's nobody behind you. Silly creature.'

Miss Weebly shivered. 'There is a finger, I tell you. On my...' She yelped. 'It moved, it moved! It held my neck, you saw it!' Yet we had seen nothing of the sort, for there was surely nobody behind her. The girl twisted, yanking her hands free, lashing into the shadows. 'Get away!' she cried. 'Let go of me, please!'

Kathleen sat forwards and clapped her hands. 'Let go of her,' she shouted. 'Demon spirit, set her free.'

'My God,' said Mr Cleaver, with an uncertain chuckle. 'What a show.'

'Who is it?' said Adelia. 'Is it you, George?'

A single knock on the wall.

'He is after the child in the grandfather clock,' whispered Mrs Weebly, before throwing her hands to her face realising what she had done, her mouth open in horror. 'Oh, I am so sorry, I did not mean to tell him...'

'Stupid woman!' snarled Adelia.

The young Ms Weebly gasped, apparently let go by her imaginary assailant, which now scraped along the murky wall at our backs in slow, deliberate, inexorable movement. It turned by the doors to my back, then slid further around the room, unseen feet drumming on the floor with each apparent step.

'No,' whispered Elizabeth. 'It is moving towards Robert. William, stop him, quickly.'

The Weebly woman stood up, pulling at my hand. 'Forgive me, I did not mean to give the boy away... not the clock, no, he is somewhere else! In the parlour! I meant to say... oh dear, oh dear, what have I done?'

Yet the figure took no heed of her, moving on, on, on around the room. I stood from my chair as the scraping drew itself to the far wall, ever closer to the grandfather clock. 'Please stop this now!' I barked. 'This is too much.'

The sound stopped somewhere in the far corner, beyond the reach of the lamp. I could just make out the dim face of the clock, its body little more than a strip of black. A squeaking noise.

'The door,' said Mr Robinson. 'The clock door is opening. The boy will be discovered!'

I clambered from my chair, ripping my hands from the circle, tripping as I flew into the darkness. I reached the corner of the room in a second, shivering as the air frosted around me, blindly swinging my arms to find the door in the clock's chest, slamming it shut before leaning my back against it panting, arms outstretched to stop the creeping thing from coming closer.

At my back, I could feel the *clunk, clunk, clunk* of the cogs beating to the pendulum's swing. The salty air was so cold and damp, I might have been standing by the sea. The table suddenly seemed so very far away from where I was standing. An island of ruby light glowing across black water, circled by concerned faces. I felt something close to me. I heard its breathing. I sensed its eyes resting on mine. *The man with the hanging bones.*

'Get away,' I hissed, gripping the clock. 'Whoever you are.'

And then it spoke.

No, William.

'Who... who are you?' I hissed. 'Who is that? Is that you, Noah?'

You know who I am.

It was a man's voice. Quiet, threatening, soft. The loamy stench of rotten fish was suffocating and I gagged, cupping my face. 'I do not know who you are, though I might guess. Why are you tormenting me? I am here to expose your tricks, I admit to that but... but I shall gladly let go, if you cease tormenting my family; I shall never cross your path again, I promise. It was Kathleen, she begged me to come and...'

It was you who put me on that ship, William.

Time stopped, the ticking of the clock still at my back. I gulped. 'No.'

The voice gave a low, dry laugh as I strained my eyes to catch better sight of the shadowy silhouette moving ever closer. 'No, it cannot be you.'

You ordered me to leave, William. Go, you said, or Elizabeth will know everything.

Who else knew about our final meeting by the harbourside, his miserable face begging me to keep his secrets? I'd told him, he had no choice but to flee, or he would have been arrested or cut to ribbons and dumped in a ditch. A Catholic girl pregnant, a pile of unpaid debts.

'Arthur, you had to go. You begged me to arrange your ticket.'

I drowned because of you.

'You were behaving like a maniac,' I hissed. 'You were a risk to Elizabeth and the children! Think of the girl you left behind, the money you owed!'

I am more of a risk to your children now, William. And I have a much grander debt to settle.

'I owe you nothing.'

The spirit voice grew hard, its unseen mouth beside my ear. *You owe me my life, William. They locked me up.*

'No, I had no idea.'

157

You told them. You turned me in.

The shadowy figure was upon me now, the smell of the sea as thick as soup.

'No, I didn't.'

The spectre's voice was sorrowful, its words submerged beneath its breath like the swish and swell of distant waves.

I cried for my sweet sister when I heard them screaming. I prayed for the children as I begged to be set free. When the water climbed my legs, when I knew that I was going to die, in the dark, to the sound of prayers, gun shots and choking, as the glass smashed and the ocean poured in, I thought of you.

'How could I know the ship would go down, Arthur? Please forgive me; I had no idea.'

The voice snapped, hard.

I will take Robert now and then you shall see what death is.

'No, please, Arthur. Do not take him, I shan't let you.'

There came a faraway voice and I looked up to see Elizabeth, standing in front of the séance table in shadow, her outline drawn by the light of the lamp. 'William, what is happening?'

The spirit voice grew sad again, the air around me shifting.

Oooooh-oooooh, my sister, what has he done to you?

I raised my shaking hands. 'Stay where you are, Elizabeth, it is... yes, Robert is safe. He is quite safe, my darling. Stay where you are, do not move.'

Trembling, I reached out like a blind man, feeling for something more or something less than the shadows. The skin on my fingers turned crisp with cold. 'Please,' I begged as I felt something move through my stomach, my bowels cramping, twisting, the thing reaching through my flesh. 'No, leave him be,' I pleaded, my voice breaking. There came the muffled sound of a child crying at my back.

Farfur, please. Uncle Arthur, stop it, I'm scared...

'No, do not take him, Arthur. Leave him be, I beg of you.'

I was about to tear open the clock to steal the boy away when, all of a sudden, something around me changed, as though the cold air cracked. The hand inside my stomach disappeared, the stench of rotten fish fading as quickly as it had come. A melody was drifting beyond the room; a familiar song keeping perfect time with the ticking of the clock.

The Elfin knight stands on yon hill,
Blow, blow, blow winds, blow
Blowing his horn, so loud and shrill.
The wind is blowing the demon away

There came a clattering sound by the séance table. Mr Cleaver shouted, 'Good Lord, the window! What is that?' I stumbled into the centre of the room to see what he was pointing at, then stopped in my tracks, falling back to the floor, my hand outstretched. Beyond the tallest window stood a woman, facing away from us looking out to sea, her long white dress billowing in the wind.

'Good lord,' whispered Mr Robinson. 'Professor, do you know who that is?'

'Yes,' I said. 'I believe I do...'

There came an almighty crash, the room resounding to discordant chimes. I turned to see the grandfather clock lying face down on the carpet, its trunk splintered across the floor.

CHAPTER
TWENTY EIGHT

I sat in my chair, quivering as Mr Cleaver brought me a sherry. I clasped the glass, humming to myself.

'He seems unwell,' said Mr Robinson. 'Would you say he is possessed, Lady Carter?'

'William,' said Elizabeth. 'Can you hear me, William?'

'Blow, blow, blow winds, blow.'

Yes. Yes. It was the ancient nursery rhyme she had sung for me as a boy. The very same she had sung as she'd lain dying.

'Smelling salts, perhaps?' said Mr Robinson. 'Parra, fetch some up immediately, quick man.'

Mr Cleaver held his pipe close to his mouth, beard frayed, his cheeks an unseemly shade of pink. 'He ought really to see a doctor, passing out like that. Did he knock his head, he seems rather unsettled?'

'He is alright,' said Elizabeth, stroking my cheek. 'He is often unsettled.'

'What a peculiar evening, Lady Carter,' chuckled Mr Cleaver. 'Here, Major Forth, old fruit, you missed quite a show.'

I shook my head, blinking to see the principal gazing down at me, a cigar in his teeth, one eye squinting. 'Is that right, Crawford? They tell me you saw a ghost and passed out. Bally childish games, if you ask me. Not good for the constitution.'

'I... I do not know,' I said, straightening my dishevelled clothes, looking about the room.

Kathleen was gone, the long curtain lying on the floor abandoned, the chairs and table vanished.

'She left,' said Cleaver. 'Soon after those Weebly women ran out screaming. Didn't like me pulling the curtain down to see who was there.'

'Who *was* there?'

'Oh nobody by that point. They must have slipped out before the lights came on.'

Adelia gave an exasperated sigh. 'There *was* never anybody behind the curtain, we all saw as much. Little wonder the poor child left; it must be impossible channelling spirits, only to have oneself questioned time and time again by amateurs. Honestly, you men; overestimating your minds, completely disregarding your souls. I should not be surprised if Paradise were completely female.'

Mr Cleaver roared with laughter, downing his whisky with a trembling hand. 'Woman, you have just given a perfect description of Hell.'

Mr Robinson was sitting opposite me, legs crossed, stroking his chin. 'Professor, I must say I envy you. As soon as Lady Carter told me about her little surprise tonight, I thought I might speak to my dear Caroline.' His voice faltered. 'Forgive me, everyone, I do love her still.' He looked at me. 'It was your mother, was it not? That's what you have been muttering to yourself in your stupor.'

Adelia snapped. 'Of course it was his mother.'

She leaned over to Mr Cleaver, tapping his knee. 'The girl insisted he be here you know. Apparently, he attracts the most powerful "friends" she has ever channelled. I wasn't convinced it was appropriate for a mere teacher to join us, though, I must say, I'm glad of it now, if only to turn the mind of another sceptic.'

She got to her feet, brushing down her dress. 'This mother of yours must have abandoned you at a very young age, William. I can well imagine her soul is in torment.'

'She died in childbirth,' I said, remembering the night I lost her. 'I was there as she passed. The baby was deformed. A girl.'

Mr Cleaver sucked on his pipe, chuckling. 'I for one am not convinced. There must have been someone hiding behind that curtain. There *must* have been! Someone else upstairs perhaps, and somebody on the balcony.'

'Wires and magnets, I expect. Hidden stooges too,' said the principal, pacing around the room, inspecting the ceiling.

'Oh yes, no doubt about it,' said Mr Cleaver. 'Any woman could have been singing that strange song.'

It was true. What proof, really, was a woman standing on a balcony on a windy night? What proof was her wistful song? Ah, but not a soul knew about Arthur. A chilly sickness gripped my stomach. At least, nobody alive. A man cannot hide from his own secrets; he might as well hide from his skin.

Mr Cleaver knelt down to inspect the girl's chair then traced his fingers over the wall. 'No holes,' he said. 'No signs of foul play at all. She was smart, I'll give her that. A very accomplished little fox. It would be a decent thing, my friends, to prove her a fraud once and for all.'

'A public service,' agreed the principal.

'You do not believe in the afterlife, Principal Forth?' Elizabeth asked him, stroking my hand.

'On the contrary, Mrs Crawford,' said the principal. 'I recruit men for war. I must believe.'

'Well then, I don't understand. How can you believe in Heaven but deny the spirits? Remember, the Lord God performs for you those great and awesome wonders seen with your own eyes.'

'I have never seen or heard a spirit, Mrs Crawford. Nor would I wish to.' The principal shook his head, solemnly. 'It is against God.'

Mr Robinson paced to the windows, hands deep in his pockets as he stared out to sea. 'There is a physician in Massachusetts you know – MacDougall's his name – who has proved the soul weighs precisely twenty-one grams.'

'Oh really,' tutted Adelia.

Mr Cleaver lifted the black curtain, inspecting it closely. 'I'm sorry, Robinson old chap, but I place my chips with Forth on this one. No chatty ghosts for me, and thank goodness, I say. If only the living were as quiet as the dead. Here though, Professor Crawford, you're a scientific man.' He turned to me, excitedly. 'Seems to me the jury's out with you. Perhaps you can put this girl under your microscope? Prove or disprove her powers once and for all?'

I blinked. 'That was my intention, Mr Cleaver.'

'Let us set a wager then, eh? I say fifty pounds she's a fraud. Robinson, are you in?'

'I forbid it,' said the principal.

Mr Cleaver growled, offering me a cigar. 'Let the boy think it over at least, Forth. It's a rather delicious mystery after all. Would you not like to uncover the rogues? Find out how it was done?'

Mr Robinson wandered back from the window, scratching his chin. 'I would gladly sponsor the professor to investigate the girl. Though a wager is rather tawdry treatment for something so important, no? Let us approach it as businessmen. We will throw in a hundred pounds and any assistance he might require.'

'A hundred pounds?' gasped Adelia.

'Two hundred pounds,' said Mr Robinson, pacing over to the smashed grandfather clock. 'It seems a fair price to prove the existence of the afterlife. Between the Institute and the department store, he will have all the equipment he needs.' He bent down to the clock, lifting a shard of splintered wood. 'My, my, this thing is completely destroyed. No little boy could have done this.'

'I forbid it,' said the principal, raising his hand. 'I cannot encourage this.'

'Will you throw your brightest star to the kerb if he defies you, Forth?' said Mr Cleaver, playfully.

'Certainly not,' said the principal. 'I simply...'

'There we are then, Forth. The boy is free to do as he pleases. I look forward to his thesis proving my gullible business partner wrong. Bad luck, Robinson.' He lit my cigar with a flick of his lighter. 'Besides, I expect the Crawfords could do with the money.'

I thought of the credit note from the department store. The cost of new pipes for the house, the children's clothes. 'My book is published next month. We won't be short of money.'

'Balderdash!' cried Mr Cleaver. 'All men are short of money, especially the rich ones. That, my friend, is capitalism.'

'We are rather poor, William,' said Elizabeth, with a pleading look. 'Even with Aunt Adelia's kind help and your book.' She got to her feet, toying with her dress. 'My husband and I spent rather a lot of money at your department store, Mr Cleaver.'

'Well then, allow me to amend my offer,' said Mr Robinson, standing before me, his hand tucked into his dinner jacket, the picture of philanthropy. 'I shall sponsor your investigations *and* waive your credit at the shop, how does that sound? I can even throw in a phonograph.' He winked, tapping my shoulder.

I looked around the room, my head aching terribly. I did not know what to say. It seemed fate was determined to force me into unending séances, no matter how hard I tried to escape them. Drawn to that damned attic, lured to the Palm House, persuaded by my own ambition to visit Lismarra House. And now, when my mind was at its weakest, my every reason confounded by impossibilities, I was challenged to apply my scientific expertise to the tawdry world of the paranormal, my growing debt the leverage. I looked up at the principal, his expression one of disappointment and derision.

'I... I don't know what to say. My book...'

'Oh, your book, your book, pish!' said Mr Cleaver. 'How much profit can you make from a paltry textbook, Professor? Forgive me, but you're hardly likely to fill the coffers with that.'

'Do you accept the challenge then, Professor?' said Mr Robinson. 'After all, who else is *possibly* qualified? Now I think of it, you must have been destined to come here this evening. You said yourself before dinner that your mother wished for her son to become a famous engineer one day. If you were to discover some unquestionable proof of the spirit world, you would be the greatest man of our age!'

'The greatest man?' I muttered, remembering Arthur's terrible account of his own death. It could not possibly have been Arthur. Perhaps I had been mesmerised. Yes, that was surely it. The girl had mesmerised me in the Palm House, with all sorts of searching questions and now the Golighers were playing me like a fiddle, blackmailing me with my own tortured conscience. I put my face in my hands, desperate to think. 'The greatest man.'

'The greatest fool,' said the principal. 'Professor Crawford has a growing reputation to protect. He is a highly valued member of my staff and operates entirely under my instruction. I am still training him up.'

I glanced at him, thinking back to the statues, the ruffling of my hair, young Blithe at the high table. Training me up to be his lapdog, while mere boys of better breeding enjoyed drinks in his office?

Mr Cleaver winked at me, sensing victory. 'Professor, will you investigate the girl or not? Let us have your final answer, or perhaps the spirits can answer for you?'

I stood up, leaning on Elizabeth's arm, before falling heavily to the wall, my foot pounding the floor. Mr Cleaver laughed, pretending to look around the room as if beset by ghosts. 'Oh goodness, a spirit rap! Come, friends, only one? Let us have a couple more.'

'Boy,' said the principal, shaking his head. 'Don't do this, I warn you.'

I held his eye, then straightened myself up, lifting my shoe with a rebellious frown, slamming it to the floor three times.

Bang, bang, bang.

CHAPTER
TWENTY NINE

A few weeks passed, following our singular night at Lismarra House, the excitement of the evening ebbing away, the proposed scheme losing its lustre in the cold light of day, as so often schemes do. I had not heard from anyone at the dinner party and had informed the principal of my decision not to pursue the matter any further after all, much to his pleasure, though my request for a raise had been given short shrift. I had been bewitched, my brain addled by drink and the all-too-intoxicating effect of Kathleen's theatrics. I? A spiritual investigator? No, it was a preposterous idea; Messrs Robinson and Cleaver had put me under too much pressure. The whole thing had been nothing more than a charade. I ought to concentrate on my work, find peace with my family, and never again confront the disquieting visions conjured up by the medium.

Naturally, I had kept my experiences at the séance to myself: Arthur's accusations, his strange story about drowning, locked away as the ship went down. The Golighers knew everything. The ticket I'd bought him to flee, the crimes he'd committed, the telegram to the doomed ship. And then my mother's song and Robert's voice. It was a trick. A clever one, no doubt, but a trick nonetheless.

My decision had not pleased Elizabeth, of course, who'd begged to return to the Ormeau Road to resume her search for Arthur and Robert, but my mind was made up. Never again would the Crawfords darken their sorry door. I had said so before, but this time my decision was final. And that is how things would – and should – have stayed, Professor Crawford continuing his humdrum life, just like any other ordinary man of his station, teaching at the Institute, playing husband and father to his ordinary family. That is, were it not for the matter of my book.

It had not sold well, you see. A few of the colleges in Scotland had shown meagre interest and a church school in Norfolk had bought a few copies but, ultimately, my career as an author had withered on the vine, the publisher ignoring my many letters, leaving us poorer than ever without Adelia's contingent generosity. Meanwhile, not to miss an opportunity, the house had burst its pipes, flooding the dining room, Rose's bedroom window had lost two panes of glass, the roof was letting in rain ready for a terrible winter and the girls were growing like beanstalks, their clothes shrinking as quickly as the Crawford finances. So the weeks passed, the strain building upon my shoulders like bricks, my headaches and forgetfulness worsening by the day.

Thus, when a letter arrived from Messrs Robinson and Cleaver one autumn afternoon, I found myself staring at it with a mix of trepidation and hope.

'My pipe,' I said, marching into the parlour. 'Girls, where is my blasted pipe?'

'In your pocket, I expect,' said Margaret, rolling her eyes. 'That's where it was yesterday, and the day before, and the day before.' She was growing too clever for a young woman, her nose forever buried in frivolous novels about trifling romances.

'No, it isn't there, damn it, and don't be impertinent.'

'What's that in your hand?' asked Elizabeth.

'This? A letter came for us this morning; it's from Robinson and Cleaver.'

'William, don't tell me we *still* haven't paid off our credit. You promised me you were sending a cheque last week.'

'No, no, never mind that,' I tutted wrestling with my trouser pockets before throwing myself to the floor, searching around the girl's feet. 'I've spoken to the bank, confound that spotty little manager. Thirty-years-old and a bank manager, I ask you? I swear if I have to go begging to him again, I shall—'

'William, tell me you're not taking out another loan?'

'Elizabeth,' I tutted from the carpet, 'have I found myself in a parallel universe where women are qualified accountants?'

'No, William, you remain in this universe where the men are hopeless with money.'

I rubbed the bridge of my nose, the usual stabbing pain cutting into the backs of my eyes. 'Helen, have you seen my pipe?'

'Yes, Father, many times.'

'Well have you seen it today?'

'No, Father. It must be in your jacket pocket.'

'For crying out loud! For the last time, it is not in my jacket pocket. For goodness' sakes, will I ever have some peace in this house?'

Elizabeth reached down to touch my shoulder. 'What does the letter say?'

'The letter?' I asked, bouncing up to check the mantelpiece.

'Yes, the letter in your hand from Robinson and Cleaver. Give it to me.'

She snatched it from my hand as I pulled books from the shelves. How was it possible for a pipe to disappear into thin air? I thought of the young medium, depositing it in my jacket at the Palm House. Was she here, in our home, the little pickpocket? I was about to march back to the study, when Elizabeth yelped.

'Gracious!'

'Have you found my pipe?'

'No, look.'

She was standing up, holding a slip of paper, a handwritten letter floating to her feet. 'It can't be real,' she said, shaking her head.

'What is it?'

'A cheque from Mr Robinson. For five hundred pounds!'

I stared at her, dumbfounded, then yanked the thing from her fingers. There it was, just as she'd said:

Mr Edward Robinson. To Pay Mr William Jackson Crawford the sum of £500.

I fell into the armchair, unable to take my eyes from the slip. Elizabeth fetched the letter from the floor and read it aloud.

Dear Mr and Mrs Crawford,
I hope my letter finds you well. I am afraid my business partner and I have been quite unable to forget our evening here at Lismarra House, and I must relay to you my profound belief that your spirit medium is a girl of the most extraordinary powers. It is my belief that the spirits continue to live within my home, and I am haunted by their incessant movements day and night. Unfortunately, Mr Cleaver remains a sceptic and our disagreement on the matter is causing the most intolerable friction between us. I can see only one course of action; that which we proposed on the evening in question. The authenticity of the medium <u>*must*</u> *be proven, and there is no man to do it but you. It is my understanding from Major Ford that you thought better of the project following your visit, and I quite understand, but I ask you to carry out your work, as previously discussed, with my utter discretion and sponsorship. Lady Carter informs me that the Crawford family is suffering financial hardship, and this brings me great sorrow. Therefore, I enclose a cheque for an initial payment of £500 with more to follow should your experiments require further investment. I also confirm that your account with the department store is settled. You see, I am a man of my word but are you a man of yours, Professor?*

Yours sincerely,
Edward Robinson

I stared at my wife, speechless. Margaret closed her book. 'Tell him no, Father, you'll fall ill again.'

'Hush Margaret,' snapped Elizabeth, staring at me, the letter shaking in her hands. 'Your father is thinking.'

'Golly, that's a lot of money, isn't it?' said Helen, speaking to her new doll, the overpriced trinket already half bald. 'Imagine how many dolls we could buy with five hundred pounds.'

'My pipe,' I whispered. 'I need my pipe.'

'Children!' said Elizabeth. 'Fetch your father's pipe, quickly now!'

Margaret rolled her eyes and threw her book to the chair, following Helen as she ran to the stairs, singing.

Elizabeth knelt in front of me, her hands on my knees. 'William, I have not asked for much in our marriage. I have moved from my home against my mother's wishes. I have borne your children and kept our house. I have listened to your lessons and sacrificed friendships. I have worn other women's clothes and suffered Aunt Adelia's comments, always defending your loyalty to the family and your tireless work. I have lost a housemaid to your moods and taken in Rose without complaint. I have nursed my dying son when you were poorly and accepted your final word on the Golighers. I have put up with more than you can possibly know. I have been a true and faithful wife. Now, I beg of you. I beg on my knees, with all my love. William, please accept Mr Robinson's kind offer. Take his gift, if not for you then for *us*. Or perhaps, for your mother. Do it for Arthur. Do it for Robert.' She gripped my legs, her eyes streaming. 'Do it for me?'

I looked at her poor, desperate face, her lips quivering. She was quite right. She had taken me on, for Lord knows what reason, and I had disappointed her. And yet, what solution was this?

'Elizabeth,' I said. 'I am afraid.'

'Afraid of what?'

'It will ruin us.'

'We are ruined without it.'

I looked at the cheque, imagining walking into the bank that very afternoon, the weight lifting instantly from my shoulders, a vision of the family sailing along the coast in a motorcar, the wind in our faces, carefree. Elizabeth, proud of her husband, the children in smart clothes. Mr Robinson my sponsor – no my *friend*. I closed my eyes and groaned. I could not do it, Margaret was right, I would fall ill again, I could feel the edges of my mind grating together like broken bone at the very thought of it. The principal's face appeared in my mind, shaking his head in solemn condemnation. Yet, what did he care for me? Would I ever be promoted by him? Had I been invited for a whisky in his office, in all his gratitude? No.

'It would be a huge amount of work, Elizabeth.'

'You have your evenings; I will support you, we all will.'

'I would need equipment.'

'Mr Robinson says he will supply it.'

'I could not do it alone. I would require an assistant to carry the equipment for a start.'

'Then we shall find you one!' said Elizabeth, clapping her hands. 'Mr Robinson will pay.'

'But who would I trust with such a thing? A boy would get in my way, prattling on about his own theories and expecting me to listen.'

Just then, the door opened, Rose appearing with a basket of washing, blowing a strand of hair from her face. She stepped inside and held out her arm with a smile, my pipe in her hand.

Elizabeth laughed, jumping up to give her a hug, then looked back at me, nodding. I took the pipe and lit it, deep in thought as the smoke encircled my head. The pain subsided behind my eyes and a smile crept over my face. How the bank manager's attitude would change to see Mr Robinson's name on my cheque. I chuckled, pulling at my moustache, as Margaret walked into the parlour, collecting her book with a pained sigh.

'I'm going to my room,' she said. 'To enjoy the damp.'

'Very good, very good,' I muttered to myself, nibbling at my lip. 'Here, Margaret, what do you think of this?' I moved my fingers through the air. 'William Jackson Crawford, Spiritual Investigator.' I pulled at my moustache. 'No, I don't like the sound of that very much.'

Margaret sniffed. 'You are a Professor of Engineering, Father; you shouldn't forget it.'

'No. Quite right, child, quite right. Well, girl, what would you suggest?'

She looked at the novel in her hand and wrinkled her nose. 'William Jackson Crawford...' she said, with the disinterest of any genius tasked with the mundane, 'The Spirit Engineer.'

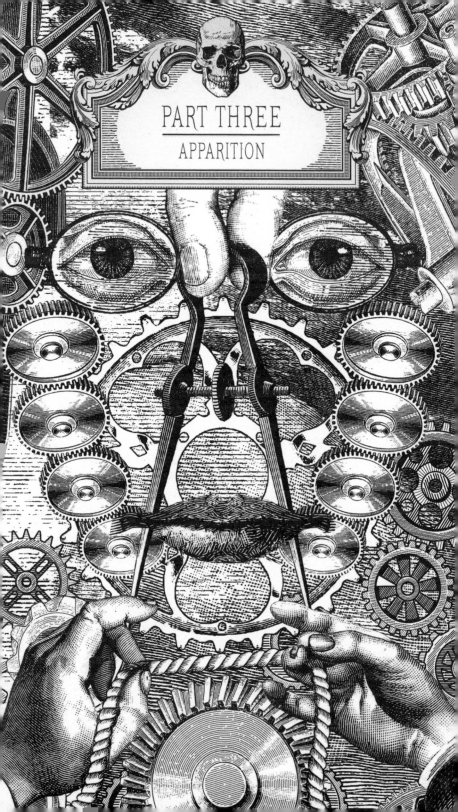

PART THREE

APPARITION

CHAPTER THIRTY

And so, one chilly morning in late October, the Crawfords hove-to outside the Morrison's hardware shop in a glittering new motorcar, chased by a crowd of dogs and excited, barefoot children. I jumped out, offering Elizabeth my hand. 'Rose,' I instructed. 'Begin unpacking my apparatus at once, precisely as we arranged, do not dawdle.'

'Here, do the horn, mister!' cheered a boy who appeared to be missing his eyebrows, teeth and trousers, a friend riding upon his shoulders. I shook my head, buffing one of the large brass lamps with the sleeve of my motoring jacket.

'Certainly not,' I said. 'It is not a toy. Move away, boy, and watch those sticky fingers.' A second child ran up to the car holding a rock above his head, flitting his treacherous eyes hungrily towards the bright-yellow bonnet.

'Don't you dare,' I growled. 'I shall have you flogged.'

'Here, get away from the prof's car,' came a scratchy voice from the shop. It was young Samuel Goligher waving a hammer, hair plastered to his head beneath a smart cap, hands still caked in grime. He stood in front of me, arms folded. 'Prof, ye want me to look after her, nai?'

I considered the lad suspiciously. A threatening gang of mud-spattered pixies was growing around the motorcar, pressing their little paws onto the bodywork. I hissed at them, scattering the little blighters like rats.

'Very well then.' I sighed. 'Hold out your hand. I placed a penny into his palm, his fingers snapping over the coin the moment it touched his grubby skin. 'Guard her well, Master Goligher,' I warned. 'I shall reward you with two more of those on my return. The merest scratch and you shall be sorry.'

PARP!

I spun about to see a little girl carrying a mangey cat, bashing her forehead into the horn. I was about to remonstrate with her when Samuel charged past me, beating the backs of her legs with his stick, ordering the lot of them back unless they wanted a hammer in their skulls. Satisfied, I nodded, beckoning Elizabeth and Rose to follow on, the maid carrying a large picnic basket with sheets and balls of string piled on top. Nothing had changed inside the shop, but for a greater conflagration of shavings, screws and myriad tools of questionable quality. Oh, and a few fresh layers of dust. I stepped inside, removing my driving gloves and cap.

'Golighers,' I announced, holding up our most recent letter. 'I am here to begin my investigation, as agreed.'

Old Mrs Goligher stepped through, feeling her way with her gnarled fingers. 'Kat is upstairs, waitin' for ye'. Yer early, so.'

'I am precisely on time, old woman,' I said, thrusting my watch under her blind eyes. She touched it with her yellow fingernails, licking her lips. 'Oh, never mind,' I said, marching past her to the tattered curtain, clicking my fingers at Rose. 'This way, quickly, no time to lose.'

I bounded up the stairs, excited by the chance to put my experiments into action. I had been planning them for weeks, inventing all sorts of clever tests to catch the family out. They would find themselves confounded in minutes and, this time, it had all been agreed in writing. No Noah Morrison looming over me, no contrived distractions. The man climbing through the house was a different person to the sorry figure who'd crept that way before. My mind was utterly clear, my purpose entirely above board and my trousers dry as a bone.

Kathleen was waiting for me when I burst into the attic, declaring my arrival. Strange, the effect she had on me. I was surprised to find myself shy, my words trailing out as she looked up from her chair.

'Hello, Professor.'

'Hello, Kathleen,' I said, removing my jacket. 'There is no need to be afraid.'

'Afraid, Professor?' she answered, arranging her skirt. 'I'm relieved. I thought you'd abandoned me. Noah has kept me busy. I've missed you.'

Old Mrs Goligher climbed through the door, panting. 'Professor, we fear for your boy. What has happened to him, since Lismarra House, eh? Kat told us all. How could you leave him in such peril?'

I sniffed, stretching my back. 'Nothing has happened to him, I'm sure.'

'Ack, I hope yer right,' she said, feeling her way to a chair. 'So many spirits comin' to Kathleen nowadays, what with the war an' all, I fear the wee dote might be lost among 'em.'

Elizabeth wrung her hands. 'Is it true? Might Robert be lost?'

Kathleen answered, her gaze on me as she spoke. 'No, Mrs Crawford, be calm. There is hope the boy will find us again. It is the power of their sadness that brings the spirits through. We must hope Robert is no less afraid than he was before. Perhaps his late grandmother found him.' She turned to me, picking her shroud from the table, draping it over her knees. 'It was your mother on the balcony, was it not, Professor? Singing that pretty song?'

I cleared my throat, moving to the window. I could see the children below, marshalled away from the motorcar by Samuel and his stick. 'It was a song my mother used to sing,' I said. 'That is true.'

'Well nai, what other explanation could there be?' said old Mrs Goligher.

'That is what I intend to find out.'

Elizabeth took my hand. 'If your mother didn't save Robert at Lismarra House, it might well have been Arthur who saved him from that dark spirit. Don't you think so, Ms Goligher? What did Robert call him?' She shuddered. 'The man with the hanging bones.'

'Oh,' murmured Kathleen, giving me a meaningful look. 'Arthur was there all right, was he not, Professor?'

'So you would have me believe.'

Elizabeth spoke on, oblivious to Kathleen's knowing smile. 'Robert adored his Uncle Arthur, didn't he, William? He positively idolised him. It was Arthur who gave him his blanket, to calm his nerves. Do you remember the little game they used to play, William? Running about in the garden making those funny raspberry noises, pretending to be motorcars?'

'This window,' I said ignoring her, scratching the rotten frame with my fingernail. 'The glass is loose. I shall have to mention it in my report.'

'Ah well, nai, that solves it then,' said Rebecca from the door. 'The professor has worked it all out, sure enough. Must be some wee spiders dressed up as the dead. We've all been found out. Game's over.'

'I do not treat this as a game, Mrs Morrison,' I said. 'I am well aware of the hostility you feel towards my experiments, but, I can assure you, they have been designed in the best scientific tradition.' She snorted and turned away. 'Ms Goligher,' I said, rounding on the medium. 'As detailed in my letters, I propose to you a series of experiments, carried out in a strict attitude of discretion, objectivity and perspicacity. I am a rational man first and a spiritual man second; so please, indulge my suspicions for now. Doubt is, after all, the mother of inquiry and the grandmother of resolution.'

Kathleen frowned as if working out a sum, then stood up, taking my hands. 'Very well, Professor,' she said. 'Thank you. I will allow it. My friends and I have nothing to hide, you can do what you like with me.'

Just then, Adelia entered, puffing and panting, dragging her voluminous yellow dress through the doorway against its will, knocking her brown feathered hat askew. 'Heavens preserve me, I came as quickly as I could!'

'Aunt Adelia?' said Elizabeth, surprised. 'Whatever is the matter, we were not expecting you?'

'Nothing is the matter, Lillie,' she snapped impatiently, craning her neck, searching the attic with her beady eyes. 'Where are they?'

'Whom?' I said, puzzled.

'Mr Robinson!' she said impatiently. 'Or Mr Cleaver. Or both?' She pressed into the room, her ridiculous bustle knocking the table against the fireplace with a hollow thud. 'I saw the motorcar at the front of the shop. A very grand thing.'

Elizabeth frowned. 'However, did you see William's motorcar from Malone Park?'

Adelia tittered, eyelashes fluttering. 'I beg your pardon, Lillie. I thought for a moment you referred to the machine as *William's* motorcar.'

I cleared my throat, with a raised eyebrow. 'Ah well, Aunt Adelia. The motorcar is indeed mine. The Crawfords are rising in the world, don't you know? Only a simple contraption, amongst many others, generously paid for by Messrs Robinson and Cleaver. How else am I to ferry my new equipment across the city?'

'A motorcar for such a middling family? I shall stop my payments at once!'

'I have stopped them for you.'

Adelia clucked like a chicken, unable to speak. I turned back to the room, rubbing my hands against the bitter cold. 'Come, everyone, time is running short, we have an hour. Ms Goligher, will you kindly commence?'

'Hold yer horses, Professor. More to come yet,' said Rebecca, pulling her shawl around her shoulders.

'More?' I said, sternly. 'This is an experiment, not a show.'

'Ack, it is what it feckin' is.'

In an attempt to control my temper, I whipped out my notebook, sketching our individual positions within the circle. Kathleen was beside the wall, Elizabeth was to her left, followed in a clockwise fashion by Adelia, Rebecca and Old Mrs Goligher. I checked the lamp, the bare walls, the gas pipe, the unblemished ceiling, the familiar door with its brass doorknob, the hearth and grate, the table and chairs. Nothing had changed. Just then, several pairs of feet came tromping up the passageway, Noah looking straight through me as he stepped into the attic wearing his long coat over his shoulders like a cape. He was growing thin in his face, I noticed, with silvering whiskers at his chin. They were difficult times at the shipyard, the Government ordering cruisers up like fish suppers. I had heard from Fforde that they were converting cargo ships into phantom battleships, complete with false gun turrets and fires hidden inside dummy funnels. Dishonesty was justified in desperate circumstances, I supposed, though Mr Churchill's ruse seemed rather dishonourable.

I took my seat at the table, crossing my legs as a pair of young men in khaki uniform entered behind Noah, chuckling to one another, swaying in their boots. Kathleen inspected them from beneath her fringe, cheeks flushing. Tutting, I hit my pad impatiently with my pencil.

'This really is highly irregular. We agreed, no spectators. And where is that damned clumsy maid of ours?' Right on cue, Rose clambered into the attic, gripping the large wicker basket in her arms, puffing and wheezing. 'About time,' I said. 'Put it down, put it down, where have you been all this time?' She gave me a sorry look, dropping the basket in the corner of the room, before sitting in the corner as we agreed, watched intently by Kathleen.

'Funny,' said the medium. 'I thought she might resemble...'

Exasperated, I cut across her. 'Enough, enough. Ms Goligher, begin.'

The young soldiers were instructed to sit between Kathleen and Elizabeth; an unseemly arrangement I decided to overlook in the interests of progress. At last, the curtain was drawn, the lamp turned low and we sang our opening prayers before sitting once again at the table, surrounded by darkness.

'Oh devilish demons, will they come charging at us again?' said old Mrs Goligher, her teeth chattering.

'Let us hope so,' I chuckled, giving Rose a nod through the shadows.

'Ack, Professor, ye don't know what yer sayin'.'

Another séance, another attempt to expose the truth. *This time*, I thought, *The Spirit Engineer is in charge.*

CHAPTER THIRTY ONE

Kathleen had barely said a word before a scraping noise surfaced on the far wall beside the two boys.

'Here,' said one of them. 'You've got mice!'

'Shut yer traps,' snapped Rebecca. 'Listen.'

The boys laughed, punching each other on the arm, making ghostly noises as Kathleen rolled her head. 'Are you with us, friends? You have been waiting a long time. Who's there? Please, do not come all at once, we must find young Robert, is he safe?'

There came a roll of distant thunder.

'Ack, Christ preserve us, here they come again,' said old Mrs Goligher, crushing my knuckles as a queer electricity passed between our hands.

Where had it come from, the thunder? Had the clear sky clouded over so quickly? Perhaps the rumbling was coming from the shipyard: a cascading tower of sheet metal from one of the hulls, a number of unfortunate men guillotined below. I smirked. How long would it take for their poor unfortunate souls to join us in the attic? Yet no, it cannot have been from the yard, for the noise had a peculiar character, not like any thunder I had heard before. Still, it grew, becoming ever more present, as a low, quaking vibration picked up beneath my feet.

I cleared my throat, shifting in my chair, Old Mrs Goligher's long nails digging into my skin as the noise grew louder.

'Elizabeth,' I said. 'Do not fear.'

'Ack, Kat,' said old Mrs Goligher, her voice trembling, milky eyes searching the ceiling. 'They're comin' nai, Heaven hold them back the poor lost boys.'

'Prepare yourselves,' Kathleen muttered. 'If they come, let them come.'

'Prepare ourselves for what?' I said, raising my voice to a shout as the thunder rattled the windowpanes.

'So many souls,' Kathleen shouted back from beneath her shroud. 'So many who died in battle; and now they fight to be heard.'

The great storm raged, suddenly blowing into the attic as though a thousand boots were beating across the floor. In the din, I could hear the howling cry of countless voices. A church bell tolled above our heads as the walls shook in the bellowing air. I tried to cover my ears, my head filled with drumming, but my hands were pinned to the table.

'George!' cried Adelia above the din. 'I can hear you, George!'

Whether she could or not, I had no idea, for it would surely have been impossible for anyone to communicate, so great was the wave of voices, filling it with...

I sniffed. Rotten fish. My heart trembled. I pulled at my hands as the air turned cold, but they were bolted fast. No. No, not again, it couldn't be. It was all a trick. All theatre. *Keep your mind, William, keep your mind.* I turned my head to Rose at the door, but it was too dark and then there was something, *someone* standing at my back. I could feel their presence as the hairs prickled on my neck. Amidst the raging thunder, I twisted my eyes into the darkness and saw him. A faint silhouette of a man standing against the wall, the outline of a hairless, translucent skull shimmering in the flicker of the ruby lamp, a pair of eyeless sockets above a gaping mouth. He turned his head towards me, moving in slow, foot-dragging steps, closer, closer to my back.

'Stop the séance!' I shouted, wrenching at my hands. 'Stop it now.' But the thunder was too loud for anybody to hear me and I was fixed in my seat. Nothing could keep his terrible form from standing at my side. Nothing could stop him from having his say, for I realised at last that everything was his design. Elizabeth's first secret meetings, my paranoid skulking to the shop, even Robert's sudden death. All of it was him. The smell was intolerable. I choked as I saw a long, alabaster finger reaching towards my neck and I gulped.

'Arthur?' I said. 'Arthur, is that you?'

The reply came clear and soft in my ear, as though the din were silence. Intimate and cruel, he spoke...

Hello again, Brother.

'Then... then you are real after all?'

Yes.

The voice was unmistakably his, muffled as it was, as though my ears were filled with water.

'Why are you here?'

I will take him.

'Take who, Arthur? Do you mean poor Robert? Please...' The cold finger moved to my back. 'Arthur, forgive me, please, I beg of you. I didn't mean for you to drown, you must understand...'

Coward.

'No...'

Cruel.

'I am not cruel.'

You watched your mother die.

'Stop this, please! I tried my best to save her, I swear it to you. I was a boy, alone...'

You watched her die, William. Oh yes. Then you sent me away to drown. You allowed your son to sicken until he was nothing but bone. The voice grew high, rattling like wind through broken glass. *Oh, William, you burnt his blanket because you hated me.*

'That's not true!'

I felt him shift from my side, watching in horror as the figure passed around the table, the red light showing his bones hanging through a ripped, glittering coat, water tumbling from his shoulders, a rusted manacle dragging a chain behind his foot. Not another member of the circle followed him, their faces staring straight ahead. He spoke, his voice cruel.

Oh now, Robert is here. There you are, my dear. Take my hand...

'Take your hand? Where is he, Arthur? Leave him be.'

'My child!' Elizabeth screamed, her voice slicing through the thunder. 'Robert! I can see Robert! There!' She was pointing towards the corner of the room, her hands outstretched.

I strained my eyes as one of the soldiers leaped up, pointing at the static figure of Kathleen beneath her shroud, her long fingers fixed over the arms of her chair. 'Here, I felt you move under the table, you witch. I saw something.'

His friend joined him, standing up, knocking away Rebecca's hands. 'Hey, who is that over there?' he cried. 'I see you.' He lumbered across the room, blindly knocking over his chair, before giving an almighty wail, crumpling to the floor like a sack of sand. The thundering stopped immediately as someone turned the lamp up, the boy groaning on the floor clutching his head. 'He hit me,' he said. 'He *hit* me over the feckin' head.' His friend stood over him, slapping his cheek as Noah stepped inside.

'What's goin' on in here?' he barked.

Rebecca cackled. 'That wee eejit got scared an' ran into the low ceilin', sure. Some soldier he'll make.'

I dashed to the window, tearing the curtain away, squinting at a bright-blue sky. On the street below, I could see Samuel, guarding the motorcar with his stick at his shoulder like a rifle, scuffing dust with his boots. He looked up, waving the penny between his fingers. Dazed, heart quivering, I waved back.

What I had heard was everything I had hoped to escape. Everything I had reasoned out. Yet I was not drunk this time. Folly to deny one's own senses and yet it could not be. I looked around for some evidence of the spirit, my chin high, sniffing the air. I mopped my brow, my voice weak. 'Rose, please find my notepad and pen, I must make some sketches immediately.'

Duly, the troublesome soldiers were ordered from the attic as I took my notepad, my pencil carving into the paper.

'Rose, take the basket downstairs please, and take care.'

'Basket?' said old Mrs Goligher, looking about the room, her hands oustretched. 'What basket?'

'Yes, Professor,' said Kathleen, sitting calmly, the shroud hanging from her shoulders. 'What was the basket for?'

'Never you mind. I shall write to you for our next meeting.'

'Very well,' she said with a shrug. 'Soon, I hope, we don't have much time.'

Adelia stood up. 'I believe I heard my George.' She nodded. 'Lillie, did you hear him too?'

Elizabeth did not reply. Nor did she utter a word as I drove her back to Park Avenue, trying my best to concentrate on the road while all around me, visions clamoured for attention. 'Rose,' I called over my shoulder as we passed over the river. 'Did you do as I asked?'

She nodded, her face pale.

'We shall be home soon, Elizabeth,' I said, patting her knee. 'Tomorrow, we shall visit Robert's grave and lay flowers.'

She stared ahead, the wind blowing her hair about her face, gripping my arm in silence.

***

Later that evening, I stood before the wicker basket on my writing desk, the door to the study locked. I was afraid to look inside, God damn my nerves. I checked over my shoulder to make sure I was alone. I could hear Rose cleaning the dishes in the kitchen below, Elizabeth praying in her room.

I crept to the basket, unbuckled the leather straps and opened the lid. The phonograph had been hidden inside, just as I had instructed. 'Well done, Rose,' I muttered, checking the recording mandrel before switching it out to play. Peering at the cylinder under the gaslight, I could see hundreds of tiny grooves etched into the wax. Evidence. But of what?

I set the machine turning, the needle following the groove as the trumpet crackled and popped. There were voices at first, Rebecca and her harsh tongue, then faint laughter from the young soldiers, followed by singing and more indistinct chatter. I moved my ear closer to the trumpet, holding my breath. There was a low rumbling, like distant thunder. A shriek perhaps? Then another. A thud. More rumbling. I frowned, about to step away, when the machine produced a high-pitched scratch, the mandrel shaking in the wooden casket. I stood closer. The needle must have fallen from the cylinder. I removed the recording, turning it carefully in my hands beneath the lamp. The faint etching was clear to see, running about the body of the cylinder from left to right. I followed it gently with my fingernail then stopped. That was queer. About halfway across, the grooves completely

185

vanished. Had the mechanism run out of power so quickly? I had given Rose clear instructions to wind the machine before depositing the basket in the attic. Perhaps someone had knocked it with their foot by mistake? Drat the clumsy woman. I removed my spectacles, peering closely at the cylinder. Aha. I had missed something in my initial inspection. Evidently, the needle had found the wax once more, at the very end of the recording. There was perhaps a quarter of an inch engraved there, far deeper than the rest, curling the wax out where the pin had sliced into its side.

Gently, I placed the cylinder back into the machine and set it turning again, rubbing my tired eyes in the mirror above the crackling fire. A second white hair had appeared in my fringe. I tweezed it out, turning to the wall. The phonograph hissed and my pipe fell from my mouth.

There was a voice, as though submerged in water, rising from the phonograph trumpet. No, not one but two voices. A man and a woman in harmony. And the sound of a violin... no, a child, weeping. I edged towards the machine...

The Elfin knight stands on yon hill,
Blow, blow, blow winds, blow.
Blowing his horn, so strong and still,
A son has lost his mother they say.
A husband has drowned a brother today.
A father has taken his blanket away.
Blow, blow, blow winds blow,
Prove me true, or Robert shall pay!

The needle moved from the end of the recording into empty space. The machine fell from the desk, crashing against the floor as I backed into the wall.

'Oh dear,' I whispered, looking around the study, before catching sight of myself in the window, eyes peeping from between my fingers. 'Oh dear.'

I heard a dull thump on the carpet and looked down to see the cylinder rolling towards my feet from the chest of the machine. I stared at it, my body convulsing in a fit of sheer terror to see, etched into the centre of the object, where the wax had been blank, four names.

Agnes, Robert, Arthur, William.

CHAPTER THIRTY TWO

'Now listen, Rose, remember my instructions, keep them at the very forefront of your mind no matter what happens, do you see?' She nodded, looking nervously around the room. We were hiding in the boy's sleeping quarters beneath the attic, having ducked inside when nobody was looking. 'This promises to be a very interesting experiment, very interesting indeed.' I frowned, searching my pockets. 'Where have I put the blasted thing?' Rose held out my pipe. 'Thank you. Now, the last experiment posed some rather troublesome questions, do you remember?' She seemed infuriatingly distracted, peering at the rumpled clothes piled up on the rungs of the ladder in the corner of the room. I snapped my fingers. 'Now listen, this is exactly what I mean about paying attention, you must *listen* to me. *Observe.* My eyes may be expertly trained in scientific observation, but I cannot be in all places at once.' I patted my head before rifling irritably in my trousers. 'Where are my damned spectacles?'

She nodded, pointing at my face.

'Ah, yes, thank you.' I pushed my glasses up my nose, checking my list. 'Don't smile at me like that please, Rose, you're not half so clever as you think. It's a pity you can't write for a start, or I would ask you to take notes. Where were we? Yes, the young men at the last séance claimed they felt the medium moving beneath the table. I have a surprise for her this afternoon to put a stop to any funny business.' I gave Rose a beady eye. 'And what else did they say?'

Again, she was peering around the room, inspecting the walls. I snapped my fingers at her. 'I'm asking you a question; nod if you recall what they said.' She mimed, giving a rather charming impression of the boy jumping from his seat and running to the corner of the room. She looked just like that talentless tramp from the moving pictures. And then she stopped.

'Rose,' I said, rolling my eyes. 'What are you looking at?' She was standing in the corner of the room, eyeing the ceiling with a queer expression. Something shifted across the floorboards above our heads. 'They're waiting for us,' I said, snapping my notebook shut. 'The question for today is this: was someone creeping about in some sort of costume, having snuck past you at the door, or... Well, I am embarrassed to say it.' A shiver crawled over my spine as I remembered Arthur's voice. His chilling words. The phonograph recording. There had to be some sort of explanation for it all. 'Or was there a spirit?' I laughed, pointing at the pile of boxes in the hall. 'Come, come, don't dawdle, I shall hold the door for you.'

***

The three women stared at me as I flicked through my notebook. Rebecca spoke up. 'Untie us, ye wee pervert,' she demanded, leaning forwards as best she could, baring her teeth. 'This in't right, so. Here, you,' she said, glaring at Rose. 'Tell 'im this isn't right.'

I checked my nails for grit. 'No use talking to her,' I said. 'You might as well speak to a cupboard. Besides, she is here as my assistant. You see.' I smiled. 'You have your accomplices, and now I have mine.'

Old Mrs Goligher stared blindly at her two daughters, shaking. 'He's gone mad, so. He'll kill us.'

Rebecca glared at me. 'Ay, he's nottin' but pure trouble from the start. Untie us now or Noah'll knack yer teeth to yer asshole.'

I took out my pipe. 'Ladies, I sent a note explaining this very process yesterday afternoon and stated to you in no uncertain or ambiguous terms that, following the accusations made in the last séance by the two young soldiers, I would need to tie you up by the ankles and that is precisely what I have done.'

I struck a match, humming a familiar little tune. There was no need to worry about Rebecca's threats. Noah was working at the shipyard all hours and I had been sure to arrive early. Besides, they had no reason to fear me. I wiggled my moustache, satisfied at the sight of them trussed up. It had been quite a tussle to subdue Rebecca, Rose helping me before trundling off to carry out an inspection of the window. The mother had been too weak to protest, while Kathleen was a perfect lamb.

'Right we are then,' I said. 'I have measured the table and chairs. Rose and I have tied each of your legs with equal lengths of string to exact measurements using identical knots. We are arranged precisely as before, save for the absence of Adelia, Elizabeth and the two gentlemen.'

'Gentlemen!' laughed Rebecca. 'Now there's a joke. Ack, they'll be back in the attic soon enough, shouting at us from Hell with the rest of 'em, the poor basturds.'

Kathleen wriggled. 'Would you say I'm tight enough, Professor?'

I pulled at my collar, tapping my foot against the séance table. 'Yes, Ms Goligher. Quite tight enough, thank you.'

The medium had taken a cold bath that morning, so she'd said, to cleanse herself for the spirits, in and out. The statement had conjured an ungentlemanly image in my mind: pale, pimpled skin, wet with grey bath water; black hair coiled about her neck. I crossed my legs as I imagined her long fingers slipping across a bar of soap before gripping the tub's hard rim, fleshy legs sloshing squirts of thick, milky water over the filthy floorboards. I shook my head, returning to the attic as young Samuel appeared at my shoulder in a loose shirt, covered in soot.

'Here, what's goin' on?' he said in his scratchy voice.

I jumped. 'Good God, where did you spring from, boy?' I said, closing my notepad.

'Mammy called me up.'

'We did not,' said Rebecca. 'Get away. Can't ye see, we're tied up by the ankles for the professor's experiment?'

'The ankles?' said the boy. He frowned, his nose wrinkled. 'Sure, that'll do it, right enough! Here, Prof. Ye need me to guard the motorcar?'

'Not today, we came on the tram.'

Kathleen lifted her hand. 'The wise professor has tied our feet to prove we cannot move the table. Isn't that clever?'

'So clever,' he said, frowning at Rebecca. 'Here, what do you want me to do then, while ye're here trussed up like hares?'

She jabbed her finger at him. 'Get away an' not be seen round here, that's what. Have a play next door.'

The boy whined, kicking the wall with his shoe before leaving the attic, clomping sulkily down the stairs. I pinched the bridge of my nose. 'It seems we will never have a moment's peace. Now, where were we?' I regarded Kathleen as my tobacco smoke encircled her earnest face. 'We had a pair of young gentlemen join the circle who made two very serious allegations. Namely, that they saw a stranger moving about in the room over there by the window and that you, Ms Goligher, were moving your legs beneath the table. So today we must introduce some controls. To wit: the door must be locked.'

Duly, I locked it, showing the women a key which I had fashioned at the Institute, along with a locking mechanism of my own ingenious design. 'Thus, we are in a controlled environment; any interference from a third party quite out of the question. Rose, are we satisfied with the window?' She gave a shove against the frame, turning with a nod. 'Very good. Now, as we have already noted, the legs of Mrs Goligher, Ms Morrison and Ms Goligher are tied to their respective chairs. Therefore, it is quite impossible for anyone here to lift the table with their feet. What next? Ah, yes. Ms Goligher, I understand the necessity for darkness, but surely the lamp can be a little brighter?' I gave her a playful wink. 'I must reassure our readers that I have a clear eye on things.'

'Your readers?' asked Rebecca.

'My readers, yes,' I said. 'I intend to write a full account of my investigations for the spiritualist newspaper, *Light*. The editor, Mr Gow, has already published one of my letters, correcting some amateur's work with a new wave detector. *Etheric vibrations,* indeed!' I chuckled, shaking my head. 'Do you know, I doubt he even considered the psycho-plasmic field?'

'The psycho-plasmic field?' said Kathleen.

I sighed, giving her a suffering glance. 'Indeed. Your abilities are sure to interest the newspapers in London. Also

Manchester, Liverpool, Birmingham, Dublin, Glasgow and – so I understand from my correspondence with Mr Gow – New York and Paris.'

'New York and Paris,' repeated old Mrs Goligher, blowing air through her cracked lips. 'Ye'll be famous, Kat.'

Kathleen shrugged. 'Well, I'm already famous in the spirit world, so sure, I may as well be here.'

Duly, we sung three hymns, the two older women swapping nervous glances throughout. I turned the lamp down, pulled the hood over Kathleen's head, joined hands with the circle, checking their wrists, and instructed her to begin.

There was no jerk; no static charge between our fingers. I stared at the space where the drunken lad had toppled after hitting his head, then at the tabletop, the edges of the room slipping away as my eyes lost focus. A twitch of a finger, the rattle and hum of the street below, the muffled voices of angry men. We listened. It continued for forty minutes, perhaps longer. Nobody spoke, for every time a mouth opened, a gun cracked or a barrel thumped and we wondered... is that them? Are they come? At last, Rebecca spoke up.

'Kat. Are they comin' or not?'

The girl was absent beneath her hood; less a person of flesh and bone, more a doll covered in a death shroud. I felt sure she was staring at me over the table and I was struck by the unshakeable notion that she was angry. There was no doubt that the séance was becoming ever more suspicious. With each passing second, I felt my heart sink. The raps, the levitations, the voices had always appeared readily, and without fail.

Another quarter of an hour passed until, finally, Kathleen spoke.

'They will come,' she said. Then, lifting her hood to the ceiling. 'We beg you, friends, come to us.'

Yet, they did not. Another quarter of an hour passed. Never had a table seemed so inanimate; never a group of women so ordinary. There it was then. It had taken no more than a few lengths of butcher's string for the truth to come out. Kathleen Goligher was a fraud after all. The phenomena were fake. One or all of them was responsible for lifting the table when their feet were free. Clearly, someone was creeping through the door to lift objects about, ring bells, knock on walls and play at spirits. I blinked. Then who had sung my mother's song? Who had spoken into the phonograph? Who had threatened me in Arthur's grim voice? Had I given away my secrets without knowing? And to whom? The thought terrified me. These people had contrived an elaborate hoax, simply to blackmail a humble professor. I was a pawn in their deliberate, carefully orchestrated rise to fame and fortune. Oh, yes. Bamboozle a highly qualified scientist to prove the veracity of the girl's powers, then sell their spirits to the rich and famous. How close I had come to enabling their clever little scheme.

I looked at Kathleen under her idiotic shroud. I imagined her cheeks burning with shame, and so they might. Grey eyes filling with tears waiting for ghosts she *knew* would never come. If the phenomena were impossible, the voices would be exposed too. What was I to do? End the séance with my sincere apologies for discovering their conspiracy? Or sit silently, indulging the witches for another pitiful hour. I tutted to myself, hands gripped still, pondering as the dark minutes ticked by. Finally, I spoke up. 'Forgive me, ladies,' I said, rising from the table. 'I am afraid that I...'

'Wait, professor,' said Kathleen, pulling the shroud from her face. The old woman spoke from the gloom, her lips drawn back. 'I hear it, sure I do.'

I had been so deep in thought I had missed the sound. A quiet, slow scraping across the floor from somewhere on the far side of the room. I settled back down to my chair. My hands were gripped tighter. A pulse shot between us. There was a jerk. A high, whistling sound like a violin. It moved closer, from left to right.

'Robert?' I said. 'Is that you?'

There was a bump, low on the far wall and then the table lifted.

Kathleen groaned deep in her chair, turning her head about in a trance. Then she gasped. I saw her belly bulge out as the table levitated. Through the red lamplight, Rebecca watched me closely with a triumphant smirk. Old Mrs Goligher whimpered, clawing at the table, looking around the room in fear. So surprised was I, that the significance of the phenomena was lost on me, yet finally the penny dropped.

'Wait,' I said. 'The table. It is levitating.' I laughed. 'It is levitating, and your legs are tied!'

I panted, looking about. So, it was not a trick? I gulped. It was not a trick! My first proper experiment had proven beyond argument that the levitations were genuine.

The table continued to float on a series of invisible, rolling waves. There was no movement to be felt around my legs. The only sensation in my arms and hands was the usual electricity between our fingers. I looked beneath the table as best I could. It was completely free of any moving limbs. No hidden levers. I wrenched my hands free, pressing the table down against some kind of elastic force.

'Here, sit down,' said Rebecca.

'No need, good woman. Can you not see, your spirits are content? This is extraordinary, I tell you. Quite extraordinary!' I searched the room, sniffing the clean air. 'Who is there, kind spirit?'

I attempted to press the table towards Kathleen, only to find it utterly rigid, as though held in place by a fixed bracket.

'Hello?' I called. 'Who are you?'

William, my little boy.

'Oh, good Lord. Oh, good gracious. Mother, I can hear you; can you hear me? It is William, your son.' I looked at the women through the red light, laughing. 'It is my mother, I tell you! I knew it must be. Mother, forgive me, I tried to save you when the baby came, but I was too young, do you remember?' The table began to fall softly to the floor. 'Do you remember me running for help, Mother? I wasn't running away.' Still the table fell, the air thinning as the lamplight flickered. 'Oh, I beg you, Mother, stay, please, I beg of you, don't go.' I tried to hold the table up, scrabbling with my knees and hands, yet the force was too strong. 'Kathleen, help me, please, quickly. Mother, you must protect Robert, can you see him? You must hide him from Arthur.' There came a knock, followed by two more, yet the softest I had heard. 'Mother, will you return?' I cried. 'Find Robert, quickly.'

And then the table nestled back to the floor, the static having departed from our hands. Kathleen sat up, blinking, pulling her shroud away. 'Did they come?' she said.

'Ack, yes,' said Rebecca. 'They came alright.'

Already I was on my knees beneath the table checking that the women's feet were tied. They were, they were. This is how

Newton must have felt. Copernicus, Galileo, all of them, my equals! I pulled the table away, lifting Kathleen's skirts to tug at the knots around her ankles. I scrambled on hands and knees to the door, pushing Rose out of the way. It was locked, precisely as I had left it.

Kathleen spoke.

'Are you satisfied, Professor?'

'What? Oh, yes, yes. Absolutely.'

'That it then?' said Rebecca.

'Hmmm?' I already had my pencil out, scribbling away in my pad.

'Ye have proof? Ye can leave us be?'

I looked up. 'Leave you be? Good gracious, no. I have proven beyond reasonable doubt that the medium is not lifting the table, but that isn't what Mr Robinson is paying me to do. Now I must prove what *is* levitating it.'

'What do you mean?' asked Kathleen. 'It's the spirits, Professor. Sure, you've just seen it.'

'My child, thousands have witnessed paranormal phenomena, yet none has explained the science behind it. I ask you, what precise *mechanism* are they using to move the table about? If I could find the answer to that, why, it would be one of the greatest discoveries in the history of mankind.' I picked up my book, chewing my pencil. 'A lever of some sort. Yes, A *cantilever*, even. Some kind of organ or limb. Just imagine the possible applications for such knowledge.'

I circled the table, inspecting the floor, the walls, the ceiling. 'Yes, a rod,' I called up from the floor. 'Emanating from the medium's body, no doubt. Rose, check the window, don't dally.' I scribbled furiously. 'A type of plasmic structure, removing itself from the medium via an as yet unknown process which attaches itself to the table? Yes, yes, it is an extraordinary thought, but a reasonable explanation.'

I jumped back up as Kathleen looked at her mother and sister with an uncertain frown.

'A rod, Professor?' she said.

I gripped her shoulders. 'Answer me this. Have you sensed something moving in and out of your body during your circles? Something growing outwards then retracting back inside?'

She searched my eyes, glancing to her sister, then shook her head. I marched over to the fireplace, kicking it in mock exasperation. 'My goodness, you are such an innocent child. No curiosity at all.'

'Innocent?' said Kathleen.

I crouched before her, taking her hands. 'Innocent, yes,' I said, laughing at her sweet face. 'Wonderfully innocent.'

CHAPTER
THIRTY THREE

What a restless, rambling sleep I had that night. Tormented by my own conclusions, I'd suffered terrifying visions of spectral men clambering the walls beyond my bedroom, pressing their bloody hands against the windowpane until the whole house was buried beneath a writhing ants' nest of faceless soldiers. A voice was calling me to the nursery, yet when I pressed the door open, a great wave had crashed along the hallway, sweeping me down the stairs, dragging Elizabeth screaming behind. At last, in the early hours, as the moonlight seemed to step closer to the curtains, I'd woken with a jump to see a woman standing at the end of my bed, only to disappear the moment I reached for my spectacles. I had crept up the mattress, shivering in my pyjamas, kneeling in prayer like a child, then whispered to her about my family, gulping tears, for it had felt as though she was listening and, oh, what a kind feeling it was after so many years alone.

There was no sleep after that, only the long wait for the slow winter dawn, and when it came at last, I rose early, driving to the Institute, exhausted and dishevelled, teeth chattering as sleet blew sharp across the river. I chugged past the men marching to the shipyard, their faces buried in iron coats, slaves to their rapacious hulls. Somehow, I kept my eyes open for another bone-rattling quarter of an hour, stumbling up the steps to the Institute, holding on to a pillar for support in the flickering light.

'Professor Crawford!'

I groaned to see Stoupe prancing towards me in a frantic state. 'William, look at your face, are you still harassed by the spirits? You look so terribly haunted, but then imagine a spirit investigator who isn't.'

'Isn't what?' I said, yawning.

'Haunted, William, haunted!' He tutted, looking about my head, waving his hand around my face and shoulders as if chasing a fly. 'Are you there?' he whispered.

'Yes, Seamus,' I said. 'Of course I'm here. What is your game?'

'Not you, Professor!' He peered over my shoulder with a mystic's eye. 'You must be surrounded by spirits, all of them desperate to be heard. Have you heard from them again?'

'Them?'

Stoupe leaned in and whispered. 'Your mother, Robert, the other spirits...'

I turned away to the stairs, making my apologies, only to have my arm gripped.

'I was in two minds; caught on the horns of the most existential dilemma, but I have decided I simply *must* show you. Come with me now, quickly.'

I followed him up to his studio, the stone steps seeming to move beneath my feet like piano keys. Presently I found myself sitting once again on the posing seat, looking about with bleary eyes as he fussed in his desk drawer.

'What game is this now?' I grumbled. 'I cannot take another photograph.' I stood up, only to be pressed back to my seat.

'Another photograph?' he said. 'Heaven forfend. Sit still, you will want to see this, I am certain of it.' He pinched his nose, shaking his head. 'The pickle you have gotten me into. The perfect pickle; I have troubled over it more than you can know, but I have come to the conclusion that I have no right to keep such a profound piece of evidence from you.'

'Evidence?' I yawned, blinking.

Stoupe fixed me with a look of utmost gravity. 'Proof of the afterlife so horribly profound I have lost sleep over it.'

Had anyone slept in Belfast? Stoupe stood back, looking me up and down. 'I must warn you, William, you will not be the same sort of a man once you have seen what I have to show you. I fear you will be quite changed, but you must forgive me, I only do what is right. Tell me.' He gripped my knees. 'Do you still have doubts about the spirits?'

I stifled a yawn, not wanting to swallow the man's breath and frowned. 'Of course. My experiments are not finished; many questions remain.'

'Indeed,' said Stoupe, as he scrambled to his desk. He made a cross on his chest, battling some terrible, private misgiving, before yanking open a drawer, shielding his face with his free hand, then stopping again to muster some greater store of courage.

'Come along, Seamus,' I said. 'I have to set things up for the day.'

Stoupe closed his eyes. 'Yes, yes, Professor, you are quite right.' And with that, he shot his hand into his desk drawer like a chameleon's tongue, whipping out a postcard-sized envelope, holding it above his head at arm's length in a cameo of Shakespearean horror.

'What is it?' I asked.

'What is it?' Stoupe nodded. 'Indeed, that is precisely the question I have been asking myself these last few days. I thought I knew but then, last Wednesday evening in my dark room, I...'

He slid his eyes to me, then back to the square of paper, pursing his lips. 'Your portrait,' he said.

I frowned, folding my arms. 'The photograph you took of me all those weeks ago? So, you finally got around to developing it.'

'Indeed I did, though Lord forgive me I wish I had not.'

I sighed. 'Am I so plain in the photograph that you cannot bear to touch it?'

Stoupe shook his head with a grim smile. 'Don't be glib, William. You never know who might be listening.' He turned to me, his face ashen, his eyes flitting about the ceiling. 'Take it,' he said, breathlessly, and thrust the envelope into my hand.

I pulled the picture from the envelope, flipping it over to see a perfectly ordinary portrait of myself with steady eyes in front of a blurred background, filled with marbled swirls. I looked very fine in my suit. Puzzled, I turned to Stoupe. 'What on Earth has gotten into you, man?' I said. 'There's nothing to see.'

Stoupe whined, clasping his face. 'But there is; look closely if you dare.'

I pulled my glasses to the end of my nose, focusing my tired eyes. I saw myself, sitting in the very same spot in the very same chair in front of the peculiar background and yet, were my eyes quite steady after all? Was my posture so very composed? Perhaps not, for looking a second time, I observed the faintest trace of discomfort around my brow. My mouth appeared thin as though I was beset by some tight, discomforting thought. Then I recalled the moments before the flash of the camera. The tingling sensation on my ear. The breath on my neck. I looked at Stoupe, frowning. 'I suppose I do look a little off,' I said. He leaned towards me with a sorrowful smile.

'William, do you not see her?'

I laughed nervously. 'I see myself. I see the chair. I see the bizarre pattern at my back.'

Stoupe spoke, voice trembling. 'But there was no pattern; only the window.'

I was just about to lose my temper when I spied something odd. There, amidst a swirl of pale-grey smoke, standing behind my shoulder, was the faintest outline of a transparent woman in a long white dress. Leaning in closer, squinting, I could make out her stretched face, her drifting hair, her mouth open at my ear as though singing a warped lullaby, her black eyes staring straight out at me. *William.* I recognised her instantly.

'Is it her?' whispered Stoupe.

'Yes,' I said, turning to look over my left shoulder. There was a chill around my jaw. An electric charge at my fingertips. A bare movement around the tips of my ears. Something brushed the nape of my neck.

I smiled. 'Mother.'

CHAPTER
THIRTY FOUR

Her portrait stayed with me always, tucked safely inside my jacket pocket. I felt certain she was standing beside me throughout my many paranormal experiments as the days and weeks rolled into a series of glad, victorious months. She was searching still for Robert, so Kathleen understood, for there were weeks when the attic stayed still, forcing me to wait in limbo for the next reassuring press of her hand on my shoulder. There were moments when I thought I could hear her singing, somewhere behind a gale or beneath a running tap. More than once, I caught her slipping around corners at the Institute. At least, I hoped it was her.

Meanwhile, much to my mortification, I was becoming famous in the world of spiritualistic investigation, my articles published weekly in *Light* magazine. In fact, none other than Sir Arthur Conan Doyle had referenced my work in his public seminars.

'You are so very clever,' complimented Aunt Adelia, admiring my equipment as I moved purposefully about the room. 'I admit it! I never expected you to become such a dear friend.'

'Hush,' I said, pushing past her to my notepad, snapping at Rose to follow. It was an auspicious day. For the first time, we were crammed together in the parlour of our humble home on Park Avenue, Elizabeth circling with a plate of Rose's delicious sandwiches. It was a clear, cold afternoon in late spring, the fire lit to fend off the last of the winter.

'Tell me, dearest William,' Adelia asked, tapping my shoulder. 'Where are you sitting at the gala this year? I do hope we can see the famous Spirit Engineer from the high table?'

I scoffed. 'We are blessed, Lady Carter, to be on table forty. I thank you for speaking to the principal on our behalf, but his scepticism abounds.'

'Shameful.'

'It matters not, I have been forced to offer my deepest apologies. I cannot attend anyway.'

Adelia glared at Elizabeth. 'What is this, Lillie? Not attending?'

I smiled apologetically. 'I have been invited to speak in Dublin. My disciples are hungry for more.'

Elizabeth shook her head. 'Disciples, William, really.'

Adelia pouted. 'Perhaps I ought to go. What sort of audience do you find at these lectures?'

I sighed, adjusting the weighing machine with Rose's assistance. 'Men and women mostly.'

'You are silly, you know what I mean. Are they my sort of people?'

'I should hope not.'

'How you tease me, honestly, you are cruel. You haven't forgotten me, have you, William?' She leaned down, her nose between my eyes and the dial.

'How could I forget you, Aunt Adelia?' I murmured, sharing a private look with Seamus as the dear man carried a tripod through the curtain. 'The spirits haunt me less than you do.'

'Well, I'm still searching for George, you see. I believe he came to me yesterday in the bedroom, what do you think?'

I straightened up, waving at Rose to fetch my pipe. 'It seems quite obvious to me, Adelia, that the Late Lord Carter, God rest his weary soul, is not searching for you at all. Little wonder, I should say. Doubtless, he'll be out of Heaven like a ferret the moment you die.'

Adelia's eyes frosted over as she straightened up, knocking the weighing scale with her bag.

Stoupe poked his head between the curtains. 'Everything's ready, William,' he said as Professor Fforde entered, pushing an elderly gentleman in a wheelchair. I stepped past him to the window, circling his companion who was propped up with pillows, barely visible beneath his blankets but for a flaking scalp, pale eyes and wisps of chewed hair. Why Fforde had brought a stranger along I had no idea; particularly one so decrepit. Still, my experiments drew fascination from all quarters, particularly the infirm. The doorbell chimed, Mr Robinson and Mr Cleaver entering the parlour, followed by a third man; tall and spindly like a furled umbrella with a jolly smile and lively eyes. He held out his hand, speaking in a refined English accent.

'Good day to you, Professor,' he said. Distracted, I turned away, watched by the disconcerting old fellow in the wheelchair, Fforde parking him in the window. I could not decide whether he was looking at me, or whether his eyes were made of glass. I smiled at him and coughed, turning around with false purpose to attend to something, anything, that might wrest me from his attention.

'Yes,' I said. 'I welcome all of you, take a seat please, your names can be found on the chairs.'

The parlour was laid out like a miniature theatre, two rows of seats facing the curtain to the dining room. I clapped my hands for attention. 'Ladies and gentlemen, hush now, settle down, the experiment is ready to begin.'

Margaret appeared at the door, looking around the room with a sceptical expression, typical of her age. 'Father, who are all these people?'

'Ah come in, child,' I said, presenting her to the room as she swung her arms and sighed. I could hardly feel angry with the clever girl, expected to busy herself with idle pastimes and menial domestic chores. I rubbed her shoulders, feeling her bristle.

'This is my eldest, Margaret. What an inquisitive, strong-willed young woman she is, already quite the mathematician. One day, I shall hand my research down to her, you know. She has already agreed to continue my work, eh, Margaret?'

She folded her arms. 'I wish you would stop your work. What's going on?'

'An experiment,' barked Adelia. 'Petulant girl, your clever father is about to show us another séance.' She turned to the smart gentleman at Mr Robinson's side, rolling her eyes. 'It really is dismal, isn't it? These modern girls wishing to be significant. None of the successful women I know do anything at all.'

'Please, Father, don't do this here,' said Margaret, hiding her face as one of our neighbours passed by the window, scuttling to the opposite side of the road, crossing her chest. 'It's bad enough at school, without you terrifying the neighbours. I can't even return my books to the library. They say the pages are possessed.'

'They'd be lucky if they were,' I said. 'It would be the first valuable thing on their shelves.'

Margaret was about to take me on, when Helen skipped in, curtseying to her audience in a fuchsia dress. 'The minister says Father's ghost book is the Devil's work.'

'Then I suppose that makes me the Devil,' I said, bowing.

'I'm going to my room to read,' said Margaret, stopping to look at the old man in the wheelchair before departing with a sigh. I laughed.

'Off to read, can you believe it? Did Da Vinci's daughter read while he fathomed the impossible?'

Stoupe reappeared through the curtain. 'Did Da Vinci have a daughter? I hardly think he was the type.'

'Enough!' I said. 'Are we ready, Seamus?' He nodded. 'Very well then, Elizabeth my darling, please close the curtains. Rose, let us turn up the lamps.'

She did so, the light glittering in our new chandelier. We might very well have been sitting in a miniature theatre, faces glowing in the gaslight, surrounded by the smart new furnishings of our happy home.

'Are we all present?' I said, swallowing my nerves. 'Very well then. Doubtless, you have read my books. If not, I shall force you to take a signed copy as you leave. No, no, I thank you for your support and encouragement.' I lifted a finger. 'Yet much of it would not have been possible without the help of a particular young woman. Her name is Kathleen Goligher. She is, as none other than Conan Doyle himself proclaims, one of the few truly pure mediums working today.'

Mr Cleaver was whispering to Mr Robinson, while Professor Fforde grumbled away beside the wheelchair-bound man. I reached out. 'Please, she asks for complete silence.' The room grew still. 'There is only one thing in all the universe so wondrous as life. That is the *after*life. For millennia, generations have gazed up at the stars, hoping to see a glittering firmament of souls.' I leaned in. 'Little did they know that their lost ones were very likely standing right next to them, staring at those very same stars. Yes...' I pointed to the empty space at my side. 'We are all, at every hour of every day, rubbing shoulders with the dead.' The audience murmured, shifting in their chairs nervously. I held my hand out to the empty chair beside Helen. 'Dear Robert, I hope you are with us tonight.' I took a deep breath, thumbs in my waistcoat pockets. 'Of course, at first, I was a sceptic.'

'Indeed you were,' called Adelia.

'Oh yes, I was. So certain of my own premature conclusions I might as well have been wandering around with a bag over my head. After all, what defence is a mere belief against a proven scientific fact?' I stretched out my arms, shaking my fists in turn. 'Belief, ladies and gentlemen, and fact. Never before has there been such an immeasurable chasm between the two. Such is the legacy of modern science, I suppose. However, tonight, you shall bear witness to something remarkable, astounding, perhaps even...' I nodded to Fforde as I clapped my hands together. 'Miraculous!' The audience applauded, the jolly gentleman sitting between Cleaver and Robinson whispering his approval.

Without further ado, I threw back the curtain to a collective gasp for there sat Kathleen, alone in the middle of the bare room, not a rug on the floorboards, not a picture on the empty walls. She wore her hair in a bun, blinking without her spectacles, for I had discovered that second sight required no prescription. She was clothed in a thin cotton shift, not a stitch underneath, her breasts pressing through the material which gathered in soft folds over her hips. Her wrists and shins were tied to her chair, a rope looped around her neck to a pole. Her stockinged feet were locked tightly within a boot-shaped box, the whole arrangement, chair and all, balanced on a large industrial weighing machine.

'Extraordinary,' whispered the jolly old fellow.

Kathleen shot me a look, troubled.

'Is everything okay, dear Kathleen?' I asked, smiling reassuringly at my audience.

She spoke through gritted teeth. 'Where are my sister and Mammy, Professor? Where is Noah? It's too early.'

'Too early, you say?' I checked my watch. 'No, no, it is the perfect time.'

'You told me there'd be dinner before the séance.'

I put my mouth to her ear and whispered, 'I lied. Do not make a fuss.'

She struggled in her bonds, the rope around her neck choking her windpipe. I placed a finger on her lips, giving a reassuring smile to the audience, before turning back to her, my voice low. 'Your family will be here later, Kathleen. Once we are done.'

'I don't want to, Professor, I—'

'Be quiet, don't embarrass me,' I said, pulling the hood over her head before she could utter another word. The audience looked on spellbound as I moved behind her, my hands on her shoulders. 'Behold,' I cried. 'The most powerful woman you have ever seen.'

CHAPTER
THIRTY FIVE

An hour later, there wasn't a steady pulse in the room.

'Extraordinary,' whispered Mr Robinson.

And so it was. Apparently *too* extraordinary for some. Fforde banged his cane on the floor, rising unsteadily to his feet. I laughed, for the fool seemed about to cry, so beaten was he by the incontrovertible proof of the séance.

'There,' I said. 'Can you doubt me now?'

'What I have witnessed here tonight, Professor Crawford...' He breathed with considerable effort. 'Is beyond words. Beyond human decency. I think... yes, I think I may have misjudged the situation. It is bloody repulsive. We should never have come.' He took hold of the wheelchair, rolling it towards the door, his companion whimpering with funny little spasms beneath his blanket. Fforde patted his shoulder. 'There, there nai, I told you this was a terrible idea, sure. The bangs and flashes have set ye off again.'

I stepped in front of them both. 'Perhaps your friend can speak for himself,' I said. 'Since he's welcomed himself into our home, I should like to hear what he has to say.' I crouched down to see his ear was missing, apart from the lobe which hung beneath a gaping hole surrounded by shining skin. In fact, all of his skin was varnished, as though brushed with egg white, patterned with veins. 'What say you, old fellow?' I said, covering my disgust. 'Did you hear the voices? The boy calling out to his father? The spirit woman, singing? The two of them, almost touching hands?' The stranger stirred, lifting his chin and I stood back, catching my breath for there was a second deep impression where his nose ought to have been. Yet still, to my surprise, in spite of his decrepitude, he had a young, handsome mouth, quite at odds with the rest of his head. He spoke in a familiar voice.

'It is a grand thing to hear you again, Professor Crawford,' he said. 'Bloody glad you didn't join us for the big game, eh?' He held up his hand, missing all but one finger. 'Not much good for trout fishing these days.'

I covered my face with my handkerchief. 'Blithe?'

'Hallo, Prof,' he smiled, handsome teeth shining. It was the only part of him left, for even his jaw hung in folds of tissue, the bone beneath it quite dissolved.

'My God,' I said. 'What the devil happened to you?'

'Truth is old chum, I can't remember. One second I was boiling some tea, the next... something was boiling me.' He gripped my lapel, drawing me close. 'Would you like to hear a joke?'

'Of course,' I said, trying to sound merry, looking around the room with a happy grin. 'Go on, man, make us laugh, just like the old days.'

He whispered in my ear. 'They say I am lucky to be alive.'

I pulled away. 'I am very sorry.'

'Ah, Prof,' he said, his throat rattling. 'Nothing for you to be sorry for. I asked the old man to bring me here, so I could witness the famous Spirit Engineer at work. I thought perhaps...' He broke off, Fforde placing a handkerchief to the side of his face as a tear dribbled over the remains of his cheek. 'I thought perhaps I might hear something from the boys.'

Fforde scowled at me, his hand trembling on his cane, thick lips shaking. His eyes settled on Kathleen in her chair. 'It is diabolical, what ye do, child.'

'Diabolical?' I sneered. 'It wasn't Kathleen's spirits who sent him to war.'

Fforde shook his head, patting Blithe's shoulder. 'I wish we hadn't laid our innocent eyes on such a thing. How many men will be destroyed before this decade is out?'

'Oh come, Mr Fforde,' said Elizabeth. 'You've ridiculed William's work for years. Surely you can admit to hearing the raps and bells? Didn't you see the table lifting?'

'I did,' he said.

'And the voices too?' said Mr Robinson. 'Say it, man, say you heard the voices.'

'I heard them, sure enough!' he snapped, stumbling on his stick.

I took his elbow. 'Please, old man, I don't want an argument. I just wish you'd concede to the evidence.' I laughed. 'You are confounded, Fforde, admit it. You cannot explain what you've seen here tonight.'

'Explain it?' He looked at Kathleen. 'I cannot.'

'Aha! Did you hear that, young Blithe? Be sure to tell the principal, will you? I insist he follows your lead and joins us for a sitting.'

Fforde pushed the wheelchair to the door, stopping to look back at me. 'I always considered ye a decent man, Professor Crawford. Serious and damn strange, perhaps. But decent. Can ye tell me, honestly, who in yer judgement is making those voices?'

I thought of poor Robert being led into some frozen sea by his uncle and wondered if my mother had rescued him. I looked up at Fforde.

'The spirits,' I said. 'How can you *possibly* doubt it?'

He surveyed the room, peering at each person in turn, a grave expression cast over his face. 'How can ye not?'

He pushed the wheelchair to the hall, Blithe's wrecked head lolling above his blankets. I was about to follow them to continue the debate when Robinson & Cleaver's jolly associate stepped up, shaking my hand, beaming from ear to ear.

'Professor Crawford,' he said. 'You have exceeded my very highest expectations.' He turned to Kathleen, hands clasped together in grateful prayer. 'My dear woman, what powers you have. Quite incredible. Incredible, I say! In all my years, I have never witnessed anything like it, and with everything tied up, too.'

Kathleen smiled wearily, hands upturned on the arms of her séance chair. She was about to reply, when the man shushed her, tapping my arm.

'Professor, this has all been most impressive work, I am proud and most fortunate to have met you. I do hope your assistant will share his photographs? I wonder whether he caught the... what do you call them?'

'Plasmic cantilevers,' I said, facing Stoupe. 'I'm sure we caught at least one of them; we must wait until they're developed, I'm afraid. It's the most torturous thing, but worth the wait. It's a pity we didn't manage to catch the spirit manifestations, though we shall try again.'

Mr Robinson stepped in, rubbing the man's arm. 'Did I not tell you? Did I not promise you a treat in my telegrams? Crawford is truly the greatest spiritual investigator of our time.'

The man turned to me, playful eyes sparkling like a miniature Saint Nicholas, offering his hand. 'Sir William Barrett at your service.'

'*Sir* William Barrett?'

'Indeed so.'

Cleaver clapped me on the back. 'Professor, Sir William is the leading light of the spiritualist movement, founder of the Society for Psychical Research.' He leaned back, sticking his great stomach out. 'King of poppycock I say, though I do wonder now.'

Awestruck, I shook Sir William's hand more vigorously than he was shaking my own, calling out to Rose to bring out our best whisky, knowing we had none to offer. Thank heavens, the great man demurred with a polite laugh. 'No need for that, Professor. I must depart. First however, I have to inform you that I am here as a spy.'

'What do you mean?'

'A secret admirer of yours, though he's rather busy and besides,' he said casting an eye over the room. 'Ireland is so very remote. He needed to be certain your experiments stood up to scrutiny, before extending a most-generous invitation to the mainland.'

I looked at him, perplexed, as a commotion started up at the front of the house. I saw my neighbours gathering in a huddle at the window. They backed away as I met their faces, a large silver Landau pulling up at the kerbside with a squeak. Presently, a valet appeared in the parlour, handing Sir William his top hat and, without further ado, the jolly fellow raised his eyebrows. 'Good evening, Professor Crawford,' he said. 'Your invitation will arrive shortly. 'London awaits the Spirit Engineer.'

PART FOUR

MANIFESTATION

CHAPTER THIRTY SIX

Snow was falling thick as feathers as Rose and I trudged our way up Regent Street, my trusty assistant weighed down by boxes and baskets as the crowds teemed around us in a disorientating mass of arms, top hats and umbrellas. She stumbled, almost falling beneath the clattering wheels of a bus, and I stopped for her, tutting impatiently.

'Look where you're going, Rose, we're late,' I said, pushing through a pack of men gathered around a newspaper stand. 'If I lose my equipment, I shall never forgive you.' I threw tuppence at the vendor and fished out a copy before striding across Oxford Circus straight into the path of a motorcar. 'Blasted place,' I growled as Rose picked me up from the pavement. 'Infernal city. Take me back to Belfast.'

On we marched, the spire of All Souls Church beckoning us to our destination and, soon enough, after a string of angry altercations with a beggar, a street sweeper, a woman selling horse chestnuts and a Great Dane – the canine variety – I stood, frazzled and wracked with sickening nerves, in front of the Queen's Hall. Today, the famous home of The Proms would play host to a very different kind of performance and it was I, William Jackson Crawford, who would take the stage.

I groaned, opening the newspaper, to see my own picture emblazoned beneath an advertisement for soap, then looked up at the legend in silver letters above the door:

Behold, if you dare, the Spirit Engineer. Never-before-seen proof of the afterlife!

We made our way to the stage entrance, climbing to the dressing room which stank of mould, cigarettes, and actors. I looked at myself in the mirror, going over my script, as Rose parted and smoothed my hair with Brillantine. Such was the nature of my schedule, three years had passed since that memorable evening at Park Avenue with Sir William, and while so many young soldiers had died, filling the world with unbearable tragedy, the spirits had pulled around us in a sort of planetesimal process, swelling in the cosy privacy of the attic. Often it was just Kathleen, Rose and I pottering about in the merry flicker of the lamp and, oh, how I preferred our intimate sessions to the vulgarity of the theatre.

Rose stood back, proud of her work, as I turned my head in the mirror, nodding. 'A fine job, good woman. Now remember, you must pay attention and listen carefully for the slides. Timing is key, do you understand?' She nodded as I stood up too quickly, almost falling over. 'Silly,' I said, mopping my brow. 'I am a little nervous, I admit. My head hurts, I didn't sleep last night.' She held out my pipe, squeezing my hand as I took it. I winked at her. 'Thank you, Rose, my dear, faithful assistant. Whatever would I do without you?' She blushed, looking at her boots, such was the sweet nature of our friendship.

Together, we had carried out hundreds of experiments, designing various methods to interrogate the spirits via letters on a wooden board or certain raps for certain meanings. I had changed the lighting, built ingenious contraptions with electric sensors, weighed, mapped and measured every inch of the medium's body, instructing the girl to search only briefly for Robert and Mother, before cracking on with the job in hand. Thankfully, Arthur seemed to have sunk back into whichever dreaded pond he had risen from, though I had sensed him in the room more than once, the smell of rotten fish preceding an uncomfortable, pregnant silence. Doubtless, he saw some personal benefit in my experiments; a sentiment clearly shared by the spirit world in general. Most of our operators were perfectly friendly, workaday sorts, well-suited to practical investigation, once they'd finished prattling about murders, lost treasures and petty grievances. In truth, I'd required little more than a 'yes' or 'no' from most of them, whoever they turned out to be and, naturally, some were better versed in mechanics than others. On one particularly exciting night, we were graced by the presence of none other than the spirit Brunel, though his thoughts on cantilever mechanics and weight transference were sketchy at best and he seemed to think the Clifton Suspension Bridge was in Llanelli.

Over time, I had become world famous in spiritualist circles, much to my discomfort, published around the world at Sir William's bequest, quoted by the great and the good. Three of my books were in print and a fourth was on the way with a tour of the United States planned. The very thought of it made me feel sick with anxiety.

'Come then, Rose,' I said, turning from the dressing table. 'Our public awaits!'

We made our way through the winding corridors to the wings, Rose setting up the projector to the low rumble of voices beyond the curtain. 'Wish me luck,' I whispered and she nodded, clasping her hands as light swept over the stage. I turned, the spotlights reflected in muffled orbs across the polished boards, then kissed my mother's portrait and stepped out to applause.

'Here, where's yer ghosts?' called a man in the front row, immediately hushed by those around him. The clapping trailed off as I gripped the lectern, pulling at my collar as my head swam. The audience spread out before me, two thousand faces in the dark. I looked into the wings for comfort, but Rose was busy preparing the first slide. I cleared my throat. 'Good evening, ladies and gentlemen.' My voice was tiny, barely a squeak in the cavernous auditorium.

'Speak up, mate!'

There was laughter, followed by a gasp. Behind me, the screen flickered, a photograph of Kathleen sitting beneath her shroud, the unmistakable outline of a spirit looming over her shoulder. I nodded to Rose, who smiled back.

'Ladies and gentlemen,' I said, remembering my script. I paced in a circle, mimicking deep thought, willing my knees to stop shaking. 'I will show you some of my controls.' The projector clicked, sending the auditorium into momentary darkness before flashing a new image onto the screen some twenty-feet high. 'Mark the medium sitting in a trance on her usual chair. All photographs were taken by an esteemed Professor of Photography at the Belfast Municipal Technical Institute and he is of a most serious and scientific mind. Next slide, please.'

Click.

Two near-identical images of Kathleen appeared above me, she sitting in her chair like the Colossi of Memnon, eyes closed, mouth twisted into spasm beneath her clasped hands, a length of white plasma pressing between her knees to the floor. I smiled nervously, knowing a gasp would surely follow.

And so it did.

'Be calm, ladies and gentlemen,' I said, my nerves easing. I stared out at the audience, nodding. They were only people, and every single one of them, a friend. That is what Elizabeth had told me at the ferry. *They are your followers, William. Do well, make us proud.* 'You can see, the medium is quite still, her knees together in standard pose, though we have the white shaft of a plasmic rod – here – extricating itself from her lower regions – here.' I smiled. 'I trust there are no children present?'

The audience laughed, whispering and nodding and I allowed myself a deep breath, wiping my clammy palms on my trouser legs. 'Note please, the medium reports a faint tugging sensation as the rod is produced. Now, I have little doubt that at the commencement of the phenomenon of levitation, a loose fibrous or thread-like structure is projected from the medium and attached to the hard under-surface of the table and that psychic force is then gradually exerted along this structure, making it sufficiently rigid. You will have seen the description in my latest book.'

How I had thrilled, the previous winter, to touch a plasmic rod's reptilian skin for the first time, catching it, tongue-like, between her parted legs. To follow it upwards, slowly, fingertips brushing across cool, scaly skin to its clammy origin.

I gestured to the wings for the next slide: a crisp magnification of a plasmic cantilever, its pale veins running around a firm limb, perfectly captured by Stoupe's camera. A shiver of excitement rippled through the audience. This was the moment to move downstage, fixing them with a challenging eye. I did so, surprising myself with my own showmanship.

'Now, it had occurred to me, some two summers ago, that the thread-like structure probably consists of a cable of thin tubes and that something is pushed into those tubes in the form of a fluid.'

The hall positively thrummed with expectation. The projector blinked. I pointed at the next image of Kathleen, her eyes closed, her legs parted. From between her stockinged ankles, three tendril-like plasmic rods spread their fingers across the floor, reaching out towards the camera. There were faint squeals from the back seats while a group of young men crept cautiously towards the stage, ready at any moment to bolt. I pointed up at the projection of Kathleen's skirt.

'At the root of the cantilever there is a shearing force and below it here...' I circled her feet. 'A bending moment. I have set scales beneath the medium. When the table is lifted, so the weight of the medium increases by the very same weight as the object. I have watched the pin move over the dial of a platform weighing machine by the light of my electric torch. This proves the cantilevered rod is, as I proposed, attached to and formed *of* the medium's own matter.'

'Doctor Crawford.'

I stopped, peering beyond the dazzling lights. There was a man, standing up at the far balcony. Clearing my throat, I ignored him and carried on. 'Ladies and gentlemen,' I said, nodding for the next slide. 'I give you the first ever physical proof of a plasmic rod.'

The projector flashed, the audience gasping to see Stoupe's photograph of a china saucer with a clear print pressed into a blob of putty. 'This saucer was placed on the floor near to the middle of the circle,' I said, striding confidently to the screen with my pointer. 'The operators were obliged to rap on the putty and, as a result, these three impressions were made. As you can see, the tips of the rods are similar in form, each consisting of an oblong cavity, about three quarters of an inch long and half an inch wide at its widest part, sloping down gradually from the periphery to a maximum depth of one quarter of an inch or so. Now, mark this: the floor of each cavity was not smooth but lined by a series of parallel grooves or waves, which showed a tendency to curl round near the long ends of the cavity.'

'It's a footprint!'

I peered through the lights again to see the man standing at the edge of the balcony.

'That picture,' called the man, 'It is a heel print, quite clearly.'

I tapped my jacket pocket, wondering if there were any ushers about, then returned to my notes at the lectern. The hall waited for me in absolute silence, broken only by an occasional, echoing cough.

'Let us... er... consider now... the time required for levitational rods to metamorphose into purposeful rapping rods...'

'Forgive me, Doctor Crawford, I must ask you some questions.'

I closed my eyes, feeling for the photograph of my mother. *Leave me be, man, whoever you are, this is precisely why I didn't want to come.* Rose was standing in the wings, waving me on. I gritted my teeth. 'My name, sir, is Professor Crawford, if you please. You are welcome to ask me anything you like in the foyer once the lecture is finished.'

'Can we not debate my concerns now, Professor? I feel I must question some of your conclusions, you see. I would never seek to offend the finer or more tender emotions of the human heart, but I wonder whether your particular ministry of consolation is based on fraud? Or inspired by greed, even?'

The audience murmured, a woman shouting for him to shut his trap. I felt my chest tighten, my hands begin to tremble. 'The medium makes no money from her séances,' I said, turning back to the screen.

'And what of you?' called the man, passing around the balcony.

I pinched my mother's portrait hard, willing her to my side, longing for a brush of cool air on my neck. 'Sir,' I said. 'I am sure you have carried out hundreds of your own experiments. Perhaps you are also a respected Professor of Engineering?'

The audience laughed and called out, 'Not likely!' and 'Tell 'im to button 'is 'ole!'.

The man shook his head. 'I am but a humble Surgeon-Captain of the Royal Navy, a fellow of the Royal Anthropological Institute, a former student of medicine at Guy's Hospital and a fellow of the Chemical Society.'

A voice called over. 'Bugger off!'

I laughed, holding out my hands, but the man would not give in.

'Professor Crawford, you will be interested to hear that I have written my own little pamphlet. Would you like to know its title?'

'Not particularly.'

'I call it *The Reality or Unreality of Spiritualistic Phenomena. Being a Criticism of Dr W. J. Crawford's Investigations Into Levitations and Raps.* I have good friends in the scientific community and the newspapers who are most keen to read it. Mr Spirit Engineer, sir, I say to you now that you are a fraud and you had better prepare yourself for some pretty difficult questions.'

My blood ran cold. He had written a pamphlet? The projector clicked and I jumped to see Kathleen asleep in her chair behind me, her black hair falling across her shoulders, the memory of damp wool, juices, faecal matter.

'For an easy starter,' said the man. 'You tell us in your book that the light in this attic of yours is perfectly sufficient for your experiments and yet you require a torch to see the numbers on your weighing machine. How do you explain that?'

'I do not need to explain it!'

'Oh, but you do, sir, and I cover the inconsistency most energetically in my essay.'

'Who are you?' I interrupted.

'Charles Marsh Beadnell, at your service. Shall I come to the stage so we can talk man-to-man?'

'Yeah,' shouted a woman from the cheap seats. 'Let 'im ask 'is questions.'

'No,' I yapped, my voice breaking. I felt my hair springing up in the heat of the stage lights, my starched shirt damp beneath my new waistcoat, a bead of sweat dripping into my eye. Rose tip-toed onto the stage, shielding her face with her hand, patting my brow with a hanky until I swatted her away, slapping her arms, to the growing laughter of the crowd. The stage tipped like the deck of a sinking ship. Down I fell, into freezing black water. I took a deep breath. 'I explain in my book that the lamp is usually strong enough to see quite plainly once the eyes are accustomed to the colour of the light...'

'Except that the table casts a shadow over a portion of the floor? You cannot see a thing there?'

'Well... yes. Hence my various controls...'

'So, the least-illuminated portion of an already poorly lit attic is precisely where your interest should chiefly lie?' The man gave an incredulous laugh, his distant shadow turning around for support. 'Professor Crawford, if you can offer one single instance of levitation in which the table, the space all round it, above it, and under it and all the sitters and the medium are plainly visible, I will give twenty pounds to any cause of your choosing.'

'I should gladly do so, Mr Beadnell,' I said. 'There are many in need of your charity. However, I have already witnessed and recorded such a thing hundreds of times with heavier and lighter tables of cane and all sorts of different materials.'

'Ho-ho! Is that so?'

'It is so!'

'Then you are either a man of extreme credulity or the very lowest form of swindler.'

'How dare you!' I thundered as the hall burst into outraged cries of 'foul play' and 'throw the bugger out!' Disconcertingly, there were people cheering him on, too.

Just as I was about to march off stage, the projector flashed, Kathleen appearing slumped over the chair, her eyes half open. Instantly, the hall fell silent as I jabbed my pointer at her. 'Why should I convince a man such as you to trust this generous, innocent woman?'

The hall applauded, cheering me on as a number of men in the far rows edged towards him between the seats. He looked both ways, realising himself trapped, and clambered over people, shouting. 'It's you we can't trust, Professor, and I shall prove it with the publication of this pamphlet. If you are a lucky man then the worst you'll suffer is a hefty fine.'

Mr Beadnell was collared and pulled to the doorway, but, just as they were about to fling him outside, he somehow wriggled free and marched forwards again, pulling pamphlets from his pockets and throwing them to the seats below.

'Most right-thinking people will prefer a much simpler explanation for your psychic phenomena,' he declared, making his way around the circle. 'Namely, that it is clearly all a trick by that girl and I hope, for your own sakes, you're ignorant to the fact. Better a famous fool than an infamous thief.'

I marched to the very edge of the stage, almost falling into the pit, waggling my pointer. 'I have witnessed phenomena beyond the strength of this girl, I tell you. I have seen no fewer than four grown men try with all their might to push the table down under the force of spirits. We might as well have tried to stop a locomotive. Do you expect us to believe this girl would be capable of doing such a thing?'

Beadnell kicked a man who was trying to get a grip on his leg and threw himself forwards, almost toppling to the seats below. '*Populus vult decipi, ergo decipiatur,*' he squeaked, tie yanked over his head, spectacles askew. 'Perhaps you should enlighten us, sir, as to why these spirits, imbued with the energy of a charging steam train, were never requested to levitate anything larger than a poxy table?' He began scattering more pamphlets, but was garrotted by a pair of young soldiers, his arms yanked backwards by a pack of rampant women who piled into him with their purses. Soon there was nothing to see of him but an outstretched hand holding the pamphlets aloft, his half-strangled voice calling up through arms and legs. 'Your claims are preposterous!' he called before receiving a thump.

I was about to call for clemency, when I caught sight of my audience picking up the man's dratted leaflets from the aisle, reading them and pointing at me. *Let those thugs tear him to shreds,* I thought. *Let them rip him inside out, the heretic.* 'That's right,' I said, folding my arms. 'Give him what he deserves.'

Click.

The auditorium was thrown into darkness momentarily, before the projector shivered back to life, strobing between a pair of near-identical images. Above me, Kathleen loomed, her head seeming to turn from one side of the auditorium to the other, eyes opening and closing, the fingers of her left hand clasping and unclasping on the arm of her chair. All the while the man Beadnell called out passages from his pamphlet.

'You people are – *oof* – no better than – *arg* – the savage who put a spirit behind the thunder-clap and the earthquake – *aiiii!* – You strain at gnats and swallow camels, oh no please don't! – *Argh!* – Every phenomenon described in this tawdry scrap is explainable in physical terms and – *oof* – either they are making a fool of you, or... *ouwww, not my fingers!...* you are making a fool of these good people!'

My audience stared between us, some horrified, some delighted, some making their way to the exit, shaking their heads and casting nervous glances back to the stage. 'Possessed,' I heard a woman telling her friend. 'The mad professor set evil spirits on him.'

'Oi,' shouted a violent-looking man, striding towards the stage, his sleeves rolled to his biceps. 'Beadnell's right, the Spirit Engineer's a fake. Here, give us our money back.'

'Yes,' called an elderly woman, waving the pamphlet. 'Gimme my money back too.'

I pulled my mother's picture from my pocket. Her face seemed to have shifted, as it often did at times of stress; her eyes blacker, mouth stretched downwards, her hand reaching straight out. I blinked.

Click.

There came a cry, the man stopping in his tracks, one boot on the stage. I twisted to see Kathleen standing before the chair, her face hard as though about to speak, her head surrounded by a crown of furious-looking spirits. 'Well done, Rose!' I called, dashing past her to the back of the stage and up the stairs to the dressing room, where I flung my equipment into her arms, then tumbled down to the stage door.

'Here, Mr Engineer,' said the door keeper as I rushed by, 'This is for you.' I snatched a card from him, flinging open the door to see a crowd of people already blocking the exit, waving their tickets in the air, demanding their money back, while others begged me to sign their books. 'We're trapped,' I said. 'Rose, protect me.'

Just then, a silver Landau pulled up, the door swinging open, Sir William shouting over the heads of the crowd. 'Hop in, Professor, quickly.'

With a determined roar, I pushed my way through, elbowing people out of the way, jumping aboard and shutting the door as fists bumped the windows. 'Go, now,' Sir William instructed the driver as we pulled onto Regent Street, poor Rose left stranded amidst the riot. I sat back, my head pounding. 'Sir William, thank you for rescuing me.'

'Excitable crowd, eh?'

'There was a man,' I said, looking at him in shock. 'He's publishing a pamphlet all about me, Sir William. He called me a fraud! I must go home at once and cancel my tour.'

Sir William spun about on his seat. 'Cancel your—certainly not, Professor! My boy, you are the Spirit Engineer. My friends and I have spent a fortune on your experiments. Cancel the tour because of a pamphlet? No, no, quite out of the question.'

'But I shall be made a fool.'

'And what of that?' he laughed. 'There isn't a successful man alive who isn't a fool. Did you expect everybody to believe in your spirits, without question?'

'My experiments are beyond doubt.'

'Well then, there you are, you see? People only *ever* doubt certainties, otherwise, where's the sport?' He tapped me on the knee as the Landau swept around Trafalgar Square, the lions wearing caps of white snow. 'Think of the many people relying on you. Think of the lost souls.'

'I shall continue with my experiments,' I said. 'But I shall never give a lecture again.'

Sir William gave a dry laugh. 'We shall see about that, Professor. Perhaps you have been wise and saved the money we've paid you, hm? We shall need every penny of it to reimburse the cancelled tickets.'

I had not saved it, of course. How could I have done? Park Avenue was as good as a new house, every fixture and fitting replaced, the foundations shored up against the mud which threatened to launch the entire street into the sea. Elizabeth had spent money on fine clothes too, while the girls were enrolled in the best schools.

'Come, Professor,' said Sir William, seeing my furrowed brow. 'You shall find your stomach for it again, never you worry. First, you have an important meeting to attend, and he'll have none of this doubtful nonsense. Believe me, you wouldn't want to disappoint him.'

I looked at the card in my hand. It had the title of a gentleman's club written in gold lettering, my name inscribed on the back. 'Who am I meeting?' I asked.

'You'll see. Out you get, quickly now. Oh, and...' He pointed a gloved finger at me, his once jolly face stern. 'Remember. You have seen the spirits with your own eyes. Felt them. Photographed them. That is why you are here. Don't let us down.'

The street was deserted, but for a flame-haired woman standing beside a nearby lamppost. I stood back as the motorcar pulled away, looking up at a set of covered windows. The snow grew thicker, flakes catching in my eyelashes as I pulled on a brass bell and waited.

'Here, you looking for company?' said the woman, stepping away from the lamppost, pulling her shawl around her shoulders.

'Certainly not.'

'Pity, I could do with some warmth from a handsome young gent like you.'

'Leave me alone,' I said, pulling the bell again.

'Don't I know you?' The woman was approaching me, treading through the slush, the bare skin of her ankles red with cold. "Ere, I do know you! You're that spirit man, aintcha?'

I looked back to The Strand, life rattling by at a deadly speed and thought of running away to the tranquil privacy of my hotel room to wait for Rose. I would watch the city turn white beyond the safety of my window. I pulled the bell again three times and stepped away, ready to dash.

'Can you find my baby, Mr?' said the woman. 'She only died last week.'

I shielded my eyes from a sudden gust of wind as the door opened, a beak-nosed footman peering out, his careful eyes struggling to find me. I held my hat to my head. 'Quick, man,' I called. 'I have an invitation.' I held out the card before being ushered inside.

The door slammed at my back, the smell of kerosene and cigar smoke gathering about me in a cushion of entombed air. The footman shook my jacket. 'Safe now, sir. This way.' We passed down a panelled hallway, our shoes padding over emerald-green carpet. An elderly gentleman in a dinner suit walked by, nodding courteously as we pressed ever deeper into the building, twisting into a longer passageway which itself gave onto a succession of private parlours until at last we came to a small room, panelled with green silk, glowing with candles in mirrored sconces. A merry little fire had been lit beneath festive boughs of holly, the window framed by heavy curtains tied with golden cords.

'Hello?' I said, pulling my jacket straight, just as a face appeared around the wing of a leather chair. I stood back, perfectly dumbstruck.

'Aha!' said the man, rising from his chair, knees popping, his eyes lusty with excitement. 'Behold. The famous Spirit Engineer has arrived at last.'

CHAPTER
THIRTY SEVEN

'Dear Professor Crawford, I cannot express to you the utter joy, spiritual comfort and reassurance my dear wife and I have taken from your experiments. You *truly* are an inspiration.'

Sir Arthur Conan Doyle's voice was rich and nutty, burred with a Scots accent, every word delivered with the sincerest enthusiasm. Never had I encountered such an embodiment of warmth and jollity; from his bristling walrus moustache to his hooded eyes there was a boisterous, irrepressible delight to the man as though his body were a machine driven by a roistering schoolboy. He let my hand go, taking me in, swelling his portly frame like a proud father.

'Look, Harry!' he cheered. 'Professor Crawford is with us at last.' He shut one eye. 'I cannot put into words the importance of your prodigious work.'

'That is most kind,' I stammered.

'Here, Harry, greet our guest, won't you?'

Sir Arthur's companion had remained silent up to this point, but with a jaded sigh he hopped from his chair, the bright fireplace crackling at his back. I peered at him, struggling to make out his face. He was a man of stocky build with a pugilistic character, perhaps five and a half feet in height, with short legs and a burst of frizzy hair atop an incongruously large head.

'I have read your articles, Professor Crawford,' he said in a peculiar accent. 'Your work is quite exhaustive, I'll give you that.'

Sir Arthur guided me to the table. 'You must forgive the manner of my invitation, Professor, but I was keen to go unnoticed. Such is the burden of celebrity, eh? You must be finding it rather taxing yourself I shouldn't wonder, what with those damned newspaper photographs and the like? It becomes increasingly difficult to avoid one's own reputation, eh, Harry?'

The stranger nodded. 'It is quite a bind.'

I picked up a glass of water as Sir Arthur chuckled ruefully. 'A bind. Ho-ho, yes indeed, Houdini. Now there's a shackle you cannot escape.'

My glass tumbled from my hand, splashing water into my lap. Instantly I recognised with complete bewilderment none other than the monstrous, box-headed denier of the paranormal and barrel enthusiast, Harry Houdini. He laughed, gripping my hand across the table, my jaw falling open like a pair of handcuffs.

'You are a Professor of Engineering in Ireland, I hear?' he said, square teeth gleaming through the dark.

'And you are a sceptic.'

Sir Arthur slapped his knee. 'You see!' he roared. 'I warned you, Professor Crawford gives no room for pleasantries where scientific investigation is concerned!' He leaned over, tapping his sleeve with an unlit cigar. 'Harry, you had better prepare to eat your words.'

Houdini sighed. 'What can I say, Professor? I have been studying spiritual mediums for years and I'm further than ever from a belief in the genuineness of spirit manifestations.'

Sir Arthur looked at me expectantly, yet I could do nothing but drum my fingers on my chair. 'Come, boy,' said the great man. 'You are a lecturer, no?'

'I am,' I said.

'Then lecture him, for goodness' sakes, lecture him! I cannot convince Harry myself, so you must do it for me.'

I thought of Beadnell and his pamphlets, my stomach turning. Houdini rested back in his chair, watching me with an amused smile, head cocked.

'Well...' I said, pushing my spectacles up my nose, preventing myself from reaching for my mother's portrait. 'The belief of many thousands of persons, and I am most certainly one of them, Mr Houdini, is that man survives death. When he departs, it is only his material body that dies or at least most of it—'

'Most of it?' interrupted Houdini.

'Indeed, I have found compelling evidence that our soul brings a residue of our physical selves with it to the next realm.'

'Have you?'

'Yes.'

Houdini sat forward, studying my face. 'Have you?' I found myself quite mesmerised by the energetic man, though he hardly moved. There was something menacing about him in spite of his pleasant features, his upper lip a perfect doll-like bow above a dimpled chin. His nose was aquiline and his broad eyebrows spanned his eyes in two perfectly arched wings. And such eyes! They were the most intense I had ever seen, glowing brightly as though made of glass, and lit from within.

Sir Arthur took my arm. 'The movement has been waiting a long time for a scientific mind such as yours, Professor,' he said. 'With your help, we shall light the fire of enthusiasm on the twin altars of imagination and knowledge. Then we might finally expose those sceptics and scoffers for the cretins they are.'

'I'm no sceptic,' said Houdini. 'I simply have the ability to recognise trickery when I see it.' He studied my face intensely, as though deconstructing me from skin to skull. I shifted uneasily, feeling myself pinned like an insect beneath his microscope. I had not agreed to this meeting, nor had I given permission for anybody to review my work at a distance. I pulled at my moustache, my arms still shaking from the theatre. I thought of Sir William's words in the car and cleared my throat. 'Only those who have visited the Goligher circle in person can have even the faintest idea of the magnitude of the forces involved,' I said. 'You cannot hope to imagine the extraordinary variety and intensity of the phenomena produced.'

Houdini lounged back, crossing his stubby legs to reveal a pair of bright-yellow socks with green stripes. 'Oh, I'm sure I can imagine them perfectly,' he said. 'Your books make some extraordinary claims.'

'Extraordinary claims with the benefit of extraordinary proof!' said Sir Arthur, thumping his fist excitedly on the arm of his chair. 'Ms Goligher is a living lamb.'

Houdini picked his teeth with his fingernail. 'I should very much like to meet your virago, Professor.'

'And I'm sure she would be delighted to meet you too. If you studied Kathleen with such perfect attention as I have—'

'Perfect attention?' said Houdini, sitting forward again, the firelight glittering in his eyes.

'Indeed,' I said.

Houdini arched his brow. 'Forgive me, Professor, but can you tell me the time?'

I sighed impatiently, reaching to my waistcoat for my pocket watch, only to look up and see the blasted thing swinging like a pendulum, its chain pinched between Houdini's fingers. I snatched it away from him irritably.

'Oh, Harry,' growled Sir Arthur. 'You are an incorrigible poseur, it does you no credit.'

Houdini clicked his tongue. 'Forgive me, Professor Crawford, I mean you no harm. I'm simply making a point. I wager I could catch your lamb rapping her foot and levitating tables with her legs within two minutes.'

'Utter rubbish,' I said. 'Sir, I have studied the operators exhaustively over many hundreds of experiments. I have had the girl on a weighing machine, I have obtained impressions of the rod in putty, I have carried out various experiments of a mechanical and electrical kind, and I know pretty well how the phenomena are produced.'

Knock

I jumped, looking around the room. Never had I heard a spirit rap without the medium at my side. Was Kathleen there? Robert? The noise had come from beneath the table. I shifted in my seat, searching the floor.

Knock. Knock.

Houdini frowned at me, following my eyes.

Knock. Knock. Knock.

The raps came louder, like hammer blows on wood, but there was no sign of movement, no electric sensation around my fingers.

'The operators,' I whispered.

Sir Arthur clapped. 'There, Houdini. The professor has brought his spirits to meet you.'

The magician lifted his face, fixing me with a broad smile. 'Listen again and watch closely.' He counted his fingers down, mouthing each number: 3, 2, 1...

Knock.

His eyes grew large, nodding. 'Am I moving, Professor?'

'No.'

'Observe,' he said, twisting to the side of the table. He rolled up his trouser leg, revealing a bald shin the size of a ham. 'Can you see this?' He pressed his thumb into a muscle, buried an inch or two from his shin bone.

'Extensor Digitorum Longus,' said Sir Arthur.

Houdini nodded. 'Just so. Now watch it, closely.' There came another rap and I saw a little explosion deep within his flesh. 'An interior muscle of the leg,' he said, slipping his heel from his shoe. His foot was quite naked, for what I had taken to be a yellow and green sock was nothing but a brightly coloured band of material which finished just below the ankle. He wriggled his long, prehensile toes. 'Spirit guides,' he intoned. 'Are you there?' I saw the muscles beside his shin travel in a wave of near-imperceptible vibrations down his leg where – in a mere momentary shiver of flesh – the ankle bones rearranged themselves like marbles, clicking the bones of his foot against the floor.

Knock.

'By jove,' whispered Sir Arthur. 'Are you saying Crawford's girl somehow chanced on the same method?'

'Oh, hardly likely,' said Houdini, rolling his trouser leg back down. 'I would normally suggest an accomplice, though perhaps the professor would have caught them by now. It may be a gadget of some kind, such as a sprung sole in her boot. I merely make the point that the professor, for all his expertise, cannot account for every type of fraud.'

'Ridiculous.' I laughed. 'She doesn't wear boots. Besides, the raps are one of many phenomena, not least the levitation of the séance table.'

Houdini pointed at me with an Elvish grin. 'I have read about Miss Goligher's table levitations. I must say, they sound very impressive for such a young woman. Still, one detail gave her away.'

'Is that so?'

'Indeed it is. How do you refer to it? The "severe spasmodic jerk" which travels around the circle, at the start of every séance?'

'I have documented the sensation, yes,' I said.

'Ah, but have you understood it, Professor? Why should you suppose there is such a movement before the table is raised?'

I tutted. 'A psychic energy passes between the sitters as the operators move particles of...'

Houdini reached across the table, gripping my hands as a sharp spasm passed between us. I jolted, trying to pull away, but his hold on me was too strong and then, lo and behold, the table lifted.

'Now,' said Houdini, perfectly still in his chair, gripping me by the fingers as the table brushed the lapels of my jacket. 'Watch me very closely.'

The table rose higher, bobbing gently as Sir Arthur clasped his cheeks, chuckling merrily like a babe in a crib.

'Look, Professor,' said Houdini. 'Look at my feet.'

I bent sideways, peering down at the carpet to see the man's toes gripping the table legs. It was the most surprising thing, for the status of his upper torso seemed completely unrelated to that of his lower half. The table levitated higher, rocking gently and then, in an expert twist, the whole thing turned smoothly to its side.

'You see,' said Houdini, poking me in the chest. 'This is something I have learned to do, after many years of practice. Someone smaller with less power in their core muscles may produce a similar effect, though they would almost certainly need to switch lower in their seat to grip the legs and, even with many hours of training, the initial tension of my feet against the table creates a jolt in the upper body.'

'Kathleen's feet are tied to her chair,' I said.

Houdini lifted his hand, my own necktie dangling from his fingers. 'Knots can be undone.'

'God damn you,' I snarled, gripping my open collar. 'The knots are as tight as they could be.'

'Then she slips out of her boots.'

'She has no boots, I told you that.'

'Then an accomplice.'

'The room is locked. You just said it couldn't be an accomplice.'

'I said perhaps. The door might well be locked. The room? Never.'

I stamped my foot, outraged by his arrogance. 'My controls are beyond all trickery.'

'Chains, wires, trap doors, hidden compartments, magnets, concealed actors. Professor, I'm sorry but I have seen it all.' He sat back, the table resting on the floor. 'You would not believe the lengths to which these villains will go.'

'Impossible, I tell you. I would have sensed someone in the room. I would have seen something.'

I heard a bang from the wall and stood up.

'And you will have seen it, Professor,' said Houdini, his voice crawling to my ear as I looked away. 'It will have passed right beneath your nose, so close you could have smelled it. But your attention will have been elsewhere at precisely the right moment. A noise perhaps, a shout, a sudden movement or flash. The art of misdirection.'

I settled back into my chair, rubbing my nose, finding the magician gone from the opposite side of the table. 'Where is he?' I said, frowning at Sir Arthur, who looked back gleefully, shaking his head.

'You are sitting on him,' came a voice in my ear. I felt between my legs for the seat, touching instead the cobble of a human knee. Outraged, I sprang away, cursing him. He straightened up, throwing a cushion to the floor, before casually tossing my necktie over my head like a ring at a fairground. 'You say in your own book that you have sensed the presence of other beings in the room. You take them for your operators, I suggest they are something more banal.'

'I have recorded the voices.'

'A switched cylinder, prepared beforehand.'

'My plans are shared with nobody before the experiments take place.'

'They are not written down? You have no study? No assistant? Nobody else in the house?'

'The voices... the spirits... *know* things. Secrets unknown to anyone alive.'

'There is no such thing as a secret.' Houdini turned to Sir Arthur. 'As our great friend has proved in his matchless stories, it only requires a smart question, a sharp mind, a forensic eye for clues and our best-hidden schemes are laid bare. A small detail, a little observation, a dash of artful speculation and, hey presto! You are exposed.'

'That I cannot deny, Harry,' said Sir Arthur. 'Though to compare these innocent spiritualist womenfolk to my detective is wholly inadequate. You may as well compare fish to a fox.'

Houdini scoffed. 'Come, Arthur, admit the professor is just as open as any of his books.'

Sir Arthur chuckled. He narrowed his eyes as I shuffled uncomfortably in my chair. 'Professor,' he said, one eye closed. 'You smoke a pipe, you bumped into a flame-haired girl outside the club and you have a photograph of a beloved woman in the left, upper pocket of your jacket. I believe the identity of said woman to be... your late mother.'

Astounded, I turned between the men, mouth gaping. 'How could you possible know such things?' I said.

Sir Arthur waved his hand. 'It is perfectly simple, just as Harry says. You are a man who finds comfort in control. Any of your readers will know that, from your exemplary, though somewhat repetitive, experiments. It is also an observation borne out by the precise symmetry of the laces on your shoes.'

'What do my shoes have to do with pipes, flame-haired girls and photographs?' I scoffed.

'Everything, my boy, everything! A controlled man is far easier to read than an unpredictable one. A passing inspection of the upper-right sleeve of your jacket reveals an area of pronounced creasing, not mirrored in the upper-left sleeve, thus belying a repeated movement of the right arm across the torso, close to the chest. A movement which might be explained by a habit of playing the fiddle, yet a cursory glance at your fingertips would disprove such inferences, meaning only one thing: that you regularly reach to your upper-left pocket. Your watch might have been the likely explanation, were it not for Harry's earlier trick, discovering the very same item in the lower pocket of your waistcoat. Besides, your jacket sits flat to your chest, so whatever you keep there must be thin enough to avoid troubling the lay of the material to your body. A piece of notepaper then, a cigarette case or a business card. Though why should a man reach repeatedly over a number of days for a piece of paper or a card? You are no travelling salesman, nor a police constable. And I can see from your teeth and nails that, if you smoke at all, it is not cigarettes. Most likely a pipe. No, it must be something of greater sentimental value for I noticed that you reached there, when you were challenged by Harry. You only ever do so under pressure. It might have been a picture of a lost child, perhaps. A wife or even a lover. Yet, no. In my arrangements for your visit, there was no request to bring your wife and family to London. I made it quite plain in my generous instructions to Sir William that you need not travel alone, yet you chose to do so, bringing a housemaid assistant of all people. I thought perhaps she was a lover, but when I saw her in the newspapers, carrying your boxes, I thought it unlikely. A secret mistress then? But no, I remembered the booking we made for you at the Charing Cross Hotel. A single room with a single bed and no adjoining apartment. No mistress.'

'It might have been a photograph of anybody,' I said.

'We do not carry photographs of people we see often, Professor. Such portraits are expensive and precious and, of course, it cannot be a picture of a lost child.'

I thought of Robert. 'Whyever not?'

'Because a grown man does not seek reassurance from his children at times of distress. He seeks purpose, yes, and protects them with all he has to his name. But a frightened man on the battlefield does not cry out to his sons and daughters. Nor does a professor under pressure from a magician. No...' Sir Arthur poked my jacket, his eyebrow raised. 'He calls for his mother.'

Without thinking, I reached for the photograph, stopping myself as Houdini laughed.

'Great show, Arthur. But how did you know about the flame-haired girl?'

'Lizzie?' The detective guffawed, waving his pipe around his head. 'There isn't a man at the club she doesn't bump into. She's as much a fixture as the lamps.'

I grew sullen while the men laughed, congratulating each other. Was it possible, as Houdini claimed, to read me like one of my books? Could the Golighers truly have guessed my darkest secrets simply by looking at my jacket sleeves? I looked up. 'I too suspected that the girl was a fraud, Mr Houdini,' I said. 'When I first encountered her. The medium keeps to a high moral standard in her daily life.'

Houdini grimaced. 'They always do. Ask yourself what she gains from this friendship. You say her spirits have voices, but where is hers, eh?'

'Professor, show him your photographs,' said Sir Arthur. 'Perfect exposures, capturing those ectoplasmic rods of yours; I saw them in your latest book, and I have the copies here, loaned to me by the Society of Psychical Research.'

He slapped them onto the table in front of Houdini, who held one of the pictures up. It was a close shot of Kathleen's boots, a strip of ectoplasm stretching across the floor. He frowned and passed it to Sir Arthur before taking up a second picture of Kathleen staring straight into the camera, a clear, white rod of ectoplasm reaching out from between her gingham skirt to the base of the séance table. He looked up. 'Have you searched her orifices?'

'I beg your pardon?'

'Saints alive, man,' said Sir Arthur. 'Search her orifices, what sort of creature are you?'

'It is a fair question. You theorise in your book that these so-called plasmic rods appear from the medium's genitals and anus and so I ask you: have you ever searched those parts of the medium before and after your experiments?'

'No, of course I haven't.'

'Well then,' said Houdini, fetching up another photograph. He smiled at me warmly. 'Maybe you should.'

I closed my eyes, rubbing my nose. 'You have written, Mr Houdini, that no greater blessing could be bestowed upon you than the opportunity to speak to your sainted mother. Well, you are looking at a man who has done just that. I am happy to have proven Kathleen an honest young woman and a genuine spiritual medium. I have found my mother and I shall find my son.'

I saw a change in Houdini's face, as though the light in his eyes had gone out. 'I envy you that, Professor,' he said. 'Sincerely, I do.'

Sir Arthur got to his feet, taking my hands. 'Success, success! Your work is extraordinary, Professor Crawford. I believe you have here, some of the most convincing evidence known to mankind. I knew you could persuade him.'

'I thank you, Sir Arthur.'

'The world awaits you, boy. Whichever world that may be.'

Houdini rose from his chair, standing beside Sir Arthur. 'I thank you for your time, Professor.'

'My pleasure,' I said, looking up at them both before realising it was time to go. I scrabbled my things together, offering my garbled thanks, before stepping into the corridor, reaching for my pipe, leaning back on the wall in the low light. Was it true? Had I just shared a drink with Sir Arthur Conan Doyle and Harry Houdini? I smiled, shaking my head. Wait until Stoupe hears about this. I leaned towards the door, pressing it open an inch to take one last look at my new friends. They must have thought me gone, for I could hear them talking about me in a low murmur. Houdini was speaking, his words barely carrying over the crackle of the fire.

'...I have watched this great wave of Spiritualism sweep the world, Arthur. It takes a hold on men, especially those suffering bereavements.'

'You make too much of it, Harry. Knowledge of the spirit world brings comfort.'

'It produces misfortunes, including suicides by men who imagine they're going to discover happiness with loved ones beyond the veil. It's more dangerous than you credit.'

Sir Arthur spoke gently as I pressed closer. 'Well then, if that is so, what do you make of our new friend, Professor Crawford?'

Houdini flicked a droplet of water into the fire. 'I must say, I am surprised. His credulity seems limitless. I expected more.' He lifted his hand. 'I mean, look at this.' He turned something between his fingers.

'Oh now, what on earth have you there, you rascal?'

I expected to see my watch, but realised to my horror that he was holding the portrait of my dear mother.

'It is the photograph from his pocket,' said Houdini. 'I forgot to hand it back to him. You were wrong, it isn't a picture of his mother after all.'

'No?'

'No.'

Sir Arthur chuckled grimly, lighting his pipe. 'What a queer sort.'

And with that, to my utter disbelief, Houdini tossed the photograph into the fire.

'Poor Professor Crawford,' said the magician, shaking his head. 'He seems mad to me.'

CHAPTER
THIRTY EIGHT

Elizabeth and I argued bitterly as we drove to the Ormeau Road.

'I order you to do it, Elizabeth.'

'I will not, William. It's beastly. It's… unchristian.'

I laughed. 'Pious, virtuous, *Saint* Elizabeth sacrificed her Christianity years ago on the pagan alter she built to her blasted brother.'

'My brother was a good man. He would never do such a thing to an innocent girl.'

'You have no idea what he got up to. No idea at all. Perhaps I shall tell you one day. Very well then, my trusted assistant Rose can do it.' I gestured to the housemaid who was stuffed into the rear seat of the motorcar, glowering at me. The sullen thing had been sulking ever since I left her at the theatre in London. 'Speak now or for ever hold your peace. No? Nothing? There we are then, that settles it.'

We trundled over the bridge, climbing the shallow hill to the shop where an expectant crowd waited for us in the shade of a smart new awning. There was a large sign in the window, *Home to Kathleen Goligher, world-famous medium and the amazing Spirit Engineer*. Two of my books were on display beside a few choice newspaper articles, one penned by none other than my confidante, Sir Arthur Conan Doyle. A newspaperman stepped up. 'Spirit Engineer, sir! This way.' I smiled for his photograph, my thumb in my waistcoat pocket, hat tipped.

'It is a grand day for the spirits,' I said as the flash popped, sending a flock of young women into a frenzy of giggles.

Stoupe pushed merrily through the crowd, clapping his hands, skipping foot-to-foot. 'A momentous day indeed, William,' he cried. 'Back away, everybody, make room!'

'It is the greatest experiment of all,' I said, polishing the brass lamps of the motorcar, watched by a gang of some fifty fascinated admirers, the lot of them held back by Samuel, his lanky arms and legs barely contained in a smart, though already outgrown, suit. 'Bout ye' Prof,' he grinned in an incongruously deep voice. I nodded to him, flicking a shilling into his hand as Noah stepped out to greet us and, together, we stood there, three men of means, hands on our hips, admiring the smart, golden lettering on the shop window: *Morrison's Famous Plumbing Supplies*.

'A lovely job,' I said.

'Ay it is that nai, Prof,' said Noah, clapping my back. 'Yer wee boys from the Black Man Tech' did us well, so they did. Here, come you in, before ye get pulled to bits.'

I shouted at Rose to hurry along with the equipment then followed inside, signing a few autographs as I passed through the crowd. Just as I was about to enter the shop, a gloved hand gripped my arm. 'William.'

I sighed impatiently. 'Yes, Adelia.'

'William, they will not let me in.' She pushed to the front of the crowd, hat askew, eyes pleading.

Noah folded his arms. 'No entry without permission. Professor's instructions.'

Adelia gave me a distraught look. 'William, I have not seen you for weeks. I am still searching for my dear George. Will you deny a grieving widow some comfort?'

I sucked my teeth, removing my driving gloves. 'The only man denying you comfort is your supposedly dead husband. How many years were you married?'

'Thirty-six.'

'Never has a man so richly earned his place in Heaven. Why, he must be a saint.' I pulled my hand away, calling over my shoulder. 'I doubt you shall ever be reacquainted with him, Lady Carter; it seems perfectly plain to me, you are as dead to him as he is to you.'

The shop was a grand sight indeed, perfectly ordered, the walls lined with smart new shelving; a long, glass cabinet running the length of the far side with a brand-new till. The wiring had been installed under my careful instruction, the electric lights bouncing off sharp plasterwork with a clean, industrial brightness. We passed through to the back, mounting the freshly painted staircase to the first floor. Neatening myself, I brought Rose to my side, pushing Elizabeth away, then rapped on Kathleen's door. It opened revealing old Mrs Goligher, her pale eyes flicking about suspiciously.

'Good day, Mrs Goligher,' I said. 'It is I, the Spirit Engineer, returned from London. Is the subject ready? Come let me see her, it has been too long.'

The old woman grimaced. 'Ack, Professor, she's pure sick so she is. Here, why not do another day?'

'Certainly not,' I scoffed, sharing a suffering look with Noah. I pushed the door fully open with my foot, poking my head inside. Kathleen was sitting on the bed in her white cotton nightdress, hands clenched between her legs. 'Come, come, Kathleen,' I said. 'No delay, this is an important experiment if we are to satisfy my friends in London. There is already a man from the press outside, along with a number of well-wishers.' I pressed Rose into the room. 'My assistant Rose has kindly volunteered to carry out the inspection of your orifices and it shan't take a moment.' I pulled the door shut. 'Book sales are going very nicely, Noah. This experiment will form an important chapter in the next edition.'

He smiled. 'Happy days, Prof.'

'Will you leave us to it, as agreed?'

'Anything ye say.'

I shook his hand and took out my pencil, calling instructions through the door, checking off each of the medium's openings. Beyond the door, Kathleen gave a little squeal. I raised my eyebrows. Presently, after a few minutes and much persuasion, the door opened a crack.

'Finished, Rose?' I asked, trying to peek beyond her bulky shoulder. She opened the door the rest of the way, revealing

Kathleen, wrapped in a long shawl, eyes wet, long fingers hanging listlessly at her sides. 'Wonderful, give me those.' I pinched away her dirty undergarments, placing them into a sealed envelope for further investigation. 'Well done.' She gave me a watery smile. I returned to my notes as we climbed to the famous attic, checking my list. 'Tell me, Rose, what did you find?' She shook her head. 'Nothing in the mouth, no? Did you investigate all of the particular places I required you to search?'

'She did,' said Kathleen, her voice flat.

'Our Kathleen was empty and true, Professor,' said Rebecca, brightly. 'Sure, she is a good subject for your experiments.'

'Indeed, she is, Mrs Morrison. And to what depth did you check her front parts exactly, Rose?' I held my pencil, ready to scribble. 'You can show me with your hand.'

She placed her index finger at her first knuckle, then slid it back to her wrist.

Kathleen sniffed. 'As deep as she would go, Professor. Deeper than she needed to if you trusted me, sure.'

I wrote furiously, desperate to hide my excitement in the page. All the while, Elizabeth followed on, chanting to herself like a nun.

'Poor Kat,' said old Mrs Goligher. 'Sure, when did it come to such a thing?'

'Shut yer feckin' trap, ma,' hissed Rebecca, giving me an ingratiating smile. 'The professor is only doing his good works.'

'Quite right, quite right,' I said, looking around the attic. 'Remember, if we complete this experiment correctly, I shan't ask you to repeat it.'

I took Kathleen's hand in mine with a squeeze, leading her across the room to the fireplace, muttering in her ear. 'You must remember the Palm House, dear girl. It was you who begged me to prove your powers.' I smoothed her hair behind her ear, kissed her cheek. She looked around the room, arranging her sleeves.

'What have you done?' she asked.

The attic looked just like the inside of a freshly wrapped parcel, beaded over with strips of tape from the Post Office. Every corner, fitting, angle, crack, cupboard, floorboard, window frame, windowsill, windowpane, skirting board, picture hook and more, sealed to prevent entry by anything larger than a puff of smoke. There was, in fact, more tape than room. I had to laugh.

'Well, Seamus?' I said.

'Wonderful,' said Stoupe, chuckling. 'Let Houdini thumb his nose at this.'

I sniggered at the thought of it, inspecting the tape around the doorframe, before tying Kathleen's feet firmly to the chair. Rose had clipped the medium's toenails just as I had instructed, for I could see that they were bleeding. How meek she had grown, the flash of character displayed in earlier experiments a distant, extinguished memory. If Houdini had been there, I felt sure he would have been impressed by her naivety. I instructed Stoupe, Rebecca, old Mrs Goligher and Elizabeth to take their seats, then locked the door to the attic, placing the key in my shoe. I set to taping the door shut, taking great care to cover the opening above, below and around the sides so that no man nor woodlouse could pass through without ripping the paper. 'Help me please, Rose,' I said. 'You know what to do.'

Before they could utter a word, the Goligher women were tied up and gagged with strips of tight muslin just like the medium. Rebecca watched her sister and mother being trussed with a superior smirk, until it was her turn and suddenly all was pandemonium.

'William, dear,' said Elizabeth. 'What are you doing, they didn't agree to this?'

'Gags,' I said. 'Another necessary control. Please don't complain.'

'What has come over you? What happened to you in London?'

'Never you mind,' I said, wrapping a gag around her head and pulling it tight.

She stared at me, confounded, as we moved on to a startled Stoupe who wriggled and struggled, held down by the maid. Kathleen gazed up at me, trembling, her fingers and toes stretching against her bindings. She gnawed, shaking her head.

'My child, trust me,' I murmured. 'Tell me to stop and I shall, I promise, but remember, you will forever be cast in doubt and I shall be forced to find a new medium.' Her eyes welled up. I cocked my head. 'Kathleen, I *must* prove to the world, once and for all, that my spirits are real. Do you not see? Harry Houdini himself will tell everybody we're frauds otherwise and what then? I must save us from ridicule.' I wiggled my moustache as a tear rolled down her cheek. 'We must claim the respect we deserve. I'll never stand on a stage and be questioned like that again. Honestly, if you knew the embarrassment you caused me that day, you would never forgive yourself. Please.' I held her chin gently. 'Don't make me cross; it would be cruel.'

Kathleen closed her eyes, shivering. To my side, Elizabeth whimpered, rocking in her chair, while Rebecca gnawed on her gag, contorting her shoulders. Old Mrs Goligher choked, lips blue, milky eyes bulging. Even Stoupe seemed unnerved, the material cutting around his pudgy cheeks.

Their fright was quite unwarranted, for I had no cruelty in mind. What had I striven for, day after day, for more than five years? To prove Kathleen's honesty, of course. To crack open death, the great divide; to spill the reservoir of lost souls into this ignorant world. Perhaps then, wretched, repentant Houdini might beg to be reacquainted with his own mother through Kathleen's unmatched mediumship.

I settled Kathleen with a gentle hand on her shoulder, duly gagging her a second time with rope across the muslin, stretching her jaw wide with the strictness of the binding. I hurt my fingers, knotting so tightly that her tongue must have been pressed to the back of her throat. I leaned in. Whispered in her ear, 'I ask you again, Kathleen. Do you trust me?' She heaved, looking up, sweat dripping through her hair. She shook her head as I pulled the hood over her face.

CHAPTER
THIRTY NINE

I dusted off my knees, asking Rose with a cheery smile whether the door was secure. She nodded solemnly. I eyed her, pulling at my moustache. It felt somehow untidy to leave one of my sitters without a gag but then, the idea of muzzling a mute seemed gratuitous.

'Let us begin,' I said, speaking to the beyond. 'Operators, this will be difficult for you, perhaps.'

I closed the curtain. 'You have instructed us for many hours, illuminating this filthy attic with your knowledge. I thank you for your patience.'

I took my seat, placed my hand on the lantern. 'This will be the strangest circle you have ever known, friends. None of our sitters today can sing hymns, none can shift in their seats nor gasp, nor call out or ask questions. None but I, for they are all gagged. Please tell your fellow operators not to fear. The controls are designed to prove that your voices are true.' I thought of my dear photograph curling in the fire. 'Mother, please speak today and with your voice we shall silence the sceptics for ever. Then I will know you are real, once and for all.'

I smiled at each of them in turn, moving the glow of the lamp around like a phantom lighthouse. There was old Mrs Goligher straining at the material between her teeth; there, Rebecca struggling against her bonds, deep in her chair; there, Stoupe looking about the room chirruping like a canary; there, Elizabeth shivering in some kind of fearful trance; there, Kathleen lit most brightly of all, her head shifting beneath her hood. Now it was I, not she, shielded by the shadow of the tin panel.

'Mother,' I said from the darkness. 'I beg you to use every ounce of your spirit energy and every plasmic fibre to appear. I hope my voice alone will be strong enough to pass through to you, beyond the veil. Perhaps you might show us your plasmic cantilevers at last...' I looked at Kathleen's lap, submerged beneath mysterious folds. '...reveal them from where they originate.'

With that, I sang out in glad prayer, full-bellowed and alone until the very walls were ringing with my solitary song. At last, when I stopped, I felt the reassurance of some fine electric charge pass between my expectant fingers. 'Ah yes,' I muttered. The table jolted with a sledgehammer blow. I laughed at the thought of Houdini witnessing such a thing. Not one person in the room could have shifted in their chair to have moved the table; it was impossible for any creeping stooge to have slithered unseen into the sealed room. I inspected their feet as a second thump rang out.

'Are you there?' I called. Joy to my heart, a series of three quiet thumps came through from somewhere beside the far wall. I repeated my question, watching beneath the table under the cloak of dim light for the click of a tendon in Kathleen's feet. There was none. Quickly, I jotted my observations down in my book before instructing the table to levitate. Minutes passed. Undeterred, I sang another hymn before calling out in greater voice.

'Operators? Mother?' Still, it seemed as though the phenomena had vanished without explanation. I whined, looking at Rose for encouragement. 'Hello, is anyone there, please?' I said and the rest of the circle watched me with frightened eyes, twisting against their chairs.

'Mother, it will undo me if my experiment fails.' I looked imploringly at the silhouettes around the table, feeling suddenly alone. Rebecca groaned, staring at Kathleen who was chewing through the hood.

'Why will you not levitate the table?' I said. 'Please, lift the table, Mother.'

We sat still for an hour at least. As we waited, the air became hot and stale, Kathleen's breath growing laboured. The circle fidgeted as I attempted to concentrate. Then, just as I was about to call a halt to the proceedings, there was another low thump at the far side of the room as something pawed against my knee.

'At last,' I said, reaching between my legs to feel it, long and slippery, the now familiar, muscular limb. Cold, like reptilian skin with a wet residue. I followed it away from my knee with trembling fingertips, slithering deeper. Slowly, very carefully, keeping my fingers in contact with the cantilever, I lowered my head beneath the table, peering into the darkness. I had seen plasmic rods in Stoupe's photographs, of course; now I would confound the sceptics with my own eyes. The table shook with a bang. I saw my fellow sitters straighten, only Kathleen remaining still. It was impossible to see anything clearly in the gloom around our feet, yet, as my eyes adjusted, I could just make out a pale-white tendril reaching through the shadows between the girl's knees. It was a pulsing umbilical cord of white, fibrous material, caked in something faintly glistening, smeared and peppered here and there with dark patches. I gasped in wonder to see it. The limb had the look of something not entirely living. A bleached, wrinkled eel, with a bulbous head.

'Yes,' I whispered. 'Fascinating.' The rod pressed beneath the table, its glistening bulb against the underside of the wood, lifting the whole thing from the floor.

'Mother,' I whispered. 'Will you speak?'

William.

It was she! Oh dear, sweet providence. Weeks had passed with no sign of her since she had burnt at Houdini's hand. How typical of her generous nature to appear at such a crucial moment.

William, I did not find him.

'No?' I said. 'Poor, lost Robert.'

Just then, I imagined Houdini in the corner of the room, his eyes glowing above the fireplace. I reached across the table, pulling the hood from Kathleen's head to make sure the gag was still in place. She was straining, staring at me in the red lamplight, gulping on the material between her teeth.

'Ha-ha!' I cried, triumphantly.

You are hurting her, William.

'I know, Mother.'

You are cruel.

'Oh, for goodness' sakes, not you too.'

Cruel to Robert. He is gone now to the below.

'Then let him go,' I sneered. 'It is not important anymore, the man with the hanging bloody bones can have him. Do you hear that, Arthur? I care not! I'm glad you drowned, you selfish, reckless devil! I'm glad I got you on the bloody ship and I'm glad I sent that telegram.'

Elizabeth gave a long, plaintive cry then fainted, hanging forwards in her chair.

I shouted. 'Come, Mother, tell me now, where are you? How are you speaking to me?'

Turn around, William, and you shall see.

'Turn around?' My shoulders prickled with icy sweat, the hairs on the back of my neck tingling. 'What shall I see?' Slowly, I moved my eyes towards the attic door, hardly knowing what to expect.

Rose.

She sat in her chair, deep in shadow. Our eyes met in the red lamplight. Her jaw... fell open.

Hello, William.

I froze, peering through the darkness. No, it was impossible. It could not be. Mesmerised by the gaping hole of the girl's mouth, I turned the ruby lamp onto her face. 'Rose?' I whispered. 'Rose, is it you speaking? Has it been you all along?'

My William. My dear little boy. It was not your fault.

I moved closer. The voice seemed to rise from Rose's gullet, quite without troubling her tongue, which sat in her teeth like a dead clam. As the voice came, her eyes stared back at mine, her head shaking.

The Elfin knight stands on yon hill,
Blow, blow, blow winds, blow.
Blowing his horn, so strong and still,
Dead so long but living today.

'Yes,' I whispered, putting my face right up to her mouth, touching her throat to feel the muscles twitching around her broken chords. 'Yes, Mother, sing on.'

The Elfin knight stands on yon hill,
Blow, blow, blow winds, blow.
Blowing his horn, so strong and still,
A mute is singing my song today.

'Do you hear that?' I turned to the circle as they watched me fearfully, Rebecca swinging herself with such aggression, she crashed to the floor. Stoupe was nodding vigorously while Elizabeth groaned, waking from her stupor just in time to bear witness to my breakthrough.

'The spirit is playing Rose like a violin!' I said. 'Do you see, Elizabeth? Oh, Houdini, you shall hear of this and Beadnell too, you fools!' I ran to the window to pull the curtain back, banging on the glass to get the attention of the crowd below. 'I have proved it at last!' I called, waving. 'Behold, the Spirit Engineer has made his greatest discovery yet!'

I dashed back to Rose. 'Speak again, woman, I'll look down your throat.' But she pushed me away, standing against the wall, her hands outstretched to stop me coming near.

'Damn you, then,' I growled, setting my hungry fingers to the tape around the door to make sure it was undisturbed. Yes, yes. I ripped it open, peering down the empty stairs to the landing below with a triumphant cheer before spinning to the floor, tugging underneath the table at the string around their feet. All tied. Their wrists? All tied, by Christ. 'Have that, Houdini, you bloody halfwit.' I sprang to my feet, yanking at Stoupe's gag.

'Did you see, Seamus?' I said, scratching my hair from my eyes. 'The levitation and the voice coming through Rose?'

'I saw,' he said, holding his hands to his face. 'I thought you told me your housemaid was a mute?'

'She is!' I exclaimed, pacing about the attic, hands on my hips, laughing. 'Let Beadnell question that.' I yanked Elizabeth's gag to her chin. 'Wake up, woman, your husband has done it again.' I turned to Rose. 'Did you feel the spirit voice on your tongue?' The maid gawped at me, chewing the air like a cow. I marched over, gripped her by the face and stuck my fingers into her mouth, jabbing at her tonsils as she heaved and gagged. 'Your throat is hot. Piping hot! It must be some sort of plasmic friction.' I wiped my hand and returned to the window to see a swelling crowd below, constables moving people away from the road, Noah and Samuel hawking charms to the onlookers. I beckoned the newspaperman up, scribbling my findings down, ordering Rose to set my brave sitters free.

Rebecca screamed: 'Katie, ye mad feckin bastard. She's choked!' She flew to Kathleen, pulling the hood away, wrenching at the rope and gag. The medium's hair was pasted to her face, her neck veined blue, grey eyes rolling, lips swollen and bitten, blood on her teeth. She came-to with an almighty gasp, gripping her throat, bewildered.

'Kathleen,' I said. 'What a powerful young woman you are.'

Presently, the newspaperman entered, looking around the room.

'Saints alive,' he said, beaming at the overturned chairs, the women in disarray. 'What do we have here?'

'History,' I said. 'That's what you have. History.'

I stood behind Kathleen, my hands firmly on her quivering shoulders. 'Come,' I said. 'Let the man take your picture. I'm still here, you're quite safe.'

CHAPTER FORTY

Principal Forth sat behind his desk, looking me over with a faint squint. He lit a cigarette, scratching his head.

'Professor, I hear you are continuing with your supernatural investigations?'

'They're going very well,' I answered, picking at my thumbs.

'So I have read.' He pulled a copy of the *Belfast Telegraph* from his drawer, slapping it on the desk between us. I smiled, looking down at a picture of myself, standing proudly above Kathleen.

'A very complimentary article,' I said. 'Republished in Chicago, so my editor tells me.'

'Is that so?'

The principal placed a book on top of the newspaper and I flushed to see that it was one of my own.

'Ah, now,' I said. 'I would have given you a copy, Principal Forth. There was no need to buy one.'

'I did not buy one,' said the principal. 'I confiscated it.'

'Confiscated it? From whom?'

He bristled his moustache. 'Never you mind,' he said, leaning across the desk to pour me a glass of whisky. 'I must ask you to be entirely honest with me, Crawford. Man-to-man. Our conversation will not leave this office.'

I gave a little yawn, waving away his offer of a drink. 'Dulls the mind,' I said, lighting my pipe.

'I have read this book and looked at your photographs. I have until now turned a blind eye to your experiments. I do my best to ignore the extracurricular activities of my staff.'

'Very wise.'

He smiled at me sadly. 'Crawford, with all the world gone mad, I had hoped you were a plain, dependable sort. I never guessed you would turn into...' He held up my book. '...this.'

'This?' I asked.

'We have all heard about your exploits with the famous Houdini. You are the talk of the Institute.'

'Hardly exploits,' I chuckled. 'I met the man briefly with my dear friend, Sir Arthur Conan Doyle, and corrected him on a few matters, that's all. In truth, I couldn't have spoken to him for very much longer, he was so slow.' I curled my lip. 'Terrible sceptic.' I pulled a sliver of fingernail from my thumb, flicked it to the floor. 'Another dull type, like you and old Fforde.'

The principal shifted uneasily. 'Professor Fforde raised some concerns with me following a séance he attended at your home. I believe it was a week before he died, may the old soldier rest in peace. And then poor Blithe, of course.'

'Yes, poor Blithe.'

'They were both very fond of you, Crawford. I don't think you appreciated that. Deeply concerned for you too. As am I.'

I leaned forwards, jabbing the desk. 'Fforde was against my experiments from the start.'

'He was against you making a fool of yourself. He told me you were hearing voices.'

'I do hear voices, thank goodness. I shouldn't be much of a Spirit Engineer if I didn't.'

'The voices of your late mother and son?'

'Yes, as it happens.'

The principal took up my book, thumbing to a page.

'At nearly all séances...' he read aloud, an eyebrow raised. 'The noise accompanying the birth pangs of the plasma is distinctly audible. With thin silk stockings, the friction of plasma on the threads as it disengages itself is unmistakable.' He wiggled his moustache. I puffed away, muttering the all-too-familiar words to myself as he continued. 'There is strong evidence of decrease in volume of the fleshy parts of the medium's body. Especially from the waist downward...'

'Master, I am quite aware of my own book.'

The principal removed his spectacles and looked at me directly. 'Fleshy parts?' he said.

I smiled indulgently. 'You are a sceptic, which I accept.'

The principal jabbed at the book. 'You are still young, Professor. A respected doctor of science at a world-leading institute. You had a gloriously sensible future ahead of you. Why, I had your name beside mine at last year's gala once that fine textbook of yours was published. All you had to do was keep your head.'

'The high table? Did you?'

'Yes, Crawford. You were going to replace that absurd Carter woman. Then, the charade at Lismarra House with those fool shopkeepers, Robinson and Cleaver. You were once a bright hope. Why did you set a match to it with all this nonsense?' He threw my book across the table. 'I hear you make a pretty penny, so I suppose I give you credit for that. Never let it be said Principal Forth is anti-capitalist but still, I find myself hoping it isn't too late for you. I am asking you now, this very second, to repent on this foolishness immediately and come clean. Forget the ghosts and tell the world it has all been, I don't know, a deliberate hoax or something, designed to test the credulity of the average working man.'

'A hoax?'

'A necessary evil, a tawdry social experiment; call it what you will but you must put an end to it. I say so as your employer but also as your mentor and friend.'

I stood, brushing my trousers. 'I'm afraid you've quite misunderstood the situation. I am an honest man and it is most certainly not a deception. You ask me what profit I make from this?' I held up my book. 'The profit cannot be measured in pounds and pence. This book, my work, will change the very meaning of life and death. It will revolutionise the human existence for the rest of time.' I sniffed. 'Conan Doyle says so himself.'

The principal rubbed his temples. 'Does he now?' He gave an ironic chuckle.

'He is the most celebrated writer of our time,' I said.

'The perfect qualification for an idiot.'

I jabbed my finger at him in outrage. 'The spirits are real and if you *truly* have read my experiments, you cannot doubt it.' I sat back. 'Come to a séance and you'll see.'

He laughed bitterly. 'I most certainly will not. Oh Lord, did I ever imagine I would suffer such madness after the War? I thought I had seen the very depth of mankind, yet here I am.' He reached back to his drawer, then paused. 'This is your final chance, Professor. Your very last chance to tell the truth. Do you or do you not believe in your ghosts?'

'More than any man alive,' I said, folding my arms.

'I see I have no choice. Answer me this: you have seen your mother in a photograph, have you not?'

'I have,' I said, puzzled.

The principal placed an object between us beside the newspaper. I looked at it with a nervous laugh, not knowing what to make of it. 'And what is this?' I demanded. 'A death mask from the trenches, perhaps?'

He gave a grim smile. 'Come, Crawford. Do you not recognise your own mother?'

I glanced at the mask. 'My mother?' I said, smile fading. I thought of her sweet face in my portrait. The object on the desk was oval, white and about the size of a dinner plate. I picked it up, turned it over and shivered. There were two eyes, painted crudely in smudges across its face, the clumsy shape of a nose and beneath it, the unsteady line of a mouth, drawn hurriedly in red chalk. There were tiny pinholes running across its scalp, a few strands of black cotton knotted to the edges.

'If you truly believed, then I am very sorry.' The principal arched his fingers, staring at the mask. 'I spoke with Professor Stoupe this morning and confronted him about his photographs. He confessed all, the queer duck, and seemed in some distress. Something about a recent meeting of yours on the Ormeau Road?' He rubbed his eyes, shaking his head. 'I ask you, Professor, who can answer for the hearts of men?'

I looked up at him, then back at the mask. I could not find the words to speak, for the meaning of the object was every bit as impossible as it was plain. The principal sighed and rapped his knuckles on his desk three times.

'Come in, Stoupe.'

I turned to see my friend, peeping around the door. He stepped inside, eyes fixed to the floor.

'Be calm, please,' said the principal. 'Now, Stoupe, I believe you owe the professor an explanation.'

The funny little man looked at me sheepishly, fiddling with his jacket. I touched the mask and turned it face down. 'Seamus? What is it?'

Stoupe shrugged. 'A little spoof, William,' he said. 'Just for fun, a little flimflam, that's all, but everything got so carried away. You came to my room for a portrait, do you remember? You were grieving so terribly for your boy and you were so sad. Then you were a little sharp with me, so I...'

'So you what, Stoupe?'

'Call me Seamus, please. One of my students had left a mask in our costume box so, when I rifled through the cupboard, well...' He looked at me, his eyes brimming. 'William, you must remember how obnoxious you were about the spirits not being real. I love you dearly but when you get an idea into your head, you become quite insufferable. You called me a fool for believing in them, teasing me and then, just as I was about to take a picture of my handsome friend, you called me fat.'

My throat was dry. I felt a dark chill running through me. I could not bear to look at him. 'You took a photograph of me with a mask above my head, then made me believe it was my own dead mother.'

'I said no such thing!' he protested. '*You* recognised her.' He stepped towards me. 'I hardly expected you to believe it at the time and I wasn't going to show it to you so I hid it away for weeks, ashamed of myself. Then you found your mother anyway, through the Goligher girl, and I thought perhaps it was a sign.'

'A sign, for goodness' sakes,' said the principal. 'A sign.'

'Yes, a sign, Master,' said Stoupe, fiddling with his tie like a schoolboy. 'I thought maybe the spirits had made me take the photograph and, besides, what harm could it do?'

The principal waved his hand in exasperation. So, Houdini had been right about the photograph after all. My treasured portrait, carried by my heart for a thousand joyful moments, had been nothing but a portrait of a fool and a tawdry mask.

'Dear friend,' said Stoupe, reaching for my hand.

'You are not my friend,' I snapped, stepping away from the table. I pushed past him, striding from the office, mounting the grand staircase two-by-two. I could hear them calling after me as I reached the third floor, sprinting along to the very end of the corridor, the bright windows flashing past me, my feet smacking hard on the polished floor. I skidded to the end, slamming into the wall, throwing open the door to the photography studio before leaping to the dark room, lit as blood red as any confounded attic.

There were photographic plates strewn everywhere, developed images piled high on the bench. I scrabbled through them, swiping discarded faces to the floor, but could not find her. And then I remembered where the lying toad had kept his most precious pictures and dashed out to his desk, wrenching open the drawer. There was a bundle of photographs of naked young men posing like ancient Olympians, beneath them a pile of telegrams. I scattered them over the desk, searching deeper. Ha. The familiar image of Kathleen in her chair, smiling as white tendrils snaked between her feet across the floor, the plasma spaced as I had never seen it before. I frowned and picked out some more. There, the picture of Kathleen from below with white cantilevers growing from her ear, her mouth, her middle, her feet. She had her eyes crossed like a clown, her face blurred, laughing. I peered closer, retching to see tendrils attached to nothing, laying around her ankles like... like cheesecloth. As I searched, bile rising in my throat, there were more, more, more damning pictures, each one of them a nail driven into my head. And then, oh cursed crypt of a drawer, at its very bottom lay a copy of my dear, forgotten portrait with Mother at my back. Clearer than mine had been. No, it was not my mother at all but the same clumsy mask from the principal's desk.

CHAPTER FORTY ONE

I sat in the laboratory on the posing chair, fingering the false portrait. For weeks, I had dreamed of holding my mother in my hands again, but now, looking down at the obvious dupe, I was pleased to think of Houdini tossing it into the fire, for – had I laid eyes on it – I would have felt greater agony than any man had ever endured. I looked at the principal's copy of my book, turning it over. I knew every word by heart and, oh, how my heart ached then to think of the pages filled with experiment after experiment. Were they all a sham? I found one of my favourite early diagrams. A plasmic rod lifting a table. I tore the page away before pressing it, finger by thumb into my mouth, chewing it into a mâché before dribbling it onto the floor.

I had spent more hours than I could recall over the years calculating weight distributions, angles of levitation, transference of supernatural forces. I thought of Houdini and the sceptic Beadnell. I stared once more at the photograph. Why had Stoupe lied? Because I had been unkind to him? It was the character of malice one might expect from a spurned lover, not a colleague or a friend. No, he had enjoyed the fame and the money, slipping into the side of my newspaper photographs, selling his amateurish paintings to ghost fanciers, attending fancy dinner parties. He had taken to calling himself the Spirit Photographer. Oh yes! I had heard him do so before I left for London. The dirty little magpie.

I heard a distant call, realising there was barely a minute before they appeared at the laboratory door. I rushed to the darkroom where I found Stoupe's shelf above the long sink, filled with little bottles. My eyes rested on one of them in particular. It was small, with black glass, the label bearing the unmistakable stamp of a skull and crossed bones.

Potassium Cyanide

I gnashed my teeth, taking the bottle down, sensing death through the brittle glass. I switched the darkroom lights on, the chorus of gloomy faces hanging from the ceiling blanched by the honesty of the light. Yes, the *honesty* of the light. I had an idea. That is how to catch them.

Laughing at the thought of it, I tapped the granules from the bottle into a square of paper before folding it into triangles and popping it into my jacket. Whether it was for me alone or for all of us, my ultimate resolve demanded sacrifice. It was such a dastardly, destructive thing, it simply had to be done but, then, could I master my own emotions long enough to see it through? I simply *had* to know, for how else would I retrieve my dignity?

Footsteps approached from the corridor. Drying my eyes on my cuffs, I smoothed my face out like clay, tucked in my shirt, flattened my hair, then stepped casually into the corridor, as sanguine as a gentleman on a Sunday stroll. Outside, Stoupe and the principal were running towards me holding out their hands. They stopped in their tracks.

'William?' said Stoupe. 'Are you calm?'

'Oh, hello there, Seamus,' I said. 'I was just looking for the posing stand from our portrait. The one you used to keep me still. I simply had to see how you managed to play your little trick on me.'

Stoupe pursed his lips, his eyes flitting around the corridor. 'You are not angry at your silly Seamus?' he asked.

'Angry?' I laughed. 'Whyever would I be angry? No, no, not a bit.' I winked at the principal. 'He was very naughty, was he not, Master Forth?'

'He... he was, Crawford. Very cruel. And he will be reprimanded for it, I assure you of that.'

'Yes,' said Stoupe, edging towards me. 'I deserve it.'

I swung my arms carelessly, turning to the window, looking across to the other side of the courtyard. 'I am perfectly calm; you mustn't worry about me.' My mind moved to the plan I had made. I breathed deeply, swallowing bile and raised my eyebrows. 'Principal Forth, I hope you will accept my resignation.'

The principal frowned. 'Crawford, that may not be necessary. Take some time away, my boy. You remain a member of staff here until you are well again.'

'Ah,' I said, pulling out my pipe, nodding as I packed it with tobacco. 'And will I sit at the high table, would you say?'

The principal stumbled. 'The high...? Ah, well... er... yes, perhaps next year, Crawford. We shall have to see. Difficult things these galas, you know.'

I strode towards him as he leaned away. 'Thank you for your good faith in me, Principal Forth, I am very grateful to you.'

Amidst so much grief, I can say that I meant it. There is a sense of calm, humble resignation to one's own demolition. A nobility to the conquered. I smiled, realising it was the first time I'd felt comfortable looking him in the eye. I nodded and he nodded back. Such was our goodbye. I turned away, stepping from the long corridor to the side stairs, skipping down to the front of the building.

My mind wandered to that night, years earlier, when Fforde had helped me to move the statues. The old man had been kind to me, I realised, and I had been impatient with him. Shaking my head, I walked to the entrance hall, enjoying the familiar smell of oil, stone and dust. The boiler thrummed far below as I said a quiet goodbye to my laboratory. To my dear Institute. I should never see it again. To have so much hope pressed into the stone and brick of a place. To have one's own fleeting existence, echoing about the high walls. I remembered waiting there for my interview with the principal as a young man. I thought of Blithe striding in, teeth flashing, telling jokes. I scanned the corridor leading down to the Central Hall. Elizabeth, dozing on my shoulder after the gala. I smiled as each little scene played out in my mind. In reality, *that* is what it means to be haunted. Ghosts are mere memories of lives passed, granted a reassuring afterlife, manifested by the pleading, grasping, fearful imagination of our own mortality. I moved to the doors and pressed them open as footsteps rang out above my head. I stopped, head bowed.

'William, please!' Stoupe called down from the balcony. 'You're frightening us, turn around so I can see your face. Will you ever forgive your poor, misguided Seamus? I am so sorry.'

I could not turn, for if he had seen my face in that moment, he'd have had a good reason to be frightened. I steadied my voice, kind and gentle as a nurse. 'Dearest Stoupe,' I said. 'Please don't say a word to anybody, we must keep your *spoof* to ourselves.'

'As you wish, William. Anything.'

'Will you come to the Ormeau Road tomorrow afternoon?'

'The Ormeau Road?' said Stoupe. 'Another séance? Another experiment?'

'Indeed,' I said. 'I expect this one to be most... illuminating.'

CHAPTER FORTY TWO

I looked at them in turn, tied to their chairs. Oh, the noxious thrill of it all; the wild, sickening, violent possibility of what was to come. They had agreed to another séance, quite voluntarily, each for their own selfish reasons. Remorseful Stoupe, Lonely Adelia, Grieving Elizabeth and The Grasping Golighers.

Unusually, Kathleen had struggled as her ankles were tied, but she had calmed down quickly enough with a dose of whisky poured from my pocket flask through her clenched teeth and some gentle shushing. I stroked her hair, patted her head, sang a little tune to her ear as her shoulders hardened to my touch. I gagged her and concealed her face beneath the hood, going through the usual motions before closing the curtain to the fading day, taking my seat in the darkness behind the ruby lamp.

'Dear operators,' I said. 'Thank you for joining us. You have given me so many hours. I am most sincerely thankful.' I scratched my cheek. 'I understand now how exhausting it must have been for you all.' I placed my pipe on the table. 'You will be sorry, I think, to know that this will be our final experiment.'

Rebecca and Elizabeth exchanged nervous glances, Kathleen turning to me with a muffled, inaudible question. I made some final notes, the pages of my book swimming before my eyes.

'Yes, the last séance for us all,' I said. 'Almost six years it has taken to reach this point. I have carried out every experiment possible to my imagination and have come to the unavoidable conclusion that you, Kathleen, are whiter than white, just as Conan Doyle says.' I hoped it was true; that Stoupe was the only imposter in the group; that the spirits were real and the only rogue to be exposed by my final experiment would be suspicious, paranoid William Jackson Crawford. I had lost the photographs, but I might still keep my spirits. 'How comforting it has been to find my dear mother in the afterlife,' I said. 'And poor little Robert of course, wherever he may be.'

I stepped to the fireplace where lengths of black silk lay smoothed over the mantel. I snapped them between my fists. 'To step so close to the veil, to press my ear to the celestial membrane and eavesdrop on the afterlife. I have received more letters this week from grieving parents, you know. Some of the stories have been quite moving, in fact. In grief we are able to see the wrongs we have done to the dead. It is an amusing thing.' I turned to the circle, the black ribbons dangling to the floor. 'We fear the dead when, really, we ought to be *far* more afraid of the living, don't you think?'

I stepped to Stoupe's side and peered down at him. He looked up, helpless as a babe, hands bound to his chair, chubby little legs kicking against their bonds, as I gagged him. The rest of them might yet be exonerated, but he... he had already admitted his crimes. A condemned man awaiting his execution, knowing all too late that he was finished. He cried as I shushed him, tying a blindfold across his eyes. Old Mrs Goligher shook her head as I gagged and blindfolded her with a double knot. Was she blind or were those eyes of hers another trick? Glass lenses perhaps, or undeclared peepholes through the cataracts. Adelia came next.

'William, dear,' she said. 'Dear, clever William. I have always held you in such a high regard. Must I be blindfolded? It hardly seems appropriate.' I tugged her gag back to her teeth before slipping the blindfold over her eyes, stepping back to enjoy the sight of the speechless, sightless woman.

'On the contrary, Aunt Adelia,' I said. 'It is the most appropriate thing I have ever seen.'

Rebecca took her trussing-up with typical insolence, knocking the legs of her chair against the floor. Let them all protest, there was nothing they could do. If they were innocent, they would be free. If not... well then. I moved around the circle.

'What experiment is this, William?' asked Elizabeth. 'The girls begged me not to come.'

'They needn't have worried, Elizabeth. They know their father.'

'I'm not so sure they do.'

'Hush now. Stay still.'

'Praise God, I am not alone in my fight against fear; I have the Holy Spirit and the angels.'

'Angels,' I said. 'Yes.'

She accepted her blindfold and gag with all the dignity of a condemned queen. Trembling, she took a peck from my lips and shuddered. 'There, there, darling,' I said, stroking her arm. 'Arthur will be pleased to see you soon. Perhaps we shall search for Robert together, you and I.'

With that, the room banged and mumbled to the noise of my struggling friends, wrenching their hands and legs, calling through their gags for help. There was nobody to hear them; I had paid Noah well enough for that. I gave trusty Rose a kindly smile. She was sitting at the door, watching me with an open mouth. I stepped over and wrapped the blindfold around her skull, pulling it tightly.

Job done, I returned to my seat, observing them as I repacked my pipe. 'My very last experiment will prove once and for all that the phenomena we have witnessed are real. We must, all of us, hope for a happy conclusion.' I waved my hand in front of Kathleen's hood and looked at the ruby lamp, the bat's-wing flame dancing behind the lambent glass.

The medium turned her head. It was a queer thing, for though she was hidden beneath layers of black material, she seemed charged with a greater character than ever before. Spooked by the possibility that she could still see me, I pulled my feet from my shoes and padded silently to her side. Her head did not turn as I approached. What a thrill, for never had I engineered such an absolute condition of power. I slid closer to her, so near our heads were almost touching. Could she sense me at all? No. I inhaled her scent, caressed the air around her body. She was utterly motionless, the only visible movement the fluttering pulse of a vein in her left hand.

Slowly, I crept back to my seat, the wooden chair squeaking as I rested my full weight into it. Kathleen's head twitched. At last, I was content to begin.

'Very good,' I said, rolling up my sleeves. 'I believe we are ready. Let the truth shine brightly through the darkness.' I began a hymn, my high voice rolling with the melody, tears filling my eyes. How desperately my exhausted, ringing heart hoped to prove Houdini wrong at this, the very last turn. Overcome, I sang a second hymn, then a third, hanging at the final note for as long as I could, afraid to finish for there was nothing but a reckoning ahead of us; nothing but the untold glory or infinite misery of the truth. At last, the song died in my throat and I shut my eyes, sucking in one long, shaking breath. We held hands.

We waited.

No sound.

No spirit breath.

No scraping foot.

No voice.

I had been there before. The spirits had often grown timid at the sight of their precious medium in peril. I looked at Rose, her lips moving to some mute incantation. The moment had arrived; it had all come to this. I peered around the murky attic, imagining beneath us, not Belfast, not a city at all, but the cavernous throat of a vast beast, waiting to swallow me down to oblivion or cry me out to salvation. To celebrate or condemn a man asking for nothing more than the truth.

'Ladies and gentlemen, I shall now turn out the light. We shall be in complete and utter darkness.' I watched their stupid heads as I reached out to the lamp and then, to the hissing and popping of the red flame, turned it *up* until the room glowed, a brilliant pink.

This time, there were no deceptive shadows, no unseen corners, no invisible spaces. The attic was filled with a scorching, inescapable light, bleached as a mortuary and, whether they were a cast of angels or villains, I was ready to begin my dissection.

CHAPTER
FORTY THREE

A brightly lit room, though only I knew it. As far as they were concerned, we were cloaked in complete darkness. Each sitter, bound and blindfolded and all but Rose gagged. I tittered to myself, sliding my eyes around the room for the first sign of trickery.

'Friends,' I sang out, voice bouncing against the gable ceiling. 'Are you there?'

I looked beneath the table to monitor people's feet, though no one moved. I righted myself with an impatient sigh, inspecting the attic with beady eyes, when I heard a faint knocking sound.

Knock. Knock. Knock.

Kathleen shifted and, instantly, I snapped my eyes to her. Stoupe jolted in his seat, his head turning about, corrupt little fingers wriggling. Elizabeth was rigid, tears soaking through her blindfold while Adelia, old Mrs Goligher and Rebecca leaned out as far as they could from their chairs, straining their ears. I looked beneath the table again, sensing something shift around our legs.

'Hello spirits?' I said, careful to maintain my trick. 'Who goes there, we cannot see you in the darkness.'

Knock. Knock. Knock.

I watched people's boots, but there was no clicking heel; no twitching muscle. With the light turned so brightly for the first time, I was more certain than ever that the sound was somehow beyond the attic. I stopped still, closing my eyes in hope. Even at such a late stage, I would give anything to believe again.

'Mother,' I whispered. 'Are you there?'

There came a faint scratching sound from the skirting board at the far side of the room. Stoupe and Elizabeth, who were closest, twisted while I, lifting high in my seat, stared at the perfectly illuminated wall, mesmerised by the undeniable emptiness of the space.

'Robert, my dear, is it you, perhaps? Don't be afraid.'

Knock.

'No? Not Robert? Mother, then it must be you.'

Knock.

'Not Mother. Then who?'

I felt Kathleen's fingers turn in my grip. The smell of the sea filled the air.

William.

My chest hardened. How odd it was to hear the voice in the light.

'Yes, Arthur,' I said, looking over my shoulder at Rose, to see her mouth hanging open still.

William, are you ready?

The words came from her, I had no doubt, yet I could see in the clear light that her lips and tongue were innocent of the sound. The spirit voice laughed at me, a dry, hacking croak.

What is this? What game are you playing?

I groaned inwardly, creeping from my chair to peer inside Rose's mouth as the spirit spoke.

You are such a fool, William Jackson Coward!

'Don't betray me, Arthur,' I pleaded under my breath. 'Did you not beg me in the phonograph to prove you true?'

Knock.

My heart stopped as I turned.

In the far corner of the room, behind Stoupe and Elizabeth, there was a disturbance in the air. I strained my eyes. Three feet in height it was, a space amidst the air untroubled by floating dust. A sort of gap in the atmosphere as though something was occupying the corner with an unearthly energy. I looked closer, holding my breath. Yes. Unmistakably, a figure had appeared in the form of a little boy.

Farfur? Is that you?

'Robert.' I dared not move, lest I scare him away. 'My boy, I see you,' I said, holding out my hand. Elizabeth gave a plaintive cry as she turned blindly, wrenching her fingers against the string to feel for her son. Would he touch the skin of her hand? I moved back to the table, yet no sooner had I done so than the notion of the child dropped through the floorboards, motes of dust drifting freely where the boy had been standing. I looked at Rose to see her mouth closed. Shaking my head, I prayed for forgiveness. I had been caught playing a dastardly trick on the spirits. I would be punished for it. Stoupe was a rogue, we all knew that, but how could I have ever doubted Kathleen?

'Forgive me, Kathleen,' I said, taking hold of her dry hand. 'I see it all now, quite clearly.'

And so I did. The cruelty of men, our jealousy, our suspicion, our craftiness in deceitful scheming. I looked up as the sound of faint singing approached from the ceiling.

'Mother?'

The Elfin knight stands on yon hill,
Blow, blow, blow winds, blow
Blowing his horn, so loud until.

I traced my eyes across the walls. 'Mother, please,' I said, checking Rose's face as the voice grew up from her belly, jumping and sticking in her throat.

The wind has blawin has blawin has blawin has blawin
has blawin
My boy, my sorry child

A clumsy noise came from the corner of the room. I looked across to where Robert had been, expecting to see the body of a white lady rising from the floor, but there was nothing there. Turning once more to Rose, I caught her shifting blindly in her chair, her lips still moving to the spirit voice as it sang, here matching the shape of a word, there mouthing something else altogether.

The Elfin knight stands on yon hill,
Blow, blow, blow winds, blow
Blowing his horn, so loud and gay.
The wind has blawin his mind astray

'Who?' I asked, tugging at my hair. 'Mother, whose mind is astray?'

You allowed me to die, William. You left my baby. She needed you. Robert is lost in the sea, with the hanging bones. I saw him go down. We will never find him.

Knock.

Rose croaked, her fingers outstretched.

Farfur?

I tore away her blindfold and she squinted in the light, surprised by the brightness of the room.

I hushed her. 'They're using your voice again, Rose, can you hear them?

She nodded, her hands squirming beneath their bonds, fingers outstretched as if begging me to follow her gaze. I turned my eye to catch a movement in the fireplace. I blinked, then looked again. There was something shifting in the grate. I stared in utter disbelief for there, where the coals ought to have been, was the torso and head of a little boy, his ashen face turned up to the flue. I recoiled, holding my fingers to my face. 'Spirit!' I said. 'Demon!'

The child dabbed at the ash before stroking grime through his curly black hair. I glanced at Kathleen as her hand fell from her chair like the stuffed limb of a doll, a second set of fingers sprouting through the front of her blouse as though growing like a tendril from her heart.

'Mother?' I muttered. 'Mother, is that you? Is this how you appear?'

Ever-so-slowly, the fingers reached through the buttons of her blouse, pointing towards the fireplace, and the boy in the grate lifted his face and blinked.

It was Samuel Morrison. I recognised him instantly. His unmistakable little face was covered all over in black ash like a chimney sweep. No sooner had our eyes met than he gawped a bright-pink mouth before disappearing back through the fireplace in a puff of ash.

I stood, in shock, unable to process what I had seen. Kathleen shifted, the arm in her chest searching, pinching, clutching at the air. The medium's head turned slowly beneath the hood. A flurry of impatient nods, as if calling someone on. I looked at her right arm, hanging dead at her side, fingertips hard against the floorboards. A crude rubber cast of a limb, its solid fingers painted peach.

There we are then, William. The Spirit Engineer is finished, do you see? Every bit as false as that dummy hand. The game is up at last.

The image came to my mind of the principal, Houdini, Fforde, Beadnell, all shaking their heads in disbelief. A chorus of newspapermen merrily typing up my farcical story as pages spread like storm clouds across the globe. I saw Adelia crowing, Elizabeth and the girls ashamed. Robert beneath the ground, neglected, putrid, alone. My own anonymous grave in some forgotten cemetery, ignominy etched into an invisible stone.

Now my path was clear. There was nothing to lose.

Turning to Rose, I put my finger to my lips then crept to the fireplace, taking care not to give myself away. I crouched down to inspect the hidden panel behind the grate, quite ingeniously masked to the casual eye, camouflaged with chunks of coal and dusted with ash. I pressed my finger against the panel, swinging it inwards on a silent spring. Peeping through, I could see the floorboards of a triangular space, barely the size of a small closet. It was the corner of the attic, sectioned off by a false chimneybreast made of thin board. I visualised the outside of the building. The chimney pot. It was directly above the false fireplace, yet I had seen it smoking, had I not? I smiled ruefully, remembering Churchill's phantom battleships at the yard, fires hidden inside false funnels to fool the Hun. Oh, Noah, how I underestimated you. I poked my head through, heaving at a sudden, all-too-familiar smell. It was an Aladdin's cave of wicker balls, masks, sheets, canes, bells and trumpets. A veritable museum of my own foolishness, every confounded object damning in its familiarity. Three identical séance tables were stacked up against the wall, the infamous bell hung on a wire above an applause of false hands. I saw bolts of black material, twine hung from hooks. A spider the size of a dinner plate... not a spider at all, but a mouldering crab painted black, rotten meat oozing from its joints. And there, sandpaper, a saw and lengths of doweling chopped to pieces. A hole had been cut into the middle of the floor, the uppermost rungs of a ladder poking through the gap. I remembered my first visit to the shop, running from Noah to the room directly below. I had *seen* the blasted ladder.

With that my heart fully broke. 'Robert,' I whispered. 'Mother. It was never you.'

Samuel Goligher's legs flashed in front of me, his bare feet jumping to the ladder. He stood on the top rungs, leering as he tugged a curly wig from his head. He was in his underwear, grimy legs wrapped in grey stockings smeared with grease. I shuddered, imagining the touch of his skin. Reptilian. So, this was my plasmic cantilever? Every diagram in every book, nothing but a slippery little boy with uncut toenails.

Just then, I remembered the cyanide in my pocket and considered emptying the whole packet into my mouth right then and there, crunching the bitter crystals like sugar. I would be dead in less than a minute. No. Too soon. Why should these charlatans live?

I pulled my head back into the attic to see Rose rapping her knuckles on the arm of her chair, straining her mute face towards Kathleen. I watched as the medium moved slowly, deftly tilting back, the loops of string around her ankles passing under the legs of her chair, the strut which ought to have confounded her, springing out on a hidden hinge. Spellbound, I watched as she lifted her feet through the loops before placing them, fast against the inside of the table just as Houdini had demonstrated. Still, her fingers were reaching towards the fireplace, gesturing impatiently.

I turned back to the hatch just in time to catch sight of the boy's head dropping down through the hole. I pulled a stick into the attic as the trap door slammed shut behind me with a loud bang. Kathleen froze, her hood turning sightlessly as I quickly pressed the stick to her outstretched fingers. She gripped it with a nod, swinging it above the table like a fishing rod, a brass bell dusted with luminous powder jingling across the table. Elizabeth's head shot up. I moved back to my seat, taking old Mrs Goligher's fingers, realising that she too had performed a little trick with the angle of her wrist, freeing her fingers for mischief. I cleared my throat, trying my best to stay my rising panic, for the boy had surely run for Noah and time was short.

'Spirits,' I said. 'It is so terribly dark as ever.' I lost my words, head hanging. 'So terribly dark.'

How it hurt to see Kathleen's mobile pelvis turning in hypnotic rolls, the table bobbing in the air on her outstretched legs.

'Dear operators,' I said. 'Aren't you clever? I never had a clue. I admire you for that, in spite of everything. I think I shall look underneath.'

No sooner had I spoken, than Rebecca jerked, hurriedly striking her own untethered boots against the table with a dull *thump*, Kathleen lowering her feet softly to the floor as the old woman rolled a length of black twine around her claws, teasing a white tendril from the medium's skirts. It grew in snaking twitches, nosing out with each twist of the old woman's knuckles.

'Fascinating,' I said. 'My operators, at last I can see you.'

I mustered what little strength I had left, and decided, once and for all, to expose the spirit voices for what they most certainly were, curious as to how they were created. Had Kathleen managed to remove her gag beneath her hood with her concealed hand? Or was there some other explanation to my mother's singing and Robert's crying out? A hidden phonograph in the ceiling perhaps or even another accomplice lurking behind a second secret wall. Impossible, surely, for the voices had come so clearly and so close when Rose had seemed their instrument. I was about to call out when there came a heavy thud against the attic door, followed by a cacophony of rapping.

'Here, open the door. Rebecca, Kathleen, quick nai, the game's up! He tricked ye!'

CHAPTER
FORTY FOUR

The women sat upright. I spun about to see the doorhandle twisting, the door bashing against the back of Rose's chair.

'Rose, hold fast!' I cried, as she struggled against it. I jumped from my chair, throwing my shoulder into the frame as it splintered.

'Professor, ye mad bastard, let me in or yer dead, ye hear? Kat, Rebecca, he's got ye trapped!'

I panicked, dashing to the hatch in the fireplace, sliding on my belly but it was too tight to squeeze through. 'Get back!' I shouted. 'Stand away, God damn you or I'll kill them all! Don't think I won't.'

The door thundered, timber ripping away from the plasterwork, the brass doorknob flying across the room as Noah bellowed, 'You lay a finger on them and ay'll chuck ye through the window!'

I scrambled to my feet, turning around in a frenzy, seizing the lamp. 'Get back, I say, get back!' With a cry, I swept the lamp at the wall with an almighty *crash*, the flame guttering, shards of crimson glass splintering across the floor, pungent gas hissing into the room. I ran to the window and tore back the curtain as Adelia and Elizabeth coughed, Stoupe holding his breath while Kathleen, the slippery eel, had freed herself entirely and was crouching behind Rebecca, untying her hands.

'Stop that,' I said, rifling through my pockets. 'God damn it, Rose, where are my matches?'

She pointed to my notebooks piled in the far corner, her back juddering forwards, shattering her chair as the door exploded open. Noah stood at the top of the stairs, drenched in sweat, chest heaving. I scrabbled the matches up, backing towards the fireplace, kicking the table over as I went. 'Stop right there, Noah! I swear on my life if you set one foot into this attic I shall light this match. They'll be picking your teeth out of the roof. And you, Kathleen. Step away from Rebecca or I'll blow us all sky high.'

Noah raised his hands. 'Alright, Professor,' he panted. 'Calm yerself down nai, let's not get excited. Sure, we can have a calm wee talk.'

'I found you out, Kathleen. I have found you all out. You tricked me for six years but in the end I won.'

'What do you mean?' said Kathleen, sliding to the window. 'What have I done?'

I snatched the bell from the table and flung it at her, the metal smacking against the wall. She squealed, covering her face. 'Did you hear that, Kathleen?' I cried. 'Did you hear the jingling of the bell?' I waved my arms in the air, dancing on my toes like a pixie, lifting the table and hurling it at Noah. 'Did you see the table levitate? Great and powerful spirits, thank you for joining us. You blasted, lying fraudulent devils!'

'He's gone mad,' said Rebecca, throwing the string from her hands and shrinking to the corner of the room. 'Noah, do something, ye big ballacks, ye.'

'Noah will get the Hell out of this attic, that's what he'll do,' I said, preparing to strike the match. 'He's done enough and so have you. Get back down those stairs, man, or this whole building goes up in flames.'

He moved away, hands outstretched. 'Okay, Professor, no need to get excited. I'm goin', see?'

I brandished the match as he descended the stairs, then turned on Kathleen.

'Admit it. Confess. Every manifestation, every voice, every rap and levitation has been a lie.'

'I can't do that.'

'You must, or I'll burn you.' I let out a stifled cry, jabbing the match at her. 'Witch!'

'I'm not a witch,' said Kathleen. 'I told you, I don't know what I am.'

'Then allow me to enlighten you! You are a liar, a thief and a monstrous, deceitful, heartless bitch.'

'No...'

I scoffed. 'But yes. Don't you realise? The lamp was fully lit the whole time. I watched you lift the table with your feet. Ha! Look at your face now.' Elizabeth, Stoupe and Adelia squeaked in surprise, Old Mrs Goligher struggling to be free. 'Yes, friends!' I said, freeing them of their gags and blindfolds as I danced around the attic, the match between my teeth. 'That's precisely what I saw.' I wriggled my fingers. 'The boy came crawling through the fireplace while she waved a bell about on a stick, thinking herself hidden in the dark. Well, you weren't hidden this time, Kathleen; I saw everything, so you can cease your lying and tell me the truth at last. The spirits do not levitate tables. Say it!'

She lowered her eyes. 'They don't.'

'Nor do they ring the bells.'

'No.'

'Or rap.'

'It's true, Professor.'

I edged towards her, jabbing my finger. 'And they don't speak.'

She looked at me, clasping her hands to her sister. 'I can't say.'

I rubbed my nose, my head filling with toxic air. 'You can't say? Whyever not? You've said so much already. Please, sing my mother's song for us. Tell my grieving wife you're afraid of the man with the hanging bones. You've come this far.'

Kathleen shook her head. 'It would be a false confession. The voices are nothing to do with me, you know that. Sure, I've been gagged every séance since last year.'

A shooting pain spread behind my eyes. 'Then who was it? You?' I jabbed the match at Rebecca.

'Ack, me?' she laughed, eyes flicking between my hand and the lamp. 'No, not me.'

'William, please,' said Elizabeth. 'Be careful, you will kill us all. Think of the girls.'

'The girls? I ask you, do the girls think of me?'

'They love you dearly. They worry for you. We all do.'

'I don't care anymore. I'm ruined. Perhaps it'll be better for everyone once I'm dead.'

'Oh well done, William,' said Adelia. 'An accurate observation at last.'

Elizabeth clenched her fists against the arms of her chair. 'Shut up, Aunt Adelia. For once, be quiet.'

I held my hands in prayer, almost dropping the match. 'Elizabeth, don't you want to die too, now that you know the truth?'

Old Mrs Goligher tutted, glowering at me. 'We may burn here fer a few minutes, Professor, but ack, ye'll burn for eternity if ye strike that match.'

'It would be worth it to see you boil, wretched grimalkin. And you, Stoupe. I never had a friend such as you and now I know why.'

He slid his chair towards the wall, voice high with fright. 'Darling William, what have you become? This is all my fault.'

Elizabeth reached out to me, her eyes fixed on the match. 'William, you don't have to do this. Put it down.'

'She's right,' said Stoupe, coughing. 'You could write another book. The Spirit Engineer's greatest experiment yet. Mystery solved! The frauds unmasked.' He grimaced, hearing himself. 'I didn't mean *unmasked*... the mask was a mistake. Oh, it's all my fault.'

Kathleen nodded. 'You said yourself, Professor, you won. And you have done what I begged you to do. It's all over for me now, isn't it?' She edged away from her sister, sliding further around the wall. 'The secret is out. I can live a peaceful life.'

'Will you tell the newspapers you're a liar, Kathleen?' I said, lowering the match. 'Tell everyone I found you out?'

She cast a nervous glance at Rebecca. 'I only ever did what I had to do.'

'It was Samuel singing, wasn't it? Samuel pretending to be my mother?'

Rebecca laughed before doubling over in a fit of hacking coughs, gripping her throat. 'He thinks it was Sammy,' she croaked. 'No, the joke is better than that; wait till he finds out!'

I ignored her. 'End the lies, Kathleen, I know you're a good woman underneath it all. You can walk down those stairs if you confess. You can go to the refuge, just as you said. Tell me which of you it was.'

'If I did that, it would be the biggest lie I ever told.'

The attic rippled, coal gas swimming like oil. The match shivered between my fingers. I pressed the tip against the box, tiny wisps of smoke and sparks sending Stoupe into a frenzy, writhing in his seat. The match puffed and fizzed as the heavy air shivered, about to blow.

'Stop!' said Kathleen, turning to her mother. 'Let me tell him, please. I have to or we'll all burn.'

'You can't, Kat,' said old Mrs Goligher. 'He'll strike the match for sure if we tell him the truth, look at him.'

I gazed at Elizabeth, my mind cracking like eggshell. 'What do they have to tell me, dear wife? Do you know?'

She looked back, defeated. 'What does it matter? Can't you leave it be?'

I could not. If it wasn't Samuel or Kathleen speaking as the spirits, then perhaps it was Rebecca or old Mrs Goligher? Adelia, even? I asked the confounded woman, but she shook her head. No, not her and not Stoupe either. I looked at my wife. She was gazing over my shoulder, her eyes settling on someone moving behind me, their shadow climbing the wall.

William.

With a gasp, I turned to see a hulking figure holding a splinter of wood, about to plunge it into my back. Her cap had fallen to the floor, her long hair resting over her broad shoulders, thick arms ready to strike the blow.

'You!' I shouted, wheeling around at Rose with a furious cry.

No sooner had our eyes met, than she took fright, fleeing from the attic with a grunt, half falling down the stairs in her eagerness to escape. I went to grab her arm but she moved too quickly for me and, as I made to chase after her, I felt something grip my ankle, only to see Noah reaching out through the fireplace. I toppled to the floor as Kathleen jumped at me with an almighty scream, grappling with my hand.

273

'No!' I cried, desperately trying to strike the match as my leg was yanked backwards. 'I shall burn the lot of you! Let me go!' I kicked as hard as I could, my foot connecting with Noah's nose as he howled and loosened his grip. I lashed at Kathleen with my elbow, struggling to the door before whirling around to face them.

I stared at Elizabeth with all the world's pain in my heart, yet all I could think was betrayal. 'Burn in Hell, the lot of you!' I thundered. 'Blow, blow, blow winds blow!' I struck the match and tossed it into the room as Elizabeth squealed and Stoupe toppled sideways. Adelia gave a lowing moan, whisps of white hair flashing in a blaze of orange sparks while Rebecca and old Mrs Goligher screamed, a whoosh of flames bursting through the air. I fell down the stairs as the sudden heat crackled around me, scorching my throat. I crashed onto my back then up, up I leapt, gripping the bannister as I ran down to the shop and onto the street, gulping lungfuls of cold, blessed air.

I stepped backwards across the road, looking up at the window, framed by the darkening sky, black smoke billowing between the roof tiles. *Goodbye, attic. In spite of everything, I shall miss you.* Smiling at my work, I glimpsed an almond-shaped face amidst the churning ash behind the glass and thought back to a dark, wet night many years ago when I crouched behind barrels. If only I had known then what portal to Hell I was staring at. *Young, innocent William Jackson Crawford, it was a demon looking down on you that night, not a girl.*

A man ran out from a nearby shop waving his arms. 'Here, what's going on up there, nai, is there a fire? Are ye hurt?'

Far away, where the road bent its back to the river, I saw a distant figure chasing after a tram, heaving her lumbering body aboard. 'Hurt?' I said, a bitter taste on my tongue. 'More than any man alive.'

Rose. It was time to talk.

CHAPTER FORTY FIVE

The front door had been left ajar. I opened it softly, stepping inside. Corrupt, silent woman, she would talk or I would silence her for good. The house creaked as my shoes tapped over varnished boards. I peered along the hallway to the empty kitchen, then stopped to listen. Where was she? Hidden somewhere, peering at me from some cobwebbed corner, a weapon in her hand no doubt. I stepped into the parlour, waving my arm around the door before springing it open. 'Rose, where are you?' My loyal assistant, her every action a veiled act of betrayal. She had contrived to burrow herself under the skin of our family, a succubus in the roof of our home, lapping up details and plans like a fly. She must have rifled through my desk a hundred times and listened to me chattering names in my dreams. That is how they knew my secrets! When I was ill, stewing in the juices of my fever, had I not spoken in tongues? I recalled the shadowy figure moving about in my office. The white lady prowling around the house, scaring the children. All Rose.

I went to the window and looked down at the shipyard, the cranes gone, hulls forgotten, tugboats in the estuary like woodlice tracing silver. A shuffling noise came from the dining room. I edged to the curtains, sweeping them open with a shout, only to find the space deserted.

'Father, is that you?' Margaret's voice drifted down from the landing; a frightened whisper. I stepped out, scanning the hallway, to see the child standing at the top of the stairs, a look of dread on her face as though she knew, somehow, that her mother was burning to death. 'Father, what's happened?'

'Never mind that, girl. Go to the nursery. Take your sister, it isn't safe.'

'Where is Mother?'

'I said *go*.'

Helen appeared at her side with her doll, pulling on Margaret's fingers. I looked at them both. What would become of them now? An orphanage, I supposed.

Margaret looked towards Rose's room as a hollow thump came from the attic. 'Why is Rose packing her things, Father?'

I climbed the stairs, my finger at my lips. 'Hush now, take Helen to the nursery at once. Do as I say.'

Margaret edged away. 'Father, your eyes are strange.'

'I expect they are; they can see for the first time,' I muttered, turning as boxes and furniture slid across the floor above. I steadied myself, balling my fists before calling up, 'Rose, I'm coming up to you now! There's no escape!'

No answer.

I mounted the attic stairs, taking a solicitous pause between each creaking step. 'You can speak to me now, Rose, you might as well. It's my turn to be speechless after all. Tell me everything, you owe me that.'

The movement of boxes stopped as I approached. I pressed the door open, stepping inside to see her, bundled in every item of clothing she owned, weighed down by a heavy suitcase in each arm.

'Here we are then, after everything. The game is up, I'm afraid. No more theatrics please, I know you're not mute.'

The room was hot, pipes glugging as dry leaves skittered over the rooftiles above our heads. The girls were right, she had been crying, rivulets of sweat joining her tears, dripping to her chin.

'Rose, you can give up the act now. It's all quite clear.' I nodded, twizzling my moustache. 'You are the Golighers' stooge. They planted you in this house. Ha! I thought you were *my* assistant, but you were theirs all along.'

She shook her head, eyes fixed to the floor. She had cared for my little boy as he had lain dying, then stolen his voice. She had spoken as my own mother, for Christ's sakes. She had camouflaged herself as Arthur to torment me, wringing every last detail from my unwitting confessions. Yes, that was the answer to it all. I stepped towards her, shaking my head in wonder that I had not seen it before. How could I have believed in such extraordinary explanations for Kathleen's phenomena? Certain men are liable to be duped, and there is no creature so gullible as the certain man.

'Were you there that night, at Lismarra House?' She stepped away from me, shaking her ovine skull, eyes bulging. I would make those damned eyes bulge if she persisted. 'Yes,' I said, following her deeper into the room. 'Of course you were there.' In my mind's eye I caught sight of her, slipping out of Park Avenue as the children slept, climbing into Noah's cart, whispering and conspiring in fits of muffled laughter, skulking beyond the balcony doors at Lismarra, camouflaged amongst the ivy, listening to us with a resolute smile, practising her voices ready for her grand entrance. Such a gloomy night, the wind from the sea rattling against the glass, any prowler could have opened them unnoticed. In she'd crept, dressed as a drowned man, smeared in rotten crab meat. Of course, it had been Samuel not Robert, hiding inside the grandfather clock. I could see it all so clearly. In every séance in the attic, it had been she, speaking in spirit voices from the door. A cold shiver ran down my spine. A conspiracy against my own wretched misery, designed in the Belfast gutters, my own friends complicit. I forced myself to look straight at her, demanding she met my eye. She deserved to be looked at. 'What was the plan then, Rose? Is that even your name?'

She shook her head, eyes like boiled eggs, shrugging her shoulders under the weight of the suitcases. I smiled. 'You certainly had me fooled. Quite a plan, I must say. Tricking me into believing in Kathleen's spirits, knowing my honest work would make the family rich and famous.' I clapped my hands together, moving closer to her and still, she shook her damned head. 'How many men did you mark before choosing me, I wonder? Was it you, watching me at the Institute? Kathleen perhaps, or Samuel. All three of you for all I know. I suppose I gave a good impression of an impressionable man, running away from squeaks and queer sounds.' God damn her, she shook her head again frantically. 'Why won't you speak?' I said, stamping my foot. 'Too afraid, poor wretch. What did they do to you, that family? Beat you, perhaps? And worse I shouldn't wonder.'

Her face split, the wretched gargoyle, her mouth gaping as she dropped the suitcases, keepsakes spilling across the floor. She fell to her knees, scrabbling amongst piles of underclothes.

'Did you ever pity us?' I said, treading over her mess. 'I can see why you used me, but Elizabeth? Losing her brother, losing her son and now...' I patted my jacket, searching for my pipe, only to see her holding the confounded thing up to me. I snatched it away, overcome by disgust and spat at her. 'Elizabeth will lose them both a second time and all because of your little schemes. Mark that on your heart.' I nodded at her. 'And still, you refuse to speak? You are a cruel woman indeed. The ugliest thing I have ever seen.'

She mouthed something, only to stop herself. I held my breath, waiting, struck by the awesome realisation that I was about to meet the true Rose. She licked her lips, eyes flicking to the door, then took a deep breath.

'Yes, Rose?' I whispered. 'Speak now. I will forgive you.'

She closed her eyes with a low moan, backing her shoulders against the wall as I stepped closer until I could feel her breath on my face.

I spoke the words slowly into her eyes. 'Rose, make the voices or I shall squeeze them out of you.' I raised my hands to her neck, pressing my thumbs tenderly beneath her slimy jaw, my fingers searching to the back of her skull. 'I want to hear my son. I want to hear my mother. Do it. Do it now, or so help me God I shall reach into your lungs and wrench them out.' She pushed against me, but I slammed her to the wall as she held my wrists, her powerful fingers digging into my skin. She gripped, but I gripped tighter. She twisted and I twisted faster as she tugged and begged with gargles and coughs, scratching and scrabbling against the fury of six shame-filled years. Every joint and sinew in my body became steel pressing in, in, in like pistons against rubber as the tips of my thumbs clamped shut, her heartbeat pounding against my fingertips and still she gaped silently. At last, her eyes held mine, jittering in their lids, and, whatever she was thinking, it was not rage, nor sorrow, for there was peace in those wide, putrid orbs. Peace and acceptance as though she knew in those final seconds that the world wanted rid of her. At last, with a kick from her shoes and a creaking breath, she hung, lifeless, in my hands.

All done in a moment. Can a life be extinguished so easily? So quickly? Yes, with a bullet, but with my own strength? A squeeze of my fingers, or the mere flick of a match? I stepped back, pulling my shaking fingers from her neck as she slid to the floor, head smacking the floorboards with a hollow thud. Her face, frozen in that final expression of placid acceptance, rolled to one side, her mouth forever fixed on the shape of a 'W'.

'What would you have said?' I asked her. 'Come haunt me if you dare, I shan't be here much longer. A dying man cannot be frightened by the dead.'

There were footsteps as someone came running up the stairs. The room went dark as a figure blocked the light streaming from the doorway. She gasped. 'William, what have you done?'

I looked up, my head swimming with adrenaline, cold fingers still gripping the empty air. It was Elizabeth, hair hanging loose, frizzled and singed at the tips, her skin bright red as though sunburnt.

'Elizabeth, you're alive,' I said, looking at the crumpled corpse at my feet. I pointed at it. 'She made a fool of a fool,' I laughed. 'Now I have silenced a silent woman.'

CHAPTER FORTY SIX

Elizabeth knelt beside the body, stroking her hair.

'She wouldn't speak,' I said.

'Of course not, she couldn't have,' Elizabeth said, her voice flat.

I threw my arms up in exasperation. 'Oh, Elizabeth, you stupid woman. It was all a lie. Don't you see? The voices were Rose all along.'

'Poor, poor Rose. We should never have kept you here. William, you will hang for this.'

I laughed. 'Ho-ho. Hang a professional man for unmasking a gang of crooks? I hardly think so.' I pointed at the body. 'That thing lived in our home, with our children, prowling about at night for titbits to feed Kathleen. I have defended myself from her, nothing more.' I nudged the maid's shoulder with my toe. 'You might call her *poor*, but I expect she was paid very well indeed by the Golighers.'

Elizabeth straightened up. 'I want you to listen to me, William, do you understand? I have left it too late, Lord forgive me, but it's time to tell you the truth. Will you stay quiet? Can you trust me?'

'I don't think I can trust anyone ever again, Elizabeth, even you. Did you know Stoupe's photographs were false?'

'No, not as such, but let me tell you everything.'

I sighed. 'Tell me whatever you like, woman, or tell me nothing, I don't care anymore. I solved the mystery; let them print that in their bloody pamphlets. I shall be a victorious man even if I do hang.' I leaned in with a wink that stuck closed until I prised it open again with my thumb. 'I tell you what, precious wife,' I said, her nose wrinkling at my breath. 'I found Hazel's letter. How about that for secrets?'

She pressed her palms together. 'Oh Lord, what are you talking about now, you hopeless man?'

'Hopeless, am I?' I chuckled, barging past her down the stairs to my study, pulling drawers out, fishing through them frantically until I found the letter. 'Here it is!' I exclaimed as Elizabeth ran past the door, calling for the girls.

'Mother!' cried Margaret. 'We're in the nursery, quickly.'

I strode along the landing after them, waving the letter in triumph. 'Right then, let's see who's hopeless, shall we?'

The girls were standing inside the nursery clinging to their mother, Margaret setting her face against me.

'Father, you're frightening us, don't you come near.'

I rolled my eyes, searching my pockets. 'As you wish, your mother can hear me well enough from where she is. Now, where are my damned spectacles?'

'On your nose, Father.'

'Thank you, Margaret.'

Helen poked her head from behind Elizabeth's back. 'Mother, where's Rose, what's happened to her?'

'Hush, Rose is packing her things to leave.'

'But, she's so quiet.'

I snorted. 'Isn't she always?' I unfolded the letter. 'Now, just you listen to this, Elizabeth.' I read the muddled letter aloud, compensating for Hazel's terrible writing, almost overcome by a fit of giggles. '*Dear Mrs Crawford, I am sorry to have to give you my notice. I have given much thought to my decision.*'

'What is this, William?' asked Elizabeth.

'You don't recognise it? What does it say next? Ah yes: *My sisters have a place for me*, so on and so on... *please don't think badly*, et cetera et cetera... my, she does go on. Aha, yes, now we're getting there.' I pushed my spectacles up my nose and sniffed, struggling to read through a growing ache in my head.

'*It is for you to say what you like to Mr C* – you certainly took her up on that offer.'

Elizabeth twisted her hands behind her back. 'Hazel's last letter. I thought I'd burnt it.'

'You didn't; I found it.'

'I don't understand, why do you have to read it now? It hardly matters, surely. Rose needs a doctor.'

'She needs an undertaker, nothing less.'

Margaret squealed as I ploughed on, tutting. 'Oh shush, girl, you're as bad as your sister. Listen to this, God damn her blasted handwriting: *I cannot sense what I saw last night and what I have heard, and it is not right for a God-fearsome woman such as myself to be part of it.*' I took out my pipe and rolled it in the air. 'Caught wind of the séances, I expect.'

'Yes, I expect so,' said Elizabeth.

I shook my head at her, delighted by the next damning line. '*I know you have been unhappy, Mrs C, but I cannot help but pity poor Mr C for not knowing about Angels.*' I glared at her. 'I suppose the silly woman means spirits. I wish I'd *never* known about them.' Elizabeth went to speak, but I shushed her and carried on, my voice rising. 'What next. Aha! *I saw you meeting that man.* Well, dearest, we know who that is.'

She nodded. 'Noah Morrison.'

'Correct! She speaks honestly, children, can you believe it? Heavens be praised. Here, listen to this then. *You are a married woman and Mr C will discover what he has been doing with you sooner or later and then what will you do?*' I lowered the letter. 'Come on then, she saw you with Noah, did she? Messing around with ghosts, was that it? Or was he messing around with you?'

Elizabeth took a long breath, her eyebrows knitted. 'That isn't what she means.'

'Ah,' I said, twizzling my moustache. 'Is it not? Then enlighten me, dearest, what exactly was it she saw you doing with Noah Morrison? Come, come, don't be shy.'

'William, not in front of the girls.'

'Whore.'

'Stop it!'

I prodded the letter so hard my finger tore through the paper. 'Look here, she writes very specifically: *Mr C will discover what he has been doing with you.* What was he doing, exactly? Tell me, or so help me, God, I shall send you off with Rose.'

Margaret wrestled free with an exasperated cry. 'You're not reading it right, Father. The letter means *you* would find out what *you* had been doing with Mother. There.'

Perplexed, I reread the words on the paper, wrinkling my nose with a snort. 'Silly girl,' I said, sucking bitter ashes through my dead pipe. 'You mean to say that *I* would sooner or later discover my *own* actions?'

'Precisely,' said Elizabeth. 'And now you shall if you will only listen.'

'Oh, pish and piffle. It doesn't make any sense.'

'None of it does,' said Margaret. 'But it's true.'

I gritted my teeth, shuffling my feet as my family shrank away. I realised it then. The Crawford family stood on one side of the nursery, I on the other, estranged, no longer father nor husband.

Elizabeth set her chin, her hands behind her back. She went to speak but stopped herself, instructing the girls to move away to the bookshelves before closing her eyes in prayer. 'Be strong and courageous; do not be frightened and do not be dismayed, for the Lord your God is with you wherever you go.'

'Come on, woman,' I said. 'You clearly have something to say. Spit it out.'

'You walk at night,' said Elizabeth in a sudden fit. 'That is what Hazel means in her letter. She feared what might happen if you found out. You have been tormenting us for years in your sleep.' She caught her breath and stood back.

I laughed. 'Stuff and nonsense! I walk at night, you say? Impossible.'

'But you do, Father,' said Margaret, pressing her back to the shelves. 'Mother don't go near him, look at his eyes.'

'Yes,' said Elizabeth, her voice tight, burnt flakes of lace tumbling to the floor as she shuffled forwards, hands clasped behind her back. 'You walk in your dreams, terrified by visions from your past. In the early hours of the morning when the house is asleep, with the bed sheets wrapped around you, wailing and shrieking like a banshee, crying like...' She nodded, her teeth chattering. 'Like...'

Helen shielded her face with her doll. 'Like the white lady.'

'Mother, don't go any closer to him,' said Margaret. 'He's dangerous.'

But on she came, smiling at me like a warden in a madhouse. 'You frightened the children when they were younger, William. Roaming in and out of their bedrooms night after night, hiding behind doors, singing your funny song. I tried to keep you from them, but they found out eventually. I gave you drugs from the doctor but they made you so drowsy in the daytime I thought you might lose your job, and we were so poor. Hazel and I locked your door at one point, but it only made you more confused.'

'Confused? I should say so, I...'

'Be quiet! Do you want the truth or not? When poor Arthur drowned, things became unbearable, and Lord I sense now you were right to be haunted by him. You didn't seem to care at all in the daytime, but at night... it was a terrible torment for you, and worse for us. How you cried and spoke of strange memories. Your mother most often. Always blood...' She lifted her eyes to the ceiling. 'Blood and a baby.'

I scoffed. 'My mother died in childbirth, it's true. The thing was crippled. I shall never forgive it. I expect it died soon after, bent little animal.'

'Stop it!' cried Helen. 'You're cruel. You hit Mother!' She jumped towards me, only to be yanked back by the collar.

'Don't, Helen,' said Margaret. 'He isn't well.'

I scowled. 'What is this? What's going on here? How dare you invent such lies?'

'They're not lies,' said Elizabeth, bringing a knife from her back, the steel blade flashing in the gaslight. 'You beat me and twisted my wrists and pushed me down the stairs night after night as we tried to keep you in bed. I married a saint with a demon trapped inside him, that's what Kathleen says.'

I looked at the girls. 'Listen to me. None of this is true, do you hear?'

'Get back,' said Margaret. 'Mother, stop him.'

Helen threw her doll at me, its plaster face smashing on the floor. A flash of pain shot behind my eyes as a vague memory came back to me. Darkness, the bannister floating by my side, a bedroom door opening, Robert on his bed crying as I looked on. I shook my head. Outside, a cloud passed over the abandoned hull of a condemned ship, the black shapes forming into a vision of shadows wrestling with me in my own bed, pinning me to the mattress. Elizabeth traced around the room, the knife shaking in her hand. 'William, you must believe me, you are not a well man.'

With a snarl, I lunged at her, hoping to snatch away the knife, but Elizabeth jumped, screaming with all her might: 'Run, girls, run quickly! Get away, get help!'

I swivelled as Margaret crashed into the shelves, flinging books into my face before escaping to the door with Helen. I howled as a novel collided with my eye, then tore after them as they clattered screeching down the stairs onto the street.

I stopped, gripping the bannister. Should I run after them, grab them and drag them back? I caught sight of Elizabeth moving along the landing towards me, holding the knife above her head. 'Wife,' I said. 'Are you going to kill me?' In a panic, I jumped into my room, slamming the door as I vanished headfirst into the bed, burying myself under the bedclothes.

Elizabeth's voice came through the door, hard and bitter. 'You wanted the truth. Now I can give it to you after all these years.' The door flew open and there she was, swiping the knife in the air like a maniac, her scorched dress ripping at her shoulders. I peeked at her from beneath a pillow as she ranged above me, her pink forehead fixed in an eyebrow-less frown.

'No,' I said, burying myself deeper. 'Please don't hurt me.'

'You've always been a strange man. Even at the start you had queer turns. My mother begged me not to marry you, she begged on her knees. So did Arthur. But I told them you were sweet and gentle, not like most men. You were honest and shy, I said. And you *were* good, in the beginning. But then you started with your headaches and one night I woke to a beating from the side of the bed so fierce I thought you would murder me. My own husband, bearing down on me, weeping like a lost boy. I should have left you the very next day, I know that now, but Margaret was still in her cot and perhaps... perhaps it was just a momentary thing, and when you woke in the morning there wasn't a memory of it, as though nothing had happened. There you sat, buttering your toast at the breakfast table, prattling on about your precious pumps and pistons while I ate with broken fingers.'

'Stop.'

'No. I can't stop. Not now. I'll carry on until you've heard it all. Then we can all be free. It was Aunt Adelia who introduced me to the Golighers, you know. I wanted to hear from Arthur, but knew you wouldn't approve so I went alone and in secret. One night, they asked about my bruises, and I told them everything. They took pity on me, offering help for a little money. You were possessed, they said. You needed to be exorcised. And somehow, Kathleen seemed to know you, everything about you, just by touching my hand. I told them what sort of man you were, that you'd never go to the Ormeau Road, but Kathleen sent her spirits to fetch you and well, didn't you come eventually? I couldn't believe it and then... then the spirits arrived. They'd never heard such voices, not even old Mrs Goligher.'

'Devils!'

'Yes, devils, just like you. But the doctor was threatening to put you in the asylum and then what would we have done? Me, a housemaid, the children as good as orphans, tainted for life. Adelia paid for the séances and they worked, William! As soon as the spirit voices arrived, your nightmares stopped and I slept soundly for the first time in years.'

'Lies.'

'Oh, you and your lies. Poor William! Did our lies strangle a housemaid? Was I thrown down the stairs by lies? Was it our lies terrifying the children? You might have been tricked, but we did it out of desperation and pity and fright and everything was better when you were working with Kathleen. Poor Robert was speaking to us and you were cured.'

'Stop talking. I can't think, I can't make sense of it!'

'Then nothing has changed.' She pulled a tuft of copper hair from her scalp, crisping at her fingertips like spun sugar. 'I thought we were safe, so long as your experiments continued, but then I realised we weren't free of your demon at all. He wasn't gone, he was stronger than ever. You had become him. No longer trapped in your head at night, he was consuming you in your waking life. I didn't recognise my husband anymore. Tying women up, molesting them, selling your experiments for money, speaking gibberish, lurking about the Institute hearing voices, filling your books with dreams. Heaven help us, we longed to take it all back, but, by then it was too late and...'

'Why are you tormenting me? I won't hear it, I will not!'

'Yes, you will hear it!' Suddenly, her fists rained down on me, flashing the knife as she raved. 'Day after day, I've bitten my tongue! Month after month suffering you! Well, now you can suffer yourself. I won't stand it any longer, do you hear me? I won't! I've seen women with bruised necks, twisted fingers, bellies filled with babies they couldn't carry, swollen eyes and brittle smiles, polite apologies about sandwiches and children's shoes. While all the while, their faces tell the same story: my husband has nerves, he's highly strung, such a temper, my husband won't leave me alone, he has his urges. Men will be men, boys will be boys. Wives will be beaten. Children will be terrified. Well, I've been terrified in this house long enough, do you hear me?'

She smashed the knife against the mirror with an almighty crack, splits hatching across the glass. 'And now my proud, jealous husband has strangled a woman to death. And for what?' Elizabeth threw herself into me, dragging the sheets away from my pinching fingers. 'For what, William? Tell me, why is there an innocent woman lying strangled in our attic? Oh, don't answer, why else? She didn't speak when she was ordered to, that's why. Tell me, wife-beater, murderer; is your mother proud of you now?'

I shuffled across the mattress to the wall, kicking her away.

'Elizabeth, I am sorry.'

'Sorry?' She turned to the broken mirror, shoulders heaving. 'I felt certain it would be me, one day, lying in a heap on the floor.' She coughed, a spurt of tar trickling down her chin.

'I would never hurt you,' I said, climbing from the bed. 'I'm a decent man, whatever you've come to believe.' I went to hold her as she wheeled about, the tip of the knife ringing cold and sharp at my heart. I waited for the steel to slip between my ribs. I spoke to her, calm and ready. 'Do it then. If I'm guilty of all these crimes. If I am so unkind. Do it. I would rather be executed by you than the hangman.' I held out my arms, speaking through gritted teeth. 'I love you, Elizabeth. Kill me and we shall rise together when you hang.'

Her face was lit gold by the lamps, a tear forming between her bald eyelids. She steadied herself, readying her elbow for the push, but just as I felt the knife prickle against my skin, her arm softened, the blade clattering to the floor. Outside, a bat screeched through the garden, swooping expertly over the rooftops, between chimneys, flitting around branches. I laid my chin on Elizabeth's shoulder, the wallpaper glowing and shifting in the gaslight.

'I will not abandon our girls as you have done,' Elizabeth said, defeated. 'And you must know the sins you've committed in this house tonight. You will have to answer for them.' She leaned back, taking my face in her hands. 'Her name was Agnes.'

I sniffed. 'Agnes?'

'In Hazel's letter. The one you were reading. When she said she pitied you, it wasn't *angels*; it was Agnes.'

'No,' I said, her hair tickling my nose. 'She must have been confused, silly woman. Agnes was my mother's name.'

'Your mother shared her name with another.' Elizabeth moved to the sink, scratching at her wrists. 'She arrived like a farm animal, covered in dirt with ragged clothes. I was cleaning the house when the doorbell rang and there she was on the doorstep, a note around her neck like a giant foundling. It was from her pastor in Dunedin. Agnes Jackson Crawford, it read:

Delivered to William Jackson Crawford. Her brother.
Care for her if able or send to asylum if God's will permits.
Blessed are the gentle, for they shall inherit the earth.

Elizabeth looked up, biting her lip.

I tutted. 'What rot, Elizabeth. My sister was a baby with a twisted neck when I left New Zealand. The little devil killed my mother and likely died soon after, good riddance, and now you have her on our doorstep?'

Elizabeth lowered her head to the sink, splashing cold water from the tap into her mouth with a cupped hand before pulling her tattered dress to her shoulder. 'She died more recently than that, William. Little wonder I didn't tell you who she was. Honestly, the things you said about that poor baby in your terrors. But do you know, I believe in your own way, you liked her very much? Heaven knows, she thought the world of you, dear thing. We hid her for a few days in Hazel's room, not knowing what to do with her until clever Margaret came up with an idea to call her Rose and dress her up like a housemaid. I thought you wouldn't let her stay when you saw her, but you have a good heart, William, it's your mind that's rotten. And then, who would have expected it? You became fast friends, playing with your experiments together. She worshipped you, as I worshipped Arthur.' She looked up with tears in her eyes.

'Why do sisters love their brothers so carelessly?' She faced the broken mirror, stroking her blistered skin in the glass as she flinched, crying quietly as an engine rumbled outside.

I backed towards the door. 'Rose?'

'You threatened to kill her every night in your dreams. I thought by hiding her from you, I would keep her safe, but I should have known. It's a wonder any of us are alive, really.'

I left her at the sink, unable to hear another word, and made my way up to the attic, pressing the door open in a trance. She was laying just as I had left her, that strange waxen face greeting me from the floor as I stepped inside, clothes and keepsakes spilled around her legs. I stood back, unable to breathe, for there, beneath the twisted jawline lay the gentle, smiling lips I remembered from my childhood. 'Agnes,' I whispered, kneeling down to brush my fingers across her heavy brow, mantel to my mother's eyes. 'Agnes, my sister.' I turned about, noticing one of the suitcases open, clothes and trinkets strewn across the floor. I shuffled over, rifling through the contents, flinging underwear and caps across my shoulder until I found what I knew would be there. A bundle of envelopes tied in blue string. I pulled them free, lifting them to the light, recognising the handwriting instantly. A familiar address in Dunedin. My own letters; those I had posted to Dunedin over the course of so many years, thinking them ignored. I looked back at her pale face, then stood away, searching in my pocket for the pouch of potassium cyanide. I pinched it in my fingers, touching the paper with my tongue, staring at it with one wide, curious eye.

I was just about to throw the whole thing down my throat when I had a sudden thought. I looked back at the body, my finger marks still red around her neck. She had never cried as a baby. The last time I had seen her with my sisters, waving at me with pudgy hands and bandy legs from the harbourside, she had been silent. Perhaps she was mute after all. Perhaps I had gotten it all wrong. Clinging to the bannister, I lowered myself back to the bedroom where Elizabeth was choking at the mirror, the glass spotted with globs of black spittle.

'Elizabeth,' I said, as she retched, tar hanging from her fingers in strings. 'If my sister was mute then she cannot have made the voices.' I stood behind her, waiting for my answer. Her neck twitched. I tapped her on the shoulder. 'The voices.

You must tell me before I hang; I couldn't bear it, do you hear? You promised to tell me everything, you must.' My head rattled. 'If Rose was not making the voices, then who? Not Samuel, his voice is too peculiar...'

Wiiiiiiiilliam.

'Not Rebecca, nor old Mrs Goligher, I was watching them today. I would have caught them at it.'

Wiiiiiiiilliam.

'Noah? Impossible.'

Elizabeth lifted her head, her face refracted in split shards of glass.

Wiiiiiiiilliam.

'Oh, my darling, no.'

Her eyes met mine.

Farfur? Can you see me?

William, please find him.

I staggered, the bed pressing against the backs of my legs.

William, it is Arthur, you coward.

'Elizabeth, what have you done to me?'

The Elfin knight stands on yon hill...

I grabbed her shoulders as I began sobbing, rubbing my shaking fingers to her face as our feet shuffled together. 'You are mad, was it you all along?'

Blow, blow, blow winds, blow...

'You planned to send me mad! You wanted rid of me!'

She trembled in my hands, her eyes on my lips. 'William,' she said, her breath hot against my face, eyes sliding to the right. 'Look.'

'None of your tricks,' I snarled.

William, save me!

Farfur!

She buckled and managed to break free, twisting past me, bolting from the room with an almighty scream. 'There!' she called. 'There are your spirits. Look!'

Blowing his horn, so loud until...

'What are you saying? Where are my spirits?'

I caught my reflection in the mirror and froze. An inhuman skull stared back from the glass. A wild man with sheep's eyes and knotted silver hair. His mouth was gurning, riven with dread-mania, and as the voices continued to speak, I realised – my betrayal betrayed – that it was I at the séances. I, creeping at night; my own voice in the darkness; my own ears deceived by my own lips; my own cold heart, chilling my own trembling flesh, the sole divide: my poor, dismembered mind.

'Farfur?' I said, in the voice of a baby, pursing my lip.

'William?' came my mother's voice, high and faint, from my own throat.

'Coward,' said Arthur, my mouth rearranging itself into a scandalous, inhuman grin.

I ran from the room, hurtling to the top of the stairs as the doctor came crashing through the front door below, followed by the girls. He held his hands up. 'Be calm, Mr Crawford,' he said. 'Don't be afraid, I have some pills.'

I ducked into the study and clambered over the desk, wrenching the window open before shimmying down the drainpipe as a pair of arms grabbed at me from the windowsill. I dropped to the grass and looked up to see Elizabeth and the doctor leaning out.

'Stop, William!' Elizabeth cried. 'Where are you going?'

'Traitors!' I spat in an alien voice, before clapping my hand over my mouth, shooting through the back gate with a deranged squeal. I raced to the front of the house as the girls stared down from the nursery window, their hands against the glass. 'Goodbye, children,' I mimed, throwing myself into the motorcar. 'Forgive me.'

The engine rattled to life as the doctor burst through the door, charging along the garden towards me. I flung the crank handle at him – the thing connecting smartly with his temple – then jumped behind the wheel, pulling away with a screech as Elizabeth ran into the road. I heard her desperate voice as I drew away, crying for me to stay, but I did not look back. I would not see her like that gazing upon me like a monster.

In minutes, I was speeding along the coast, the estuary swinging at my side in the darkness, the spirit voices still whistling in my ears, chasing me through the wind. What then, had I discovered? That there is nobody so duplicitous as oneself? That certainty is nothing but unreasonable belief? That there can be no answer to death? That there *should* be no answer to it, at least not for the living? That we have in all of us, written into our very matter, an unpassable divide; and if there is a bridge between this world and the next, then surely there is only one toll to pay.

EPILOGUE

THE BEGINNING

One's consciousness passes into a new realm on the brink of death, whether the soul does so or not. Anger, jealousy, hatred, ambition, regret, none of them matter in the end.

Is it time? Must I do this horrible thing?

A wave crashes onto the rocks. I scrabble backwards, shoes scraping over wet stone. *Take it, William. Drink it quickly.* I shiver as the sunlight sparkles in rockpools, glowing in coins of golden lichen. It is a brave thing to die.

Trembling, I pinch the envelope from my pocket, tap the potassium cyanide crystals into a bottle of scotch, rolling the mixture until the poison drowns and vanishes.

A spirit to create a spirit.

I whimper, burying my face between my knees. The water whispers, slapping between legs of sharp stone. I am a failure, a fraud. I have travelled far to arrive nowhere; to become nothing.

Take it, William. Drink it quickly.

'Is it time?' I ask. 'Is the final experiment about to begin?'

I rub my thumb over the mouth of the bottle, rap it three times.

Knock. Knock. Knock.

So, I am done.

There is no escape now.

I drink the whisky to the very last drop, licking the foul stuff from my moustache for good measure. Gurning at the bitter taste, I wait, head swimming. Where is the poison amidst the burning liquor? The swelling waves brush the soles of my shoes. I think of our little home above the shipyard and of the Institute. I think of the attic above the shop. My wife. My daughters. My mother. My sister. Kathleen. The séances play out, one atop another like shifting prints on plates of glass. Nothing but a mess of tables, bells, and my own insensible chatter.

A dull pain spreads through my fingers and toes. My arms grow heavy, muscles cramp. I gulp as my chest tightens. A pain takes hold around my ribs. 'Oh dear,' I whisper. The ache spreads quickly, skittering like spiders across my bones. I hear myself cry out as my fingers bend, knuckles snap. A curtain draws across the seafront, blotting out the light. I cough blood, my very existence consumed by searing agony, and suddenly, I am away...

Shrugging off my skin, I drift merrily into the breeze, warm and gentle like smoke from a pipe. In a babbling moment, as though every blink is the glad passing of minutes, I discover myself, whatever my *self* may be, floating amongst the gulls. I am looking down at a dead man strewn across the rocks beside the pressing fingernail of a wave, his mouth foaming, a bottle toppling into the drifting gravel. There is a package at his twisted hip. A letter slips into a pool of clear water at his shoe, blue writing seeping through the paper. A policeman climbs down to him from the path, reaching out as the white sky wraps around my face like damp tissue, and I am gone...

***

'William, are you there?'

I turn to see a light flickering in the darkness.

'William, can you hear me? Come to us.'

I am standing in an attic. Two figures are sitting at a table, illuminated by the glow of a ruby lamp. I squint at them through the darkness. One is a familiar woman with copper hair, deep lines around her eyes. She rubs nervously at her wrists as she prays, turning her head about scanning the ceiling. 'Is he there?'

she whispers, leaning to her companion who sits beneath a long, black shroud.

'Yes,' comes the reply. 'Yes, he's here.' The figure pulls the shroud away to reveal a woman with an almond-shaped face, spectacles framing keen grey eyes. 'Welcome, Professor,' she says. 'You have returned to us at last; we've been waiting for you. Now do you see?' She stares at me through the gloom. 'Death is a beginning.'

ACKNOWLEDGEMENTS

With thanks to Matt Casbourne, a visionary editor who believed in me and my ghostly true story when sceptics did not. Your faith, wisdom and tireless support proves the impossible can be achieved.

Huge gratitude also to those who have helped me research and write *The Spirit Engineer*. Friends and first readers, Andrew Goff, Pauline Morris and William Hollinshead, Northern Ireland researcher, Catherine Millar, historians, Henry V. Bell and Gareth Russell, book blogger par excellence, Victoria Hyde, and family and loved ones, you know who you are. Also to my husband, Nicholas, for supporting me always.

A special thanks to the families of Kathleen Goligher and William Jackson Crawford, particularly generous Bronwyn, William's great-great-granddaughter, history buff, Clare, his great-granddaughter and the ever-patient and kind Cathryn, who remembers Kathleen as a most gentle, though perhaps mysterious, grandmother.

For interviews with William and Kathleen's descendants and to find more about my research into their story, visit: ajwestauthor.com

AUTHOR'S NOTE

I first encountered William's strange story in Harry Houdini's memoir, *A Magician Among the Spirits* (1924). It would be excessive to state that I was instantly fixated but, somehow, the name William Jackson Crawford haunted me. Over time, with an archive visit here and a little curious delving there, I came to realise that one of modern history's greatest paranormal mysteries had been almost completely forgotten, relegated to a frivolous, maniacal blip in an Edwardian era beset by far noisier, far more violent, events.

I have done my best to tell his story, and that of Kathleen, Elizabeth, the children, Stoupe and all those characters who existed in real life. To save you time in your research, I can state that all main characters in *The Spirit Engineer* are based – to varying degrees of historical inaccuracy – on real people, with the exception of Lady Adelia Carter and Albert Blithe, who are both figments of my imagination.

To discover more about the true story behind *The Spirit Engineer* and to connect with A.J. West, visit www. ajwestauthor.com